Ideas have a life of their own

Preface
When one out of many billion humans has something to say,
he needs to invent a story. This is mine.
I hope you will enjoy it.

English is not my mother tongue,
so I hope you will forgive me the flexible
use of this beautiful language.

The plane landed near the blue sea. It could have been a place anywhere apart from its unique location near a mountain that every passenger sees once the plane's door is opened. It's a hot afternoon and all passengers are let out before Enzo, escorted by the two Italian police agents, is allowed to stand up and walk towards the door. Enzo feels the warm air touch his face and the mountain opposite the runway welcomes him to Palermo in Sicily. He had not been to Sicily for more than 20 years. Enzo turned to the two agents and asked: "Why on earth have you brought me here? You also know that I am now a US citizen. I want to speak to the US authorities. Please inform the US embassy."

One of the agents looked at him with a smirk and said: "Don't worry, they certainly know you are here and this is where they want you to be. We also know you now prefer to be called Vince, but here on this island you are still Enzo. Now stop asking stupid questions and move along."

The other agent did not seem to like Enzo or was just keen to finish his job and fly back home. A police car drove under the plane and once Enzo went in with his two companions in uniform, it drove fast towards a complete different back exit fit for VIPs and criminals like him. It was clear that those two agents who had arrested him after he had landed in Rome were convinced he was a criminal. He still had no idea why he had been put under arrest. Despite asking the agents several times, the reason for his detention, they just told him that he would be told once he arrived at his final destination. They had also warned him that if he resisted his arrest, things could get worst for him and his family back in California. Enzo thought long and hard about anything he might have done, or maybe it was something to do with his job. The fact he was taken to Sicily made him think that they probably had mistakenly arrested him for some mafia related crimes he knew nothing about. The police Alfa-Romeo drove around the outskirts of Palermo, then took a smaller road and started to drive towards the interior of the island. Houses and people got scarce and the roads continued to get smaller. It must have been an hour and half drive when suddenly the car went off the dirt track. At this point, Enzo lost his cool and shouted: "Where the hell are you taking me and are you real policemen or some kind of mafia gangsters taking me for someone else?"

Both agents laughed out loud and the one who had already spoken at Palermo airport said: "Listen, we are not loving this job either and will soon deliver you to a smaller and secret prison where we usually keep some mafiosi to be interrogated. But today you will have the honour of being a special guest of the Italian state. Now be quiet, and in 10 minutes max we will be there."

They kept their promise and the car stopped in front of a gate of what looked like a high security location with an Italian flag at the entrance that reassured Enzo. He thought that the mafia would not have decorated one of their villas with an Italian flag. Now someone would finally explain to him why he was kidnapped, whisked away so abruptly. The agents seemed happy to deliver that important packet. They looked at Enzo and told him to walk towards the entrance of the building.

"Go on, someone is waiting for you inside. Once you are in, we will leave. Be prepared to remain here for some days."

Curious to know more, he quickly went into the building where someone that looked like a security agent of some sort asked him to put his wallet, watch and smartphone on the reception counter. The phone or intercom rang. The guard answered simply: "Yes, he has arrived."

A man followed by two agents or guards come down the stairs.

"Good afternoon, Signor Dangelo, please follow me to my office. The two agents will make sure you won't get any funny ideas or try to escape. Please note that the fence around this building is electrified, so it can cause a painful death. The suitcases you landed with and the stuff you left downstairs at the reception will be returned to you as soon as you leave this place."

Then, he carried on: "I am inspector Cammarata, please take a seat. You might be wondering why you were taken here without explanation. Well, to be honest, I am not totally sure myself, as you were arrested in Italy, but the request actually came from your new country, the USA. We were asked to take you to a high security location to be interrogated because of an international issue you seem to be involved with. We were also told that someone else is being arrested and will soon join us. This person will also be investigated on a related issue. We might be told more about the reason for our new guest's arrest, as he seems to have only Italian citizenship. Do you have any idea yourself, or any questions?"

Enzo was puzzled. Why on earth does the USA want to arrest me? Then Enzo started to think of the work he had done for the US army. Could this have anything to do with his medical research, partly financed by the US Department of Defence? Well, it seemed that he would have to wait. "Yes, I have a question. Have you informed my family in the US?"

"Sure, Mr. Dangelo, your family has been informed of your arrest. At this moment your family knows that you are being interrogated by the US army to disclose to the enemy some secret US research information. Due to the nature of the investigation, the news of your arrest has not been passed to the mass media. Your work colleagues have been informed of your suspension due to an investigation. I am sorry, as I said earlier, I do not know more and I hope you will not be our guest for long. The prison cells are not the worst here as they are mostly used to host mafia people who we hope join our protection program. Ah, do you have any food allergies?"

"No, luckily I have no allergies and would not mind eating some Sicilian dishes that I have not eaten for more than 20 years."

Inspector Cammarata laughed and pointed to the door with his right hand where the two agents were waiting. The cell was at the end of a long corridor. It looked like a US motel room, but had no television or air-conditioning in it. The windows had metal bars on them, the door was of solid metal and the window looked at the bare grey stone of the mountain that had been excavated to accommodate the building. Luckily a tree had managed to grow unplanned between that grey stone wall and the building. Amazing what a difference a small tree can make if this is the only thing you will be looking at for who knows how long. Then Enzo's mind went back home to California where his wife, Carmen, and his daughter, Mary, must be puzzled and concerned about him. What would Carmen think? Would she believe whatever she must have been told about him? What would Carmen think about him being back in Sicily after more than 20 years? Well, they probably did not tell her his whereabouts. Carmen knew he had to attend a medical convention near Rome, but he had not managed to call her to say that he had arrived. He normally called home once he checked in to whatever hotel he was staying at. As he had been arrested as soon as he had landed, there had been no time to call home. He had met Carmen not long after moving to Boston to join a medical research team that was interested in his work. There were other good looking women in the office, but Carmen had the warmth he missed from Sicily and the Sicilians girls and friends he had left behind. The fact Carmen had a darker skin made her more attractive to him. Not so much to his parents and relatives when he decided to bring her back with him to Sicily on one of his holidays. Some relatives and friends had complimented him on her beauty, but in the small town most had shown their disappointment and some even dared to ask how, as a doctor, he had not managed to get a blonde, American girlfriend. Carmen, at first, had not noticed, and had enjoyed the extra attention and the warm Sicilian climate that reminded her of her parent's island. The Sicilian language also seemed similar to the Spanish she had learned as a child. So communication had not been an issue. A couple of years later, an older cousin who had gotten a bit drunk suddenly asked if it was true that the girls of the Caribbean islands were all easy. Carmen was stunned and asked for clarification just in case she had not understood correctly. Well, the old man carried on saying that he had meant that maybe all girls in the Caribbean had less inhibition about sex. By the time he had come out to the terrace, Carmen had thrown a glass of sticky Coca-Cola at the face of the old cousin, who was now shouting some nasty Sicilian swearwords at her. Enzo escorted the old man out of the house and told him never to show his face again in his parent's house while they were visiting. After that, Carmen had never wanted to go back to Sicily and after visiting his parents alone a couple of times, he had told them that his life was now in the USA and that they were more than welcome to visit him there. Carmen's family had welcomed him in Santo Domingo in the Dominican Republic, but when they realized they were serious and wanted to get married, they had gotten worried. Carmen's father and brother told him that they were no mafiosi, but would be prepared to kill for their daughter and sister. They wanted to make clear to him that they had not invested so much in her studies for someone to marry her, get involved with the mafia and drag her into it. The few Sicilians they had known about on their island were some mafia guys who had invested some drug money in some hotels and had gotten investigated by the US FBI. So they had liked Enzo, but had had some second thoughts about his home land and the clichés that went with it. Enzo was used to having to excuse himself wherever he went in the world for the work of a minority of Sicilians. For many around the world, Sicily is synonymous to the mafia, so he was not surprised about Carmen's family's worries, but he had been able to convince them about his good faith and his non-involvement with the mafia, in Sicily or in the USA. What would they think now? Would they feel confirmed in their doubts? Finally, he managed to fall asleep and forget where he was, at least for a moment. The birds were loud and the grey stone was bright. That lonely tree was still there, visible through the barred window. Enzo thought it must almost be lunch time, as he felt a bit hungry and his stomach was complaining about the lack of food. In the room he had only found a couple of plastic bottles of still water. After all, it had not just been a nightmare. It was true, he had been arrested and flown to Sicily by force. Maybe today he would finally be told the reason for his circumstances. Was there any point in getting up before being told to do so? Why not enjoy the seldom rest he had been longing for in the last years? Despite not wanting to, his mind started to investigate all possible reasons that could have put him in this predicament. What could he have done and not have realised, that must have caused him to be seen as an enemy of the United States. The more he thought about it, the less he could make head nor tail of it. Maybe some relatives that had visited him from Sicily or the Dominican Republic were involved in some criminal activity and now they thought he might be part of their illicit deals? Other people he knew could also have been arrested without him knowing. Maybe things would solve themselves once they found the right culprit. What a nightmare. Had I finally killed that bastard that twice scratched my new car in the office garage, then I would at least know why I got arrested. Maybe I should have done that and now I will probably never have the chance again to liberate the world from one more idiot driving a SUV and thinking he owns the road he drives on. What a missed chance, he thought. Suddenly a trolley being dragged along the long corridor could be heard. Well, he thought, it could be food. A flap at the bottom of the metal door opened and a tray was pushed through it. No word was exchanged just the sound of the metal tray scraping the floor. Noisy enough to force one out of bed. To his surprise, the food looked good. A plate of pasta with lentils and a second dish with "Melanzane alla parmigiana" - a traditional Sicilian dish that strangely uses parmesan cheese made in the north of Italy. The dish put Enzo in a good mood and made him realise that Inspector Cammarata had kept his word and provided good Sicilian food. Only in Sicily had Enzo known dishes totally made of vegetables being highly celebrated by everybody, not only by vegetarians. In America, and in the north of Italy or Europe, he had seen vegetables being always relegated to the role of a side dish and never taking the main role in a dish. He knew he was supposed to eat the pasta as his first dish, but he dug straight into the "Melanzane alla parmigiana" and to his surprise, the dish was perfectly prepared. Well, he thought out here, between the mountains, there must be someone cooking for all those poor souls playing their roles of prisoners and guards. The building did not look big and there did not seem to be many people either. Probably not more than 20, so he might be getting some decent food out of this strange experience. While he was attacking his plate of pasta, he could hear a car that sounded exactly like the Alfa-Romeo he was driven in, coming always closer. He thought this must be the second guest the inspector Cammarata had told him about. He could hear the car stopping in front of the gate and someone shouting in Italian: "Where the hell have you brought me, and what is the reason for my arrest! Leave me! Leave me alone!"

Well, it seemed that this other gentlemen did not want to move alone to the reception as he had done. After some silence he could hear some people coming up the stairs, dragging something along. No one was complaining any longer. Suddenly, a loud noise announced the opening of a metal door not far away, opposite his cell. Then the noise of someone or something being dragged in and the door being slammed closed. Well, he thought that maybe he had been right in not complaining much and walking the way they wanted him to. He then tried to open the food opening to see the other side, but no chance - it was locked from the outside. Now he looked around for anything to read, but nothing. Outside of the window was the same grey stone wall and the lonely tree with some birds freely flying around it. All his life, he had wondered about those birdwatchers and what could drive them to such passion. Now he felt ready to join their ranks. I wish I had taken an interest in this. There seemed to be two different type of birds that kept on coming back to their nests. Now he wondered what type of birds they were, what they ate and how long they lived. Throwing himself down on the bed, he started to think about his youth on the island. Since he was a young boy, he had wanted to learn a profession he could use anywhere in the world. He had first looked at electrical engineering or information technology, but there were no information technology courses in Sicily at the time. Studying IT at the time would have meant leaving Sicily and studying somewhere else in Italy. In the north, he thought the weather was horrible and people were racists to southerners, so he had discarded that option. Maybe Rome or central Italy, but to study something in Sicily was what he had preferred. When he had told his parents that he wanted to study medicine, they could not hide their approving smiles. They felt they had won the lottery or God had answered their prayers. They were very happy. Like many young men, even Enzo had had his doubts about what to do with his life, until he had met Annamaria. Annamaria was the girl he saw at Palermo University the day he went to enrol. She had not been to Palermo before and was originally from a town in the east of Sicily. She had decided to study in the island capital to be as far away from home and yet still study in Sicily. Her family was quite conservative, and while she loved them, she wanted to have some distance between them and her. With her curly long hair and short skirt, it was hard not to notice her. Enzo saw her being a bit dizzy and confused, so he decided to pounce and offered his help. She looked at him and with a half-smile and a cheeky look and told him that he had better be sure he was able to deliver on his offer of help, as she would need a lot of it. Enzo smiled back, saying that as long as he was allowed to take her to eat some ice-cream or pizza, then he would be her slave for the day. She smiled back, turned around and dropped the heavy books she was carrying on him, saying: "Be a gentleman and start with carrying these."

Well, he had asked, so he now had to keep to his word. She rushed through different buildings around the university, then told him that she was going to share an old and small flat with another two girls from the same town she came from. But she needed to still buy some small furniture and a lamp. Maybe he was the exact helper she needed to carry the stuff to the third floor with no lift? He answered: "Yes. Sure, I did offer to help and you have promised to come out with me later."

He had to help her for a whole week, getting all she needed to settle down before he was allowed to take her out to eat some ice-cream. She did not waste time and she knew what she wanted. After the ice-cream, she kissed him like he had never been kissed before.

"Well," she said. "Was it worth all that work you had to put in?"

He smiled, still in dreamland, like someone that had lost his mind. Actually he probably had. She proudly kissed him on the cheek and pushed him out of her front door. See you tomorrow, if you want. Pick me up after lunch. Annamaria being there and studying the same course, had made it clear to him that he was studying the right thing. Destiny had wanted them to meet. This made it difficult for him to leave Palermo and visit his parents in the nearby province of Trapani whenever there was a holiday break. She could not join him as she had to also go to see her parents in the far away Syracuse province. Wanting to spend more time together, they had sometimes hidden from their families during their time off school. Suddenly the opening of the cat, or food flap, noise took Enzo back from his daydreaming. Finally, someone talked to him, even to just say: "If you want your supper, just push the lunch tray out first."

He stood up, pushed the empty tray out, got the new one in and, before the flap closed, he managed to shout: "Say thank you to inspector Cammarata for the good Sicilian food. A glass of wine would not be bad either!"

The flap closed with no response, but the supper tray had a plate of lentil soup with some good bread on the side. Of course, he thought, this was a similar supper to one his mother would prepare when she was still around. Cook enough lentils to have some with the pasta at lunch and the main part as a soup for the evening. Proper Sicilian food it was, and he was imagining the chef in this prison to be just an elderly lady like he remembered his mother, sweating while cooking in a small kitchen in such warm weather. He had missed his mother since she had gone. She never forgave him for moving so far away and partly blamed this on Carmen being from the other part of the world. Of course, her doctor son could never be at fault. It was always someone else leading him astray. It did not matter how many times he had tried to explain to her that if he wanted to progress in his medical research field, Italy, and especially Sicily, had little to offer. Mamma could not understand why he had not just specialised in something and opened a practice in their town, or at least in Palermo, where she could have visited him more often. If it had not been for him meeting this Carmen, he would now be closer to her. Mamma had never cared about Carmen's skin being a bit darker and had appreciated her attempt to learn to cook Sicilian dishes, especially when they had visited him in Boston. But why would she not agree with her mother in law and move to Sicily? Eating that Sicilian earthly food took him back to his childhood when he was running around the country side with his friends, picking whatever fruit they could find, on whatever tree. Most of the field owners did not care about a couple of children picking fruit. But some did, and tried to shout them away from their fields. Some just shouted: "Please leave some for me! In those fields, we felt most embarrassed and tried not to go the year after, while those where they had to run away from had become a challenge to steal the fruit without being caught. Those fields guarded by dogs were the most challenging, and the one that really earned one a badge of honour for their bravery among their friends. It was getting dark and he still did not know why he was held, nor had he seen a lawyer as he had requested in Rome, straight after his arrest. Would his screaming for news at the metal door have changed anything? He did not even know if they could have heard him down that long corridor. He decided to give it another night and hoped to know more the day after. All those years he had longed for some rest, and now he was forced to have one. Maybe this was not so bad after all. Or at least this is what he convinced himself. Jumping back into bed with his eyes fixed on the light blue ceiling, he remembered what a butcher's son, Marco, had told everybody in his elementary class - that in the past, houses were painted white on the outside to protect them from the strong sun and keep them cool, while the inside of the houses like his father's butcher shop, where painted light blue to emulate the sky and confuse most insects to not try to land on what they regarded as a piece of sky. Well, he hoped this also worked for the mosquitoes that usually liked his blood. Now he started to wonder what happened to Marco and all those people he had grown up with, and if they had seen him being arrested on the local news. Well, who cares, but why on earth is the US asking for my arrest, and in Italy? Why not stop me directly before leaving US soil? He had no more idea than 24 hours earlier. Maybe if he had listened to his mother and become a local GP he would not be here now. When visiting Marco in his butcher shop he had thought how unpleasant his father's job was when he was cutting the different parts of a cow that had been recently slaughtered. Then, separating the bones from the different meat cuts to give him a couple of bones for his dogs back home with greetings from Marco's dad. Several such experiences would prepare him for when he had started his medical studies and the human body, including bones and muscles. Especially at the end of the first year in the medicine faculty, when almost all students attended their first autopsy, almost as a dare for every prospective young doctor. Annamaria was not worried and had laughed at Enzo's unwillingness to accept this as a normal part of life or a normal part of being a doctor. Enzo had tried to be strong and the only way he could cope with this was by comparing the dead human body to the body of a slaughtered animal, like he had seen at Marco's butcher shop. The professor performing the autopsy was aware of the fact that at this point some young student would decide to study something else and was used to performing the act with some humour to distract the audience from their more gruesome thoughts. So the professor started to say that despite what everybody was thinking, this human body is no longer an individual and should not be regarded as a person. Then the professor carried on saying: "While this is just a lifeless body, we will still treat it with respect and use it for our study." The professor turned towards all the students and said: "Please pay attention to every action and detail as this is very important." But also that they should keep their experience to themselves, as all previous medicine students had done over the years. Then he quickly inserted his index finger inside one of the body's sphincters, took it out and put it in his mouth. The horrified audience reacted with disgust. Then the professor turned to the student and asked if there was someone willing to try the same trick. Many boys lifted their hands, but Enzo was not one of them. The professor choose the bravest looking and invited him into the middle of the operation theatre. Then told him: "Let me see if you have paid attention." Without hesitation, the young man put his index finger inside the cadaver's sphincter and then straight into his mouth. A new loud sound of disgust arose in the theatre. Then the professor thanked the young student and turning to the spectators saying: "Well, I had asked for your full attention, and maybe some of you have given it to me, but judging from your disgust, few must have. I had asked you to pay attention to detail. If you had, you should have noticed that I had put my right hand index finger into the sphincter and later my left hand index finger into my mouth." The whole class exploded in laughter and the brave young man was left looking stupid. The professor told him to quickly disinfect his mouth and he hoped this lesson would teach him and all those looking to pay more attention in the future. Then, he said: "Imagine if removing the wrong kidney from a patient would mean killing that patient.

You would need to be very sure, you know if it is the patient's right hand side of the body and not your right hand side you are talking about."

Enzo had never forgotten that experience and with this funny memories, he was now able to fall soundly asleep. Day two and the food flap opened again, asking once more for the tray exchange for breakfast this time. Just a cappuccino and a jam filled croissant. Grey bare stone wall was still there outside of the window with that single small tree between them. No shower in the room or cell, just a toilet in the corner and a sink. Well, time to wash a bit in the sink. Just in case he got a visit, he had better stop stinking. The room was not luxurious, but not the worst of the places he had spent some time in London or Boston while studying and looking for a better place to stay. After he had finished his breakfast, he had decided he had had enough, and started to hit the metal door with the metal tray. This, he thought, would make enough noise to attract the agents' attention. After a while a voice outside said: "Please stop hitting the door. This afternoon, someone will come to see you."

"Well, good to know!" He shouted back.
He sat on the white-painted, wooden chair eating his croissant and looking outside the window, wondering if the same birds were also flying today around the tree. Biting into his jam filled croissant he remembered the first time he had visited his uncle in Bologna in the north of Italy and had gone with him to the local bar. After having avidly bitten into the croissant he had turned around to his uncle and told him that they had been cheated. The croissants were empty! His uncle had started to laugh aloud and the other people in the bar had turned around. Then, still laughing, he explained that in the north of Italy most croissants were not filled. Enzo had been spoiled by the bars in Sicily where croissants were always filled - with jam, custard or chocolate cream, and people used to go to the bars that provided the better filled ones. In comparison, eating an empty croissant seemed to him like biting into some strange soft bread. He had carried on eating empty croissants all over the world and had got used to those. Now he was forced to eat one filled with jam. He certainly never dreamed of eating one in a prison before and had had no plan to fly down to Sicily from his meeting in Rome. He had always thought of a croissant as something that maybe the French had left behind in Sicily after they had dominated the island. Only years later, he was told by an Austrian that croissants were first baked in Vienna to celebrate their defeat of the Turks that had managed to come close to their city gates. The Austrians celebrated by baking a half-moon shaped piece of patisserie. The half-moon represented the half-moon of the Turkish flag. Eating the half-moon made it less scary. Enzo thought that

without something to read or write, in the long run he would have gone mad. So he made a mental note to ask inspector Cammarata for something to read and write. Better still, if he could be freed and let go home. He would have loved to make a list of the last projects he had worked on to better focus on what could have caused his arrest. He had enjoyed a time without his smartphone, but now he kept thinking of getting his phone to check the latest news, his last messages, emails, Facebook, WhatsApp chat groups and now nothing. How strange to be disconnected. How would people react, not getting any answer from him? Maybe he could start thinking of all the latest projects he had worked on, and start from there. Or maybe it was his pet project he had dedicated most of the last five years to, but why would a weight loss product interest the US national security? Soon after moving into research, or better, after finally getting the chance he had been looking for, he had started to work on a weight loss product. Typically, healthy diet plans supported by some plant extracts, such as the hoodia cactus of South Africa, long used by the San people (Basarwa) before going out to hunt. The San people have long known that eating a roasted hoodia cactus would stop them getting hungry. Some western pharmaceutical company had tried to further investigate the issue and created some types of food containing the key ingredient that stopped the San people getting hungry. It was a great experience and he loved working in an international team. But every good thing also comes to an end. Due to some disagreement with the South African government, the project soon came to an end and he had to quickly find a new project to work on. Another department in the same company was working on physically removing the accumulated extra fat from overweight patients. Some operations had already started providing help to voluntary patients who had agreed to be studied and analysed, free of charge. But the best studies were happening in the USA, where many more overweight people were willing to pay for any type of operation that would improve their health without having to undergo a very hard and long diet. It was clear that the best career opportunities for him were in the USA office. This is when he had decided to move to Boston. His family, especially his mother, had not been pleased he had moved to Milan. Moving to the USA reminded her of all those Sicilians who had emigrated to the USA decades earlier and nobody had ever seen them again. Convincing his mother that he would come back often to see them was not easy. His father was saddened by his moving away, but he knew that a man needed to follow his dreams and make them happen. All his friends knew already he was never going to hang around in their small town. Enzo had always felt a citizen of the world, and saw the world as his playground. He kept on repeating: "You live only once, and not for that long either! So make the most of it." The noisy metal flap announced once more that it was time for the next meal. The breakfast tray was exchanged for the lunch one. Pasta with fresh tomato sauce followed by "sarde inpanate" or pan-fried large sardines and salad. Not a bad hotel were it not for the strong metal door and the barred window. Looking at the barred window, he had never understood not even as a child, how someone could voluntarily put himself or herself behind metal bars. He remembered when at the age of six or seven, he was taken by his grandmother to the nearby convent where the nuns sold their home made biscuits. The exciting thing for him was to catch a glimpse of the nun's eyes who was turning a wooden table to deliver the biscuits in exchange for the money his grandmother at put on it. When he asked Nonna, she said that those were "monache di clausura" or nuns who had voluntarily abandoned their normal lives and locked themselves up to serve Jesus. They were living a life of prayers and work for their community. "Why would someone do that?" he thought then and still now, looking at the bars on his room window. "How can someone lock himself up and throw away the keys?" He felt much closer to the free flying birds on the small single tree he could see from there. He even pondered whether it would not be better to have the shorter lifespan of a free flying bird and enjoy the natural world. Now he felt he had come full circle and had changed his mind again. Then his mind wondered to a long haul flight where, when asked by the stewardess, he had chosen a chicken dish instead of the soggy pasta. This made him think about how far we humans have gotten. This felt like an evolutionary victory, eating a bird while flying. Behind those metal bars, he was no longer so sure about the evolutionary victory of humans. Maybe there was something to be said about prioritizing the quality of life above longevity. At this moment, he felt very keen to trade his life with one of those free flying birds. Had he, as a doctor or medical researcher, worked more to stretch the human's life or to improve it in the short run? He was not sure. Maybe by losing weight, some patient's life had been stretched and he had contributed to it. Some maybe did not manage to live longer, but by feeling better about themselves they had lived happier lives. He had not studied medicine just to get rich. He, like many other of his fellow students, wanted to do something good for others and the world, and they also wanted to feel good about themselves. So where had he gone so wrong, that he had done something to upset the security services of his new adopted country? With that thought he nodded off, helped by the warm air coming through the metal bars of his window. A loud noise woke him up and this time it was not the noise of the food flap, but that of the door being unlocked. Inspector Cammarata walked in sat on the only chair in the room and the agents slowly closed the door behind him. Inspector Cammarata started by apologising for keeping him under arrest without explaining the reason for him being there. Then, he carried on, "I am afraid your new

American friends and family have not shared much with us and I had to concentrate on dealing with our new guest - you probably heard arriving last night. It seems that, despite him being an Italian citizen, he was also living in the USA like you and his arrest was also requested by our dear American friends. Looking into his past, I see that you have not worked together or met in the USA, but he is someone you have met in the past here in Sicily."

Enzo asked for his name, or whether he was one of his relatives, but Inspector Cammarata stopped him, saying that he was not able to tell him more, but that he should not need to worry as they would soon have the pleasure of meeting again. Then Inspector Cammarata turned to Enzo and carried on: "First of all, after reading about you, I want to compliment you on your career achievements. Not bad for a Sicilian country boy turned doctor and medical researcher. It seems that until now you have done everything right. We are now here to find out what you did wrong and why. First of all, please tell me why you decided to take US citizenship?"

Enzo wanted to remain friendly but, after two days waiting, he exploded: "Does this mean that you still do not know the reason they asked you to arrest me?"

"I am afraid," the inspector replied, "what I know or do not know about the reason for your arrest I cannot share with you until we have investigated the issue further and you have told us what we want to know. Should you decide not to speak with us, this room could be yours forever. I know the food is not too bad, but I do not think you would be able to appreciate this for years to come. Don't worry, we will not torture you, we could just forget you are here. On the other hand, should you decide to collaborate, then you might have a chance to come out of here as soon as we are done and your new country persecutors agree with our findings. So, what is going to be, a friendly, daily chat, or do you want to become a reclusive monk?"

Enzo, looked up at Inspector Cammarata and started to talk: "Well, I had been in the US long enough, my wife and I had both decided to create our new family there, and I was at the time not allowed to work on some of my company's core projects used by the US military. Not that I was too keen to get involved, but it was annoying not to be included in some of the key discussions or meetings, just because I was holding a foreign passport. Once Italy started to accept dual citizenship in 1992 I, like many other Italians citizens living and working in the USA, decided to apply and become a US citizen. I had no intention of changing my job, but by being a US citizen I would not be bound by a work contract to be able to renew my green card.

After telling my managers that I was finally one of them, I was allowed to sit in every meeting with my other US colleagues. On many occasions, I had been disappointed as I could not understand the sensitivity of the issue and why someone foreign could not hear. Probably one of those ground rules, by which if the US army was paying for the research or project no foreigner was allowed to listen in."

"I see, then," Inspector Cammarata carried on, "There is an instance here that I am not sure you are aware of. This is the first time the US authorities noted something about you and I am not sure you were ever told."

Enzo turned around and asked, "When was that?"

"Well, it's now a long time ago, but in 1987 you flew from Palermo airport via Rome to New York and were bringing some packets to relatives of people in your town."

"I did that several times, so I cannot remember exactly and, by the way, those were all people, friends and relatives I trusted," Enzo answered.

Inspector Cammarata then carried on: "Maybe you should not have trusted all of them. For example, in the summer of 1987, you were given a small packet to give to a certain Michele Bongiovanni that was supposed to come and pick you up at the airport in New York and had offered to drive you to Boston. Do you remember?"

"Do you mean the time that someone did not turn up and I had to catch a train?"

"Yes. Anyway, why did you not fly directly to Boston?"

Enzo, annoyed by having to explain what for him was obvious, said: "At the time, flights to New York were much more affordable, so I often flew via New York."

"Did you ever meet this Michele Bongiovanni before or after?"

"No, never, and if I had, he would have certainly paid the consequences of not turning up at the airport like he had promised. Because of that idiot I turned up late at work the day after and I lost the chance of working on a great project promising an extra bonus to those working on it."

"Don't worry, you had your revenge. When you landed, the Italian police had already informed the FBI in the US about a two kilogram packet full of heroin coming their way and you were the carrier. At the time, the Italian police, like the FBI, were not sure if you were aware of the content of the packet and would have arrested you after landing, had it not been for the fact that Mr Bongiovanni had not got stuck in traffic due to an accident on the highway and you decided to go to the information desk asking to call his full name aloud, just in case he was somewhere else in the airport. Better still, you gave the information desk Mr Bongiovanni's car phone number with which the US straight away were able to tracked him down and arrest him. So this is why he never turned up and was never able to contact you. If you remember, some kind of relative of his came later to Boston to pick up the packet. Well, the FBI wanted to see your moves and after a week, they decided that you were clean and sent an FBI agent playing the part of Mr Bongiovanni's relative to pick up the two kilogram packet full of heroin. They had decided in New York, that if you had had any part in it, you would have not gone to the information desk and had Mr. Bongiovanni's name advertised to the whole airport, nor would you have passed his car phone number to someone else. After a week of observation, they were sure you had nothing to do with them and had only been unknowingly their drug mule. I must say it was a lucky escape then, but one cannot always be lucky. By the way, I am sure the people sending the drugs were also observing you the whole time and would have killed you, had you made the wrong move. So let me say, you are, or better, were, double-lucky there!"

"I am impressed and shocked. I cannot even remember what relative of my mother or some cousin had given me the packet and I wonder if they knew what was inside or if they had done someone else a favour, just friends of friends spanning the whole island. Any more interesting stories you know about my past that I do not?"

"Just a small thing still, but it is drug smuggling again."

"Another relative's packet from Sicily?" Asked Enzo.

"No, this happened nine years later, in 1996, and it is about your wife's brother Julio."

Enzo very surprised. "Julio? He works for the police in the Dominican Republic and seems to be proud of it!"

"It seems that Julio did not know either, but that year he accepted the invitation to sail with a wealthier friend all the way from the Dominican Republic to Boston and Julio accepted because he could come and see his sister, your wife. What Julio did not know is that his wealthier friend did not make most of his money just by selling alcohol to the island tourist's hotel, but he sometimes used his sailing boat to smuggle drugs into the USA. So when Julio was staying at your home, the FBI raided their sailing boat and arrested the boat owner. This is why Julio received a call saying that the boat needed repairing and could not sail back."

"Yes, I now remember Julio being very upset and annoyed about having to pay for a flight back to the Dominican Republic. We even had to lend him some money. I should tell him this story as I am sure he would feel better now about paying for his flight back."

"I am afraid he will have to wait until we are done here."

"Any more lucky escapes for me or my family?"

"No, not really just some traffic speeding fines here and there. Just be careful with your daughter's friends as some are not really clean people if you know what I mean."

"Who and what do you mean?"

"As much as I understand your curiosity and worries, being a father myself, we are not your private investigators, so we would need to concentrate on what we want or need from you. So let's please carry on. Have you ever shared information about your work with people outside your company?"

"Not really, maybe sometimes with my wife because of being frustrated with something at work or maybe for being happy about some innovation of breakthrough in our research. Why?"

Inspector Cammarata was insisting and trying to give him another chance to come clean. "Are you really sure about this?"

"Yes, pretty sure."
"Do you happen to know Mrs. Julie Wilson?"

"No, the only Julie I used to know was called Julie Anderson. Why?"

"I see, what was your relationship with this Julie you knew or still know?"

"Well it is probably unnecessary to lie to you as you know this already, but Julie was the reason we moved to California. Knowing that I missed south Italian food and the fact that I was under pressure at work putting in long hours every day. My wife Carmen suggested I take a cooking class once a week to get out of the rat race. At the time I was new in a company and I had not yet learned to stand up for myself as one needs to do in the US. When my relatives and friends used to ask me if I liked my new job in America, I remember answering them that in the USA they liked the concept of our European 40 hour-week so much, that they did it twice a week. Anyway, it was at the cooking course my wife Carmen had suggested I attend, that I met Julie."

"What was your relationship with Julie like?"

"As I am sure you know, Julie and I started to see each other outside of the cooking classes and sometimes instead of the cooking classes."

"Were you meeting Julie always after work and did you ever discuss your work with her?"

"No I never spoke to her about my work, apart from telling her that I worked in this or that research project, but I don't think the names of those projects meant much to her. She used to tell me about her job at a beauty salon, but as you can imagine I was not much interested in that either."

"Did Julie ever talk about her family or her parents to you?"

"Only once, when she told me that her parents were both from Maine in the US."

"Mrs. Julie Anderson's actual name is Julie Wilson and while her father was from Maine, her mother was a beautiful Russian lady from Saint Petersburg where your Julie still has some relatives. Mrs. Julie Wilson did work in a beauty salon, but she did not mind using her good looks to earn some extra cash through industrial espionage, sometimes for the Russians and sometimes for others. Have you ever heard about a honey trap?"

Before Inspector Cammarata could carry on asking, the noisy food flap opened again with a voice asking for the empty tray. Inspector Cammarata turned around and shouted, "Wait a minute while I open the door and let you in, I think I have squeezed enough out of this lemon for today. I think if we keep on feeding you well, you might decide to stop talking to me so you can enjoy our cuisine for longer after having spent so much time in Yankee-land."

He smiled, saying "Buon appetito" and left the room.
This time they had delivered pan-fried artichoke hearts and a "caponata di peperoni e melanzane" with some good local bread that he had not eaten for more than 15 years. After being squeezed he felt he had earned this food. Now his mind was trying to go back in time and think what and when he could have shared with Julie that could have got him into this mess. And in what trouble was his daughter or her friends? How great he had felt when that beautiful girl who was ten years younger had fallen in love with him. What a bloody good actress she was and how stupid and easy it had been to catch her. He never thought someone would be interested in his work. Well, yes there was enough money to be made in producing a drug or a way for people to quickly and easily lose weight. But engaging a spy for that? And who was this other prisoner whom he might be knowing from his past? These were enough thoughts to keep him awake all night.
At least it seemed he would not have a boring day tomorrow either and who knows how many more secrets they had dug out about him that would reveal some more truth he himself was unaware of. Looking at the bright side, had he not been arrested, he would never have discovered the truth. What was hard to discover was the fact that Julie, the woman who had almost caused his divorce and made him consider leaving his wife and children, was a fake, a fantasy of his mind. What an idiot he had been. Luckily Carmen had forgiven him and he had gone back home. Had he followed through once Julie had got what she wanted, she would have certainly dropped him like a stone. Another lucky escape he thought to himself. Normally he would be attracted by darker ladies with long curly hair, but Julie's long blonde hair and sweet smile had melted his heart the first time she had decided to join forces with him in preparing their first team dish. Then she did not mind him giving her a lift back home and going upstairs to her flat to help with hanging a shelf. Carmen did not notice anything in the beginning and was happy to see him a bit more relaxed and keen to be going to the cooking class she had found for him. She was even happier to see him carry on the course for longer that she had booked him for. Thinking about it, strange that this younger good looking girl was always well dressed and carrying nice jewellery, never asked for anything, nor wished for any presents. Having two beautiful women waiting for one was a dream too good to be true. Carmen had done nothing to deserve this. He was getting older and wanting to experience one last spring season. He had

not been looking for an adventure, but Julie had just appeared on the scene and had been difficult to resist. He will never forget that day when he came out of the evening cooking class with Julie hanging on his neck and Carmen being just there looking at him after having seen the whole romantic walk and kissing down the corridor through the stupid glass doors. Carmen was there looking on in disbelief, she did not even look hurt, just frozen. Then she quickly seemed to wake up, slapped him very hard and ran away crying. She had wanted to surprise him and surprise him she did. Julie's reaction was even better. She just told him that she understood, told him to go home to his wife, but to also remember that she would be in her flat waiting for him.

Going home had been hard, but Carmen deserved some kind of explanation. Carmen did not allow him in but did send out their little 5 year old boy, Johnny, with a letter for him. He hugged little crying Johnny who did not know why daddy wasn't allowed to sleep at home that night. With a heavy heart he said to the boy that daddy had fought with mummy, but he will soon be back. The letter just said to stay away. "At the moment I do not want to see you. I need some time to think about what to do next." He drove back to Julie's flat where she was more than welcoming of him, even talking of a common future, should he decide to leave his wife. That night he was not sure if he wanted to fight to keep his family together or embark into a new future with this woman who had declared her love for him. He was not sure if he loved her or if he was just sexually attracted to her. God, she seemed very kind and understanding. Even then he had thought this was almost too good to be true. It felt almost like a nice Disney happy ending story. But she was gorgeous and willing. He was stupid and vulnerable.

Three days later Carmen had called him at work wanting to meet for lunch. They met in a place just outside of the office, where she appeared very serious, but with a bunch of flowers. As soon as she arrived he asked her who those flowers were for. She said those were for him as she had been thinking those past days and realized she still cared for him, but wanted to know if he loved this other woman. Not being yet sure, but not wanting to upset Carmen, he said that it had been just sexual attraction. She put her hand in her bag and took out a very black picture, and when she turned it around it was a pregnancy ultrasound scan with their baby daughter in it. Carmen had kept this surprise for him and had wanted to show it to him after his cooking class. Now she said, it's time you decide what to do with your life. I believe you had told me about an opening in your company's California office. This would be a good new start for us far away enough for you to forget that bitch. The Californian weather would be better for us both, a bit more like back home where we come from. Once Carmen had put the ultrasound scan in his hands, he knew what he had to do. California, here we come! When he told Julie, she did actually cry and he had to spend some hours calming her down. What a fantastic actress he thought again. Maybe she had cried because of losing a revenue stream. He thought into the night, still scratching his head for whatever secret he might have disclosed to Julie that had guaranteed him a room in this special Sicilian hotel.

The food flap worked once more as an alarm clock with the usual request for the old empty tray in exchange for the breakfast one. Once more a cappuccino and a croissant. This time it was a custard-filled one. How many times was he told all around the world that not eating in the morning or just having a coffee was a bad thing to do? Finally nobody was questioning his breakfast habits. But he was also aware not to ask for a cappuccino after lunch time where, in Italy, cappuccino is seen as a breakfast-only hot drink. In his new country he had got used to ordering a cappuccino even in the evening or afternoon without the server looking at him as if he were deranged. His old companion was still standing strong with the usual birds flying around. Somehow he was looking forward to Inspector Cammarata's visit to take him out of his boredom. He started to wonder if this was the plan. Keeping someone alone for a while might just do the trick, at least with Italians, as he had met some strange Scandinavian in his life who did not seem to think of speaking as one of the things that humans were supposed to do. When asked, one of his Swedish friends once confirmed to him his feelings. Sven had told him that when visiting his father after years they would open and drink a couple of beers together and stay in almost silence for two or three hours just enjoying each other's company. He had then told his dear friend that if he observed such behaviour in the south of Europe, he would have been labelled with having some kind of syndrome and a doctor of some sort would have been called. After that Sven decided to share with him a joke about some Italian soldiers taken prisoners by the allied forces during WWII. The American army sergeant turned to his captain and said, those Italian soldiers are very hard to crack and despite some beating do not want to reveal where they have hid their ammunition. The captain went to see the Italian prisoners and turning back to the sergeant major, said of course they did not tell you anything. These are Italians and they cannot speak with their hands tied behind their backs. As soon as the sergeant cut the ropes holding their hands together the Italians started gesticulating and pointing to where they had hidden their ammunition. Sven was right, but after living for so long outside of the country, he had noticed having almost lost his capacity to speak with his hands. An opening door noise attracted his attention, but the noise came from further down the corridor. It seems prisoner number two was being visited. Maybe he got Inspector Cammarata on the morning shift and he will have to wait for his afternoon chat.

Boredom started to set in and he remembered that he had wanted to ask for something to read and write. By now he had read every single label on his clothes, noticed every single crack in the walls and counted all the floor tiles. There was nothing more around to exercise his mind and not lose his marbles. From the outside some cars were leaving and entering the site again, probably shuttling the people and agents working at the prison. Judging by the isolated road along which he was driven there, this building might be the only employment opportunity for miles. He wondered if the people working there actually knew what the site was used for. Would they care? Probably not, like many people in the world who are only working towards their next pay check. This is what he never wanted to end up doing. Working just for the money, whatever the amount. He had considered himself lucky being able to choose his carrier path, thanks partly to his parent being able to pay for his university and accommodation in Palermo. He was free of debts when he accepted his first job. A different start from his many US colleagues who had left university with huge loans to pay back. They often did not take the job they preferred, but the one that paid more, to shorten the amount of time needed to repay their debts. His brother did not want to study as he had. He had seen too many of his friends armed with a degree, then beg the local politician for a job in the local administration. Salvatore preferred to work in his parents' fishing and sports equipment business. His sister had decided to become a teacher and had been lucky enough to be transferred back to Sicily after a stint of five years' teaching in Ferrara in the north of Italy. Both Salvatore and Maria had been visiting him in California from time to time. They had brought their families with them, thus keeping the family ties. He had not told them that he was coming to Rome as they would not have appreciated his not flying down to Sicily to see them. They would probably be partially happy to know that he had been dragged down to Sicily paying for his white lie. Now he started to feel guilty for not having called his sibling much since his parents had passed away. Their almost biennial visit to the US had become a fixture, like their Christmas and Easter best wishes calls. He had got a bit fed up with his friends and family expecting the person who had left the island to call back home to speak with friends and relatives. For some strange reason, probably due to the fact that those Sicilians who had left after WWII were expected to be wealthier than those left behind, the one who left had the burden of keeping in touch with the people on the island. This seems to be a tradition still alive today, still expecting everybody who has left the island to call back home and when visiting, being the one getting in touch first to be asked: when are you leaving? For years he kept on answering I or we will remain for two or three weeks. Everybody had also asked him if it was true that in the US one only gets two weeks of paid leave in a year. When he confirmed what they had heard, they all reacted surprised and responded that they thought the US was rich enough to afford more holiday days. Maybe he should have stayed in Italy or at least in Europe where he would have got at least four weeks' paid leave a year. Well, at least this was stopping many envying him and some even felt sorry for someone condemned to work with little paid time off. Finally someone at the door again. Inspector Cammarata was a very welcome site.

"Buongiorno, Mr. Dangelo". Before he could come in, Enzo told him that he would be very grateful if he could get something to write and something to read to avoid going mad. Inspector Cammarata answered, "Well I am afraid I cannot give you anything to write just in case you manage to pass your writing to someone else out of this building, nor can I give you some new newspapers that could change what you decide to tell me. Downstairs there are some books which those mafia guys who were our guests for a while left behind. I will ask the guards to bring you some of those. I hope you will find something interesting between the books we have. Those ones have been pre-approved, any others you might wish to read would have to be checked first. Honestly I do not fancy reading all the books before you, just in case you use those to fabricate some half-backed truth. Anyway, where did we get to yesterday? Ah sorry, I came a bit early to see you today as it is my wife's birthday and I will have to be home earlier to avoid getting the third degree myself. So I have arranged for you to get a snack while we chat and I apologise for your missing a proper lunch today. Here is our snack. I got some "arancine" and some "calzoni" you can pick between your answers. If you do not mind, I will have some as well. I have not yet eaten either."

"So Mr. Dangelo, have you finally remembered what kind of secrets you passed to Mrs. Julie Wilson and how?"

"Sorry, I still don't even have any idea about what she could have wanted from me or my work and I never shared with her details about my work."

Inspector Cammarata turned around from his chair and grabbed a bag he had brought in with him and from it, got out a large folder. Pointing at the contents he said, "Those are the details of some of the projects on which you worked, photocopies of which were found in Mrs. Julie Wilson's apartment after her arrest. To be honest, they are of little interest. Who knows, maybe she did really like you. Anyway, yesterday after her arrest, she did admit to passing the rucksack you took to work to a neighbour who would photocopy everything while you were having a good time in her bedroom. Mrs. Julie Wilson did not know what she was looking for either, she just had to provide a copy of every document you carried with you. At least this is what Mrs. Julie Wilson is currently telling us as we have not yet been able to identify this neighbour she is talking about and the FBI still wonders if you passed the copies of the documents to her. Anyway, when did you decide to join or better, when were you assigned to the "dripping" project?"

"Seriously, this is why I am here, for the DF project?"

"So it seems or that is what my US colleagues have been telling me until now."

"I did not even know the US Ministry of Defence had any interest or was paying for that."

"Could you explain to me how you got involved with this DF project?"

"Sure, the DF project sounded interesting and as Carmen and I had started to think about buying our own house the project had a nice bonus waiting at the end of the tunnel if we would have managed to find a better way of doing things."

"Doing what?"

Enzo sighed and started to spill the beans, "With an always larger part of wealthy countries' populations becoming obese it was clear for the pharma industry that there was loads of money to be made in producing a way to quickly lose weight and I did not only loved the idea of working on a project that would make money for me and my company, but also to do something good for millions of overweight people. We had first studied people who were being operated on to remove extra fat by surgery. It became clear to us that we needed to find a better way of doing things if we wanted to corner the market. So we worked on a way to melt human internal fat, while simultaneously diverting the melted fluid (streaming fat) from the stomach to an inserted funnel and pipe. The patients would take some of our special medicine, not eat for the day and sit on a comfortable chair with a hole in the middle where all their fat would end up. People could lose or drip 10 kg in a single day. Better still, after having been cleansed or filtered, we sold the patients' fat to the cosmetic industry. The patients were so grateful that they never asked what we would do with their dripping fat, nor did they care. It was great to see them so relieved. Some of them, days after the dripping procedure, would straightaway enrol for cosmetic operations to get their outer skin back in shape. Of course, our company made sure we had the large part of the cosmetic surgery done by our daughter company dealing with that."

"Do you mean you worked together with the daughter company called Cut&Run?"

"Yes, well some thought that Cut&Run sounded much better than Drip & Run as we had started to call it at first. So yes, cut the worst bits of you, cut the past and run to a new lighter future. This was the idea and slogan in the US TV ads. But I rarely had contact with the daughter company. My job was to improve the way we were doing things as the fat dripping procedure was an advance at the time, but did not appeal to all of those who wanted to lose weight. Sitting on a chair for the best part of a day while some fluid was dripping out of you was certainly not the most pleasant of experiences. So we knew we needed to work harder to improve our procedure."

"I can tell you already that our second guest here used to work for Cut&Run, so you were kind of colleagues. Anyway, reading into your past, I see that you were also investigated for inside trading. What was that all about?"

"I see. As soon as we realized that the human fat drained from our customers, once filtered, was a new expensive raw material for the pharma and cosmetic industry, our company was keen to have a cut of this new business and decided to create a new daughter company to sell the human fat, better marketed as HL-formula for human lipids. All those working on the DF project were aware of this and of course bought many shares at a lower price as soon as the new company went public."

"Did you not think that by making half a million US$ in just one year you were going to be investigated?"

"Well, I did not think I was doing anything wrong or had something to hide, nor did all my other colleagues and my own financial adviser. I am sure you also read that I was cleared of any wrongdoing on that account."

Inspector Cammarata, keen to know more, asked "Why did you decide to sell the HL-formula shares just three years after and just before the share price collapsed?"

"I guess because I still have some ethics. When HL-formula was born our new company customers were from the pharma and cosmetic industry and I was happy to earn some extra cash. Later we found out that at HL-formula they had started to sell the human fat to the food industry. I did not like the idea from the start and I knew once the media would get hold of that information that they would start talking about some kind of cannibalistic practice. So this is why I decided to sell my shares while the price was still high."

"So it was not really about your ethics then."

"I was fine with passing one individual's fat to another, but not in oral form. I am not sure I would have taken or eaten it myself."

Undeterred, Inspector Cammarata continued, "Were you aware of the fact that a hedge fund linked to recycled mafia money had invested in HL-formula just after you had and sold those shares shortly after you did?"

"No, not at all. I have nothing to do with the mafia and I have always kept away from them. But wherever you are in the world if they know you are Sicilian, they always suspect you to be one of them. I did not expect this from you, here in Sicily."

"Mr. Dangelo, you might have tried to keep away from them, but it seems that they have not kept away from you and I am sorry, but we need to find out if you were really unaware of this as you say now. Like you, as a researcher and scientist, in the police we also work on facts and have to examine the issue and only after an in-depth analysis can we confirm or discard a theory. I am sure you will agree with that. Anyway it is getting late and I need to go home. I can tell you already that tomorrow or maybe the day after, you will meet our other guest of honour here. I will mention his name to you now so you can prepare for our session. I do not want you to get bored and maybe we can save some time. The person in question still works for Cut&Run and his name is Francesco Lombardo. Mr. Lombardo has been working in the USA for the last 12 years. By the way, I have not forgotten and I will ask the guards downstairs to bring up some books for you. We don't want you to lose your mind. Have a good evening and wish me good luck with the traffic getting back into Palermo at this time. She will kill me if I don't manage to get there on time for her party."

The door slammed closed and Enzo was puzzled by what Inspector Cammarata had said. What was that son of a bitch Francesco Lombardo doing there and why after so many years did he have to meet him again. Before he could dedicate some time and energy to this new thought, the food flap opened and someone requested the empty tray in exchange for supper and a couple of books. The Sicilian, a book about the bandit Salvatore Giuliano and a biography of Giovanni Falcone the Sicilian judge who fought against the mafia. Swordfish and tomato salad, and even a carton of wine. Why was Francesco Lombardo there? When had he moved to the US? And when had he started working for Cut&Run? What had happened to Annamaria? He had met Francesco at university, Francesco was from near Syracuse like Annamaria. All three were on the same medicine course and used to meet during the lessons or exams. They had got on fine and had spent some time together outside the university. They had become friends. Francesco's family was wealthy and had bought him a new car with which he managed to impress many of the girls at the university campus apart from Annamaria who seemed not to be impressed by his car or wealth. But being from the same area, whenever he was driving home he offered her a lift back home. The journey to the other side of the island, even using the motorway, would take more than three hours. Many journeys back in the car with Francesco seemed to have slowly changed Annamaria's view and feeling for him. He believed Annamaria loved him, but she never liked it when he talked about travelling and working outside Italy. She might have liked to have some work experience out of the country, but she could never seriously consider living somewhere else. She loved Sicily, the Sicilian warm weather, the friendly people, great food and history and she found the people in the north too cold to be real friends. Apart from that she made it clear many times that after all her parents had done for her, she would not like to leave them alone. She was the only child and felt fully responsible for them. Her parents were a bit older than his and she had a different sense of responsibility from what Enzo had ever felt for his then younger and fitter parents. Eventually she had got tired of him talking about all those places he wanted to visit or move to. Francesco's dream was to become his town GP, just 35 km from her town. One day after coming back from Syracuse, she dropped the bombshell saying that she was sorry, but her heart was no longer in it as she could not think of a possible common future and she no longer wanted a relationship with no future, just for fun. Annamaria had wanted some freedom away from her parents, but deep down she was a bit old fashioned and a conservative girl, probably because of her older parents from the deep province. He was still a young boy at heart and not ready to commit to a serious and long lasting relationship, but seeing her walk into the university hugging Francesco had killed him. He had lost his girlfriend, his best university friend and his trust in friendship all at the same time. It is probably not his fault, but it had taken him a long time to digest. He had been so in love with Annamaria that he decided to even disappoint his own parents by changing his university course. Mostly because of her, in the second year of his medical study, he had decided not to become a doctor, but became a medical researcher instead. His parents were devastated despite his explaining the great job opportunity he had going into medical research. He had always known that he had never wanted to become his town GP, like his parents were wishing he would. Now he is being told that Francesco Lombardo who was supposed to become a town GP and who managed to steal his girlfriend from him has been working in the US almost for the same company. So what happened to Annamaria? Did he just leave her after stealing her from him? He could not wait to meet Francesco and ask him about Annamaria. He was tired and looking forward to a good night's sleep. Every evening before he fell asleep, he was wondering about Carmen and his two kids back home. He knew that complaining about seeing a lawyer or having his rights respected would not get him anywhere with the Italian authorities. He had learned from his father as a young boy to show respect whenever the police or Carabinieri would stop them on the road. Even when asked stupid questions, show respect and try to respond without offending. That was what his father always told him. There was nothing to be gained by antagonising a policeman or Carabiniere.

Food flap alarm once more. He had got used to his life in captivity and he had not even been there a week. He started to think about his own grandfather's hunting dogs locked up in the house terrace. This is probably how they must have felt. The difference was that at the time he was one of their guardians bringing food to the dogs, so happy to see him that they always jumped around him. He wondered how long it would take until he would be so keen to see Inspector Cammarata and dance around him every time he came in. Strange how one's mind starts to think in a different way when the tables are turned. Maybe this is the injection of empathy he had always needed. Now it was time to discover what was inside today's croissant. A big bite uncovered a flow of chocolate cream. Well, not his favourite, but he thought the cappuccino would round up the taste. The morning was long and the solitary tree out there did not look as splendid in the rain. The birds were quiet too. A rainy day seems to perfectly start one of the books he had been given. He had noted people in Boston or in the north of Europe reading more than people did in Sicily. Well, what can people do when the weather is bad and they are alone? Now there is the internet and smartphones, but up to just 10 years earlier the only refuge would have been a good book. People in Sicily, the Dominican Republic and all other countries with some decent weather were offered far more outdoor activities than just to lock themselves in and read. Reading is rarely a group activity and mostly is associated with sad, lonely people who cannot or will not socialize. It is not considered good manners anywhere to visit friends or have friends over, sit down and then read a book in silence. He remembers reading the most when he had been ill in bed. What else can you do? The rainy winter days were good reading time, but those were rare in Sicily where even in winter the blue sky was only a couple of hours or a day away. Now he could choose between a biography of Giovanni Falcone or one of Salvatore Giuliano. As a young man he had followed Giovanni Falcone's career as a judge and always had mixed feelings about the way Falcone had decided to fight the mafia. On one hand he saw him as a Sicilian hero trying to clean up his island, on the other he found him a bit naïve. Every Sicilian knows from birth that some politicians in Rome are supported by the mafia. Therefore taking on a fight alone against the mafia was a clear suicide mission. Falcone's enemies were not going to be just in front of him, but also behind, stabbing him in his back. Sooner or later he was going to be left alone. And so he was the day he was killed the 23 May, 1992. Enzo remembered crying like many other Sicilians living on and off the island the day that happened. Since then he had always stopped at the autostrada Falcone memorial where he and his wife together with their police escort were blown up to pieces. Despite many Sicilian including himself knew that this was eventually going to happen, they still had a tiny winy hope that he could change something. Maybe with his death, he changed how Sicilians perceive the mafia. Since then in Sicilians' eyes the mafia was never again a Sicilian tradition to be partly proud of, but just a band of ignorant criminals whose only purpose is making money. At the time of Falcone's killing, he was already living in the US and had started to ask himself why there are mafia in Sicily and in the USA, but not in other countries where the Sicilians had emigrated. In Sicily the mafia seemed to be a cancer that had spread to other regions of Italy and into the Italian government, while in the US at first sight it seemed just one of the criminal organizations mostly kept under control by the US authorities. Why was the USA far more powerful against the mafia than the Italians had ever been? Sicilians and the mafia knew that killing Giovanni Falcone and later his colleague and friend, Paolo Borsellino, would have stopped their investigation and the state battle against the mafia. The Italian state put its judges on the front line. Those individuals and not the Italian state institutions were fighting the mafia. In the USA the state institutions were fighting the mafia. It seemed clear in the USA that killing a judge like Giovanni Falcone or Paolo Borsellino would not have stopped investigation as the US government enforcement machine would have carried on relentlessly. In Italy after the killing of Falcone and Borsellino the investigation into the colluding of mafia and politics ground to a halt as the investigation was not carried out by the Italian state, but by those brave individuals. This is why for the mafia it is pointless to kill a judge in the USA, but makes lots of sense in Italy. Giovanni Falcone surely knew that, but he carried on. He probably knew he would never get the full support of the

Italian state, but he might have felt that he had no other option. In Enzo's town everybody knew who the local mafia guys were. Even the Carabinieri knew who they were. They would only intervene when the order came from above, to be sure someone else would take the blame for arresting a mafia guy. He remembered being fourteen years old when, together with his friend Mario, they were waiting in a queue at the local post office. Behind them they saw an old Carabinieri still in uniform, but off shift who was waiting in a parallel queue. Mario whispered in his hear, "Look who is queueing in front of us." It was a local mafia guy that the Italian state was looking to arrest. He remembers spotting an old Carabiniere behind them who was staring at the wall to avoid looking in front of him. They were only fourteen and they had already learned what a joke the Italian state was, as represented by that Carabiniere. Now and then the Italian government would send down the army for a show of force for a couple of weeks. The extra police and Carabinieri on the Sicilian streets made sure to fine every young and old Sicilian for a faulty indicator or a broken light, while the mafiosi stayed away in their villas. This was a great way of alienating the local population.

Enzo's mind was wandering and he started to remember when his younger brother, Salvatore, had asked their father why the Carabinieri Alfa-Romeo number plates everywhere in Italy always started with the letters "EI". Their father explained that the Carabinieri belonged to the "Esercito Italiano" or Italian army. This might have been the reason why Salvatore wanted to enrol with the Carabinieri instead of spending a year with the regular conscription army. Salvatore liked Alfa-Romeo. Their father dismissed the idea from the start and explained that to get into the Carabinieri they needed some good political connections he did not have. He had no intention to beg some corrupt politicians for their favours either. Begging the local politicians would have meant promising them, that he and the whole family would have voted for him or her at the next election. This also meant making a questionable political choice and having to ask all relatives to do the same. Not something he really wanted to do. Free elections had never existed in Italy, where everybody knows where you live and the address of the local school where your whole family has to vote. A family of five must correspond to at least 5 votes to a given person or party at that specific school. No exit polls are required in Italy. Salvatore was very sad for not getting his father on board and tried to convince his mother who straightaway dismissed the idea saying that as a Carabinieri he could be in danger of being killed. Better to spend a year as a regular soldier. Maybe boring, but it was unlikely he had to risk his life. Telling his mother that most army barracks were in the north of Italy where they did not like south Italians was not enough to change his mother's mind. Enzo had tried to console his brother, but it was not easy. Then he explained that being a Carabiniere or policeman meant obeying the order of the state whatever form this would have in the future. Enzo explained that while Italy was currently a democracy, what did he think would happen if Italy would become a dictatorship or a communist country in the near future? He would still be a Carabiniere and expected to obey, not for a democratically elected government, but for a dictator.

"What did you think happened to all those soldiers and Carabinieri when Mussolini had taken over the country? Or what happened to those German soldiers or policemen when Hitler suddenly came to power? Please think about those soldiers and policemen who had joined earlier and suddenly found themselves serving a dictator. Would he like to be serving a dictator?"

Salvatore had never been one to think too much about the future and dismissed his words as pure fantasy. In the end Salvatore went to serve a year in the regular army, stationed on a mountain in the north Italian east border. Salvatore was not interested in the fact that to have political connections in Sicily often meant having mafia connections that can easily drag somebody into some dangerous friendships. So joining the Carabinieri could have easily tainted him and this is what their father had tried to avoid. Nothing is free, especially not a mafia favour that comes with never ending interest to be paid back. Thinking back, Salvatore was either too young to understand the implications for him and his family or had decided that this was the way of living in his land and he had no intention to fight the system. It was after all a thousand year old Sicilian tradition. Who was he to tell him otherwise? Enzo had just opened the book when the opening of the food flap announced his lunch time. One more dish he had not eaten for years and reminded him of his dear mother who had passed away only five years earlier. It was pasta "finocchi e sarde" or pasta with fennel and sardines followed by a ricotta omelette and a green salad. The food was so good that he thought that once out of there, maybe he should keep the address and come back to eat there. While he liked eating vegetables or fish, he started to wonder why all those days he had been there he had never been served meat. Was the cook vegetarian with the exception of fish or had they read somewhere that he was a vegetarian? With the food in front of him and the Falcone biography on his right hand side, his thoughts went to his daughter Mary. He had spent years telling Mary not to read while eating at the table. If she could see him now. Eating at the table together is something that he still cherished as it reminded him of his childhood days when most people still went home for lunch and ate together. From his arrival in the US he noticed that there people ate when they had time and some managed to eat together only at breakfast, a big problem for him who, like many other Sicilians, cared little about having breakfast and more for lunch or supper. All other colleagues and American friends he had spent time with seemed to draw their energy out of their heavy breakfast. Because of his upbringing having a heavy breakfast meant feeling too heavy and was a bad start to the day. Once back in Sicily, staying with some relatives he had been disappointed to see that even in Sicily this custom had changed and most families only ate together for lunch on Saturdays and Sundays. The older generation were still holding on to their traditional lunch time and could barely adjust at their children's place like when his parents had visited him. His father had been the one mostly annoyed by the lack of a fixed lunch or supper time. Grandpa, while visiting them in California, when watching a television programme about obese people trying to lose weight in a training camp, shouted at the television making sure that they were all listening, "No wonder they are so fat if they keep munching and drinking sugary carbonated drinks all day long. Keep them busy all day and let them sit down to eat only two times a day."

We all laughed aloud, but he reiterated that he was not joking and he had very little sympathy for anybody who could not stop eating. At this point his grandson, little Johnny who was 9 years old at the time, took grandfather's plate away from him and announced, "Today grandpa will lead by example and stop eating."

Everybody laughed including grumpy grandpa. Enjoying one more Sicilian meal, he wondered if the food would carry on being as good if he stopped answering Inspector Cammarata's questions. On the other hand, feeling that he had nothing to hide, he could carry on collaborating and keep on enjoying the local cuisine. Reading and flicking through Falcone's biography was not bad. The door was being unlocked and he felt a smile coming to his face that resembled his grandfather's dog's tail wagging. He hoped Inspector Cammarata would not start to stroke him, or he would have to start dancing around him in the hope of being let out to meet Francesco Lombardo. Inspector Cammarata walked in looking tired.

"Buongiorno Mr. Dangelo. I hope you had a good morning and some time to think about Mr. Francesco Lombardo."

"Did you make your wife's birthday party on time?"

"Yes I did, thank you. But I had forgotten to confirm her birthday cake order and we were left with no cake. Luckily this is Sicily and I could raid a couple of patisserie shops. She was not pleased, but luckily there were enough relatives there for her not to explode. Well, yes, I survived. By the way, I am sorry, but today I cannot keep the promise to let you meet Mr. Lombardo. He has not been willing to speak to us as much as you have which is not surprising with his recent history. Maybe tomorrow, but today we might start talking about him in his absence. So, have you had time to remember how you met him and if you have met or contacted him while in the USA?"

"Inspector, that guy stole the first love of my life! The first time I really fell in love was when I met a girl called Annamaria at university in Palermo. Then Mr. Lombardo came along and, a year after, she was together with him."

"Is this the reason you changed what you were studying at the time?"

"Yes, you are right."

"Thank you, as this confirms what Mr. Lombardo told me. A bit stupid to change a career because of a broken heart, but maybe that's just me. Are you sure you have never contacted Mr. Lombardo in the US or maybe during a holiday in Sicily?"

"I swear that after the incident with Annamaria, I broke up our friendship and have avoided any chance to meet him. I still hate him for what he did."

"Well, as I mentioned before, Mr. Lombardo works for Cut&Run in their New York office and this is where his wife Annamaria lived with him for five years before filing for divorce. Were you aware that Mr. Lombardo, after practising few years as a GP, had returned to study to become a plastic surgeon?"

"As I said, I tried to avoid him and as I am from the other side of Sicily, we had no reason to even bump into each other during our holidays here, as you have suggested."

Inspector Cammarata looking puzzled, carried on: "This seems strange, as when he applied for his job at Cut&Run he put your name down as a reference. He must have known you worked for the mother company."

"That son of a bitch! He got lucky I was never contacted or asked about him."

"So it seems. By the way, he even invested in HL-formula, but was not so lucky to sell his shares when you sold yours. Maybe he does not have your ethics or did not have your insider information. Mr. Lombardo did try to get into any lucrative job opportunity that came along. For example, Mr. Lombardo became a top surgeon for the gender change operations or, as it is called now, sex reassignment surgery. Mr. Lombardo has turned many a he into a she. Mr. Lombardo was even sent to Europe to open a new branch of Cut&Run in Denmark to take advantage of a new Danish law that dealt with rapist reoffenders. Did you ever hear about Cut&Run branches being opened in Europe?"

"No I did not. I used to just pass on to our Cut&Run offices in Boston and later in San Francisco the names of our patients that had lost a lot of weight and wanted to make some adjustments to their extra skin. Internally we used to joke by saying that we sent the list to Cut&Run of those customers that needed ironing a bit. By the way, what were they doing in Denmark?"

"As you know, the Scandinavian are famous for being a bit more open minded about sex, so they can speak more freely about it in politics and make some logical decisions without the obstacle of the Catholic Church, as we have in Italy. All over the world, people do not want to live close to someone who has served his time in prison for rape. This is why there is a rapist register. People might want to live close to a criminal, even a mafia killer that has eliminated several people, but nobody wants to live close to an ex-rapist. Understandably, especially not families with small children. Keeping them locked up forever was also not a good solution, so for years in that country they had voluntary castration of male rapists. Some young politicians, most likely women, came up with a new idea. As people were scared about male rapists being released from prison, some suggested a state sponsored sex reassignment surgery. They turned male rapists into new women. Of course, being Scandinavian, this was only a voluntary procedure that got them out of jail in a third of the time they had to serve. It seems to work, and now no one is worried to have them as neighbours."

"Inspector, that is not a bad the idea. Denmark is a small country, it certainly cannot have all those rapists that choose to become women? Was it really worth for Cut&Run to open a new branch there?"

"Yes, you are right, but other Scandinavian countries were thinking about a similar law, maybe the Netherlands and even Germany. So I guess there was enough money to be made in turning males into females. Apart from that, Cut&Run in Denmark was also passed the customers list from your company for those obese Europeans that had undergone the weight loss or fat suctioning procedure. Isn't it strange that you weren't aware of Mr Lombardo's working in almost the same company? Are you sure there is anything else you want to share with me?"

"Inspector, I have nothing to hide and I have not refused to answer any of your questions. I seriously do not understand what you want me to tell you that I do not know myself? Do you want me to invent stuff?"

"Maybe I need to help you along the way. Did you create a Facebook user and a group to support a global vegetarian diet and online campaign against eating beef or meat, in general?"

"Yes, I did. Ah, now I understand why all dishes served to me since I have been here were vegetarian ones. If you got all that information, you must have read that I did not advocate for total vegetarianism, but for all of us eating less meat to better preserve our environment. Especially less beef, as cows are responsible for lots of the damage caused to the environment. But I must say that, maybe once a month, I eat beef myself. I am no Hindu. I also eat very little pork or lamb, mostly chicken and turkey on thanksgiving and Christmas, as many US families do."

"Mr. Dangelo, I understand you probably do not know personally all those who write to you in your 'Less meat, better lives' online group, as many do not use their real name, but you might like to know that Mr. Lombardo is in your group under the pseudonym Casanova, and his ex-wife Annamaria was also in the group until they split up, under the pseudonym Exy. Just for your knowledge, this Facebook group has been under the observation of the US authorities as they think it might be linked to some animal protection activists that have damaged some farms and meat production plants in the US. Some of those activists were arrested and some have confirmed belonging to your group. Remember that whatever you do or say can have consequences for you and for others. Now, you must excuse me. Last night I was late and I will need to write down my report for today and yesterday. So, I will leave you in peace to enjoy your books. Tomorrow, you will be let out of this room and into another to meet your dear old friend, Francesco. I apologise already for the kind of cells you both will be put in, but this is to make sure none of you go mad and try to run out of here, turning my last five years of service until I retire into a nightmare for me. Don't worry, after we meet tomorrow morning, you will be free to come back to this room. See you tomorrow, and I will tell the cook that you do also eat meat sometimes."

Then, inspector Cammarata pulled the door behind him and with a loud noise he had left the room. Enzo was confused and cross. Annamaria had left him to stay in Sicily, or so she had told him. If what inspector Cammarata had said was true, she had married and followed Francesco to New York. She had even joined his Facebook group and mockingly used the pseudonym Exy. Despite all these years and being happily married to Carmen, he still could not digest this new uncomfortable truth. He needed time to get used to that. He could also not believe the importance inspector Cammarata had given to his "Less meat, better lives" Facebook group. It was something he had created to raise awareness about the consequences of the habit of meat eating on the environment. He had decided to do something about it after reading an article about cows emitting so much methane that they represented a stronger threat to the environment than fossil fuel powered vehicles. Then, looking further into it, he had read that most of the Amazon forest clearing in South America was in order for cows to be farmed. He had once visited friends in São Luís do Maranhão in Brazil and had assisted at the "Bumba meu boi" celebration. The "Bumba meu boi" festival had been celebrated since the XVIII century to remember the coming of the Portuguese. What he had found funny at the time was that nowadays people of different ethnicities were dancing with what seemed the wrong ethnic group for the specific dancing group representing the Indios or the Portuguese. Some people with white skin were representing the Indios and some mixed race dancers were representing the Portuguese. He loved to see that and had erroneously thought that racism must have disappeared in Brazil. Racism had not disappeared, but it certainly seemed that it was going to in the not too distant future. What he had been most fascinated by was a dancing, colourful bull, which was hollow on the inside where people were invited to ride through the crowd. The bull or "boi" had to dance through the crowd and people kept on touching it as it seemed to bring luck. He, himself, had been invited to wear the bull over his head and dance between the crowds. At first he thought this was a kind of carnival celebrated in the north of Brazil, but this is celebrated in June, while he knew even in Sicily, carnival is celebrated in February. He asked his friend, Bene, he was staying with. What was the meaning of the bull? Was this a religious or carnival symbol?

Bene explained that the bull ate the native Indian forest. The bull ate their habitat. The bull represented the Portuguese conquest and their destruction of the forest that was cleared by Portuguese slaves to feed the cows they brought with them. During the "Bumba meu boi" celebration, he noted that was the "boi" or bull that had the prominent role and not the people. It seemed if the cows had tricked humans into taking them to America where they even cleared the forest to create pastures for them. The all-powerful bull was eating their habitat. It took time for him to understand that the whole powerful grazing "boi" had also started to eat the world's atmosphere. That is when he thought he ought to do something with the limited amount of spare time that he had. Social media, he thought, might be the best way of doing this. He had never thought of destroying factories or animal farms, and he had never advocated for total vegetarianism. What he wanted, was just for people to eat less meat, especially less beef. He thought that raising awareness might convince people and reduce the size of the meat market, forcing farmers to switch to other products. He was clear not to fight the meat industry as he had learned in Sicily as a young man that the meat industry, especially the expensive beef sector, is a lucrative market where the mafia plays a big role. So, the last thing he had wanted was to provoke a fight with the mafia bulls back home. Any doubts cleared when he read about eating red meat being linked to cardiovascular diseases. His own father had died of a heart attack. The food flap announced that it was supper time - Sicilian or Italian supper time, a time around 7:30pm or 8:30pm. He remembered spending some time in the north of Europe and being served supper after 6pm and feeling hungry again at 8:30pm. Luckily, Carmen had also grown up in a warm country and liked to eat late like him. People kept on telling him to have a proper breakfast - that is supposed to be good for you and mean you don't need to eat too late. Clearly these were rules dreamed up by doctors who were not from the south and sunny places of the planet. Instead of listening to those guidelines, he preferred to look around places he lived and realised people were much unhealthier in places where they had a bigger breakfast, ate their supper earlier and went to bed earlier. Eating more in the morning and going to bed early seemed a rule invented by the owner of the fields and industries that preferred a wide awake worker who does not even needs a long lunch break. What a fitting idea, he thought. Similar to the vows of some monks and nuns' religious orders: "Ora et labora" or pray and work. For supper, he was given a chickpea soup. Once more, he was taken back to the old times in his parents' home. Then, a sudden moment of happiness come over him, after he remembered Francesco Lombardo had an allergy to chickpeas. He hoped the guy would be given the food. He remembered his time back in Palermo, driving around on Francesco's Vespa when they stopped to eat a "panino con le panelle". The delicious panelle made of thin slices of deep-fried chickpea dough. At the time, Francesco choked on those and he had needed to be driven straight to the hospital where he swiftly got better after a quick injection they had given him. It was time to get into Falcone's book again and waiting to hear if Francesco choked across the corridor. The day after he realized to have woken up alone without the help of the food flap. Maybe he was now rested enough or maybe he was excited to see Francesco again and ask him about Annamaria. They had brought his suitcase with his clothes into the room. Maybe he thought he would wear his suit for a change. He had nothing else there. The flap person soon shouted asking for the empty tray to exchange it for his breakfast tray. He started to wonder when the commissar would appear. He had said he would come to see him in the morning. He thought he had better be ready as he could not wait to get out of his cell, even if it was for a short time and to get into a different one. He had just finished putting his suit on, when someone tapped at the door to say that he should be ready in 30 minutes. Half an hour later, the door was unlocked. Two agents came in saying that for security reasons, during the transfer from one room to the other, they would need to put him in handcuffs. He voluntarily stretched his hands forward and they did their job. They asked him to follow them and pointed him in the right direction. The room he was now in was larger than the one he had been in previously. It had two large cages at the opposite ends of the room which could fit several people in them. One agent asked him to choose one and walk in there, where, as promised, his handcuffs were taken off.

"Inspector Cammarata will be here soon," said the grim looking agent, before leaving the cell. After a while, he could hear another door opening down the corridor and someone swearing loudly, asking to see his lawyer. Francesco Lombardo walked into the room, looked at him and shouted:

"What the hell are you doing here?" It seems that, unlike him, he had not been informed of this meeting. Then he carried on: "I hope you did not dressed up for me as I prefer you in shorts and a t-shirt. God, you have gotten old."

"You are right, I might be getting grey, but at least I still have my hair. Where is yours?"

"If you must know, lovely Annamaria made me lose most of my hair. Do you remember her? The girl you thought I stole from you? You never accepted the fact she had wanted to move on. Believe me, if it hadn't been me, she would have left you for someone else."

"Thank you for that. Do you think it was normal to use my name as a reference to apply for a job at my company without me knowing about it? What do you think I would have said about you if they had asked me?"

"Come on, I am sure you would have done the same, and there was no harm as the worst that could have happened was that I had not gotten the job. It was worth trying. Stop being bitter about Annamaria. I still liked you. Sure, I understood you not wanting to be my friend anymore. So, someone has now told you about my job then? This means that you must have told them far more than I have. Do you think they will let you out earlier because of being nice to them? Have they told you yet why they have arrested you?"

"Not really, and the commissar does not seem to know much either. He is just supposed to squeeze us and send the juice back to the US."

Francesco laughed aloud. "Yes, like two Sicilian lemons or oranges. Send the juice to the US and later they will resell it to us as Fanta or Sprite. Clever they are. We can certainly say that. They even get our own people to squeeze us. That is clever. I have always admired them for being the best at screwing other countries. That's life - either you screw or you are screwed!"

"What a great philosophy of life. Do you teach this to your children as well? What is your motto, screw the world?"

"What children? We never had children and I did not want to run the risk she might want to name her son Enzo like her father, or you. I am only joking. We tried, but we could not have children or maybe we did not try hard enough. Once they did not come naturally, we did not want to try anything that could have helped. I guess we were not that desperate to have kids. Maybe her parents dying took her mind off kids once and for all. As this happened at the time we were trying to have kids."

"I am sorry to hear that. It must have been devastating for her. She did not have many relatives."

"Yes, it was. Three years after we married, they both died in a car accident. A lorry drove straight into them. Yes, it was a bad time, but they were the only anchor that had kept her in Sicily. So, in a way, this was a blessing for our careers."

"I see, that is why you left Sicily."

"Yes and a new start was what we needed. Annamaria asked me to call you for help, but I knew how much you hated me and honestly I did not think while she was so vulnerable it would have been a good idea to let you meet up again. She reminded me of you and I looked you up. It was a great idea.

When I saw a job opening in a company linked to the one you were working for, I applied straight away. So thank you for your involuntary help."

"Do you happen to know why we are here? Did you also involve me in some stuff without me knowing about it?"

"Maybe just a bit, but I am not sure about the extent of it."

"What the hell do you mean? Did you want to ruin my life and why? Was it not enough to steal my girlfriend and take advantage of my good reputation in my company?"

"Enzo, you probably won't believe this, but I was actually trying to return you the favour by involving you in a project that could have made us both pots of money. I decided to suggest your name, before things started to go wrong."

"Whatever you have done or said, did you not think that maybe it was time to let me know and let me decide if I wanted to participate in a project or not? I am not you. My main aim in life is not just to make money!"

"Listen, I did not want to cause you any trouble and I am sorry if I did. I am not sure I am the one that got you in here. Why were you in Italy, anyway?"

"I was invited to a congress in Rome at the Food and Agriculture Organization (FAO) of the United Nations. They were interested in the new food directive our company was supporting to stop the worldwide spread of obesity. Now I am not sure if this was a real appointment or just a trap. I guess I will eventually find out. Anyway, in what dirty business did you get me involved?"

"Well, it's a long story and maybe we should wait for Inspector Cammarata."

Moment later, an agent entered the room saying that Inspector Cammarata apologised, but he was called to attend another urgent matter and that today they would be left alone to reacquaint. Inspector Cammarata promised to come tomorrow.

"It seems we now have enough time and I would be bored just looking at the walls. So start telling me how you got me involved in this."

Francesco thought about it and realized, that he had nothing to lose and was better to talk than to wait in silence.

"I guess it is only fair for you to know the full story. As you were probably told, I specialized in cosmetic plastic surgery and, probably thanks to you, I started to work in New York for Cut&Run. I made enough money and I got a good reputation that led to the company asking for my help in setting up their branch in Denmark. The job there was different, as it involved mostly sex reassignment surgeries that were not necessarily the customer's life dreams. It was a way for rapists to be, so to say, recycled into normal society life. I got interested in this Scandinavian way of fixing things and I was asked to follow the lives of those released onto our society. So, we started to track them for a while, offering counselling to see if they managed to return to their normal lives in Danish society, but as women. Of course, we were not doing the counselling, but some Danish government social agencies were doing that. A lady called Sofia was helping day and night, and we became very close, especially during the night. Sofia was the Scandinavian stereotype, blond and beautiful. I was spending too much time away from Annamaria and Sofia was too beautiful to resist. I had to invite her out and we did have a good time together. Her younger sister was going out with an American guy who had something to do with the NATO. I got to know Jack, whose real name I never bothered to learn. The four of us went out several times while I was in Copenhagen. Jack and I tested all sorts of European beers, but he was much keener on the Whiskey and I did join him sometimes. Jack was involved in all sorts of military projects and I never found out for what exact US state department or institution he was working for. We had many great discussions about many things, as our interests were various and did not involve sport, so we had loads in common. One evening, we were talking about the many wars in the Middle East and the Islamic fundamentalists. We both agreed on the fact that young men who cannot get rid of their testosterone are trouble in any society, and in a conservative one certainly much more. I mentioned that in Europe during the middle ages, rulers were aware of this fact and they would send young men to battle, to keep them fit, eliminate the bad warriors and make sure their own realm was not put under pressure by those young, restless men. At the time, sexual customs were in Europe as they are now in many Muslim countries. We also joked about the fact that in 2017, the Islamic calendar was in the Islamic year, 1439. So the Islamic world was at the end of their middle-age period. Then, talking about the wars in Iraq, Syria, Afghanistan, we were agreeing that the Muslim religion was being used to unite people of different cultures and costumes, such as the Egyptians and the Saudis. We remembered reading that in the Middle Ages during the crusades, to terrify their Muslim opponents, the Christian crusaders used to bury the killed Muslims in pig skin and they believed they would go to hell. So we thought that it would be a good idea to have a piglet flying on every plane so that any Muslim terrorist would be sure if he or she was killed in a plane crash, they would be dying together with a pig, which would have to turn up in his paradise or hell. We agreed that such a rule could be effective, but would be difficult to enforce. Then I said that I thought that there was a much simpler way to win the war in the Middle East, against the Islamic fundamentalists. Jack said: "Come on, tell me your great theory," and took a large sip of his double whiskey on the rocks. I said: "Imagine those young Islamic fundamentalists blowing themselves up, or going to fight thinking that they will be going to paradise where 72 virgins are supposed to be waiting for them. Why not send 5000 prostitutes to the Middle East as an army battalion for the soft or pink power. Imagine how many lives this would save?" "How?" he asked me.

"Just make sure everybody on the enemy side gets to know that if they leave their fundamentalist group and swap teams, they can have sex in our harems for free and for a whole week. No need to die to have sex. No uncertainty. Sex now, for sure, not maybe, later."

He knocked down his whiskey, looked me deep in the eyes and said. "You know, you might have something." "Yes," I said. "And I think it would have been much easier to convince a north European country than the religious conservative USA. I think this is when our problems started."

"I don't see how I am involved in this?"

"Be patient, I told you it was a long story. I mentioned Sofia and her sister. Jack did not forget about what I had suggested and did mention this idea to other people somewhere. So three months later, he started to be very interested in Sofia's work. He kept asking her about the amount of people that were going through the sex reassignment operations and how they were doing after they had become women."

Suddenly, someone walked into the room with two trays with bread, cheese, ham and an onion omelette. "This is today's lunch. Please move to the other end of the cage and I will slide the tray underneath." Then, the agent left them alone again.

"Did you like the chickpea soup yesterday?"

"Very funny, and I guess you wanted me to choke, but then you might have got stuck here forever without me. Let's eat and remind me of where I was later. I must say, that for a prison the food has not been bad at all. Just the cook must be vegetarian as I have not got any meat, have you?"

"No the cook is not vegetarian, it has more to do with you joining my Facebook group 'Less meat, better lives' under the pseudonym, Casanova. Better still, your wife Annamaria joining with the pseudonym, Exy. Kind of nasty, isn't it?"

"They must be stupid, your Facebook group 'Less meat, better lives' was not advocating vegetarianism, and I did like what you supported and wrote there. Had I given my real name, I am sure you would have complained and unfriended me. By the way, I did not know Exy had joined the group as well. You can guess that if I knew, I would have not been happy for her to call herself as your ex. What do you think? Or maybe she missed a 's' and she had wanted to write 'sexy'."

Both laughed.

"Why did you leave her or why did she leave you?"

"Well, I still don't know. Maybe she found out about Sofia in Denmark, but maybe we had just grown apart. She was away for work and so was I a lot. We did spend less time together, and, honestly, I do not know if in the end she got someone else to fill her empty slot."

"Now, stop your innuendos. Somehow I still care about her, even if I am happily married. When did you split up?"

"It was a long time coming, but I moved out almost two years ago. Now, it's a year I have not heard from her. I am afraid we are not on good terms."

"Maybe we should both forget about her. You were saying that Jack had got more interested in Sofia's social work with the 'new' women. Why?"

"Ah yes, there I was, so some of those had embraced their new body and being a woman. A good part had started to work in the sex industry. This was, for them, the easiest way to make money and differently from those that were naturally born women. Those 'new' ladies having been brought up as men had little or no inhibitions about their bodies and making use of it. Sofia did explain to us that while women grow up worrying about getting pregnant, those new women never had to worry about this as they could not get pregnant, anyway. So they had a female body with no female social or physiological worries that came with it. One of the evenings, Jack told Sofia that he had been impressed by her work and gave her a contact name and phone number and said that she should pass this to any of those new ladies looking for a job opportunity that would change their lives and make them rich. When I used to ask Jack how someone like him had become so concerned, he always answered that we all get older and gentler, especially in the company of beautiful ladies. This of course, I knew was utter bullshit, but I did not want to push too hard as it was none of my business, or so I thought, at the time. Months later, I found Sofia at my door with a distressed, big lady. They were looking behind their back and quickly came through the door of my apartment. Sofia seemed to be cross with me and I asked her what was wrong.

"She will tell you what is wrong," she said. I quickly said that I had never seen her before. Sofia looked at me very annoyed and said: "Just sit down and listen to her." The big lady looked at me and said: "I have been told that this was all your idea and now I need your help to get out of it."

I was lost and had no idea what she was talking about. She then carried on saying that she had called the number Jack had given to Sofia, but I still couldn't understand how I was supposed to be involved. She carried on, saying that they offered her good money for a half military mission in the Middle East and after at least two years in service she could get a relocation package, starting a new life in one of several countries. She had worked out that those were mostly NATO countries. I complimented her as I had not yet realized she had been re-engineered as a woman. She did not care about my compliment and carried on. She had agreed and signed a contract that meant she was taken to Iraq. As agreed, she and many other ladies were lodging in a house protected by some security forces. Most of the ladies were blond, as this seemed to be the preferred choice down there and she was one of the few real blonds. So she was booked a lot and she made loads of money. She said that many of the men were young Arabs that never had had sex before and did not speak a word of English. She said that she did not want to pleasure more than 12 of them each day. But they were put under pressure with promises of more money to do more, but she never did. Some Iraqi older men, now and then, also took advantage of our services and later she had realized some of those were public servants or officials from the Iraqi army. She of course, was not allowed to disclose to anybody ever that she had once been a man. Despite her being a bit bigger for a woman, men in the Middle East had little idea about the average size of a north European woman. So nobody ever suspected about Georgina, ever having been Jörg or George. At this point, I realized that Jack had made something out of my idea and had never told me. They wanted this practice to remain a secret, so not to upset the US public opinion or blow up their cover, should the Arabs have learned that at least half of the ladies they had slept with were once men. Georgina carried on saying that one of the Iraqi officials kept coming back and even forced her not to provide her services to anybody else. For a while, she liked the idea as she was still getting the same money for hanging about and waiting for her single lover's visit. The problems started when he asked her to marry him and move out of there into a house with him. He declared his love for her and said that he would forget and forgive her past. But, from then on, he wanted to be her only lover and was prepared to travel to Europe to speak to her parents. She tried to let him down gently, but he kept coming back and eventually said that she must either accept his offer, or he would ask for the closure of the ladies' house. At this point, some American guy appeared on the scene and tried to convince her that maybe this would not be a bad idea and that they would pay a lot for her commitment. She was too scared about moving out of the compound in a country still at war and taken to God knows where. The disguised army guy said that once their operation came to an end, they would have made sure they would have gotten her out of Iraq, but he could not say how long exactly it would take. He had been very forceful so she did not dare to say no, but she answered that she would think about it. They shook hands, and after her evening meal she had gone to sleep, as she had done every day before.

She woke up in a different place and thought at first she was still asleep and dreaming. Her lonely lover appeared smiling and with some food to wish her good morning. He told her in his broken English how happy he was about her decision to move in with him and he said that he understood her parents not agreeing to a marriage with a man of a different culture and someone they did not know. So, in his mind, he had made peace with the fact that they would just live together in their love nest. He hoped that maybe later, after the war was over, her parents could come to see them and then they might be able to marry, after she had converted to Islam. She could not believe what she was hearing, but it was clear she had been drugged and moved there while she was deep asleep. She knew she could not trust the local US army guys, as they had sold her to have this local official's favours. Worse still, she remembered that for their own security before being dispatched to the Middle East, they had agreed to have injected a GPS trackable chip that would allow the army to find them anywhere. This no longer sounded like a great idea and now it was too late to be able to do anything about it. Despite this, she was determined to

escape. She just had to wait for the right time. The moment came when her companion, proud of his blond woman, wanted to introduce her to some relatives living near the Iranian border. The women of the family, trying to convince her into becoming a Muslim, took her to a nearby Mosque, closer to the Iranian border. Behind the Mosque, she had eyed a young man with a small motorbike. She excused herself saying she was going to the ladies toilets and ran like mad to the back where luckily she still found the young man that had been admiring her from afar. She kissed him on his cheek and asked him in the few Arab words she had learned to save her, by running away from there. Once they were far from the Mosque, she hugged him and gave him the kiss he had probably dreamed of and, while caressing him, asked him to take her quickly to the Iranian border. The young man did so and dropped her there, where she wanted. A long thank you kiss and he drove back as fast as he could to probably tell all his friends about the adventure he had just had. It was a small border station, but heavily armed. The Iranian soldier patrolling it seemed more than surprised to see this blond woman running towards the border. They questioned her in broken English and took her to their commander. She was then let through and managed to reach Europe. He asked her how on earth she had managed to get through all those borders and back into Europe. She answered that the whole way on her journey back home, there was a string of peaceful, smiling, relieved men. As an open minded, good looking, woman, one does not need to have money or a purse - at least not in the Middle East.
Sofia interrupted, saying: "Yes probably, but not all women are the same. Now that you are one, do not feel like you can speak for all of us. You might look now like a woman, but I think you still think like a man. So, please keep me out of your equation."

Sofia was not pleased, but after saying her bit, she did shut up. Once Georgina managed to get back to Denmark, she went straight to Sofia and told her the whole story about the sex workers being recruited by a company working for the US and other western armies. Sofia was close to her little sister and shared the story with her, who remembered me talking to Jack about sending prostitutes to the Middle East, instead of soldiers. I told both of them that Jack had never informed me about his plans to recruit customers from his 'Cut&Run' company looking for a new life opportunity, and, anyway, how was I supposed to help them? Sofia told me that it was my moral obligation to help her as it had been my idea and one must be responsible for one's own ideas, especially if those end up affecting other people. Well, I thought this was farfetched, but I liked Sofia a lot and didn't like Jack not telling me about turning my idea into reality."

"What about your trackable chip?" I asked?

"Yes," Georgina answered.

"They certainly know I am here and I am sure someone will come to see you about this meeting. I had no idea what to do and I decided to wait for someone to come to see me. So I suggested they both stay at my place and we would talk to whoever turned up at my door. They agreed, Sofia slept in my room with me, while Georgina camped on my sofa. The night passed and, by morning, nobody had come. Sofia decided to go back to work and asked me to be careful. I did call the office and said that I might be late as I did not feel well. As soon as Sofia had gone, Georgina came totally naked out of the shower into the kitchen. I liked what I saw, but at first I could not get out of my mind that she had been a man. Looking at her figure, I started to forget she had ever been a man and had to look at the opposite wall not to get aroused. They had done a great job and her smile killed me. She turned around and said: "I like Sofia, and she is helping me, but I wanted to thank you at least by showing you my new, great female body. If you need, I can relieve you of some of your internal pressure? I was stunned by the fact that despite knowing she had been a man, I found myself attracted by her body. It made it clear to me what Annamaria had always told me, that men were like children. Men are more interested in the wrapping rather than the actual toy inside. I had always denied this, but this in front of me was the proof she had been right all along."

"Did you end up sleeping with George then? Did you also betray Sofia who you were betraying Annamaria with?"

"Of course, I am sure you have been always faithful to your wife. No, I did not sleep with Georgina there and then, but on another occasion later after I had already split up from Sofia. But this is another story."

"Did someone eventually come and get her?"

"Not yet. Georgina came closer and I think on purpose touched my back with her breasts. I turned around saying that yes I was under pressure and that she was a good looking woman, but I also told her that at any moment someone could enter the apartment thinking I had some kind of relationship with her. I told her then that she was a bit too risky for me. I asked her what she meant with man pressure. I would have rather called that thing, desire or maybe attraction. Georgina explained that, the man pressure was the reason why she now stood in front of him as a woman. She said that, as a young man, he often felt the pressure of the excitement too strong to resist, despite knowing that he might be getting into trouble. So, this is why, when he had come close to some ladies at work, he had found it too hard to control himself. When they refused his advances, he just carried on and raped some of them. The first time he got away with it, as his victim was married, and from a conservative, south European family. Worrying about breaking up her family if the truth had come out, she cried and asked for his promise that this would never happen again. The second time he was not so lucky and was first sued by his second victim, then arrested. At this point, his first victim seeing him already in jail, found the courage to sue him as well. As this was the second time. He was locked in jail for a while. Having suffered for his behaviour and seen the pain he had caused, he eventually agreed to be turned into a she. She carried on saying that it was that man pressure that you are feeling now, that got me into trouble. "So, I do understand you like no woman ever will. Any pressure down there?" Then she laughed. A call from the office interrupted us. A colleague asked for me to quickly come for an urgent issue, because some client was complaining about a botched job. I told Georgina to stay in the apartment and gave her my number to call me if she needed. Once I got into the office, I realized that the client waiting for me was Jack, looking serious and not at all pleased with me. I invited Jack into my office and after sitting down he said: "Why the hell are you helping this guy or woman?"

I answered that I was expecting someone to get in touch with me, but I was not expecting this to be him. Jack asked me to tell him all she had said. I repeated the whole story and congratulated him on turning my idea into reality. Then I asked him to leave the woman in peace, as long as she did not tell anything to anybody.

"I could," answered Jack. "But I need to be sure you both would keep your mouths shut, as, if not, the damage could be enormous. Your idea is working and is saving many soldiers' lives, so you can be proud of it. Sorry for not telling you, but it was better to keep you out of it. After all, you are not even a US citizen."

"This is a very long story and I am really interested, but I need the toilet."

"It seems a good idea. I would not mind going either. Hey, you out there, we need the toilet."

An agent came quickly into Enzo's cage, asked him to stretch his hands and into the handcuffs. After their toilet break, supper was served. Half a chicken each with some potatoes on the side.

"Hey, it seems that inspector Cammarata did pass on the message, and we got some meat for the first time. I have never been in an Italian prison before, but if this is the standard, it is not bad at all. I might give up work and settle in here." They laughed like in the old times.

"Francesco looked to the door of the cell, "I guess that one can squeeze more out, by doing it gently, than by crushing a lemon and getting all sorts of crap out of it. I am sure they are recording our conversation, but who cares, I want to get out of here and I have done nothing wrong. DID YOU HEAR ME? Well, I am sure they did."

"Okay, please carry on as I still don't know why I am involved. What did Jack propose or do to you or to her?"

"So, I was saying that Jack was not sure how to trust me, so while I was waiting for him to break a long silence, I told him that I had another great idea that might help him. Jack laughed and said: "Come on, tell me this new fantastic idea of yours. It has probably got something to do with sex again, right, you pervert?"

"Kind of," I answered. "Maybe my idea will change some extremist Islamic fighter view of the world."

Jack looked at me intrigued and said: "And how would you do that?"

"Well, I said, imagine if any other leader we capture is not imprisoned and tortured, but we put him through the sex reassignment operation, let him/ her recover and then throw him/ her back to where he came from. With some extra hormone injections so they cannot hide their new beautiful breasts either. Would you not think they would change their opinion about women? Would you think those returning leaders would be welcomed back into their old roles as ladies? I do not think so! This would scare the hell out of the rest of them. No more killing them off or throwing them into Guantanamo Bay, or similar. No, let's create some new Muslim ladies and see how they like being locked up and having to serve their men."

Jack looked at me seriously, then exploded laughing. "Fucking brilliant," he said. "And I did not know you were so cruel. Keep Georgina at home with you until I have cleared this out with my people and be prepared to get involved. Only this way, we will fully trust you both. Do you get me?"

I nodded and he left me. When I got back, Georgina was more than happy to hear about my deal and kept on walking around naked. After a while I got used to her and loved her moving around the flat. Sofia came by and that was the only time Georgina put something on. Sofia told me that she did not want to get involved in anything that had to do with a war or army. She said that she liked me, but while she had put up with the fact that I had a wife back in the US, she could not carry on seeing someone that was working for the US army. She kissed me goodbye and left me with Georgina who was happy to console me and who I was no longer willing to resist. She was great and she knew exactly what a man wanted. I wonder why. She also said that, if relieving Jack from his pressure would help, I should keep this in mind, as long as she got out of the deal and was free to do what she wanted again. I told her that I did not think this was strictly necessary, but I would keep this in the back of my mind. One day, she asked me if I, as a young man, I had ever felt that pressure so unbearable to think about using violence to obtain sexual satisfaction. I told her that like many young men, even I sometimes had to masturbate to keep the pressure down and keep on behaving in a civilized manner even if my young, male instinct was telling me to jump on every good looking girl.

"Well," she said. "Maybe I should have done more of that."

She carried on saying that she did not really mind being now on the other side of the fence and making the most of being a youngish, good looking woman. At this point seeing that she was keen on talking about pressure relief, I told her an old Sicilian joke you might know already.

"Which one?"

"Do you not remember, the one where a man from Milan was travelling to the south of Italy and decided to stop near Rome to fill up his car? A Sicilian came near the car, knocked on his window, and asked him where he was going. The driver answered that he was going on holiday to Sicily, so the Sicilian took out a gun, pointed it straight at the driver, and said, you need to masturbate. "What?", replied the shocked driver.
"Yes", the Sicilian retorted, "you either masturbate or I kill you now".
So the driver did what he was asked and once finished said, "I am done, please let me go."
The Sicilian asked him again, "Where are you going?"

The poor man answered, "I told you already - I am going on holiday to Sicily."

The Sicilian took out the gun again, pointed it at the driver, and said, "You need to masturbate again."

The driver pleaded to be let go but could do nothing except obey. Once finished he asked for permission to finally leave but got the same response. After the third time, the poor man from Milan, all covered in sweat, asked to be let go as he had done nothing wrong. The Sicilian asked again, "where are you going?"

"To Sicily", answered the driver again.

"Good", said the Sicilian, then turned around and shouted behind him, "Rosalia, my lovely daughter, come here. This young gentleman will take you to Sicily with him."

They both laughed aloud and Enzo had forgotten the hatred he had felt earlier for Francesco. In that moment they felt nostalgic, telling jokes like they used to when they were still friends at university. Enzo had started to think that maybe it was not all his fault. After all, Annamaria had decided to leave him for Francesco.

"Tell me what you did for Jack."

"Jack turned up a week later, said that Georgina was free, but would be kept under observation, while I had to fly to Iraq and perform the first sex reassignment surgery specially arranged down there in some military hospital and then go to Afghanistan to do the same. I also had to train some local doctors in the procedure. I spent a month in Iraq and at a later point another month in Afghanistan. We helped those countries' growing their female population. Some "new" women committed suicide, not being able to cope with their new reality, while others were raped several times by their ex-partners and went into hiding. Some have managed to hide their new gender, but sooner or later it will come out. The scare factor seems to be working as they now prefer suicide over being captured and turned into women. It works better than burying dead Islamic fighters in pigskins as the crusaders used to do in the middle Ages. Maybe it will do something for women's rights down there as well."

"Why do they want to keep the whole thing a secret?"

"I guess they are worried about upsetting the US public, being unable to speak as freely about sexual matters as they are accustomed to, or maybe not to upset the sensitivity of some Islamic countries allied to the USA. But who knows, I thought I had given them enough to trust me, but look where we are now."

"It's 9 PM already and I still do not know how I got involved in this."

"I said it was a long story. Bear with me. Jack and I kept in contact, not as much as before, now that our girlfriends were no longer sisters. We did go out the odd night for a drink, just the two of us. After several drinks he was asking now and then if I had any other crazy, sexy ideas he could use. I always read our company's internal discovery bulletin to see what was cooking and what shares to sell or buy. One day I happened to read an article about your new project regarding moving from the fat dripping procedure to a new, more comfortable procedure that would use some drugs. One where you did not need surgery to divert the dripping fat from the stomach. It seemed that you had found a way to bypass the stomach and discard the surplus fat that way. The fantastic thing I read was the speed by which this was happening. I happened to tell Jack about this and I just said that I wondered what would happen if this same compound was given to people that had no extra weight to lose. Or even an overdose of it. Would those people literally melt away? Jack stopped drinking and fixed the whiskey bottle on the table. Then asked me again what the name of the researcher in question was. Well, I gave him your name and told him that I knew you from when we were still studying back in Sicily. I thought he might decide to develop my idea, but I still do not know why you ended up here."

"Thank you, Francesco. Maybe now I know why I am here. When I published my findings in that bulletin, the head of my department decided to go against my idea as her husband was managing the DF procedure. It seems that whatever one does or changes it will affect someone somewhere. At the time I told her that any innovation is disruptive by nature, and if we did not make any further progress ourselves other companies would have done so anyway. She said that she was determined to block my project as my idea would cost the company loads of money and we had a 20-year patent on our procedure anyway, so we did not need to worry about our competitors. At this point I upset her by going over her head and to her manager saying that if I would be forced to stop my project, I would take the idea with me, change it slightly and apply for another patent, backed by a keen competitor I had got in touch with. They asked me to reconsider and they guaranteed me that my project could go ahead with the full support of the company. My head of department was unwillingly forced to let me carry on as I pleased. I wonder now if she has something to do with me ending up here. I must say that I never thought my discovery could be turned into a weapon. But now that you mention it, I guess I must have been a bit naïve. It is true to say that ideas, once uttered, seem to take on a life of their own."

"Maybe, but had I not pointed this out to them, I am sure that sooner or later someone else would have done so."

"Do you know if they have already used my invention somewhere?"

Francesco, looking at the floor, "I am sorry to say that they have. They used a kind of bomb to spray several Islamic fundamentalists in a cave in Afghanistan. It seems the bodies they found there were skinny and the ground was wet from their human fat. They even burned the cave very easily as the fat in the ground lit up straight away, eliminating any trace. I only know this because a guy I met when I went there was part of the search expedition team to see if the bomb had worked. By the way, they call it the ED bomb."

"Shit, I feel like crying. The product I invented to improve many people's lives got a name from our marketing department, while the fucking bomb got my name?"

Enzo was holding his head between his hands and fixing the floor while swinging his head. Only after ten minutes did he feel like saying something.

"Ironically, this reminds me of a book I read a long time ago about the Mongols of Genghis Khan. People everywhere were very scared of the Mongols. When necessary, they used the fat of the people they had killed in battle. They melted human fat, dipped old clothes into it, lit it up, and catapulted it onto their enemies' buildings. I remember how cruel I found this practice and never thought that I would create something like that. I think I've had enough for today."

Enzo called the guard who happily escorted them, one after the other to their cells. Enzo could not sleep and felt very bad for what his invention had been used for. He did not feel any sympathy for those killed in the cave, but he had not wanted them to be killed with a weapon that used his invention. While some people would be grateful for his invention others would die. He knew it was going to be a sleepless night full of nightmares. He almost felt he had partly deserved this. He had always been of the opinion that we only get one ride on our blue planet and his aim was to leave a positive mark on it. His own father had always told him, the world is like a toilet, leave it cleaner than you found it. Instead, he now felt like Alfred Nobel, who, despite having invented many good things during his lifetime, had mostly become famous for inventing dynamite and causing the death of many people. The "Nobel Prize" invented and financed by his family was a way to clear their bad reputation. Did he have to start working on creating a "Dangelo prize" now? Going on a long trip down memory lane with the help of Francesco had tired him out and only the clang of the food flap delivering his breakfast woke him up. A new day and the sun shining on a lonely tree out there. He wondered what else he was going to find out on this new day. He was aware of the fact that he had learned far more about his life in the last few days than he had done years before. How could he have been so blind? Or had he really had any chance to find out earlier? He was not sure, but he was sure he had been a puppet in an act he had not written. Had he been blind or had they been too clever for him to find out. Maybe some of those conspiracy theories some friends had told him about were not all fantasies. But who was pulling the strings?

He bit into his custard-filled croissant and enjoyed it with a hot cappuccino. Not a bad way to wake up and wondered if inspector Cammarata would turn up. He had not even had the time to wash when someone knocked at the door and asked him to be ready in half an hour. He got excited, maybe something would finally happen to get him out of there. Half an hour later he was moved once more to the room where he had met Francesco the day before. Francesco was also brought there. They were happy to meet again and not having to spend the time alone in their cells. Inspector Cammarata interrupted them greeting each other. The commissar started apologizing for not having turned up the day before, then he carried on by saying that, despite their case being an urgent one, he was happy to give up his normally free Saturday, but not the Sunday. Enzo and Francesco told him that they had not even realized that the day before had been a Sunday. The commissar half laughing, "Remember we are not in America here. Here we work for a living. We don't live to work."

Then he carried on, "I never understood why a rich country like the USA cannot afford to give their employees four weeks paid leave a year as is compulsory in the EU. Isn't it strange that the same US companies operating here can afford this and still make a profit?"

With an ironic smirk he carried on, "I guess if like me you have a job you like a lot, you need no holidays, right? Anyway, I am glad you two have met and cleared things up between each other. Mr. Lombardo, I am pleased to see that you have now calmed down. I take you enjoyed meeting Mr Dangelo again?"

"Yes, you sure are right. Not that I am too happy to be here. I like tasting some good Sicilian food again, resting a bit, and meeting an old friend, but what the hell am I doing here and why can I not see my lawyer? You know well it is highly illegal what you are doing here!"

"Mr. Lombardo, please calm down as this attitude won't get you anywhere. The quicker we get through what we have to do, the faster you will be out of here. But I am afraid we are not done yet... Mr. Lombardo, I need to ask you about an interview you gave to an English journalist who came to see you while you were based in Copenhagen."

"That was years ago. It was a journalist from a British newspaper. Why?"

"What did he want to know?"

"They wanted to know about me opening the Cut&Run branch in Denmark for my company. I told them also that later I was sent to other countries to do the same."

"Did you go to Mumbai, India to set up the Cut&Run branch there?"

"Yes, I did. They offered me a lot of extra cash to do that."

"I believe the journalist had come to see you because of an investigation in the Cut&Run branch's unethical activities in India. Isn't this true?"

"Yes, it is true. I hadn't a clue of the application of the law in India and what they were going to do in the Cut&Run branch there."

"Mr. Lombardo, may I remind you that the English journalist had come to see you, because it seemed that the Indian government had found the Danish idea of turning rapists into women a good one, with the main difference being that, in India, this was not a voluntary decision made by the perpetrators. The sex reassignment surgery was forced onto those men. True, they did not have to serve a single day in prison but instead were delivered straight to the Cut&Run branch there. Were you aware of this practise? And were you not still the manager-director responsible for the Cut&Run Mumbai branch?"

"As I said before, I did not know how they were going to implement the Cut&Run services in that country. Certainly, I cannot be blamed for this and I am sure this cannot be the reason you are keeping me here."

"Mr. Lombardo, was this not the same reason another Cut&Run branch was opened in China after you had been made aware by the English journalist of what was going on in the Indian branch of Cut&Run even after you had returned to America?"

"Inspector Cammarata, who am I to tell the Indian or Chinese how to apply the law in their country. I remind you that I was not the general manager-director of Cut&Run, but just the director of the Mumbai branch for a short duration. If I had not opened those branches a colleague of mine would have gone instead. Apart from that, I have no sympathy for any rapist. By the way, like you, I am aware that in Italy, rapists put into prison are used as women. At least in India they now have the right genitalia to do so."

"Could you tell me if Mr. Jack Wolton was involved in the Cut&Run operations in India, China, or any other country?"

"No, I don't think Jack was involved with Cut&Run."

"Are you telling me that, as his good friend, you were not telling him what you were doing when flying out to India?"

"Again, I did not tell him anything and we were not good friends, just acquaintances."

"Then I guess it must have been your girlfriend, Sofia, who told her sister, who then passed the information on to Jack. By the way, Sofia is the one that contacted the English journalist and caused the whole investigation into the issue. Mr. Wolton flew to India and helped to set up an office there to organise the new Indian women to be sent to Afghanistan to lure out some of the lonely men there. The problem was that there weren't that many rapists to recycle in India alone. After the Chinese government refused to allow Mr. Wolton to recruit the new women created by the Chinese branch of Cut&Run, the common reoffending Indian criminals suddenly ended up receiving the same treatment from Cut&Run as rapists. This is when the lid blew off and the English journalist jumped onto the story. Did you ever perform a sex reassignment surgery in India? Note that after pressure from outside, the Indian government is now trying to persecute some Cut&Run surgeons."

"Yes, I executed the first ten sex reassignment operations of Cut&Run in India, but I was sure those were all reoffending rapists. I did not spend much time in India and have not returned there since."

Enzo waited and patiently listened to his point, but then... "Inspector Cammarata, I certainly find this interesting, but I am still puzzled by my presence here. I had nothing to do with Cut&Run and as you understood Francesco got his job there by mentioning my name without me being even aware of it. Why am I here listening to your interrogation? Please understand that I would rather be out of here. If Francesco is the one involved and not me, I cannot understand what I am accused of. What did I do wrong?"

"Mr. Dangelo, you are only partly right. Yes, at this point we have much more evidence about Mr. Lombardo's involvement. Maybe, Mr. Dangelo, you can help me out by telling me who Mrs. Janice Thompson is and how you met her?"

"This is a very old story, but I see that you managed to dig it up. When we rolled out our dripping procedure called 'melt away' or DF, we were very successful and the only company in the world offering the treatment. For a short time after I was interviewed in the USA, by some journalists from women's magazines. I suddenly became famous and many people, but mostly women wrote letters to me to thank me for my work. They told me how my discovery had helped them and changed their lives. Some ladies wanted to thank me personally, so much that my wife got very uncomfortable with all those ladies' letters. After my photo was printed in a few magazines some women even stopped me in the street to kiss me. This is not what a pharmaceutical researcher is used to. I guess I got carried away and started to meet some of those admirers privately."

"Do you mean that you took advantage of them?"

"If you mean having sex with them, yes. I did have sex with some of them. I did not force any of them and they were all adults. I made a point not to meet any woman under 18. I knew the trouble I could have gotten into and to be honest I had not gone out of my way to find those women. If they had not contacted me personally nothing would have happened. Nevertheless, I cannot deny enjoying being in the spotlight for a while. Sure, I knew this would end soon, and yes, I took advantage of the situation."

"It seems that even after your fame faded you kept meeting Mrs. Janice Thompson for more than a year. Why?"

"She was a good-looking, greatly appreciative lady and I have to admit that I found it very difficult to resist her. Janice told me that she really enjoyed sex and felt that she had to catch up with all the chances she had missed because of being overweight during her youth. When I met her she was 32 years old and she looked like 22, at least after going through our treatment."

"How did she pay for her 'melt away' treatment?"

"It seems you know everything. Why are you asking me then?"

"Mr. Dangelo we know part of the story and we need confirmation of some of the facts. So please carry on and answer my question."

"Janice had contacted me saying that she was dreaming of the 'melt away' treatment that she could not afford and had asked me to help her out. Maybe to take her into our research program and possibly pay her with a free-of-charge 'melt away' treatment."

"Did you end up paying for her treatment?"

"Yes, I did but I never told her. Still, she was more than grateful to me, for over a year as you say."

"Did she not ask you for any other financial help or maybe a job?"

"Yes, she did and I helped her by passing her name to the Cut&Run branch in Boston. I believe she got a job with them shortly after. Later she left Boston and probably saved my marriage. I think my wife had started to suspect something."

"Mr. Dangelo, do you not know where she went or where she is now?"

"No, she never got in touch with me, as we had agreed to part ways. We had a great time, but she wanted to earn some money and change her life. She told me that, being much lighter, she felt she now had wings and could fly as high as she wanted."

"Yes, flying she did, as she joined Mr. Jack Wolton's operations or the so-called EDF (Enemy Distress Forces) troops."

"I see. I thought that only refurbished men were sent there."

"No, the money was good and foreign ladies can even get a US green card after six years of service in the EDF. Plenty of poor women around the world are keen to serve in those troops. Are you sure you were not aware of sending Mrs. Janice Thompson straight to Mr. Jack Wolton's operations? It seems too much of a coincidence that you sent away someone who started to be a problem for your marriage. Especially with you being an old friend of Mr. Lombardo. Mrs. Janice Thompson has disappeared and we cannot find her. She was last seen in Iraq from where she has either gone into hiding or is no longer alive."

"I am really sorry to hear that, but as I said before, she never got back in touch with me after leaving Boston."

"I think I have enough for today as I will need to put this all in writing. Tomorrow we will have a third guest and will meet him as well. If all goes well he should be arrested today in Rome, while changing flights and be here this evening. I assume you both know the person in question. We will see tomorrow how well you both know him and how involved you are. Have an early night and enjoy your supper."
Inspector Cammarata left the room and the agents came to take first Francesco, then Enzo out of their cages and transfer them to their cells. Soon after that the food flap opened with a beef steak and salad on the plates. Enzo started to wonder who the third person to be interrogated was going to be. A work colleague maybe. Maybe it was time to relax and get into Falcone's biography again. The night was broken by someone swearing heavily in English from the entrance to the cell. He had not recognized the voice, but the new guest sounded American. Then once a cell door was slammed closed, it was time to sleep. The usual food flap woke Enzo up with a warning to be ready in one hour's time. A croissant filled with custard and a cappuccino, followed by a wash at the basin. No time to shave with the cheap razors they had provided. He decided to wear his suit once more to meet the new American guest. At around 09:00 AM two guards knocked at the door, put the handcuffs on, and took him to the same room again with the two cages at the opposite side of the room. But this time they picked up Francesco and put him in the same cage as him. Once their hands were freed they hugged each other like friends that have not met for a long time. Inspector Cammarata came in, apologising for putting them both in the

same cell, as he was sure they would not mind and he was not sure how aggressive the new guest was going to be. The new guest was soon escorted in by the two guards, who freed him in the second cage. Recognizing the new guest Francesco looked far more worried than Enzo, who seemed to be puzzled.

"So gentlemen, I believe you all know each other. I am not sure you know Mr. John Austin by his real name."

Francesco surprised, "John Austin? This is Jack Wolton."

Enzo looked at both and shouted, "John Austin? This is James Williamson."

John smirked, then looking at inspector Cammarata said, "Well done inspector, so now you know some of the names I have been using to do my job."

"Please tell me Mr. Austin, why do you feel the need to use names other than your own?"

"This is certainly none of your business and I want to speak to the US consul in Palermo."

"Mr. Austin, I told you already that you have been arrested and will be let go as soon you have cleared a couple of doubts we have about your activities."

"I work for a US national security agency and I am sure you will pay for the consequences of your mistakes. I want to speak with a lawyer and the US authorities."

"Mr. Austin, I am sure you are used to doing what you want and with impunity. I do not work for a US agency, but for the Italian government and you are now in Italy. The USA is a faraway country that does not care about our laws nor do we care about theirs. Once we know you are clean we will let you go. For your information, the US security department is aware of our investigation."

"Is this the Italian justice system? Is this a democratic country? What a joke!"

"Well, Mr. Austin, at least we kept you in Italy and did not send you to an Italian Guantanamo Bay. Mr. Austin, while I respect your country, please let me tell you that my father and grandfather were both members of the communist movement here in Sicily. I am well aware of your country's dirty games, starting with the landing in WWII when the allied forces liberated all mafiosi that Mussolini had put into prison. Your great country liberated the island to give it to the fucking mafia. My grandfather and father suffered for what your great country did. Do not listen to fairy tales they told you at your school back home. Every country tells its people the story they like to hear. Go and find the notes of General Charles Poletti about what he had to do in Sicily. He certainly was not proud of it. When I was a boy I went to the funeral of Pio La Torre and Piersanti Mattarella, two Sicilian politicians killed by the mafia with the support of your CIA. We all knew the killers had come from the US, first of all, they wore snickers that no Sicilian wore at the time. The police were not allowed to investigate. It was paramount to keep Italy on the right and avoid any politician leaning left, who cared about the bad and corrupt political system on the island. Once I had been lucky enough to listen to a lecture from one of your greatest countrymen, the controversial Noam Chomsky who told us that, between 1970 and 1980, the CIA spent 70% of its budget to keep Sicily and with it the whole of Italy on the right, and so making sure Russia had no influence over it. I wonder how much of that money was paid to the Sicilian mafia to play the guard dog for your country. I am no friend of Russia, but I don't want to hear any rubbish from you. You won the war. Winners write the history in the shape they like. The loser has to live with it. A dictator freed us of a parasite called mafia, a democratic country re-introduced the parasites. Now start answering my questions or I will send you to another prison where I will make sure you will stay for a long time, till they find you again. We have many small inhabited islands. Am I clear?"

"What do you want to know?"

"Why did you have the need to conceal your identity while working in another NATO country such as Denmark?"

"This was arranged by the US agency I work for."

"Is it possible that you are not actually working for a US national agency, but rather for a US private security agency that does, from time to time, provide services to the US and other countries? Are you a kind of modern mercenary, Mr. Austin?"

"We work in close contact with US national agencies, so we are not so different."

"So you are not working directly for the US government like you had told Mr. Lombardo. Am I right?"

"Yes, you could say that."

"Mr. Austin, why did you feel the need to conceal your identity from Mr. Lombardo and Mr. Dangelo? Was this necessary to gain their trust and support in some of your illegal dealings?"

"Mr. Cammarata, I do not know what your role in this investigation is, but before you arrested me I am sure you looked me up and are well aware of the fact that I have been working closely with US national security agencies for a long time. Therefore it should come as no surprise to you that during some operations I needed to conceal my identity."

"Mr. Austin, are you a spy? Or working for the US Secret Service?"

"If I were, do you think I would answer with "yes"?"

"Mr. Austin, why were you in Libya just before the US and UK government decided to attack it?"

"I was trying to help liberate the world from a nasty dictator. We were doing what you Italians were not brave enough to do."

"Do you mean destroying a wealthy country, causing a humanitarian crisis with millions of people fleeing that country? Is that what you are proud of?"

"Sure, just look at the lame Italian response to the refugee crisis."

"Do you mean the refugee crisis that you American and British caused in the first place? Your memory is very short and you have the cheek to even complain about the refugees trying to make it to your countries? Even someone as brainwashed as you, should recognise that your country is one of those that caused this refugee crisis."

"Why are you not showing us how to deal with the refugee crisis, as you think you can do better?"

"Mr. Austin, have you noticed that most refugees speak English or French and no Italian at all. This is because their countries were mostly colonised by the British and French by killing some of their grandparents and relatives. I think this is just payback time. The refugees want to go to France or the UK or even to the land of opportunities, which everybody thinks is the USA. You must certainly need some of those people to work in your armaments factories? Had you not gone to Libya to convince some Libyan politicians to cancel some of their contracts with ENI and replace this Italian company with some large US petrol conglomerate? I believe that, apart from a large sum of money, you arrived there with a team of girls ready to please the right politicians. Were some of those girls provided by Cut&Run via Mr. Lombardo?"

"Yes, they were. Some were originally born women whose names and contact details were given to me by Mr. Dangelo as he helped an association trying to help women looking for jobs."

"Mr. Dangelo, what kind of association is Mr. Austin talking about?"

"First of all I want to say that I had no idea what kind of jobs these girls were being offered by Mr. Austin. Remember that he introduced himself to me as Mr. James Williamson. After the success of the DF project and me being interviewed by many women's magazines, I was contacted by a social worker in New York who told me that some girls coming out of prison could do with some help losing weight. They said it would be good for their self-confidence to start anew. She was convincing and I agreed to support their association that tried to help female ex-convicts find a new job and restart their life without falling prey to the same people and ending up committing new crimes. The association was using the funds from some donors, but put together a plan by which those women coming out of prison would sign a contract with our company guaranteed by this association. We would wait a bit longer to get paid for our services and we could write off part of the charges as donations. I passed the names of those women on to many agencies trying to help them out and one of those agencies was run by Mr. Austin or Williamson. Anyway, I do not think Mr. Austin forced them, so they must have chosen to serve his agency and its clients. Sorry, but I do not think I am responsible for any of this."

"Mr. Dangelo, I am reading here in your dossier, that you tried to get a young girl, who had never been in prison, through the same program as ex-convicts. I believe the association found out about this and complained to your company. Why did you do it?"

"Fine, one evening a black girl turned up at my office parking lot and begged me to help her. She told me that she had gone through the ex-convict association program and, thanks to her losing weight, she could get a job in a night club where she was earning enough to have a decent life and not rely on some dodgy man. She begged me to help her with her younger sister, who had just given birth and given her child up for adoption. She said that she would do anything to help her out. I answered that she could just pay for her sister's DF treatment. She suggested to me that I could put her sister in the same program she had gone through. She also said that she knew someone at the association that could push her application through if they see my signature on it. So I signed and helped her out. After all, I thought the association owed me something for helping them out."

"Mr. Dangelo, I would certainly admire your readiness to help people in distress, were it not for the fact that you ended up sleeping with that black girl who had come to ask for your help. Is this correct, Mr. Dangelo?"

Enzo: "Well, she was grateful and beautiful. I did not want to seem racist by not asking her out."

"I see, what a big heart you have. Mr. Austin, why were you in Rome when you were arrested?"

"To meet some Albanian and other Balkan politicians."

"To do what, Mr. Austin?"

"They were interested in helping us out on a project."

"Mr. Austin, the people you wanted to meet have now been arrested. They were arrested for human trafficking and for selling girls into prostitution. Were you buying those girls?"

"I have never bought a girl for myself or for any agency. I was told those girls were looking for work in the sex industry. I did not interrogate each of them. I only gave them plane tickets and contact names. I thought I was helping them out."

"Mr. Austin, you are being accused of forcing girls into prostitution and helping criminal organizations to smuggle people. The families of those girls did not know the job their daughters and sisters were engaged in. The girls had been told that if they tried to escape, they, along with their families, would be killed. Those criminals get about 70% of what the girls make while serving in your EDF special forces."

"You cannot accuse me of this. I only provided them with airplane tickets and contacts details. You will need to deal with my lawyer and I am sure my US agency will be happy to defend me and my actions."

"Mr. Austin, I am sure you have friends in high places, but luckily not so high like those people in Rome that you wanted to meet."

"What do you mean?"

"Those criminals, even if they are minor politicians, were flown back to the Balkan via helicopter. Sadly, many seemed to prefer suicide by jumping in the middle of the Adriatic Sea during their night flight there. It seems our colleagues in the Balkan have learned a thing or two from the Philippines' president Mr. Rodrigo Duarte. Consider yourself lucky as they were really keen on taking you with them. The only reason you are alive is that we still need some information from you. Of course, if you prefer, let me know and I will ask them to pick you up."

There was an awkward silence while inspector Cammarata was looking straight into John Austin's eyes. Then, he carried on, "You are not a clever man, Mr. Austin, or perhaps you have started to feel untouchable. Why is your agency paying those men and not the girls directly as you do in all other places? This I am afraid is what makes you their accomplice. You made payments directly into their Swiss Bank accounts. You should know better than me that an anonymous Swiss Bank account only exists for criminal or illegal money that you want nobody to know about. Why does neither of our countries allow an anonymous Bank account, Mr. Austin? Because it is perfect for criminal activities. Even a kid could figure that out. And you pay them into a Swiss Bank account? Do I still need to explain in what a mess you have landed?"

"Fine. What do you want to know?"

"Mr. Austin, Denmark is a bit of a strange location to settle down or live if you are mostly working for some US land security department. As far as I know, you are divorced but have no real relationship that holds you down in Denmark. Nor have you any ancestry or relatives in Denmark or nearby countries. Why are you based in Copenhagen?"

"There is no specific reason. I am originally from Chicago, so I prefer the weather in northern Europe and, like many men, I love blonde girls. For my job it does not matter where I am based as long as I am in Europe."

"Mr. Austin, I realize that you underestimate Europeans, as well as Italy's security services. Please remember that we have an open border. This is the sea that separates us from North Africa. Believe me, a land border with Mexico would be an easier border to have. Maybe you need some experts from Europe to patrol it. This means that despite what you might think we check who steps into the EU even if that person comes from the USA like many mafia killers did in the past and may still do today. Please stop wasting our time and try to answer truthfully."

"I am telling you the truth!"

"In that case, it's time for me to help you a bit as we are all getting older and forgetful. Mr. Austin, why did you travel to the Baltic ports of Gdansk in Poland, Riga in Latvia and the Russian enclave of Kaliningrad?"

"I have never been to Kaliningrad."

Inspector Cammarata put his hand into a bag he had brought with him and pulled out a couple of photos.

"Mr. Austin, have a look at those pictures and please tell me if this is maybe a twin brother of yours being photographed in Gdansk, Riga, and Kaliningrad. It seems to me that apart from working for an agency that provides services for the US National Security Service, you also have other activities. Now I need to find out if this is an extra job on the side or if the US or another government is paying you to do that. To me, it seems that you got lured into some very lucrative criminal activities. Some people like to have an exciting life and maybe start to think they are above the law. I am not paid a lot, but I take pride in my work. I like to think we should all be the same in the eyes of the law. Who knows, maybe this is the same communist gene my father and grandfather had. Like you, I live a risky life, but the difference between us is that, should I be killed in action, I will go down with a smile as I have a clear conscience. You, on the other hand, if my feelings are right, are just a piece of shit that should be flushed down the toilet and so return your misused cells to Mother Nature. Maybe you can read between the lines that I am not a fan."

"Is this supposed to be your tough talk?"

"Not really, sometimes I just need to vent my anger. Despite all these years I still seem to care. I do sometimes surprise myself. I guess this is what keeps me motivated. Anyway, it seems you had been going to meet some Russian criminals with high connections in the Russian army and other ex-soviet countries. Russia was never properly able to feed its own people, but have developed many good weapons to kill them. After the Soviet Union collapsed, plenty of armaments were seized by some well-connected ex-army people that have turned themselves into businessmen of some sort. Now, this is logical, as when all falls down around you, you try to grab onto whatever is still floating to avoid drowning. Arms trafficking is a lucrative market, but I think you decided to participate in a much larger market, the international drug market. Am I guessing right?"

"Inspector Cammarata, you are really not as clever as you think. Everyone knows that most wars are financed by selling drugs. What's new?"

"Did you sell drugs or get a cut of any of the deals? Or did they pay you with their artificial diamonds that Russians can manufacture and have paid their spies with for years."

"I do not know what you are talking about."

"Despite being younger than me, you seem to have a worse memory. No worries, I am here to help you remember. You see, while Mr. Lombardo's Danish girlfriend Sofia is a keen pacifist and tries to improve the world, her sister Cristina, who you are acquainted with, is altogether a different type. It seems that you were prepared to take Cristina with you to Poland and Latvia. Cristina was even with you in some of the meetings you organized. We know how valuable her Russian knowledge was to you. My advice to you would be not to mix work with pleasure. Cristina was told of your criminal involvement and she decided to tell us all she knew. You see, innocent Cristina had stabbed her previous Russian boyfriend with a knife for sleeping with her best friend. As she did this under the influence of alcohol and her ex-boyfriend did not press charges she was let out of prison after only 12 months. Being involved in some dirty deals with you would have caused her to land in jail for a long time. So dear Cristina decided it would be better to talk to us. I must say that you seem to like a complicated life. While working mostly for some US security agencies, for reasons that are not yet fully known to us, you got in touch with some Russian gentlemen that, through their contacts, were able to sell or rent to you a Russian submarine."

"She will never come out alive."

"I would not be so sure about you either. You left behind too many traces, so for whoever you are working for, you are no longer a clean person that can be trusted. You are now tainted and unreliable. Now someone might think of disposing of you. Anyway, we still need you alive and will protect you here. Please, tell me how you met Mr. Dmitry Klukiev and if he was the person that introduced you to the Russian general Sergei Ivankov."

"Mr. Dmitry Klukiev is a Russian ex-army man that now lives in Riga. Yes, Dmitry was the one that introduced me to General Sergei Ivankov."

"Why were you so keen to meet the general and what were you trying to achieve?"

"As you can imagine, I might be risking my life on this one, so you will understand if I will not collaborate too much on this issue."

"Mr. Austin, by now they know you are in the hands of the Italian police. I am not sure they will trust anything you say to them. Mr. Austin, you have been brought to this place where the so-called 'pentiti' or people that have testified against the mafia were kept away from the eyes of the public and from where some 'collaborators' were given a new identity and a new future somewhere as long as they stayed out of trouble. So the choice is yours. As you know, our laws do not allow us to torture our prisoners, nor is this something I would like to do. Nevertheless, I could easily invite some journalists, publicise the story of your confession in the main Italian newspapers, and release you. No law stops me from doing so. Would you like to be released tomorrow and not only be on the front page of the Italian papers but the international press as well? Mr. Lombardo and Mr. Dangelo are here to listen to what you are saying as they want to know how deep you dragged them into your dealings. At the same time, they are here to witness you being treated fairly and if necessary the witness to your deposition."

John changed colour and became very uncomfortable. For the first time, he had lost his cool. He suddenly realized that, even if he would be released on that day, his life had changed forever.

"How are you supposed to protect me? Will the US authority enrol me in a protection program?"

"Mr. Austin, we will do what we can to protect you while you are on our soil and the US authority will keep you safe on the other side of the Atlantic if that is where you want to go."

"I met General Sergei Ivankov because I needed to hire or buy a Russian submarine."

"Mr. Austin, why does someone working mostly for the US security agencies want to hire or buy a Russian submarine?"

"I am getting older and do not fancy travelling to war zones. I am divorced, but still love my three children who are all very smart, therefore expensive to maintain at school. As you know, higher education in the USA is for those that can afford it. My parents were unlucky and both had lost their jobs before retiring. My father got cancer and, for a while, my mother had to take care of him. Because of his illness, she could no longer work the long hours she used to, so she was let go. This means that I have been supporting my parents for a long time. Something that put a strain on my marriage and probably caused the divorce. You see, I help my country by helping other countries keep their democratic values. The reward is being able to work harder and harder to help my own family."

"I am very sorry about your family issues, but as you understand, we all have our stories and families and our job is to stop people using illegal shortcuts to riches. Otherwise, we would all try the shortcut and end up in anarchy or like Sicily." Inspector Cammarata laughed, then carried on, "As I imagine you prefer to travel by car, plane or train, so for who did you try to hire or buy a submarine?"

"I never met someone in person, but an agency based in the Cayman islands contacted me and offered me a lot of money to seal a deal with the Russians."

"Were they going to pay you in a bank account of the island or somewhere else?"

"They offered to transfer the money to a Swiss bank account for me."

"Is this the reason you have been travelling to Zurich once a year?"

"Yes."

"Is this the only reason?"

"Yes."

"Not really. Mr. Austin, you went to Switzerland to check on many of your deals, arms sales, people smugglers from the east of Europe and the purchase or hire of a Russian submarine."

"I thought the Swiss Bank account was secret and not accessible."

"Mr. Austin, just look at the European map and you will understand that despite its wealth, Switzerland is a buffer state between three big European nations, Germany, France and Italy. In short Switzerland exists because its neighbours want it to exist. Now that those three nations are coming together and the EU surrounds Switzerland, this country's being is questionable. In short the lovely Swiss either collaborate with our investigations or they will face the consequences for not doing so. Long gone are the days when Falcone begged them to stop selling Kalashnikov to Italians. These were often used to kill Italian judges and politicians. Not to mention the mafia and corrupt politicians' bank accounts in that country. I have been several times to Switzerland, always following the trail of dirty money. You see, like you they think that money does not stink. Well, I think it does and once you've touched dirty money, you also stink and for me you are one of them."

"Great story. What are you trying to hang on me?"

"Mr. Austin, how did you manage to earn the five million US$ deposited into your Swiss bank account? By the way, the US authority does not seem to be aware of any of this either, so I bet your country's Inland Revenue might be interested in your business."

"Why should I carry on answering your questions if you have already reported this to the US authorities and told me that the Russians already know I have been in the hands of the Italian police?"

"Mr. Austin, please try to focus and remember that we can offer you the only way out with a new identity and a new life. If you stop collaborating, I will be unable to help you and tomorrow you will be picked up by our colleagues from the Balkans. They would either sell you to the Russians or as I said earlier test your night swimming skills. So what is it now, nocturnal swimming lessons or a new life as John Smith somewhere quiet?"

"You are right, the Russian submarine was going to be used to transport large quantities of drugs around the world. Different criminal organizations were going to collaborate in the deal. Every time a big delivery was successful, I got a small cut on the deal."

"You know I have been suspecting for a while that all those incursions of Russian submarines near the coast of Sweden or other countries were no real military operations, but commercial ones. Special drugs delivery. I knew it! It makes me laugh thinking of all those governments wondering why a Russian submarine was detected close to their shores. Of course, the submarine was Russian and detected as such. That also explains the various packages of abandoned drugs near the British coast and other places. So the submarine goes near the coast and discharges its load near some boat that is supposed to pick those packages up. I wonder what went wrong in the UK that they could not pick up the packages on time."

"They were unlucky as the weather changed quickly and the coastguard was nearby trying to help some heavy loaded ships come near the shore. Someone already paid with his life for that error."

"Are the Russian authorities or army involved? Or is it just a criminal organization with the support of some corrupt Russian officials?"

"I am not sure, but General Sergei Ivankov seemed to me to be proud of his country and working for its greatness. I guess the Russians can only learn from this, causing troubles in the west and profiting from it as well. They get the largest cut on the deal."

"Who hired you to rent or buy the Russian submarine?"

"As I said earlier, I never met anyone and my cut was always transferred to my Swiss bank account."

"I believe you have a niece who has been arrested and locked up in a clinic for treatments after an overdose of a class 'A' drug. Maybe you are helping her addiction, have you ever thought of that?"

"Do you think my niece would run out of drugs if I stopped hiring the submarine? The USA is the largest drugs market in the world and as long as there are users of that stuff there will be people risking their lives to provide it as long as they can make loads of money in the process."

"You know what, this is probably the only thing we probably agree on. But you yourself know that this does not make it right either. Were it down to me, I would make sure drugs are sold in state-controlled shops, but every authority in the country and employer should have the right to test applicants' blood or hair for traces of drug usage. Everybody should be free to use drugs and be aware of the consequences. If young people would know that taking drugs would bar them from getting a driving license, enrolling at university or getting a good job, they might think again before doing so. In my opinion people will always find a way to get high. Forbidding it makes it more attractive to a teenager. I say, feel free to take it, but at your own risk. Of course, don't expect for any national health service to pay for your detoxification care afterwards, nor should you expect any leniency after you commit a crime under the influence of drugs or alcohol. Once you decide to drink heavily or take a heavy drug, you have made your choice. The mafia and many other criminal organizations would run out of money to buy their arms and corrupt our politicians. Best of all I would not have to investigate drug-related crimes. Luckily I am no politician otherwise trying to spread such ideas, someone would have already killed me. Anyway, it's getting late so please carry on telling me at least who you think might be behind the submarine deal."

"I am glad we agree on something. I thought you just hated all Americans."

"Why should I hate all Americans just because of the politics of their government? There are good and bad people everywhere. As a Sicilian I know that well. Probably just 10% of Sicilians give the island a bad name. In the same way I make a mental effort not to throw all of you in the same bunch. Some people from your country have done great things and I am glad you won the war and not the Germans, British or French alone. Otherwise we would have just become one of their colonies. Or simply some second class citizens. Of course once you won you tried to keep us far from communism and Russia, but we have been more or less free to move and many Sicilians not to say Italians were welcomed by your country. I am actually sorry about some bad apples we sent over there such as Al Capone, Lucky Luciano or the Gambinos. Now tell me, who do you think placed an order for the submarine?"

"Maybe some mafia guys in the US or even the Mexicans."

"Are you sure that no US government agency was involved?"

"Why should some US government agencies smuggle drugs into the USA and use a Russian submarine to do so?"

"Mr. Austin, are you proud of the US army and its power?"

"Yes of course."

"Mr. Austin, do you think the US army is the most powerful in the world?"

"Yes, I think so. At least until now."

"So would you say that the US army failed in Iraq, Afghanistan and Vietnam because it did not use its full capacity? Or because it is not capable?"

"I guess because they never fully engaged with those enemies."

"I am getting worried as we seem to agree again. If the US military has the power to really change things, then I might be forgiven to believe that some people somewhere might be taking advantage of the US military power. Those people could for example corrupt or simply lobby some politicians to start a war somewhere so that the US army can get involved, then steer the army operations towards their indirect aim."

"A great conspiracy theory, but I still do not understand."

"Mr. Austin, you are probably aware of the fact that the US army has been operational in Colombia helping the local army fighting the local drug lords. This operation has been going on for many years and during all those years the production of cocaine has not decreased. So either the US army is useless or someone, somewhere likes the status quo. Do you get me?"

"Just for that?"

"Not really. The Taliban had almost eradicated the production of opium and heroin in Afghanistan, but strangely since the US army put their boots on the ground there, the production of heroin in Afghanistan has increased dramatically so that today 90% of heroin is produced in that country. Better still, western soldiers including Italians sent there were told not to destroy poppies fields so as to keep the local population friendly on their side. Strange that they do not stop burning poppy fields in Sicily to keep the inhabitants on their side. Now again it could just be a coincidence, the fact that while US soldiers are in Colombia and Afghanistan those countries' illegal drugs production increases or maybe not. What do you think? Is the US army really unbeatable or useless? If unbeatable, then you must agree with me that the production increase of those illegal drugs is kind of strange, don't you think?"

"You might be right, they might not be as strong as I had thought before."

"Strange how people like you, involved in all sorts of crimes just to make money, still want to hold onto a belief of a trustworthy country and government. Well, I guess even the pirates of the Caribbean while they were still killing and robbing people, dreamed to send their children to live in a safe country with a government that worked and protected their children from people like themselves. Even those stupid mafia guys who destroy their country send their children to colleges in Switzerland, England or the USA. The problem is that once they are there, they try to change those countries too and destroy everything. As I said money does stink. Anyway, it seems we came to a good stopping point. I am tired, so all of you must be too. I apologise to Mr. Dangelo and Mr. Lombardo for keeping you here, but I am sure you found my conservation with Mr. Austin interesting. The agents will take you back to your rooms. If Mr. Austin decides to collaborate we could be done in two or three more days. After this hard day I think you deserve some good wine. I will ask the agents to bring you some of my own wine. Gentlemen, I thank you again and have a good evening."

The police agents took all three back to their cells. Enzo and Francesco shook hands, while John just looked back at them and said, "Sorry guys, I had to do what I had to do. I did not want to get you involved in this shit."

This time Enzo was happy to be taken back to his peaceful cell and rest. He had started to feel at home in there. He went straight to look out of the window to see if the smallest of the birds perching on that lonely tree had already come back to its nest. Then stretching on the bed and staring at the ceiling he wondered why inspector Cammarata had invited him and Francesco to listen to John's questioning. What was the purpose of the show? He felt now even more involved than before by knowing stuff that he had not known before neither had he wanted to know. All his life he had avoided getting dragged into mafia or drug smuggling and now the Italian police were turning him into a witness for a major international drug smuggling cartel. It was a curse. His deep thoughts were interrupted by a noise. This time it was not the food flap. An agent walked in and rested a tray on the table. On it, was a bottle of white wine. Inspector Cammarata had kept his promise. The simple fish dish served with a lemon and a salad was a perfect complement to the wine. He wondered if at the end of his stay he would have to fill in a card marking the quality of his accommodation and food. He thought that for the food he would have certainly given it at least four stars out of five. It had been a long day and he was tired. It was going to be difficult to fall asleep while his brain had to somehow store somewhere all this information he had mostly preferred not to know about. Staring at the ceiling was not helping. He could not even watch the lonely tree out there in the dark. Tossing and turning, he then made an attempt to read the book about the bandit, Salvatore Giuliano. That finally knocked him out to sleep.

Suddenly Enzo was woken up by an explosion that had rocked his bed. There was dust everywhere. He jumped up and saw his cell door half open. The explosion must have been under the corridor as this seemed to have given way. There was little flour-like dust left and his room door was barely hanging on just one hinge. He was slowly gaining consciousness and at the same time trying to understand what had happened. Finally he grasped that someone must have bombed the place, maybe the mafia for revenge or maybe a gas bottle might have exploded in the kitchen downstairs. Whatever had caused the explosion, had now put him in a difficult situation that required a quick decision. Should he run away from the place and try somehow to reach his home and family in the USA or should he stay tight and wait for someone to turn up? Running away would have made him a fugitive and implicitly made him guilty of whatever crime they were accusing him of. What if those causing the explosion had intention to kill one or all of the prisoners? His instinct and stomach were telling him to run, while his brain was saying stay there and don't move or you will be a criminal on the run. There was no time to waste, but he felt frozen. The dust around him was still settling. What was he supposed to do? He started to move out of the dust and near the open door of his cell, there he could hear his newly found friend Francesco asking for his help. "Enzo, please help me out of here, I am hurt!" Enzo slowly push the door open with little difficulty. Francesco's cell was opposite and its floor had almost entirely fall down. Francesco was holding himself at the bars of his windows. Those bars that had kept him prisoner all those days were now keeping him alive. The prison guards could not be seen or heard. Then Francesco called again, "Come on Enzo, please help me come down from here! Come on, Enzo? What are we waiting for?"

John had already run out of the building, his room looked empty.

"Francesco if you are hurt you better stay here. Eventually someone will come to take care of us and will fix you."

"For God's sake do you really trust the Italian justice system? Who knows what they are up to? Come on let's get out of here."

"Okay, then hold on until I am downstairs. You can then slide down but before that, let me move some of the stuff from down there."

Enzo went down and found it very strange not to hear from the agents or guards. The situation was hairy and he realized it was better to get out of there. Once downstairs and having made sure there was nobody looking for them, Enzo pushed a cupboard near where Francesco was hanging from above.

"Finally. I thought you had run away and left me hanging here."

"Stop talking and slide slowly down. Let's get out of here before someone arrives."

Nobody was there to stop them, so he told himself that fate had decided for him. Francesco had been hurt on his leg where part of the falling roof had hit him. Looking at the damaged building he realized that it must have been a bomb planted to rip the place apart. It was still dark outside. They started to walk down the track along which the police cars had driven up to bring them there. There was no light around, but a three-quarter moon allowed them to see where they were going. Francesco was struggling, but still pushing his leg forward. After they had followed the track for a couple of miles they saw a house that looked lived in. Trying not to make any noise, they walked around the house, where they found a couple of children's bicycles. Better than nothing, as where they were the track was mostly winding down. This helped them gain some speed in running away from their prison. They had to duck down behind some bushes when they saw a fire truck driving up their road at full speed. The firemen were too busy to see them. After some more miles they found a house that looked empty, more like a holiday place. They walked around the back of the house and used a broken tree trunk to push it through the terrace glass door. It made a noise and an alarm start going. They knew it would take some time before someone would get there. They found what they were looking for. A couple of sets of men's clothes, so as not to look like some runaways in their dirty clothes and Francesco's bloodstained trousers. The siren was screaming, but the place was very remote and they slowly walked out of the place, cleaned up and with some fresh clothes. The sun was still rising when they arrived at the outskirts of Palermo. Suddenly their nostrils were filled with the smell of freshly baked bread.

Enzo looked at Francesco and asked him, "What the hell are we going to do now?"

"I think I will try my luck by calling some old friends here in Palermo. Do you remember Carlo from our university course?"

"Carlo the sex obsessed one who was addicted to porno films and prostitutes?"

"Yes, that Carlo. We got on well and I did get him a couple of times out of troubles. He does not like the police much, so he might be alright in helping us."

"Do you know where he lives or do you have his phone number?"

"Yes, funnily enough his phone number is 69696969."

"You must be joking! Anyway, I have no money or phone."

"Let me walk into this bar. Good morning! Sorry, we had a problem with my car and worse still, we forgot our wallets in our jackets in the car. Could I just ask you a favour and call someone here in Palermo to pick us up."

The young barman just handed over his mobile phone after unlocking it. "Sure as long as you are calling someone in Italy it's okay."

"Thanks a lot!"

Francesco dialled that memorable number and despite being just 06:30 in the morning someone picked up. It is true what people say, the best thing about calling people in the night is that they are at home.

Enzo looking at Francesco with curiosity, "So, was Carlo in?"

"Yes and he is happy to come and pick us up here now. I heard his wife or woman arguing in the background, she probably wonders who the hell is calling at this hour, but he said that after some explaining he will come to pick us up. He said it will take him half an hour or less."

"Did he ask why or did you tell him anything?"

"No, not really, maybe he has seen us on the news already or he just does not care and is coming here for old times' sake and as I said he owes me one or more favours."

Twenty minutes later Carlo was there hugging both of them and asking what they had been up to. They slowly told him the truth. They had been in prison, but had no idea why? When asked Carlo answered that he had not read or seen any news reporting their names. Carlo told them that he could not take them home to his wife as she did not trust him to bring home trustworthy people and maybe if someone was after them, maybe it would better for them to leave Palermo. Carlo offered to take them to Trabia, a nearby sea town. He had a fully furnished summer house there where they could stay. They thought and discussed for a while, but came to different conclusions. Francesco wanted to accept Carlo's offer and wait to see if things would calm down, while Enzo decided to be driven to Mazara del Vallo where the largest Sicilian fishing fleet resides. So he thought that from there he could try to reach Tunisia. Enzo thought that if some fishermen were prepared to earn some extra cash illegally transporting refugees into Europe, he would certainly find someone willing to take him the other way. Carlo could not offer money, but he said he was willing to give him his gold bracelet and necklace, hoping to get something similar or even a better one, once Enzo would have made it all the way home. They arrived at Carlo's summer house where Enzo and Francesco hugged like good old friends forgetting altogether the Annamaria episode that had broken their friendship years earlier. They wished each other good luck and parted. Carlo then drove towards to the south Sicilian coast, after having reminded Enzo not to wear his seat belt while crossing the city of Palermo. He wanted to avoid arousing the Carabinieri or the police's suspicion that they were hiding something. In the city nobody wore a seat belt or better, only tourists, outsiders, or those who wanted to hide something did.

"Carlo I hope you do not mind my asking. Why on earth do you have a telephone number 69696969?"

"Well, maybe you remember my attraction for the ladies?"

"Sure, do ladies like to call this number?"

"No, you are right. It is mostly men who call this number. I have an escort agency that in theory is illegal. Practically nobody has yet understood the reason prostitution is the oldest profession in the world. Where there is a need, a product or service will be provided. This is how it works and how I see it."

"Now this makes more sense. How did you get into this business?"

"You see, when I was still a young man at university with you and even earlier I was a client of many prostitutes who over time I came to know very well. One time I even became the boyfriend of dear Maria who was one of the older but very good looking ladies. I guess I made her feel younger and in return despite my young age she made me feel like a real man. So I guess we were a good match and we had great fun. Through her I got to know several other ladies working in the same sector and many started to trust me. After several years they asked me if I knew much about the internet, something that was still new at the time. We set up a website showing only parts of the ladies and I advertised in many schools full of young men eager to prove their manhood. I organised a couple of parties where some of the ladies would turn up and sing, dance or just hang around in skimpy clothes. A couple of hugs and kisses and the young men were hooked. For closer contact, cash would be required. That is how it started. Then some stag night parties and some business meetings with extra massages. All went well, until a jealous wife who had hired a private investigator ended up calling the police. So I ended up in prison where I spent five years. Thanks to my lady's friend I did not suffer much in jail. It is amazing that while all talk about the future digital currency, nobody has ever spoken about the oldest international currency in the world, sex. Do you know had you called at another time I would have been able to lend you some money, but at the moment the police are checking any of my movements especially money movements. Anyway, you should be able to make it to Tunisia using the gold bracelet and necklace. I am sure you will need more to fly from there to the USA."

The motorway to Mazara was empty and it was a beautiful day. Enzo remembered when he used to live in this beautiful island, he was now trying to escape. He was now running away as the mafiosi were many years earlier from prefect Cesare Mori. The fascist regime had given prefect Cesare Mori the task of clearing up Sicily from the mafia. The Mori tactic was a siege. He would put each town under siege until the population gave him the mafiosi names. As expected, nobody obeyed his order at first. After weeks babies and the elderly in the town started to die for lack of milk, water or medicines. This did not deter prefect Mori nor the fascist Italian government. Eventually the town inhabitants started to give Mori the names of all mafiosi or bandits. Mori lined them up the town wall and had them shot on the spot. Then he moved to the next town. Like rats and bandits, mafiosi were running away from Sicily. Some managed to escape and embarked on a trip to the Promised Land, where many turned into gangsters who thrived in the American prohibition era. Of course, mafia movies partly financed with dirty money never show mafiosi running for their lives with their tails between their legs. It would probably give Mussolini too much credit or maybe because it would inspire someone else to do the same. Now he was trying to embark on a journey for America, but he was not sure what he was running from. Enzo kept on talking to Carlo to whom he was now very grateful. He tried reminiscing about the time they had spent together back at university even if it was not really much. Enzo was now realizing that having fallen in love with Annamaria soon after starting university, she had stopped him from spending more time with extravagant people like Carlo. Enzo's mind also wondered about calling home, but he did not want to give away his location or put his family in danger. Maybe he thought he should contact Carmen's family in Santo Domingo. Then again that would probably not be helpful to Carmen either. At this point Carlo asked him why he did not even think about asking his relatives in Sicily for help. Enzo replied that he did not want to involve his family members in whatever he was accused of. Anyway, he was sure the police were certainly expecting him to do exactly that. Now that he had run away from his cell he had no intention of going back there. He longed to see his wife and children. Mazara del Vallo was getting closer and they were lucky not to meet any police or Carabinieri patrol on their way there. They arrived at the harbour and they tried to find a bar where fishermen went to drink their espresso. It did not take long and Carlo invited Enzo for a coffee.

"Do you still drink espresso or have you got used to the American black soup they call coffee over there?"

"I drink both now, but I know that ordering a long coffee here is stupid and would taste bad. Believe me, a watered down espresso is as bad as an espresso made with American coffee."

"Well, I have never been to the US, but in all their movies we see people drink coffees out of what I would call buckets."

Carlo laughed out loud with the two baristas behind the counter joining him. They decided to hang around there and started to chat with the bartenders until someone who looked the part came in. After almost an hour and three espressos each, they finally decided to ask the bartenders for some help. Carlo, wanting to drive back home to his wife, "Sorry, do you know someone who could take this half American friend here on a boat tour to some islands?"

The bartender looking helpful, "I am sure we can find someone prepared to take you out to sea. It is just a question of agreeing on a price and time. Wait here, while my colleague Salvatore goes to fetch some small boat owners out there."

Salvatore did not take long to find someone who wanted to earn some extra cash. Calogero introduced himself by shaking Enzo's and Carlo's hands. Enzo thanked the bartender and Salvatore, pointing to the door, walked out of the bar. Calogero asked if they wanted to see the boat. Enzo pointed at the sea separating Sicily from Africa, "Well the truth is that I need to get to the other side of that."

Calogero laughed then said, "I think it is better if you catch the ferry from Trapani. It goes every second day to Tunis."

Calogero looked up and saw that none of the two was laughing. Then he carried on,
"Guys if you are in trouble, I cannot help you, but I know someone who could. I recently married. I have a pregnant wife and I have not been clean for a while. So a little misdemeanour and I am in jail. Gaetano, a friend of mine is now out fishing, but should be back before six o'clock. So let's meet here at the same bar at half past six."

They shook hands and agreed to meet later.

Enzo being worried, "Do you think we can trust him or his friend Gaetano?"

"Listen Enzo, we don't have much of a choice and I think we can trust him. The police might be looking for you, but not for me. At half past six I will walk alone into the bar, while you wait in the car."

"Thanks a lot. I am very sorry for your having to wait here for me. I hope I can make it up to you."

"Don't worry, I do not mind helping you out. My wife will probably kill me for being late. She will not believe me when I tell her that I spent all the time with a man. I guess I should not call her either. If you get caught, they might trace my call back home. I need to get some cash out. It will take them longer to trace my cash withdrawal. If they do I will say that I came here to buy some fish. So please remind me to get some fish and keep the receipt. We need to kill some time. Have you ever heard of the dog man of Mazara?"

"No, who was the dog man?

"Let us read this article of today's 'Giornale di Sicilia'. It says that the dog man of Mazara was a homeless person who lived on the streets of Mazara until he died in 1973. The local people got used to him as he always refused food and money. He only collected the cigarette tips he found on the street and never accepted a whole cigarette. He lived on the streets of Mazara like a stray dog. This is why they called him 'Uomo cane' or the dog man in English. He died as Mr. Tommaso Lipari, but many think he was in reality the physicist Ettore Majorana who disappeared in 1938 under mysterious circumstances. Tommaso or Ettore wandered around Mazara making use of a stick at the end of which he had put a nail to collect the cigarette ends. The same wooden stick had some carving on the side that resembled a graduation of values that could be interpreted as a Fibonacci numbering sequence only a physicist would know about. Someone once claimed that he had asked dog man to help his son pass a mathematics exam and he did, but asked the child's father to keep this to himself. Some say that he had bought his new identity from a man released from the prison of Favignana. A certain Edoardo Romeo asked the Marsala chief public prosecutor of the time, Paolo Borsellino, to check if Tommaso Lipari was in fact Ettore Majorana. This was the same Borsellino who was later killed by the mafia in Palermo. Paolo Borsellino stated that a month after Ettore Majorana disappeared, Tommaso Lipari was released from prison. In fact nobody ever confirmed that Tommaso was in fact Ettore. Nobody knew why he, whoever he was, had decided to punish himself by living like a stray dog. In 2006, the Majorana Prize was established in his memory. Mathematically gifted, he was very young when he joined Enrico Fermi's team in Rome as one of the 'Via Panisperna boys', who took their name from the street address of their laboratory. In 1932, Majorana was the first to interpret correctly the experiment as requiring a new particle that had a neutral charge and a mass about the same as that of a proton; this particle was the neutron. Enrico Fermi told him to write an article, but Majorana didn't bother. James Chadwick proved the existence of the neutron by experiment later that year, and he was awarded the Nobel Prize for this discovery. Majorana left Italy early in 1933 on a grant from the National Research Council. In Leipzig, Germany, he met Werner Heisenberg. The Nazis had come to power in

Germany as Majorana arrived there. He worked on a theory of the nucleus (published in German in 1933) which, in its treatment of exchange forces, represented a further development of Heisenberg's theory of the nucleus. If you ask me, I think he was involved in the development of the atomic bomb and he regretted what happened with the project he had contributed to. Or maybe he was just very disappointed by friends and colleagues and decided to withdraw from it all. I believe Tommaso was actually Ettore Majorana, but the only way to find out for sure would be by getting his remains out of his grave and checking the DNA. Some people say that there were too many people from outside Mazara who just came for the funeral of what was supposed to be a homeless person. What do you think, was he really Ettore Majorana the physicist born in Catania on the other side of Sicily?"

"It could be possible, but as the atomic bombs were dropped on the Japanese cities of Hiroshima and Nagasaki in August 1945 it does not seem plausible to me that he disappeared in 1938 seven years earlier for feeling guilty about working on some possibly related nuclear physics projects. He could not have known at the time. But as you said, he could have been deeply disappointed for some reason or just lost his marbles. It does happen even to well-read people if not more. Anyway, it is a nice story and looking at the town now, I can see why one might think that disappearing here nobody would care to look for them. I know there are many illegal immigrants from Africa the authority worry little about. I guess it is important to have enough workers on the fisher boats of the largest Italian fishery fleet. So in theory the police here are most likely to stop men with a darker skin, but we'd better be careful and not walk much out of the centre of town."

Late after six they went back to the bar near the harbour. Carlo went into the bar as they had agreed earlier and Enzo waited in the car parked not too close to the place. Carlo worried when he saw the Carabinieri car parked near the bar entrance, but thought that if they would have been there to catch Enzo they would not have parked exactly in front of it. Carlo walked in and found Calogero and his friend Gaetano waiting for him. The Carabinieri were just having their coffee break there and did not seem interested in them. They looked happy to have reached the end of their shifts and were talking amongst themselves. After having drunk their coffees, Gaetano followed Carlo to his car and got in it.

Enzo who had been waiting patiently, "So you are the one who can take me to the other side?"

"Yes, I can. I am Gaetano, by the way."

"Great to meet you Gaetano. When, how and how much will it cost me?"

"Going that direction nobody cares, but once the coast guard sees me go to the other side they will check the whole boat when I return to Italian waters. It is a pain and I do not want to be accused of smuggling refugees. Therefore I will come back empty. This means you will need to pay for both ways. A thousand euros plus the diesel we need would do it."

Carlo being the one with the cash, "I understand that, but let's see what we can do with the price."

"Not much really. I have no idea in what troubles you are right now nor am I interested. You understand that this has its price."

"Sure we do, but I am also not sure you won't have a full load of refugees on the way back as well. I know they pay a thousand each. I do not really care as they want to move north to the countries that taught them French and English in the first place. Anyway, what about five hundred euros and a great night out in Palermo with a lady working for my escort agency? A young man like you might sometimes get bored in provincial Mazara, right?"

"It does not sound bad, but seven hundred euros and a full night out in Palermo with an escort of yours sounds good and like a final deal to me. I would even leave this evening at around nine o'clock. Do we have a deal?"

Enzo could not believe his ears. He had already wondered what to do and where to sleep in the town if he could not have left straightaway. His happy face said it all and Gaetano stretched out his arm to shake his and Carlo's hands. Then Gaetano, directed the two to the coast near a little bay and explained that this was where he would have picked up Enzo after nine o'clock. They drove Gaetano back to the bar. He turned around and seriously looking into their eyes, "See you here after nine with the money and we will go for our boat trip. The sea is supposed to be good tonight, so plenty of fisher boats will head that direction. Bring food and water for yourself as we could need one or two days depending on the Tunisian coast guard."

Carlo drove near the place they would later separate, but not before having stopped at a "rosticceria" to buy a couple of panini with panelle. Every Sicilian loves a bar where they can eat sweet or savoury bakery. Many love the "rosticceria" shop where panini or white bread buns can be filled with all kind of ham and cheese or deep fried food including panelle. Cooking with chickpea flour was something that some Arabs brought to western Sicily hundreds of years earlier or maybe a local invention as on his travel to Arab countries, Enzo had never found panelle. Falafel could be found around the world, but even if those were also made from chickpea flour, their taste was very different. He was hungry and that panino with panelle disappeared so quickly that Carlo ordered four more to go.

Carlo looked at him devouring those panini, "Those taste good, right? But these will make you very thirsty. You better buy plenty of water for your journey. Listen, Enzo, take the money and I am sorry I cannot give you more. Once over there, use this gold watch I was given by my brother. Don't worry, I never liked it. It should be worth something. Maybe you can trade it for a passage to America, but I doubt it will be enough. I am afraid I cannot withdraw more cash without getting into trouble myself. Let me say that I would have helped you anyway, but should you make it back home, I would love that you could help me in setting up a branch of Cut&Run in Palermo. In Italy there are one in Rome and one in Milan. Believe me I know plenty of ladies in my business who would love to use their services. I already tried, but they gave me some lame excuses why I could not represent them in Sicily."

"Might this have to do with the problem you have with the Italian justice system?"

"Maybe, but it would be ridiculous if you think how many criminals run legal businesses in this country. Anyway, it would be great if you could help."

"Sure I will. For old time sake and for all you have done for me today. By the way, my phone was taken by the police, but where did you leave yours?"

"As I said, I had some problem with our justice system and nowadays it is too easy to be tracked down with a smartphone, so I left it in the garage and this is where I am sure my wife has been ringing for a while. Something else I will have to explain to her which she will never believe. Whatever I say, true or false, she does not believe me. I might as well tell her the truth. It saves me time having to invent something."

"I think there is nothing I can say now that can tell you how much I am appreciating what you are doing for me. Even if this is because you aspire to get a license to open a branch of Cut&Run in Palermo. This would be the minimum I can do for you and I will be grateful to you forever. Should you be stuck with the Italian justice system come and find me wherever I am as long as you have nothing to do with those bastards from the mafia who have ruined this beautiful country."

"Enzo you know how it works here. If you want to survive we need to try avoiding those bastards and provide them something for free. This is the only way they leave you in peace. Since you have left, little has changed. The Italian government is still not in charge in the south of Italy. For us living here, we need to come to terms with two governments. The one that is taxing us is worse than in Sweden, but providing half of the services and the other charging us for life insurance. Like you, I might not like this system, but if I want to live here I need to deal with both of them and shake some dirty hands."

"Carlo, do you remember our discussing Sicilian history while sitting outside an ice-cream parlour? This was a time before the Internet and smartphones. We used to discuss it into the morning, annoying those people who wanted to sleep. Do you remember? How could just one thousand 'Garibaldini' have taken over the island from the Bourbon army? I remember being naïve and thinking that the strong ideals of one thousand men and the forty five Sicilians amongst them had been enough to encourage the Sicilians to rebel against the Bourbon. If I remember correctly, you were already much more practical and sceptical about the Garibaldi landing story. You said that they had not got a chance in hell if they had not joined the devil in the form of Sicilian criminals and bandits. Now it is clear to me that thousands of poorly armed young men could have been easily killed during the landing at Marsala. I think you were right and I owe you an apology."

"I like to see you still getting passionate and louder when talking about the political situation in Sicily. This means that despite having gone away and becoming a US citizen, deep down you still care a lot about this island."

"I guess you must be right again."

The two talked for hours and soon it was dark. They could no longer distinguish the dark Mediterranean Sea from the sky above it.

"Listen Enzo, as soon as we see the boat coming near the shore, you should discreetly get out of the car, go down to that little beach and keep to the right of it. Those few trees there should keep you hidden from people living nearby. Please take care of yourself and somehow let me know when you get home safe. You have my easy-to-remember phone number and it is better you don't carry my address or phone number written anywhere on you. Should you get caught, please do not mention my name as I have enough troubles of my own with the Italian justice system. I also don't need the Americans on top of me as well."

"Don't worry Carlo. I won't mention your name. I will certainly let you know once I manage to get home."

The time had come. Enzo hugged his friend and got out of the car making sure not to slam the door. Now he was on his own hoping Gaetano would keep his promise. Walking down the beach in the dark was not easy. Walking near the trees had been the worst advice he could have followed as he was pretty sure he had stepped on some human's not-too-old faeces. He knew that he could not waste time cleaning his shoes, so he carried on walking towards the sea water he could hear well if not yet see. While he was wondering how he could attract Gaetano's attention, he saw what looked like a small rubber boat which had detached itself from the fisher boat and was nearing the shore. Gaetano himself was on the rubber dingy and after stretching his hand pulled him onto the swimming device without saying a word and putting a finger in front of his lips to suggest to remain silent. Gaetano rowed a little bit offshore and then turned a small overboard engine on. Once he reached the fisher boat, they climbed on a rusty metal ladder hanging on the boat side. Gaetano looked at him, laughed and asked why the hell he was holding his shoes in his hands. Was he worried about stepping into the water and dirtying his new shoes?

"No, not really, it is just that walking down the beach between the trees I think I stepped on something that could potentially be very smelly and spoil our cruise to Africa."

"No worries. On this boat you now have a choice to smell like fish or shit. By the way, I hope you have not hidden your money in your shoes like many people do?"

"Normally I would have done, but I only thought about it at the last moment, so don't worry I got the cash in my jacket."

Enzo opened a zip inside the jacket and started to count the money. Then, walked near to Gaetano and gave him the seven hundred euros in €50 notes as he had requested.

Gaetano, looking pleased, "Thank you and I am looking forward to the night out in Palermo. I am sure you have already made use of your friend's escort services?"

"No, I have not had the chance. I am sure that after you take me over there, you will certainly have deserved a good massage. Being a fisherman must be a hard job."

"Yes, it is and this is why most people working on our boats now are foreigners. It's happening here, the same as what happened a long time ago in US cities like San Francisco, New York and Boston where many Italians moved at the time to do jobs the Americans were no longer prepared to do, like fishing. The difference is that here, even those who have no job prefer to beg their parents instead of earning little money. I guess they don't want to be looked down upon by the other people in town, especially by the girls. There is no pride in work. Just money now."

"You are young. Why did you not do the same?"

"My luck was that I had nobody at home who could help me, so I had to do something or starve. As you know, this is no Germany or France or any other European country where you get a minimum unemployment benefit to live on. Here, if you have no work and no family who can help you, the only safety net is the mafia. It is a kind of second extended family for those who have nowhere to go. If you work for the mafia and you get caught, they help you with the expenses and keep your family fed. Until now, I have been lucky not to need their help. Of course, you know how it works here. Sometimes to avoid troubles, I give something for free or do a little favour."

"Yes, you are right. I know how the system works here. I left this country years ago, but I see that little has changed since then."

Their fisher boat was slowly sailing towards Africa through a very black night with almost no moon and a quiet sea. Enzo got an old jumper from Gaetano to make sure he looked like a poor fisherman. The Italian coast guard was busy enough preventing outsiders from coming into the Italian waters and the EU coast to care about those leaving it. Gaetano only answered Enzo's questions probably to avoid asking the wrong thing and involving himself in whatever he thought Enzo was running away from. Nevertheless, Enzo felt the need to tell Gaetano that he was not helping a mafia guy or a real criminal, so he started a new conversation on his own.

"We are certainly lucky with the weather as with these calm waters the coastguards do not see the need to be out at sea if not called, right?"

"Yes, indeed, but as we need to pretend to be fishing, you will now need to help me to throw out the net. In this way our fishing trip looks real and we might even catch something."

"Can you still make a living out of fishing?"

"Well, we are all overfishing everywhere and I should probably get into aquaculture, but as with everything in Sicily, if you have no connection you cannot do anything."

"Yes I know, it is frustrating. A friend of mine used to say that we have a great sports car and even the petrol, but prefer to move it by pushing it. And still now, like then, the bastards are keeping people in poverty in order for them to keep their power and buy the Sicilians' votes. They are like a cancer that cannot be cured."

Gaetano laughed aloud and shouted over the diesel engine noise, "You sound like an optimist."

"I am glad I was able to leave this behind me and I feel sorry for those who cannot and have to live in this situation. I often thought that there is an advantage in playing ignorant and just enjoy the simple things in life: good food, beautiful scenery and some sex. Who cares who is in charge of what? But I cannot do that. I could not see the cancer getting hold of the island and the rest of the country. Ignorance is bliss. It was too late for me. I had already opened the can of worms and I had seen the shit inside it. So I had to leave."

"I think there are advantages and disadvantages everywhere. We are poor, but I love my family and friends. I could not just leave it all behind. I knew some guys who worked with the mafia, but few make it to their pension age. I might have a poor life, but you will see tomorrow morning at sunrise how beautiful it can be to be alone out here on the deep blue sea. It makes me forget the shit back on land. Here I could be anywhere. Here the sea is in charge and no one else. Respect the sea or it will kill you, whoever you are. For Mother Nature, we are all the same. So I go on land and listen to some of those monkeys, but I prefer to come back to my fishes out here."

"Sorry Gaetano, do you have a toilet up here?"

"No sir! There is no first class on this boat. Go to the back of the boat and you will find two hooks slightly raised. Get up there, make sure your legs are both inside the hooks, then sit with your bum sticking out. It's a calm sea, so you should not get the automatic bum washing service tonight."

"This is one of those things I have not yet done in my life and now I can tick it off. Thanks."

Enzo made sure he locked both legs before sitting down with most of his body leaning outside of the boat. He felt lucky that being dark nobody could see him dangling out of the side of the boat. While he was enjoying the sea breeze on the part of his body that is normally covered. Then he thought he heard some voices in the distance. It sounded almost like screaming. Once he got his new experience under his belt, he walked up to the bow of the boat to find Gaetano.

"Listen, I think I could hear some shouting while I was at the stern of the boat."

"Maybe, but we should mind our own business out here. I certainly don't want to be accused of being your accomplice for whatever you have done. So keep quiet and low."

The voices kept getting louder and shouting could be heard. It seemed a boat in distress. Maybe some refugees. Gaetano kept ignoring the noise while pretending to fish and sail south. After a while the sound turned into fuzzy images far away.

"Is there anything else we can do to help them?"

"Do you want me to go there and be on the news? They are running away from shit and you want me to get into it? Do we know who they left back home trying to save themselves?"

"I get this, but can we send a signal somewhere for them?"

"We could get a bit closer and flare a rocket, then get the hell out of there, but if a boat comes to find us, I will let you out alone in a dinghy and good luck. Do you want me to do that?"

"Yes!"

Without saying anything Gaetano changed the boat direction and started to blow up a dinghy. Then he opened his mouth, "It's your choice and your life and we all pay the consequences of our actions."

"What if they get me in the dinghy and I tell them about you?"

"As I said, I do know some of those bastards you were talking about and believe me they owe me a favour or two. We might both end up in a jail, but you won't come out of it. Anyway, thanks to your stupid question I won't help them at all."

Then, he turned the boat back south ignoring the raised voices shouting in their direction. Enzo regretted the stupid question that might have killed some people and had granted him a silent passage all the way to Africa. The voices slowly faded into the distance. Suddenly Enzo started to hope that Gaetano would not play a trick on him and leave him on another Italian minor island like Pantelleria, Lampedusa or even back to the Sicilian coast. He now remembered reading in one of Verga's books about those poor Sicilians who had paid large sums for their passage to America, only to disembark days later and during the night near where they had departed after circumnavigating Sicily. Some impostors had stolen the poor people's money. Was this going to be his fate now that he had annoyed captain Gaetano? That stupid question might have ruined his chances to get to freedom. The captain started to play on his phone and from then on disregarded his guest. In a cabin corner he found a kind of mattress onto which he throw himself exhausted from the long day. Before falling asleep he wondered what Carmen and his kids were up to. Had Carlo made it back home already and was he arguing with his wife? Was the Italian police looking for him? It was morning and the strong sun was shining straight onto his face. This woke him up early. Out there, there was a beautiful blue sea all around. Gaetano just lifted his hand to acknowledge his presence. Enzo walked towards him.

"Listen, I am sorry about that stupid question yesterday. Your suggestion to let me drift away on a small dinghy must have put me under pressure."

"Let me get this straight, you wanted to help those people, but wanted me to pay the consequences together with you? You wanted to help them, not me! Why should I pay for your actions? It's like those well-meaning politicians who want their children to go to the best schools, but want my one to share the few resources with the refugees' kids. They can afford private doctors and clinics and I have to share the hospitals with the newcomers I did not want in the first place. If you mean it well, then you need to show it. Do you want to help refugees, then start with taking a family into your large house and share your children's school facilities, not mine? Then, I would believe you. You know what we say in Sicily don't you?"

"What?"

"A dick in someone else's ass always feels like a piece of straw to you!"

"I did not know that one, but it certainly conveys your point. Anyway, sorry again and you might be right. I wanted to involve you. I guess it's like the Germans saying to the east European members of the EU, you have to take in refugees because we have already done so. I cannot imagine what the German public would say if it were the other way around. If other EU countries would tell Germany what to do and how many more refugees to take in. I found this a funny way of doing this and now I behaved in the exact same way. Yes, you are right."

"It's okay, no need to apologise. As I said out here, we are all the same, but I am the captain and I decided to turn the boat away. Anyway, listen, we could get to Africa or better Tunisia during the day, but that would be stupid. So we will have to wait for darkness and only then will I let you out. I know a place not too far from Tunis the capital. There are some hotels there. That would make it easier for you to look like any of their other guests. Some might think you have turned up during the night. In the evening they usually have loud disco music on. That should make it easier for you to walk off the dinghy and onto the beach. Go to the back of the hotel where some of guest clothes might be hanging for laundry service. Then try to steal some swimming trunks and try to look the part. Some holiday t-shirts would also be better than what you are wearing. Then I would advise you to find your way to Tunis in the north or Sfax in the south. Those are large enough places to find some passages wherever you want to go. If you want to go to America, maybe you need to get all the way to Casablanca in Morocco where they have plenty of cargo boats going all over the world."

"Thank you for your help and while I know you are doing it for the money, please let me say that I am very grateful to you."

"No worries, look around you and enjoy. Did I say it was going to look great? Is there anything else more beautiful? Of course, sex, but it does not last this long. At least not for me."

Gaetano was in a better mood now and laughing. Enzo's apologies had certainly helped improve the mood on board.

"What about the escort that is waiting for you in Palermo?"

"I am looking forward to that night, but it's like sea and sunshine in a bedroom. Better still having sex in the sea. Have you ever done it? It's great!"

"Yes, but I am sure not as much as you have."

Suddenly far away they spotted a boat with a dark blue bottom. It could be the Italian coast guard. Enzo looked at Gaetano pointing at the fast-moving boat.

"Listen if this is the coastguard there is little we can do as their boats are very fast and if not, they will call a plane or a helicopter. So stay calm and wear one of those cheap looking cappies from inside the cabin. The net is out and just follow what I am doing. OK?"

Enzo nodded, but his blood pressure shot up. It was definitely the coastguard and was coming closer. Once just few metres away, they slowed down their engine and shouted towards the boat: "Buongiorno, tutto bene?"

"Sure, all okay thank you. It's a beautiful day and let's hope we get enough fish today to fill the boat."

From the coastguard boat a smiley agent answered, "I wish you good luck and try staying away from the Tunisian coast. They don't like us fishing in their waters. Have a good day!"

Gaetano and Enzo waved back, while the coastguard's powerful engine got louder and faster. They disappeared in little time while Enzo's blood pressure started to normalize.

"Well, it seems they do not yet have your picture and you managed to keep your pants clean."

Gaetano was laughing loudly again.

"You must be right or I have other reasons why I want to leave Italy in this way."

"Sorry, you are right, it is none of my business. To me, you are a fisherman. So come back here and help me pull the net."

They managed to pull some fishes out of the water and Gaetano went straight into the cabin and started to take them out. The boat had a little galley, but had all it needed to prepare a meal. The smell of garlic and fried fish filled the air around the boat and Enzo could not wait to be invited in. He had asked if he could help, but he was sent out to avoid him starting to smell of fried fish. It seemed that Gaetano was keen on him to succeed in getting away from the Tunisian coast, so relieving him of any likely involvement. His smelling of fried fish would have probably give him away as an Italian fisherman rather than an Italian tourist. Or maybe he simply wanted him out of the galley while cooking. After a while, the long expected invitation came and Enzo was more than happy to oblige. There was enough fried fish for a large crew, but Gaetano reassured him that until the evening they would have got through it. Then with a full mouth, "Do you see why I love it here? Great sea, mostly great weather and fantastic food."

"I sure do miss this, but there is more to life than just eating, singing and dancing. Well, at least for some like me."

The full stomach and the gently rocking sea convinced Enzo to just lay down on deck and sleep on the spot. Hours later Gaetano was steering the boat that slowly went south.

"Sorry to bother you captain, but: is there any way I could wash here? Do I need to lower myself overboard or should I pull some buckets of water. What do you usually do here to wash?"

"We have enough time and there is no one around. If you want we could stop the engine. There is a ring buoy on the other side of the boat with a rope attached. So throw it down, jump in and hold the lifebuoy. I'll give you no more than half an hour. Remember that this is salty water and we have no fresh water on board for a shower. So you are going to be clean, but a bit sticky. Do you still want to jump in?"

"Yes, sure."

Swimming in the middle of the blue sea reminded him of his childhood. After having washed in the small cell basin for a week it was great to have a swim. In the basin had been too little, there was too much water to wash here. Once back on board, the boat steered its south course again.

"Get ready, as soon it will be dark we will carry on towards the Tunisian coast."

"Will the Tunisian coastguard stop us?"

"In the past they did, but now they do not have many boats and at the moment most of those are near the Libyan border making sure no terrorists comes in, I guess?"

In the early hours of the morning they could see the Tunisian coast and the great weather allowed them to see very far. They got worried that they could also be seen from afar. There was no Tunisian coastguard in sight.

"Now I will get close to the coast and let you out behind that hotel you see on the right. I will leave you on the other side of it close to those rocks. So walk slowly towards the hotel seafront and look like one of those weird tourists who cannot sleep when on holiday. If someone asks you something before you manage to get some beach wear, pretend to be drunk having had a long night out. Whatever you do, try not to alarm them for your sake and for mine. I will go back to international waters as fast as I can, pretending to have fished in Tunisian waters and not caught anything."

"Understood and thank you for all your help."

The rest was a silent journey on an empty blue sea with the shimmering sunrise on it. Beautiful, if not for the risks Enzo thought were ahead. In part this made him feel young. At his mature age, life was giving him one more opportunity for adventure. While coming very close to the coast, Gaetano started to lower a dingy at the back of his fisher boat. He threw all of Enzo's stuff into it and asked him to come to the back of the boat. They shook hands, a sincere look into each other's eyes followed by a good luck and a sign to climb down. Enzo started rowing fast to reach the rocks Gaetano had pointed out to him. At that moment he remembered the scenes of Syrian refugees landing in Greece and cutting their dinghies as soon as they arrived. While at first this action seemed odd, he had then read that under maritime international law, stranded people cannot be turned away if they have no valid means of travelling. He was not worried about that, but he started to think that maybe it would be good to break and hide the dinghy after landing. Luckily nobody seemed to have seen him. Searching in his bag and pockets, he realized he did not have a knife with him, so he resolved to let the dinghy air out slowly. He jumped on a different continent, the coast of Africa. He managed to deflate the dinghy and leave it behind a rock. Then he tried to walk across the rocks and to the beach in front of the hotel. Without shoes he managed to cut his foot badly. As usual he thought that while trying to save time he was actually slowing himself down. He then found his shoes, wore those without socks and with plenty of sand in it, absorbing his blood. Finally he had made it onto the sandy beach and started to walk towards the other side of the hotel. There was an old man sweeping the beach clean and looking at him in a suspicious way. Being worried he would call a guard or even the police, instead of hiding he started to walk towards him and play drunk as Gaetano had suggested. Then shouting "Bonjour, bonjour, puis-je aller dans ma chambre?"

The man smiled, then opened the back door for him mumbling something that sounded like, stupid, drunk tourist. He was impressed with how much French he could remember. His school days were long gone. Luckily there were plenty of tourists around who seemed to be ready for an early morning trip on a bus. That helped him look less conspicuous. He found the downstairs toilet where he could use some of the clothes that Carlo had brought for him and clean his bleeding foot. The bleeding had stopped, but to make sure not to ruin the only shoes he had, he put some toilet paper under his sock and in it. It was a great day and after being kept in a Sicilian cell for about ten days, he wanted to get on with trying to go back home. He walked together with all the other tourists out of the hotel, but did not jump on the bus. He carried on following the only road out of the holiday resort. Once he was far enough from the hotel the bus passed him at great speed with many tourists looking down at him. Nevertheless, he thought he had made it out of there and now needed to find a way to reach Morocco. After walking for a couple of hours, being passed by a few cars at high speed, he encountered a village where he was hoping to buy something to drink. He went into a small shop that was also the local petrol station. At this point he realized he did not have any dinar, the local currency. So he got the smallest note of five Euro that he found in his pocket and waved this to the man behind the counter after pointing to a fridge with cool bottles in it. The man showed his thumb up and said something in Arabic, then seeing that he had only got two bottles of cool water out of the fridge, even gave him some dinars back. He uttered the only Arabic word he could manage - "Shukran" - and left the shop. After coming out of the shop he noticed something that looked like a gang of young men, which did not seem to have come out of any vehicle. They seemed also too trendy to be from the village and too well dressed to be local farmers. They seemed to have spotted him straightaway as soon as he had got out of the shop. Not good he thought.

Pretending not to notice nor look at them, he started to walk towards what seemed like the road to Tunis, from where he thought he could somehow leave Tunisia. After walking for almost another hour he noticed the entrance to a road that went to what looked like another holiday resort. While he was attempting to cross the road a young man came close to him, but this time he spoke English. The young man had a knife in his hand and asked him to hand over his wallet. Suddenly Enzo recognized the young man as being one of the gang he had seen near the shop. While he was looking for his wallet in which he had left only a few notes, having foreseen such type of encounters, a car stopped near them. It was a police car. At this point the young man hugged Enzo and gave him a kiss. Then looked at the policemen and said in a very camp English voice, "Sorry officer, we were just going for our morning walk."

Disgusted, both police officers looked at them and shouted back, "Aller à l'hôtel, les gens d'ici n'aiment pas les homosexuels."

The young man answered "Merci", then took Enzo's hand and started to walk towards the hotel. The police car drove off and both felt relieved.

"Great safe and good acting!"

"I knew you had something to hide. Why on earth are you walking all alone on the road at this early hour? If I had not been there, you would have had to explain this to them."

"Are you really saying that I should feel lucky that you were or still are trying to rob me?"

"Kind of. Anyway, where are you going?"

"I need to go back home to America."

"That is a long way from here, but maybe the airport in Tunis might be where you need to head to. Why did you not take a taxi? Are taxis expensive here for an American?"

"Where are you going and why are you an English speaker here in Tunisia? Where are you from?"

"I am Joshua and I am from Zimbabwe."

"Joshua, I need some help going to America and you could probably help me getting there. Maybe I could help you in return once I get there."

"America is a long way away, so I prefer you also start to help me here."

"I do not have much money here if that is what you need."

"I am not looking for money, but I would love to move to Europe or America and I think that like you, I cannot get there legally either."

"I see that we have something in common and we could benefit from working as a team. I think you had a great idea. Should they stop us again let's play the gay card and pretend to be a western homosexual couple on holiday. I am sure they don't like gays, but will leave foreign tourists in peace. If you help me, I will do what I can to get you out of Africa."

Joshua turned around, looked him in the eyes and gave him a hard handshake, then said "This is a deal." That way of doing things seemed to Enzo so peculiarly similar to what he knew from Sicily that he had to ask.

"Where did you learn to sign a contract in this way?"

Joshua laughed out loud, then he said, "In South Africa from my Sicilian boss."

"What, you worked in South Africa for the Sicilian mafia?"

"No, no. In South Africa I worked for McDonald's and the area manager was the son of a Sicilian immigrant who had made some money there. He taught me that every man, poor or rich, can sign a valid contract that if broken entitled the other one to put a long knife through him. It seems you understood well my gesture. Are you a Sicilian?"

"Yes, you can say that. I have just arrived from Sicily."

"We can chat later, now let's get to this hotel and see when some employees leave for the nearest town. We could get a lift for a few dinars."

They walked to the hotel and to the back where Joshua started to discuss with someone who looked like a kitchen chef. Then he came back with some food and the news that in half an hour some employees who would have finished their night shifts will be able to give them a lift to Tunis. They sat near the kitchen on a bench and waited for them in the shade. The hotel employees kept their promise and invited them to jump in a minibus in the parking lot. After what seemed a long time travelling, they reached Tunis "Jardin Habib Thameur" bus station.

"And now?"

"I thought our plan was to go to Morocco and from there to America on a container ship right? Or do you have a better idea?"

"No, I don't. Good idea, let's do that."

Joshua walked through the old town and went into an Internet café, booked a desk for both of them, turned around to Enzo and said, "Now let's try to find a holiday resort near the Algerian border to justify our journey there. In the past we could have gone via the desert, but now because of all the refugees like me and the stupid religious fundamentalists the desert is far more guarded than the north of the country. Believe me, I have been stuck here for a while. I arrived here via the desert and it is not a safe place there especially not for someone with your skin colour. Wait, I found one. Look this is the 'El Mouradi Hammam Bourguiba four-star hotel'. Now it is your turn to get the money out and book a room there."

"I don't have that much money on me especially not for a four-star hotel."

"Damn, you are slow! We will never arrive there, but if they stop us on the way, you can tell the police that we are booked at the hotel and if they call the hotel, they will confirm. Just use your real last name and a fake first name, maybe Joe or even Joshua."

"I see. Let me send them an email and ask for a room for tomorrow evening right? How far is this place? I see only about 200 Km from here, but four hours' drive. How will we get to Algeria?"

"I think a fisher boat from the nearby town of Tabarka is probably the best bet. Some poor fisherman will certainly be keen to earn some extra cash throwing us over the border."

"How does a clever boy like you end up as a refugee?"

"How does a middle aged white American like you, end up walking on a dusty road near Tunis? Anyway, please pay for the half hour Internet and let's get out of here. We need to catch a bus."

They walked back to the bus station and wandered around for a while trying to find a minibus that would take them near Tabarka. A bus driver seeing this mixed couple suspiciously asked where they were heading to. "El Mouradi Hammam Bourguiba hotel" said Enzo. The driver smiled and told them to wait for a couple of hours as the bus would leave then. They had enough time to buy food and water for their journey ahead.

"So tell me, Joshua, are you on the run or just looking for a better future? South Africa is one of the wealthier countries in Africa. It seems a strange place to leave for Europe or America."

"Don't forget that I am not South African. There, I was a Zimbabwean, a barely tolerated refugee. For a while I lived on the streets of Johannesburg, until a McDonald's manager gave me a chance. There were criminal gangs in that area of Johannesburg and some youngster kept on breaking into the McDonald's after dark to steal and break stuff. The manager had spotted me living in an abandoned part of their car park. One day he called me into his shop after everybody had left. He looked straight into my eyes and said that he had a job for me. Then he handed over a loaded gun to me and asked me if I would prefer to sleep inside the McDonald's. He would arrange a bed in his office behind the kitchen. He asked me to shoot, but not necessarily kill anybody attempting to enter their premises. I had nothing to lose and someone I did not know was trusting me with his own loaded gun. I nodded and shook his hand. For a couple of nights I did not hear anything, but one day someone tried to break in and as I was requested to do, I shot in their direction and heard them running as fast as they could. The day after I got promoted to a day job in the joint and I got a monthly salary. The owner never asked about my past and told me that he was only interested in me now."

"So I am right! You had a job and no need to run away. Or did they want to kick you out of South Africa?"

"Not at all. The manager managed to get a work permit for me, so I was a legalized immigrant."

"So why are you here?"

"Gino the manager of the McDonald's never asked me for his gun back and I never returned it. That was probably my mistake. He trusted me and I thought it could be useful should I need to guard the place again. You see I wasn't born poor and I was lucky enough to be able to attend university in Zimbabwe. My family's political involvement meant that suddenly we were living in danger. After they killed my father, my mother asked me to leave the country. My sisters should be safe there, but as an educated young man, I was in danger. Ironically before leaving my country I might have looked down on those less fortunate bringing me food. In South Africa things had changed and now I was one of the poor guys. I knew why some of those arrogant rich trendy kids who were coming into the McDonald's looked down on me. I had been one of them before. I think the big difference for me was that I was not a local, had no family there and altogether not much to lose in South Africa. Like a little hamster on a wheel I was doing my daily run minding my own business until a stupid rich boy started to come to our shop. He came in always with a new girlfriend and to impress his new girl he treated anybody around him like a slave. I knew he was just a stupid spoiled boy, but a sentiment in me kept on growing. One day I decided that our planet would be a much better place without assholes like him stealing our good air. I started to believe that I would have helped humanity by eliminating someone I regarded as a waste of space. That feeling grew stronger every day and every time I had the pleasure to meet that stupid individual I was always more certain that I was right. Seeing how much I liked him, one day a colleague told me that he was the son of a local politician. Believing most politicians to be corrupt and useless, this new information turned him into the perfect target for me."

"Did you kill him?"

"Yes, Sherlock, eventually I did. One morning that idiot came in with his new girlfriend. This time he was unlucky. The evening before I had called home and heard from my sister, that my mother had died. The government had made sure no member of my family would be allowed into a hospital or to see a doctor. A doctor could have saved her, but she could not see one. After that spoilt brat come in, I knew that this time I would not just take his insults. As expected he came to the counter and shouted at me to gain attention. I pretended not to hear him and asked the customer behind him for his order. This enraged him. I carried on ignoring him. His friends and other customers started to look at him getting very angry. He came forward and beat his fist on the counter. All sorts of stuff flew around. I was unlucky as the manager was out, so I was left alone to deal with this bully. I again asked the next customer behind him. He became furious, asking me if I was trying to be funny. I answered that I was a McDonald's employee and not his servant. Should he decide to behave like a normal customer, I would serve him like one. At this point he grabbed my t-shirt and lifted me towards him. I let him lift me up, jumped on the counter and behind him with the cold barrel of the gun on his head. I enjoyed it then and I will never regret that moment. He shouted fucking foreign to me. I shot his foot and with the gun on his head, I asked him to take me to his car in the parking lot. He opened his car, gave me the keys, but made the mistake of trying to take the gun off my hands. I smiled as I had been wishing for his action and shot him three times in his heart. I wanted to make sure he was dead. Then drove as fast as I could towards the Botswana border. I later abandoned the car and set it on fire. With my gun I convinced the owner of a different car to drive me closer to the border and let me out. Luckily for you I made it all the way to Tunisia."

"I guess so. Have you ever regretted killing that idiot? Or have you ever thought of his mother and family?"

"Not really. He got what he deserved. I think that day he paid for what Mugabe had done to my family and what all white idiots have done to Africans."

"I see, so he was white. Maybe it felt for you more like revenge than like a crime."

"You are probably right. How do you know?"

"I lived in Brazil for a while and when I got there I wondered why there was far more violence in Rio, Sao Paolo and other cities in the south compared to where I lived in the north. Later I realized that in Brazil some of the rich white people in politics today are still the direct descendants from slave traders. I understood then that it is obvious that robbing from white people or killing some of them must feel more like revenge than a crime. Black Brazilians from the cities are more likely to have studied or at least to have learned some of their history and understood how they ancestors were brought there in chains from Africa. In the countryside, few know their country history. Some were even illiterate so they took the world as it is and never questioned it. If I were a black person in Brazil or South Africa I might have thought the same. Like you, I did not choose the colour or religion to be born into, nor the country."

"Now that I told you about me. It's time you tell me why you are on the run?"

"I wish I knew. I went to Italy on a medical conference and I was arrested shortly after I landed. They locked me up and never told me the full reasons. They said I was involved in some US military stuff and then put me in a cell and interrogated me for days. I still have no idea why. One evening someone blew up the prison and we all ran away. I had to leave Italy and I will go back to the USA to face whatever I have to as my family is there."

"So will you be able to help me?"

"I will certainly do what I can. I cannot guarantee I can get you into the US, but let's try to get to the American continent first."

"Where then? To Brazil? Are Brazilians racists?"

"We will see where. In Brazil things are changing. Their famous black or brown footballers have done a lot to change people's attitudes towards black people. You see Brazil was a Portuguese colony and the Portuguese did not take their own women to the colonies. This meant that they had children with black or indigenous ladies. Many Portuguese recognized their brown offspring as legitimate. When I lived in Brazil they called me blond. I told them that I was not blond, but they replied that I was. They explained to me that all white people there were called blond to make brown the new regular skin colour. Brown might be called black in the US, but not in Brazil. Of course, there are still black people in Brazil. Their lives are getting better, but there is still some racism. Compared to other South American countries I have visited, Brazilians of every class will speak to anybody, rich or poor. They might not invite them to their homes, but outside of their houses they are not scared to talk to each other. Today in Brazil like many other places in the world, money is what makes the difference. Even in the USA, the black people who are doing better are not locals, but Nigerians who mostly have a school degree. Did you manage to finish your studies?"

"Almost. I had to run away to South Africa before I could."

"Do you have any brothers?"

"Well, yes I had."

"Did he die?"

"No, he did not. I guess I could say I now have a second sister."

"What happened, did he decide to change his gender?"

"No, someone decided that for him. You see my brother is older and was together with my father far more involved in our country politics. After my father started a movement to modernize the ZANU—PF from the inside he started to have problems with some of his best friends who were worried he wanted to split the party. My brother, being older, was saying aloud stuff that my father was slowly trying to change. One day my brother was arrested and taken away for interrogation. My father used all his connections to have him released. Three months later he was released, like they had promised to my father. When my father picked him up, he could not believe his eyes. They had operated on my brother. They had turned him into a woman and even put him in women's clothes. They wanted to strongly warn my father, by destroying his son's life without killing him."

Enzo knew this started to sound familiar and uncomfortable, but he could not show that. He kept the conversation going, hoping Joshua would not notice him feeling a bit uneasy.

"Did your brother ever recover?"

"Not really. He had a long-time girlfriend who was ready to marry him. I told him that they could have killed him and at least he could try to learn to live as a woman. Not easy for my bigger brother who was always a bit of a macho. Before I left Zimbabwe he or she was still a mess. Maybe he should leave the country and reinvent himself as a woman. If he stays there he will go mad, maybe he already is. I do not really know. I think my sister is trying to spare me more bad news."

A couple of hours had passed and it was now time to jump on a bus to "Ayn Darahim" near the holiday resort and the Algerian border. The bus was half empty and they both stretched on a double seat. It was going to be a four-hour drive. They felt safe enough to fall asleep. After two hours' solid sleep they were in the middle of the countryside driving through a dusty road. A young man came closer to Enzo and asked where he was going. Enzo realised the young man wanted to just practise English.

He pointed at Joshua and answered, "I am here on holiday with my friend Brian. We want to see the Tunisian countryside or better, we want to explore Africa."

"Your first time here?

"Yes, this is our first time. What is the coast like near the border?"

"It's great, I am from Tabarka and some relatives will pick me up at Ayn Darahim."

Suddenly Enzo thought the conversation was worth pursuing and even the newly baptized Brian was keen to get into the chat.

"Really, we looked at the map and we were wondering if it was worth going there. Someone in Tunis had suggested to us the El Mouradi Hammam Bourguiba hotel, but it is a bit expensive."

"If you want, I can ask my school friend. His family have a guesthouse in Tabarka."

"That would be great. Thank you. Is there a bus from Ayn Darahim to Tabarka?"

"No, je ne crois pas, oh sorry, I don't think so. This is no problem, you can come with me. It is just my uncle coming to pick me up."

"That would be great and we can pay for the petrol."

"Thank you."

Enzo and Joshua could not believe their luck. They carried on talking to the young student for the rest of the journey. The uncle was there and happy to take them on board his old car. The uncle did not speak English, but looked proudly at his nephew who could. The young man dreamed of becoming an English teacher and liked to practise. He said that he watched English TV channels and YouTube videos, but he had few chances to practise with real English speakers. Luckily his English was not good enough to recognize Joshua's South African accent. Tabarka was a three quarters drive away. The countryside was beautiful and from afar they started to see the Mediterranean Sea. They arrived in the late afternoon and were driven to Mohammad's uncle's guesthouse. When asked for a document, Enzo pretended to search through his pockets. Joshua showed him a British document with his photo and the name Steven Bennett underneath it. The guesthouse keeper was happy to see just one passport. Enzo looked worryingly at Joshua, wondering where he had got that British passport. Once they were in their twin room with sea view, he enquired "So Mr. Steven Bennett, I did not know you were British?"

"Don't worry, I did not kill Steven. I just stole his bag at the hotel golf club. I don't think this little hotel will check the passport validity, at least not in the next couple of days and then we will already be out of here."

"I hope you are telling me the truth. Let's have a shower and then go near the port to see if some fisherman will be able to take us to the other side of the border. A boat to El Kala would be perfect."

Once clean, the two men decided to wander into the town and near the seafront. After spending a couple of hours walking around, they saw a lorry with what looked to them like an Algerian number plate. And then one more and more. They started to wonder if it would have been easier to just catch a lift to the other side. Those lorries were certainly there to load or unload something and go back. Joshua decided to hide away and let Enzo deal with the lorry drivers. He thought that Enzo's white skin might be less suspicious.

"I do not speak as much French as you do?"

"Just speak Italian, add an S to the end of each verb and you are halfway there. I think it is better if they do not straightaway see a mixed team. You start, I'll wait here near the sea. Call me when you think it is safe for me to come."

Enzo slowly went close to the lorry drivers who were drinking tea and smoking shishas.
"Bonsoir. J'ai une demande? Demain vous retourne en Algerie? "

"Oui, pourquoi? "

"Je voudrais aller en Algerie avec vous. Se possible?"

They seemed to understand that he wanted to go back with them to Algeria.

"Vous devriez prendre le bus."

"Yes, oui, le bus. Mais pour moi c'est mieux avec le camion. "

They suggested he take the bus, but he replied that he preferred to go on the lorry. They laughed and asked, "Combien?" or how much?

Enzo took his golden necklace off and said "Cette pour deux personnes."

One stood up and nodded, then said, "Oui, mais demain matin à 6 heures ici."

With his hand he gestured to follow him to the back of the lorry and said, "Ici, avec les moutons."

Departure time was six o'clock and they would have to share the back of the lorry with some sheep. They shook hands and they went quickly back to the guesthouse. They needed to sleep and make sure not to miss their lift to their next country.

"You see, your French is not bad at all."

"It seems that I remember more than I thought I would. You are right, it is not difficult for an Italian, but I have not used my French for a very long time."

"I never studied French. I picked it up travelling through French-speaking countries. I found it easier than Arabic. Especially the writing. "

It was a sleepless night, worried as they could miss their lift to Algeria. They woke up early enough to get dressed, but when they went down, the front door was locked from the inside. After pulling it for a while the owner came down mumbling some Arabic swear words that did not sound good. Looked at them like they were mad wanting to get up that early while on holiday. But he let them out. The locked door stole a quarter of an hour of their time, they now had to make up by walking faster towards their appointment. The lorry was there and was loading sheep. The lorry driver greeted them, then stretched out his hand towards Enzo's neck, who understood quickly and handed over his gold necklace. Then the lorry driver pointing at a map and showed them where he was driving to. He was going to a place just outside Algiers. Joshua and Enzo both showed their thumbs up and jumped in the back of the lorry where the driver had arranged a couple of palettes behind his cabin. They had their own pen so as not to be crushed by the sheep. They made themselves cosy, but at that early hour it was freezing. The driver threw at them a plastic lorry cover. They put the cover on top of the palette and built a warmish den. They were well hidden and hoped to go over the border without problems. Half an hour later they were on their way. They were about to fall asleep when the light got stronger and loud noises were all around. They guessed this was the border. It seemed that someone jumped on the side of the lorry briefly looked into it and shouted what sounded like, "All fine". They were happy to be on their way and driving in the right direction. Both fell asleep and only woke up under the scorching sun that now made their plastic cover smell of burned rubber. Taking it off had not been the right thing to do as now the sun was shining directly onto them. After the bumpy road had given way to what felt like a motorway, they could sit comfortably without having to constantly jump up to avoid every pothole. The sheep looked curiously at them between the wooden planks of the palette. They both had no idea how far Algiers was from the border, but they knew that Algeria was a big country. Only once they were both rested did they turn to each other for entertainment.

"Are you OK?"

"All fine. I never felt like a sheep, but today I am. I have eaten many of those, but maybe I should not say that too loud while sharing their bus."

"Did you not feel inspired by Mohammad's optimism back in Tunisia?"

"Who, that young student from Tabarka?"

"Yes, his dream from a modern, democratic and successful Tunisia. He gave me hope."

"Why? I think he is just a dreamer."

"Yes, exactly. I hope there were more dreamers around dreaming up a better world."

"My father was a dreamer and this got him killed. Maybe if he had dreamed less I would still be in Zimbabwe and my brother would not have gone mad."

"Think big, Joshua. Your father died trying to improve the lives of the people living in your country. Your father died trying to give you a better future. Maybe he did not succeed, but your father was one of the thousands falling on the hard granite that would eventually give way to the flow of water dripping down. I am sure you admired Nelson Mandela."

"Of course, I do."

"Do you think Mandela's family enjoyed having him locked up in prison for decades? Do you think his children had a good life without a father being there for them? In the same way your father was a hero even if he is not a famous one. At least not famous to me, maybe he is already. Sorry, if I did not know about him. I am aware that Nelson Mandela is a more famous ANC fighter, but I also know that thousands of others fought together with him. A man alone cannot do anything. Mussolini, Hitler, Stalin, Mao, Mugabe, none of them could have done anything at all if they'd been alone."

"Thank you. I just cannot stop thinking how my father's fight changed my life. I was never asked what I thought about it. I am paying the consequence of his actions."

"Sorry to ask, but what did you think of Mugabe before you left?"

"Listen Enzo you are from another world and probably will not be able to understand me. In Gweru where I grew up, I went to a primary school called the Cecil John Rhodes School. I am sure you know who Mr. Rhodes was, right? My country was once part of Rhodesia, a country that was more than a colony. It was the propriety of a wealthy English man. In England they still have statues of him. In short, my great grandparent became the property of a few white men who had on their side far more advanced technology and a far better organization. I am not surprised they won. Even understanding this I cannot excuse them for what they did. How is it possible that after hundreds of years there was still a complete white population in Zimbabwe? The Arabs mixed with the Africans on the continent's East coast as did the Portuguese in Mozambique and Angola or Brazil where you lived. So we got the worst racist British people. They were no better than the Boer or Dutch in South Africa. If they felt white and did not want to integrate in their new continent, then they had no place in Africa and should have been kicked out. We cannot change history, but I think we need to move on. If you are of European or Asian descent, but feel African, then we need to work together to improve our lives in our countries. If you feel better than an African, feel free to leave tomorrow. Mugabe had no choice but to take over the land of the racist white minority in Zimbabwe. Those white racists are idiots like Hitler was. How can you win a war if you kill your own people just because they have a different religion? Did you know that the inventor of the German mustard gas that was used in WWI was a German Jew? Did you know that Mussolini's lover was a Jew? So I understood why Mugabe and the ZANU-PF party behaved the way they did and why they were isolated by the international community. The international community and the British colonizer did not ever apologize to us, but even told us that we were in the wrong when taking our land back. Have you ever seen a white colonial power being taken in front of the international court of justice in Den Haag? You never will, as those judges are not African, but racist westerners. Have you heard of any colonial reparation for Africa? Look at DRC and other African countries still in the hands of western countries' businesses. Sure, it's partly the fault of our corrupt politicians. Those I would like to hang, but the day after some western journalist writes to me about the danger. I supported my father's idea in modernizing the party he so much loved, but his ideas were not the most modern ones. He also accepted support from some British and American NGOs that we all know are the modern Jesuits of our times. The NGOs come with foreign ideas and tell us what is best for our countries. They love to drive around in their big cars and tell us how we should do things. They do not know our culture nor are they interested in learning anything. They want to teach stuff that works in their countries. To us, they are ignorant people who want to teach others. Of course, not all are bad, but I am not sure if we would not have been better off if they had all just packed up and gone. We need African solutions for our African problems. We will ask for help when we want it. Don't force your help on others. I still cannot understand how a British person who is the offspring of the colonizing power could ever pretend to speak to us about a fairer society? The only possible explanation is that they have a useless education system that teaches them no real history. How can they pretend to teach China human rights? Imagine a country that destroyed a Chinese generation by selling them opium even when the Chinese authorities were begging them to stop that trade. The British won the opium war killing millions of Chinese. Now they want to talk to them about human rights? Do you have any idea how stupid they sound in the eyes of the rest of the world? They might have forgotten the past but we haven't."

"Wow, you certainly love history. It must have been hard just working in McDonald's for the last few years."

"Not really. I loved the fact that working in the shop I always had access to the PC in the office and the manager let me use it. I could read all I wanted online. I love history and I love to understand why things are the way they are."

"My history teacher in Sicily told us once, history teaches us that we have learned nothing from it. He was no optimist. I think we do repeat some mistakes, but we slowly learn from those otherwise we would not have had any progress and we would still be cave men. Anyway, I hear more traffic. I think we must be getting closer to Algiers."

"I hope so as we are running out of water and I feel that if we stay here longer we will start to smell like sheep. By the way, how did you pay the lorry driver? Was that a golden necklace?"

"Yes, my parents gave it to me when I turned forty. They wanted to thank me for having paid for their kitchen being redone. It was probably worth more, but I had nothing else to pay him with."

"I think we should ask him if he knows someone who could take us all the way to Morocco on a lorry like this one. Maybe he knows someone. I just wonder how to pay him for the next trip."

Enzo put his hand in his front pocket and pulled out what looked like a golden coin.

"What is that?"

"This medallion was hanging on the necklace before I gave it to the lorry driver. I thought maybe this could pay for taking us over the next border. It weighs as much as the necklace."

"Great! I knew you were the right guy to rob and I am so happy the Tunisian police stopped me. Otherwise I would have probably taken everything off you and carried on travelling on my own. I am not sure I would have made it here so quickly. It is good to have a white ass like you travelling with me."

"Well let me say that I am glad I met this black asshole in front of me."

They both laughed aloud, while all the sheep were staring. They were looking at what to them must have seemed like a strange two-headed zebra.

"From what you are telling me, you don't like the Brits?"

"I never met one, apart from the one whose bag containing his passport I stole. Anyway, I don't think he even saw me. I saw him only from a distance. I guess he is just partly compensating me for what his ancestors did to mine. I don't care where people are from and their past. Like me they did not choose the family into which they were born. The past is the past as long as they know their past and don't try to tell me how I have to behave in my country or continent."

"Would you like to live in the UK?

"Why not? I guess I would probably beat the crap out of anybody proudly telling me about their grandfathers being stationed in one of their colonies. Apart from that it seems a good country to live in. Of course, after Brexit they seem to have changed their attitude towards foreigners and being black would not help me much. Maybe America is a better bet."

"You are probably right. It is a small island with an island mentality. Coming from Sicily I know something about that. Like the British, we in Sicily call the rest of Italy the continent. The major difference is that over thousands of years we have learned that we are small and to keep our independence we would have to constantly fight stronger armies. So we ended up letting everybody in and making their lives difficult once they are in charge. Sicilians still distrust any kind of government as foreign, even their own. A tradition of mistrust that ruins the lives of those living there. One of the reasons I left."

"Is the United States your adopted country?"

"Adopted, yes, that is the right word. You see if my father had told me that I was adopted, I would not have cared much. The way I see it, the one who brought me up is my real father. My real father is the one who was there when I needed him and not the one who had fun for five minutes and provided some cells in the shape of sperm. For me, that one is just the sperm donor. In many cases the sperm donor and the actual father match, in some they don't. With the same logic my country is not the one where I was born, but the one that provided me with a roof and gave me the best opportunities. Who helped me most? The USA, so this is my home country now. Of course, I have respect for my country of origin, but that is respect like the one you have for a relative. Friends you choose, relatives you don't, they just are. The same goes for my country. I chose the USA. I did not choose where to be born."

"What do you like most about the USA?"

"First of all it is a country of immigration with people from everywhere and of all races. In Europe or even in the north of Italy, every time I said something people always put my words through their clichés filter and said that I wrote that because I was a Sicilian, even years after I had left the island. Even now people in Europe do that if they know I was born in Sicily. In the US and in Brazil, it was not the same. Once you are integrated and speak their language well, nobody uses any cliché filters. They will not say Enzo says that because Enzo is Sicilian. They just say Enzo said that and this is his opinion. In Europe we are very sceptical while in the US the first reaction is positive. People are more willing to accept change and embrace new ideas. Things are changing now, but in essence the core in the US is still good. In my opinion the whole world is changing and the US is not immune. Globalization is affecting us all."

"Do you like Trump?"

"I am not a fan of his policies, but I fully understand why many Americans voted for him."

"Why?"

"What I am sure is that it was not for his hairstyle. In Italy many people who voted for Berlusconi had done so because they thought that him being already rich, he was not in it for the money. In the same way, the US middle class was tired of seeing their income remaining at the same level, while politicians enriched themselves. When I went to the US as a younger graduate, there were maybe five thousand foreign graduates entering the US economy every year. Now, thanks to countries with larger populations like India and China, there are more than one hundred thousand foreign graduates moving to the US every year. These were the reasons why US businesses had no incentive in making higher education more affordable to US citizens. They instead import foreign graduates. I started to wonder how some conservative white Americans would react when I always saw more dark skinned graduates sitting at the tables in fast food chains and restaurants. The children of the American middle class were serving those newcomers. Nowadays few Americans can afford their children's school fees. So there is no social ladder to be climbed anymore, it was just a question of time."

"It is not the foreigners' fault if they have such a stupid system in place to discriminate against their own people."

"Yes, you are right, and clever young people like you understand this. Tell me, how would the people in your country react if thousands of young well-educated graduates from Malawi or Mozambique came and stole the best jobs and left the locals with servers' jobs to serve them?"

"Sure they would react like the South Africans reacted to me and others like me moving to their country. Funnily enough, it was a white guy who gave me a chance in black Africa. Stranger still, was that he was a Sicilian and so are you. The second who crosses my path."

"Consider yourself lucky!"

"Sure. Let's see how far we will get together."

"By the way do you know that Sicily is on the African land mass? So I am also a kind of African. African is also what some people in the north of Italy called me when they were trying to offend me. Believe it or not, I took it as a badge of honour and was never offended by it. Racism or discrimination also exists between people with the same skin colour."

"I know, even in Zimbabwe people sometimes discriminate between people of different tribes. Probably like you, I also read Mandela's book 'Long Walk to Freedom'. Even he writes about the discrimination between black people from different tribes. I know that the slave traders bought the slaves from black people belonging to different tribes who lived on the coast. The ones sold as slaves to the white people were often captured in the interior of the continent from other tribes they were at war with. Despite knowing this, it doesn't make it okay. I know the Romans had white slaves and enslaved the people they conquered. This does not justify slavery. All those involved were bastards and none of their descendants should be proud of what they have done. If they are proud of their grandparents or great grandparents then they should be condemned even today. Just because it was in the past, we should not forget. They have no fault of their own, if they distance themselves, but not if they are proud of them. This makes them guilty."

"Well that is certainly a way to look at things."

Suddenly the lorry stopped and brought them down to earth. The back of the lorry opened and the sheep were let, out one by one. The lorry driver made a sign towards the two on the palette that suggested they still had to wait there and so they did in silence. Eventually all the sheep were gone and the lorry started to drive again. They wondered where they were going to. Half an hour later the lorry stopped again and the back was opened again. This time the lorry driver shouted in their direction asking to get down. Enzo pushed Joshua to the front telling him to ask in French if he knew someone who could take them to Morocco. The lorry driver had stopped in the periphery of Algiers where lorry drivers stopped to fill up their machines and their bellies. There was even a toilet they could run to. After talking to Joshua, the lorry driver said that he would see what he could do. They should wait at the bar while he went eating with some other drivers who might know someone who was driving to Morocco. The driver took a long time, but when he emerged after almost an hour he did so with a smile on his face. He told Joshua that he had found someone who would drive to Morocco in two days' time. They would have to go with him to the interior of the country. Once there, as part of their payment they would have to load the lorry with gas bottles to take to Morocco. Once in Morocco, they would have to help to unload the lorry and load it with car spare parts manufactured there. They would have to pay for the journey with their work and the gold coin Joshua had told him about. Not having much choice, Joshua had already agreed to the deal.

"Did he tell you at what time and where we should meet the new driver?"

"Calm down, the new driver will be here in about an hour and we are supposed to leave from here. In two days we need to be here before the sun rises."

"Then let's wait and drink some tea. The food does not look bad either. I am not sure I can eat lamb today. All those sheep looking at me seemed to say, I know you have eaten many of us. I need some time to forget their questioning eyes. Or maybe I should become a vegetarian."

"I eat anything. Believe me, it will certainly be better than what I found in Johannesburg's restaurant bins the first days I arrived there. Incredible how much food people throw away."

"This is certainly a different perspective."

They went to eat and Enzo went for a chicken and potatoes dish. Later the lorry driver arrived and went straight to their table. He introduced himself. When Joshua asked him how he recognized them, he answered that there were not many black and white couples of men in the place. He said they looked like foreigners anyway. He sat at the table and asked to see the coin. Then they shook hands and agreed to meet there at 6 AM, in two days' time. Before he left they asked him if he knew of a cheap place where they could sleep. He suggested a place a couple of Km south of the restaurant, but he did not have time to take them there now. Then he went.

"Should we go to check that place out?"

"Not sure. We have little cash and we cannot show them your stolen British passport."

"Why not?"

"Joshua, I don't think there are many British tourists coming to Algeria, so they will be suspicious. The weather is good, let's try to spend the nights on some beach under the sky."

"Or maybe we should find some business hotel near the centre of town."

"Why? I told you that I don't have any money nor do I have a valid passport with me."

"Did you not hear when Ahmed said that we look very foreign? If they don't have many tourists around here they might have some business people in town to buy their gas or whatever they export and import in this country. I think that if someone sees us near a hotel where foreigners are often seen, they won't suspect us. I am sure some people looking at us are thinking that you are the clever man and I am just your driver. Come on, let's get closer to the centre before some police car turns up."

"Okay driver. Where is the car? And where will we go to sleep?"

"I don't know yet."

Both started to walk against the flow of traffic that made them think they were walking towards the centre of the city. They thought that it was probably a long way away, but after sitting for hours in the back of a lorry without being able to move, they were happy to use their legs and walked for miles. They had plenty of time to kill.

"Do you know that I always wanted to see Algiers? I was put off when some years ago they killed some Italians. This country must be beautiful. I heard many old French colleagues still crying about their families having to leave this place after independence."

"Listen, I like to hear your stories as it kills time, but please stop when people are passing by. Or speak some French if you can. We shouldn't attract more attention than we already do with our mixed look."

« Bien sûr que oui! »

"There you go. So you were saying that you wanted to come to Algiers. Why?"

"In 1943, the son of a Sicilian, General Enzo Castellano, came here probably with some Sicilian mafia guys to discuss the possibility for Italy to change sides in the war. I am sure they sent him because he also spoke Sicilian and probably still had relatives on the island. The Americans had started to work with Lucky Luciano who helped them land peacefully in Sicily. My grandparents told me the day before that the Americans who were landing were bringing food. As a sign of peace, everybody was told to hang white bedsheets outside of the windows. My grandmother told me that she did. Algiers is where the Italians or better the Sicilians met to stop the war in Italy or sell out Mussolini to the Allied Forces."

"This is certainly not what I have read about WWII."

"Joshua, by now you should know better than me that the winner writes the history books the way they see or like it. The loser has to live with it and carry on. It took me years to find the real history and forget the fairy tale they fed me during the history lessons at school. Not everything Mussolini or Hitler did was bad, but that is the only part they teach. Churchill, like them and many European men of the time, was also a racist. He was asked once by an Indian why the British were oppressing his country. Churchill replied that the British were superior people and that India was British or better belonged to the British. Anyway, I have no idea where they met in this city, but I am sure it was in some grand hotel in the centre."

"What about the fighting of some fascists before the landing in Sicily. Was that not true?"

"Yes, the British did not trust the mafia and they attacked the East of Sicily near Gela where the rest of the fascists on the island where resisting their doom. They even managed to sink a large allied ship. The west of Sicily where the mafia had undisputed control was not much fought over. Of course, there are always a few hard liners, but not many to provide a real defence against the Allied Forces."

"Why did the mafia help the Americans?"

"Mussolini had put most of the bandits and mafiosi behind bars. Many of them had run to America. At the end of the war the Allied Forces had liberated all mafiosi or bandits. After the Allied Forces left, 90% of Sicilian town mayors were mafiosi. You are right, the mafia never does anything for free. A small favour here, a small favour there, this is how the mafia works."

"Look, there's the sign for the 'Cathédrale du Sacré-Cœur', this must be in the centre of town. Let's follow that sign."

"Should we not follow the mosque sign?"

"This is a Muslim country, maybe they have more mosques than churches here. I am sure the church was built by the French before they got kicked out of here. So it must be old and in the centre."

"Not bad at all for a black boy from the streets of Johannesburg."

"Slowly but surely I am starting to think that you might not have survived without me. Just call me bwana."

After two hours walking, they had finally arrived in the centre of Algiers. It was almost dark and they decided to go into the church after following the sign that took them there. The church was empty and they could hear their steps. Sitting down for a break was good. Then a voice in French surprised them. "Bonsoir!" It was a catholic priest who told them that the last Mass of the day had finished one hour earlier, but they were welcome to come back tomorrow. Joshua looked at the priest and explained that they had no money and nowhere to sleep. The priest asked: "Êtes-vous deux bonnes personnes?" Are you two good people?
"Nous essayons." "We try," answered Joshua. To that the priest replied, "c'est tout ce que nous pouvons faire, mon fils". That is all we can do, my son.
Then the priest asked them to follow him. In his little office at the back of the church he showed them a map of the area and pointed at the harbour. Then to a specific area and mentioned the name of a boat "Algérie Libre". He told them that that is an old boat, but they could find a cabin to share in there. They just needed to tell them that Father Alexander sent them there. Enzo could not believe how easily Joshua had found a place for them to sleep. Years of travelling through most of Africa had taught Joshua a trick or

two. They walked to the harbour and managed to find the boat in a short time. They had not eaten for the evening, but decided to make sure they had a safe place to sleep. They decided that their night sleep was more important. On the boat they found some other people sleeping there. They looked like local homeless people. They nodded their heads and walked in. A guy called Marcel asked who had sent them there and once they had mentioned Alexander's name, Marcel pointed them to a corner of the boat where some old empty hammocks were hanging down.

Enzo was relieved, "I expected worse. I can sleep two nights here. I think we were very lucky."

"You would be surprised, but most people are nice. Travelling all over I have met plenty of idiots, but the majority of people mean well and want to live in peace."

"You must be right and I am going to test this hammock straightaway."

They both started to swing gently in their hammocks while chatting away in English when a younger guy came up to them and shouted something that both could not understand. It was probably Arabic, but Joshua asked him in French what was the problem? They got shouted at again, but this time in French. He told them to go home and that Americans were not welcome in his country. Joshua explained that he was from South Africa and Enzo was from Italy and they just used English to communicate and understand each other. The guy was still not happy, shouted at them fucking Christians, told them in French that his grandfather had fought the French pigs for his country's independence and moved to the part of the boat from where he had come.

"I think he just does not like us to be here."

"I am not surprised. Thanks to American and British bombing everywhere, speaking English can be dangerous. Don't be loud and avoid speaking when other people are close to us. Imagine my getting stabbed because someone thinks I am an American, while I am still trying to reach America. That would be funny. Anyway, I think it would be better if we took turns in sleeping here. I wonder how many people like him are on this boat. I thought it looked too good to be true. So please stay awake while I have my turn now."

"Good idea. I will stay awake to protect my robber's belongings."

Enzo fought his sleepy eyes even if he thought they were probably safe now. Now he was alone and his mind went back to the inspector who had probably been killed. The time he had spent in a Sicilian prison seemed so far away now. Carlo's lift to Mazara and crossing the Mediterranean Sea. All seemed a dream. What were his wife and children thinking about him? He would have loved to call home, but he did not want to put his family in danger or give away his own location. He had to try to make it back on his own. Nevertheless the thought of just walking to the US embassy in Algiers and handing himself in was tempting. He really did not want to go back to prison for whatever they wanted to lock him up for. Having run away he knew he was now in a worse situation. For a moment he looked out of the boat window trying to find the small lonely tree he had got used to. Strange what one can get used to and miss. Joshua eventually opened his eyes. Now he could close his.

Joshua had woken up hungry, "Come on, we need to go quickly to have breakfast."

"Breakfast at 6 AM?"

"Quickly. Come on, old man. Wake up!"

Joshua walked quickly towards a hotel they had passed the day before near the church. He went straight to the car park of the hotel and stopped there. Now instead of hiding the fact he was speaking English, he did so very loudly. He started to talk about imports from South Africa and the customs duties they would have to pay. Enzo just played along as he understood his clever companion was up to something. At a certain point, he stopped and asked Enzo to follow him once more. They went into the hotel lobby where again Joshua kept on talking about non-existent business deals and company names. While doing so, he was scanning the downstairs floor of the hotel so as to spot the entrance to the breakfast hall. Once he was sure of himself, he hinted to Enzo to walk in his direction and as soon as a server asked them for their room number, Joshua answered, 249, to which the waiter replied good morning, Mr. Taylor, after having consulted a room list with customer names.

"How the hell did you do that?"

"Old man, learn from a young one. People who leave the hotel in the morning just after 6 AM have not yet had time to have their breakfast, even if in such a hotel it is always included in the price. Better still in this expensive hotel, two breakfasts are included. So you are included. Eat now. Remember, they serve breakfast from 6 AM. So simple really. Now stop talking and start eating. Remember, this might be the only free meal of the day, so make the most of it."

Enzo was certainly impressed by his travel companion and at the same time he was aware that he needed to be careful not to get involved in any new crimes. They walked out of the hotel with two full bellies and no idea of what to do in the city for a whole day. Enzo wanted to take advantage of the opportunity and just play the tourist by visiting sites that were not expensive or were completely free.

"Follow me now into town and let's find the tourist information office. It's sightseeing time. By the way, yesterday that guy swore at us because he thought we were Christians. Are you a Christian?"

"Why do you care?"

"I am just wondering, no reason really, just you decided to walk into a church instead of going to a mosque."

"Most Zimbabweans today are protestants and this was the way my parents also raised me. It seems that in the past many Zimbabweans worshipped Mwari, the supreme god of the Shona religion, but who knows and who cares. Are you a catholic?"

"I am a catholic by birth, but like you I am not really practising. I go to church for weddings, funerals and when babies are baptised."

"Is it true that you hate Muslims in Italy or Europe?"

"Who told you that?"

"Well, that is what most people here think."

"I think there are good and bad people everywhere. I have to admit that in Europe or in America we do have a problem with some Muslim people. To be honest, I also have a problem with conservative Christians and orthodox religious people from anywhere really."

"Why? Live and let live! You live the way you want and let them live the way they want."

"I wish it were that simple, but it is not. You see I moved to the US and did not expect the Americans there to adjust to my way of living. Instead, I try to fit in myself and behave like a good guest. Some Muslims expect us to change our traditions to accommodate theirs. It is not easy."

"Well, you do sound like you don't like Muslims."

"I repeat that I don't care what people believe in as long as they don't want to change the way I live. When my children were in kindergarten, we had two Muslim children in the class. One day we had to organise a kindergarten party and the Muslim mother asked for the pork sausages to be replaced with chicken ones, this to accommodate the fact that Muslims do not eat pork. We offered to put on the barbecue some pork and some chicken sausages. They said that this would not work as we could not use the same barbecue where the pork sausages were cooked. We ended up only buying chicken sausages that were mostly not eaten as the majority of the parents did not like those. The kindergarten lost money. Normally they used the money they charge for the hot dog to finance small trips with the children. No trips possible that year because of two immigrant children. During another meeting one of the Muslim children's mothers said that she had a problem coming to future meetings because some other mothers drank alcohol at the end of that meeting. Note that nobody had asked her to drink any alcohol. She said that she could not be in a place where alcohol is served or drank. An immigrant who had just moved in, requested the majority of the people there to change their way of living to accommodate them. Imagine if such people were to move to Zimbabwe and expect everybody there to stop drinking alcohol, eat pork or expect the women to wear a veil. What would Zimbabweans do?"

"Some would probably be killed."

"Exactly. With orthodox religious people of any faith, you cannot speak rationally. Once you are winning the logical arguments, they will invoke some religious scripture to justify the stupid things they do. I think they are just racist or discriminating against people with different beliefs."

"Are you saying that Muslims are racists?"

"First of all, don't say it too loud. Remember where we are. Yes, I think conservative religious people in general are just racists hiding behind old religious scriptures."

"Well, they say you are racists."

"Listen, if a Muslim girl in the West falls in love with a Christian man, her parents will first try to dissuade her and if she still wants to marry him, they will ask the man to convert to Islam. In my eyes, this is racism against Christians."

"I think they just want their daughter's new husband to respect and accept her traditions."

"Why is she then not accepting her host country and new husband's traditions instead? Also, what do you think the Muslim parents of a young man living in the West would say if their son would like to marry a Christian girl, but her parents were against the marriage to a Muslim? They would call them racists. They would not think that the groom's family have their own traditions and expect those to be respected. It cannot be that the newcomers' traditions are superior to the traditions of the majority of the people actually living in the country to which they moved. Before demanding your traditions be respected, you need to be prepared to respect the traditions of others."

"Are you sure your European ancestors colonizing the world had the intention of respecting the local traditions and not forcing their own on the local population?"

"As you said, that was colonialization. If the West thought the newcomers would not want to integrate but colonize, believe me, some killing and expulsion would have started to take place already. By the way, if you think the West hated all Muslims like you said, why have they not converted or killed them all? We have had the technology long enough to kill as many people as we needed and turn the whole world into a Western one. I don't think the Muslim world would have had a chance in hell to survive the slaughter fighting on camel back with weapons produced by non-Muslim countries. Nowadays, in the West, we don't care how people live in their own country, but we don't like their telling us how we should live."

"I think they believe the West is imposing on them your way of life."

"You are probably right, but it is not our fault if they have technologically fallen behind and their youth dreams of a more modern world like ours. They should stop watching Western films or reading Western books. Stop using Western medicine and Western-produced weapons. You cannot use modern medicine invented by people of many different faiths relying on modern technologies and then say that those people providing those medicines are evil. Those people were able to develop those new drugs and cures despite their religious beliefs. Those people did not have the fatalistic view that God would solve everything for them. They tried to do something to improve their lives now, on earth. If you are a radical preacher believing just in the supreme will of God, you make me laugh if you read the sacred scriptures using glasses developed by people who decided to do more than just look at the sky and pray. If God wanted you to go blind, why are you wearing the glasses developed by someone who did not just rely on the power of God, but used his own knowledge? How can they complain about idolatry and then watch television or videos on the internet? Sorry, this religious crap makes me mad."

"You don't believe in God or traditions?"

"I believe there is a God and it is the same for the whole world or universe. I don't think my life is very important in the scheme of things. We may put ourselves at the centre of the universe, but I believe that we are no better than other creatures on this planet, just one of them. Believe me, once we have made this planet uninhabitable for ourselves, it will carry on turning without us. We are not as important as we like to believe. Just enjoy the ride while you are here."

"What about traditions, should people not care about their thousands of years of old traditions?"

"Remember that traditions are invented by people. There are good and bad traditions. Traditions change all the time. The British love their traditional tea time. They forget that tea does not grow in the UK and that tradition was imported. The first Europeans to drink tea were the Portuguese. The Portuguese Catherine of Braganza married King Charles II of England. She brought with her in 1662 the habit of drinking tea to the British. This changed their traditions by enriching them with tea. This is just an example of what we believe to be traditions over the millennia. Those are just habits that change all the time. So are religious beliefs."

"I think traditions are far more important than you think."

"Listen Joshua if I would respect old Sicilians traditions, I would think black people are inferior and I would certainly not talk to you. In the Sicilian language we call people, 'Cristiani'. That stands for Christians, meaning that those who are not Christians are not people. Do you really want me to respect those old traditions? By the way, remember that most people in the world did not choose their faith, but were born into it. Some of those same people who are ready to die to defend their religious values or traditions, would do exactly the same defending the other religion if they had been born on the other side. It is not religious beliefs, it is just tribalism. What do you think would happen if we were to swap a new-born baby of an orthodox Jewish family in Israel with a new-born baby from a fundamentalist Muslim family from Saudi Arabia? Each family would raise that child with their own strong beliefs. The child from the family in Saudi Arabia would become a convinced Jew and would probably be ready to die for his country and religion. The exact same would happen to the Jewish baby raised by the Muslim family in Saudi Arabia. He would be ready to die for his country and religious beliefs. That is because religion or traditions are a layer on top of our human condition. We are born equal, we screw things up. Religions and traditions were invented to control people's behaviour. I never said that all traditions or customs are wrong, I am just saying that those things should never completely rule our lives."

"I guess I had never thought that way about traditions. In Africa we have many of our customs and traditions. In Zimbabwe some people still marry only those from the same tribes as we sometimes have different traditions. The younger generation care less about those traditions. You are probably right, there are good, but also weird or bad traditions."

"Are you coming into the tourist information centre?"

Enzo was happy the lady there spoke English and could explain how to walk to the different sites from there. They got a map so they could finally walk around like real tourists.

But as soon as they walked out of the tourist office, a voice from behind called,
"Bonjour, pourrais-je voir vos documents s'il vous plaît?"

Two police officers in uniform were looking in their direction with inquisitive eyes. It was clear that they wanted to see their documents, so they asked back, "Parlez-vous anglais? Do you speak English?"

Just a small English, one of them answered. Then carried on, "What you here for?"

Joshua promptly, "We are here on business and this here is my boss Mr. Taylor."

"Where is hotel sleep?"

Joshua again, "We are at the Hotel El Djezair, room 249. We share the same twin room. I am sorry, but we have left our documents in the hotel room."

At that point one of the officers made a call and they could hear him asking to be put through to the Hotel El Djezair reception and then a receptionist confirmed a Mr. Taylor does stay in room 249.

"Qu'est-ce que vous faites maintenant? Oh, pardon. What doing now?"

Enzo, politely, "We have a bit of free time and wanted to see some tourist sights. This is why we were inside the tourist information centre."

"Bien, merci et bonne journée."

After the officers left, they felt much relieved and once they were away from their sight Enzo found the courage to say aloud, "That was a lucky escape!"

"Thanks to you old man they almost caught us!"

"Why?"

"I am sure one of the ladies inside the tourist information centre pushed a button to call them. They are probably not used to seeing many black and white tourist couples here. Anyway, we were lucky, so let's play tourists and stay away from the hotel now."

They went again to see the Notre-Dame d'Afrique, the church where they had arrived the day earlier, then they walked to the Martyrs' Memorial, Algiers, finally to the Jardin d'Essai du Hamma and the Palais des Rais. They walked enough to be ready for their hammocks they hoped would still be free for them. For a moment they had embraced their tourist spirit and had forgotten they were both on the run. They knew they had a short night and a long day ahead. Once back, they jumped on their hammocks and pretended not to need any food. Water was free on the boat. The same man greeted them with fucking Christians and they just waved peacefully back with a "Nice to see you too."

They left the boat in the middle of the night, making sure not to wake up anybody, especially not their new found friend who loved Christians. They knew they had two hours' walking to meet their friendly lorry driver Ahmed who had promised to pick them up there. It was too early to talk. They were just pointing directions to each other and walked like two remotely controlled zombies. Two hours later they arrived at the lorry driver stop. They walked in and to their relief, Ahmed shouted towards them to attract their attention. After shaking hands they walked to the lorry and started to drive south. Ahmed spoke no English so carried on in French hoping they would somehow understand. The zebra couple soon fell asleep. Three hours later they were far from the capital at a place that looked like a gas bottles factory. Ahmed jumped out of the lorry and asked them to wait a moment. Then he jumped on again and drove the lorry where he had been told to. When the lorry stopped he invited his two guests to jump down with him and climb out the back of the lorry. The lorry was full of empty methane gas bottles that Ahmed needed help unloading. Enzo and Joshua worked hard in the hope of speeding up the process and being on their way soon. After they finished unloading hundreds of bottles, they were allowed a break to drink some water under the now strong sun beating down on them. Ahmed moved the lorry again. This time, it was to load the full bottles of gas. They both were surprised how much a substance called gas can weigh. Loading took much longer. At the end, they were exhausted. Ahmed called them to the front of the lorry and handed over to them a plastic bag with some bread and cheese. Once they had finished eating, Ahmed asked them to follow him. He showed them the toilets and behind there they discovered some showers. They asked if they could shower and leave their sheepish smell behind. Ahmed nodded and said that he had to go to speak to the manager about the gas bottles they had just loaded. It was great to feel the fresh running water over their sweaty bodies. Enzo's mind went back to his jump into the Mediterranean Sea and what Calogero had told him. It was finally time to get that salt off his skin. They came out half an hour later trying to find something to dry themselves with. The industrial paper roll from the toilet did the job. They went for their clothes and were surprised to see them on the ground together with their emptied bags. It looked like someone had gone through their stuff while they were having a shower. They got dressed and ran out to tell Ahmed about it. Ahmed was no longer there nor was the lorry they had fully loaded.

"Do you still have your gold medallion?"

Enzo searched his pockets repeatedly, but it looked like his golden medal had gone.

"How could you be so stupid to leave it in your trousers after showing Ahmed that you had it in your pocket?"

"Did you not say that most people are good?"

"Yes, if you don't put them into temptation and I did say most people, not all."

Enzo started to frantically touch his belt and soon seemed relieved. Joshua understood that he must be hiding some money in it, but probably didn't want to show this to the guy who had tried to rob him."

"It's getting late and we need to get out of here. We do not even know where we are."

"Old man, look there. There are still many lorries that are loading. We will catch a lift."

"Would you pick up two strangers from the middle of nowhere?"

"Probably not, especially if they are foreign and don't even speak my language. Just come out of the gate and help me."

Once out of the gate, Joshua started to pull some heavy bins towards the road.
"What are we doing?"

"Come on old man, just do as I say. The lorries are driving too fast out of here, but if we manage to slow those down we will manage to get a free ride on their back. Understood?"

"Fine. Come on now, you pull and I push. Not too close to the gate otherwise someone will see us."

They were not waiting long, when a lorry drove out at full speed, but soon hit the brakes. It was slow enough for them to run and jump onto the back of it. They managed to find a space they could hide in between the gas bottles. They had no idea what direction they were driving in, or for how long, but they knew that a lorry full of cooking gas bottles must be going to a place with plenty of people to sell it to. They were just hoping the lorry would travel west towards Morocco. They were driving on exactly the same road for a while, and they were worried that they would be driven back to Algiers. The sun was strong, and they had only their bags to protect themselves from the direct sunshine. They had to move away from the gas bottles that, despite the blowing wind, were reaching too high a temperature to comfortably lean against, or even touch with bare hands. Suddenly, Enzo's thoughts went to the possibility of a road accident that could blow up one of the gas bottles. Nobody would ever find his remains and his family would never know what had happened to him. What a thought! Better to sleep on it. And he nodded off again.

Hours later, the traffic became noisy and they started to wonder at what point they would jump off the lorry without the driver noticing their presence, or worse, alarming the police. While on board, talking was not an option. They had had no time to bring any water with them and they were getting thirsty. They thought the driver was going to stop, but he soon drove out of that town. The countryside gave way, and they were again driving on a major road. Leaving the town, they spotted a road sign written in Latin script with the town's name, "Tiaret". It was late afternoon. The sun was on their left-hand side, and that told them that they were driving north. Then, a new road sign saying "Algiers" confirmed their worst suspicions. Over an hour later, they reached a big junction to what looked like a motorway. To their surprise, the lorry did turn towards the sun, and they both smiled at each other, knowing that they were driving west. More than two hours later, the traffic started to increase, telling them that they were close to a large city again. At the entrance of the city, a loud siren greeted them. There had been a small car accident, and a car of the Gendarmerie had its siren on. They made sure they were well-hidden. It was evening, and the traffic from the end of the working day forced their lorry to drive very slowly. They looked at each other and decided to wait until the next busy traffic light for the best opportunity to jump out of their hiding place. That worked well. They found themselves on the periphery of what seemed to be a large town.

"I really need a drink."

"Me too, but first I need to let some water out. Do you know where we are?"

"I think so. After the car accident, I saw a road sign saying welcome to Oran, but I have no idea how far it is from Morocco."

They followed the road signs pointing to the "Centre de la ville", taking care not to be too loud when people were passing close by. Hours later, they arrived at the centre of Oran. They were happy to see the sea in the distance. At least, they hoped it was the sea, as it was almost too dark to be sure.

"How the hell will we get out of here now? Maybe I've reached the end of my line."

"Hey, listen. I haven't been helping you all this way just to have you give up and leave me stuck here. We will find a way. When do you think a middle-aged man like yourself will have another chance at such an adventure? Are you tired old grandpa?"

"Have you ever thought about becoming a motivational speaker?"

"Is that a real job? You sure have a whole load of crap in the West. Maybe you could help me get a job in a women's clothing store, measuring their breasts before they buy their bras. Maybe you have that kind of profession in the West, too?"

"I am sure we do have it, but I know that same person must also have to measure men's testicles before they buy their underwear. Are you still interested?"

"That's something for you, then. Anyway, it looks like there's a port with some ships down there. Surely there is a place nearby where the lorry drivers who load and unload their cargo go to eat."

"It's late, but we have nothing to lose. Come on, let's walk there."

Near the end of the harbour, they found a coffee shop with some lorries parked in front of it. They walked in and ordered a tea. In a corner, they saw three tired-looking men who fit the lorry driver stereotype. They were speaking French, so communication should be fine. After a while, they started to look their way to attract their attention. They looked back at them, then Joshua got up and walked over to them. After introducing himself, he asked if they knew of any lorry drivers that were planning on driving over to Morocco and might be able to give them a lift. The three lorry drivers looked at each other and started to laugh. Joshua asked what was so funny about his request. They answered that everybody around here knows that the border with Morocco has been closed for years. Joshua and Enzo both felt stupid and started to laugh themselves. That meant that Ahmed also must have known that he could not have driven over the border. After they had finished laughing, one of the men said that, for the time being, there was another way to go to Morocco. Joshua asked how expensive it would be. The man replied that he did not know, but he gave them an address where they could go and ask. They walked for what seemed like an eternity, and finally found the address in an alley behind a fishermen's shop. An old man who did not speak French asked them to wait, using a kind of sign language. A man came out. "Que puis-je faire pour vous?"

"Quelqu'un nous a dit que vous pouvez nous aider à aller au Maroc."

Someone told us that you could help us get to Morocco, Joshua asked in a subdued voice. The man invited them into the house, and then asked, "Quand voulez-vous aller?"

"As soon as possible, or better, the next time you can take us," replied Joshua.

"Je suis Pascal et si vous voulez je peux vous amener là ce soir."

"Did he say 'tonight'?"

"Yes, he did. Combien ça va nous coûter? How much is it going to cost us?"

"$500 chacun."

"We are not rich people. We don't have that kind of money."

"Pourquoi perdez-vous mon temps? Why are you wasting my time?"

Enzo touched his belt and asked, "Wait. Can I pay you in euros?"

"Qui €400 chacun."

"J'ai 700 ici."

"OK, ca marche. Voulez-vous de thé?"

"Yes, thank you. Some tea would be good. Quand, alles nous ou Maroc?"

"Plus tard. Later! Puis-je avoir l'argent maintenant? Can I have the money now?"

Enzo looked him straight in the eyes, showed him the money, and said, "Once we are in Morocco, you will get the money."

"Ok, ca marche. Nous allons traverser la frontière avec mon bateau de pêcheur. Vous vous cacherez tous les deux dans une cabine, mais si le Moroccon vous attrape, je ne vous connaîtrai pas. Avez-vous compris?"

"What did he say?"

"He said that we are going to cross the border with his fishing boat. We will hide in the cabin, but if the Moroccans catch us, he doesn't know us."

"Qui!"

"Très bien!"

Hours later, the three men started to walk towards the sea. Eventually they reached an old boat, and all three jumped on board. Pascal gave them some cappies to wear to avoid someone from afar seeing their skin colour. It was dark, but the sea was calm. The monotonous beating of the boat's engine combined with the sea breeze made them want to sleep, but Pascal asked them to help him with the fishing net he was preparing.

"Do you think we can trust him?"

"Do we have any other option?"

"I guess not, but I was wondering if you had a good feeling about the guy."

"I think so. But I also trusted Ahmed before."

They had been travelling for almost five hours when another boat seemed to approach. Pascal was on his phone, speaking in Arabic. Enzo and Joshua went to hide, and Pascal allowed them to. From their hiding place they could hear the boat approaching, and shortly after, they heard when it touched their boat. They could only hear people talking in Arabic, then silence, and some steps walking towards them. Then, a bright light and a voice asking them in French to get out. There were no men in uniform.

There was another person on board that seemed to be a friend of Pascal's. Pascal made a sign, asking both of them to help load some of his cargo onto the other boat. They did so, without even knowing what was in the different boxes. It looked like Pascal was more of a smuggler than a fisherman. Who were they to uphold his moral conduct? When they had finished loading all their cargo onto the other boat, Pascal demanded in English, "Money!" He continued, explaining that they were already in Moroccan waters. Now they would have to pay him €500 and give his friend the other €200 once they reached Moroccan soil. Enzo went to the back of the boat so as not to show where he was hiding the money, and came back with the money for Pascal, who thanked them and wished them good luck. Both thanked him in return, and happily jumped onto the Moroccan fishing boat. A couple of hours later, they arrived in a small harbour near the town of Saidia. They soon left the area and started looking for a way to travel west. Casablanca was still a long way away. They had read online that it was the largest cargo container port in Morocco, so they were hoping to catch a ride on one of those. Now they had learned how to travel on the back of a lorry, so they went to look around for a place filled with lorries . There wasn't one. Saidia was not a large, heavily-populated city like Algiers or Oran, but a small town with only a few thousand people. Soon, they realized that it was time to check if there were any buses going west. Eventually, they met a young boy that was keen on trying out the English he had learned at school. Talking to him, they discovered that they had to first travel south to Oujda on a local bus, and then from there to Fes. They thanked the boy who, like the one in Tunisia, was also called Mohammed. They walked to where he had told them they could get a bus to Oujda. The tickets were cheap and their journey did not take long. Luckily, they only had to wait a short time in Oujda before taking a bus to Fes. They were happy they were travelling west again. After their sleepless night, they were more than happy to fall asleep and enjoy the long ride to Fes. At their next stop, a boy came on board, shouting out his wares to sell to the travellers. They were happy to see that he had food and water at a cheap price, and he was very keen to accept euros. Enzo asked him for his name, and the boy answered, "Mohammed".

"What's the point of having a name if everyone is called Mohammed? The reason our common ancestors invented names was to be able to address different people without having to point at them. Later, even names on their own became confusing, so we added last names. Like Stephenson, which means the son of Stephen. Some added the places they were from as their last name. Leonardo Da Vinci was Leonardo from the town of Vinci. Imagine if everybody then decided to be named after the great inventor, Leonardo Da Vinci. That would be pointless."

"Stop ranting, old man. They just want to name their children after the prophet Mohammed, whom they all respect. What's wrong with that?"

"In Italy, if you call your son 'Jesus', they would think that you have no respect for the Son of God. So nobody does it. But you are right, some people in Spain call their children 'Jesus'. Well, they can call their children what they want, but I wouldn't like to give my children a name that the majority of other children have. Not very special, really."

"Do you remember what traditions are?"

"Yes, I do, and as the bus is departing again, I will follow my tradition of sleeping at least eight hours out of the daily twenty-four."

It was early afternoon when they finally made it to Fes. They felt rested and ready for their new adventure of trying to find their next means of travel that would bring them west. To their disappointment, there were no buses leaving till the next day. Fes was going to be the place where they would have to spend the night. They walked through Fes' old town market, where Enzo felt catapulted into an old, medieval world were it not for some of the modern products sold there. What was good was that the place was full of tourists, where they could fit in well. They stopped to have a drink on a rooftop terrace, and discovered that many house's rooftops overlooking the Medina and old town had been transformed into coffee places and bed and breakfasts. On their roof, there were other tourists having a good time. Two women looked in the direction of their table for a while, and eventually dared to speak to them, asking where they were from. Enzo said that they were two American colleagues on holiday there. The women, Helen and Rose, were from Manchester in the UK, and had driven up from Marrakesh where they had first landed, and hired a car. All four enjoyed each other's company, and continued talking and sipping tea until the owner told them that it was time to close. The ladies looked like they were up for a good time, while the men had nowhere to sleep. When Rose and Helen suggested they come to their hotel to look at what they had bought and see whether those clothes fit them well, they accepted wholeheartedly. They both had a good, sleepless night enjoying the ladies' company. They met at breakfast, and the four smiling faces enjoyed the rising sun on the terrace. The local waiter explained that in the past, the terraces of Fes were women's territory. The roof was the only place outside of the house where women did not have to cover themselves. Enzo and Joshua apologised, and explained that they had no intention to look at the other women on the roof. The waiter (another Mohammed) laughed, and explained in perfect

English that things have also changed in Morocco. He carried on praising King Mohammed VI, who he said had done a lot to modernize the country and advance women's rights. The waiter was not sure that this was a good thing, but there was no way back, or at least, that was what his wife told him. With a disapproving look on his face Mohammed, told them that from 2004, a man must prove his financial standing before being able to marry his second wife. Worst still, he needs the approval of his first wife.

Joshua had to ask, "Do you have a second wife?"

"I am sorry to say that I don't earn that much working here as a waiter, but who knows? Maybe with the help of your tips I might come closer to that goal."

They all laughed, and Mohammed went back to the kitchen to fetch more food. During the small talk, Rose and Helen said that the next day, they would be driving slowly back to Marrakesh via Morocco's capital city, Rabat, and then, Casablanca. They wondered what their plans were. Enzo answered that they had no fixed plan and an open mind. He added that they would not mind joining them, if they so wished.

"How long do you want to spend in Rabat?"

Helen said, smiling, "Don't worry, you won't get bored. Just a day, sightseeing. If it's OK with you, you don't have to worry about looking for a room. We'd love to share ours. What do you think?"

After he pretended to think about this proposal, he replied, "We'll need to change our itinerary a bit, but you are reason enough to change our whole holiday plans. What time should we leave tomorrow?"

"No hurry, just after breakfast. Of course, it depends on the kind of night we have. On the way, we'd like to stop near Meknes to see the Roman ruins of Volubilis. Is that OK with you?"

Joshua was surprised. "Did the Romans manage to conquer as far as Morocco?"

"Yes, and I am sorry they didn't stay longer. Otherwise it'd easier now to read the road signs in Latin script." The old wise man then added, "Most are also in French nowadays. That's a kind of Latin, right? So we should be able to find our way around. Volubilis sounds great. I'm looking forward to it."

Helen carried on, "I just don't expect everybody to be interested in history. We like a bit of history, sunshine, good food and a couple of uncomplicated guys."

"No complication, just fun. We like that, right Joe?" said Joshua, looking at Enzo, then suddenly remembering that he was supposed to be Joe.

Rose glanced at Joshua. "Tom, you mustn't have spent very long in the US. You sound more South African to me."

"Yes, you're right. I'm originally from South Africa, but I moved to the US about five years ago."

Helen looked back at Joshua. "Don't worry, Tom. We don't really care where you're from. I like you, and that's all that matters." She stood up and kissed him. Then she announced, "Guys, we have some tours already booked for the day, but we should be back here after four in the afternoon. Can we meet here after six o'clock?"

Enzo, showing his interest, replied, "Sure, we will be here at six. We'll need some time to re-book our accommodation and tell the hotel we are staying at that we want to leave earlier. We might have to still pay, but who cares? You're worth it."

The men stood up and walked down to the steep staircase and into the street. They wandered around the market and found a peaceful place to sit down and drink a very sweet tea.

"So, Tom, did you have a good time last night?"

"Sure, Joe, I did. And I think you did as well."

"Is Helen the first white woman you spent the night with?"

"Yes, the first white woman, and the first woman old enough to be my mother."

"Was that a problem for you?"

"Not really, just at first I felt a bit insecure, so I let her be in the driver's seat. I think she liked that, and after a while, so did I."

"Helen is a mature woman, and by now, she certainly knows what she likes and what she does not."

"You see, in my country or South Africa, women need to be careful about what people in the community think of them. Helen and Rose don't seem to care about what people think of them. Aren't they worried?"

"Worried about what? Women in the West fought hard for the rights men have had for a long time. Women that earn their own money can also decide when and with whom they want to have sex. Of course, the invention of the contraceptive pill helped, as they can now control when they want to get pregnant. For us men, having sex has always been mostly fun, but women had to consider the consequences of getting pregnant and having to spend the rest of their lives raising children. Nowadays, men in Western countries need to also be very careful about getting some girl pregnant, as they will have to pay child support their whole life. Didn't you pay attention last night? What if Helen gets pregnant? She'll track you down in America and you'll have to send her money for the child you conceived last night."

"What? Are you mad?"

"No, not really. You said you had fun last night and, after all, the newborn baby will be your child. Sorry, but little baby Joshua will also be your responsibility, my friend. Are you ready to be a daddy? If you want to live in the West, you'll need to respect the rules of the Western world. Whether you like it or not. Our game, our rules."
Enzo was laughing on the inside while teasing Joshua. Joshua's face drained of colour, and his world seemed crumbling in front of his eyes.
"Sorry, I'm only pulling your leg. I'm sure you're sterile. Sorry, joking again. Helen must already be fifty, and I'm not sure she can still have children. Anyway, I'm sure she doesn't want any, so you should be safe. Helen is here to celebrate her fiftieth birthday with her friend. They just want to have fun without any commitment. Rose told me that they are colleagues. They're nurses, and work together in a hospital in the oncology unit where they deal with final stage cancer patients, where they see many people die. They are here to forget about their normal life and just have fun."

"This is Africa and I've seen many people suffer or die, but I haven't seen many African women using this as an excuse to have sex whenever they wanted."

"I understand that if every day you have to think about how to feed yourself and your family, you have little time to think about fun or the fact that your life is short. In such circumstances, it's hard enough to stay alive. And of course, let's not forget about the traditions you love and defend so much. As I said, women in the West have fought hard to gain the right to behave like men have done for thousands or millions of years. One day, even the women on this continent will ask for the same rights men have. Men in the West resisted gender equality for a long time as well, but now only a few do, as they saw that equality is good for them as well."

"What do men gain from women having more rights?"

"First of all, think about women having sex whenever they want with whoever they want. If, of course, these women aren't lesbians, then there's a good chance that you end up being their sexual partner. If women can have sex whenever they like with whoever they like, men end up having more sex. As simple as that. Apart having more sex, one day you might have children, and then you'll feel better knowing that your daughter will have the same rights as your son."

"Those are Western, rich country problems. Don't forget that I had to leave my country because of my father and brother's different political views. Sure, women's rights are good, but they aren't at the top of my agenda at this moment."

"Didn't you have fun last night?"

"Sure, and...?"

"That, my friend, only happened because of the rights women have gained in the last fifty years. Remember, women's equal rights means more sex for you. Women's segregation means men's masturbation! Got it?"

"If you put it that way, then I am all for women rights. It's just difficult for me to understand why she doesn't seem to need or want a husband. Do women in the West not want a family or children of their own?"

"Some do, some don't, but it should be their choice, like it is your choice to get married or not."

"Where I am from, it is often the case that you need to be wealthy enough to be able to afford a wife and children of your own."

"Believe me, this is not just an African problem. In Italy, there are plenty of adults that at the age of 35 or 40 still live at home with their parents because they cannot afford to rent an apartment. Despite that, not everybody necessarily wants to get married."

"I think that without a woman in the house, there is no family."

"You might be right, but that doesn't mean that we should lock women up in the house and regard them as a dishwasher or stove."

"So do you think things are better now in the West, after women gained more rights?"

"It's not perfect, but I think we are still figuring out a new model. The other just lived in the past. Things have changed and moved on."

"Why not stick with the old model we have used for thousands of years already?"

"Because whether we like it or not, things have changed, people have changed. The past is in the past and we live in the present. Even if the past was better (and by the way, I personally don't think so), we live in the present. And we need to get on with our lives and find a way to work it out with what we have now. You see, I think there are four types of people. There are those that look up to the sky for their answers and often do little here on Earth to solve their problems. Their problems are often solved by those that look forward and try to build a better future. Then there are those that look back on the past, and sometimes, dwell on it. For those, the past was always better, but instead of drawing inspiration from the past to build a better future, they just want to stop time or roll it back. This does not work. Finally, there are those that look down and are depressed. Sometimes they were just beaten down by bad circumstances and never had a chance to lift their head. I try to always look forward. If there is a God and He wanted me to look backwards, then I would have been born with eyes on the back of my head. I haven't checked your head yet. Will you turn around?"

"Good one, old man. What about those that can look forward, but need glasses to see anything?"

"Come on, I was just joking, no need to be nasty now. After all, it's not bad if you keep on watching our backs. As I just said, I keep on looking forward, even through glasses."

"What about your family? Do you have wife and kids?"

"Yes, I do."

"What would your wife think about you spending last night with Rose?"

"I guess she wouldn't be thrilled, and that's why I won't mention it to her."

"What if she finds out?"

"Maybe I shouldn't help the only person who knows about this to come to America. What do you think?"

"Come on, now. It's my turn to joke. No need to be nasty. Listen, it's time we get a move on. Have you noticed that sometimes there is a whiff of a bad smell coming in our direction? What the hell is that?"

"This morning while I was waiting for Rose to come out of the shower, I read her travel guide and saw that there is a leather tannery near here. It seems that they still use pigeon poo and other natural products to treat the leather they sell all over the world. I was wondering if we should go, but I'm worried about getting smelly as we don't have any other clothes with us. Maybe we should at least try to buy some cheap T-shirts and look more like tourists."

"Why, buy those! Wait here, I'll get some."

Enzo tried to stop him, but Joshua had gotten up and was gone. Almost an hour later, he came back with several T-shirts. They did not look like they came from the local market.

"Where the hell did you get those?"

"Keep them please, and let's wear them after we leave Fes."

"So, you stole those?"

"I borrowed them from some tourists that I am sure were eager to support us in our poor state."

"So these aren't from a shop in the Medina, then?"

"No, don't worry. I found a large enough hotel and blended in with the crowd walking in. I pretended to be one of them, till I saw the courtyard where I was sure they were drying some of the guests' clothes. The only problem was that I didn't have much time, nor much choice. So some of those T-shirts might be unique here in town, and I wouldn't like the owner to spot us in the market."

"A part of me thinks you have done a bad thing, but another part of me is very grateful. So, thank you very much, and I hope they fit. Listen, let's walk around town for a couple of hours and then it'll almost be time to meet the girls again."

"Hey man, I am much younger than all of you. If those are girls I must be a baby."

"Come on, baby, let's go for a walk. Or do you need a pushchair?"

They walked for a long time and enjoyed the old market. Finally, it was time to meet the girls again so they started to walk back towards their hotel. Rose and Helen seemed happy to see them again. Luckily for them, their tour had included visiting a restaurant where the ladies had eaten. They didn't want to eat anything else for the day, just have a drink. This made it easier for them, as they also pretended to have eaten earlier. Offering a few drinks would not strain their funds too much. Their friendship was fresh enough for all to be keen on having an early night in. After one more breakfast on the rooftop of the B&B overlooking the old Medina, they gazed at another beautiful sunrise.
Rose, looking at their luggage, said, "Why did you bring just those two little bags with you? Don't you have any other luggage?"

Enzo, trying to save the situation, replied, "Yes, we have more, but we left it at the hotel here as we will fly back home from Fes. We don't need more for the next couple of days. We'll come with you all the way to Casablanca if you like. Then we'll find a way to come back here."

They all walked to the car. Helen looked at Joshua and Enzo.

"It would be great if you could drive, but I guess the insurance is in my name. I suppose you'll have to entertain me instead."

Thank God for the insurance, Enzo thought. The last thing they needed was to be stopped somewhere and be asked for a driving license or document he did not have. Then, he suddenly remembered that he did indeed have a copy of his driving license, and a password that he sent himself via email so to have a copy online, as he always did before going on a trip. Why had he not thought of that earlier? Half an hour's drive away from Fes was the already less-touristy Meknes, and from there they drove to Volubilis. They pretended not to be interested in historic ruins to avoid an expensive entry fee. It seemed that Volubilis had been a Berber city before the Romans had conquered it. It was incredible to imagine the Roman soldiers that had been posted to this faraway place on the edge of a huge continent they probably knew very little about. At the entrance, a poster showed the mosaic of the Roman houses' floors, as a testimony to the wealth of the Roman town at the time. The mosaic represented women in more relaxed clothing than most Moroccan women were allowed to show now. Enzo regretted not having the chance to go in, while Joshua was very happy that he did not have to.

Joshua asked Enzo, "Was this the first European attempt to colonise the African continent?"

"What about the Homo sapiens coming from Africa and probably causing the extinction of the Neanderthal men in Europe? Did they colonise Europe?"

"Who were these 'Neanderthal men'?"

"Another human species that lived in Europe before the Homo sapiens turned up there. Of course, we cannot blame you, because we in Europe are now all descendants of Homo sapiens ourselves. Well, mostly."

"Were Neanderthal men white-skinned and blue-eyed?"

"Probably, but as I said, we are all Homo sapiens living in Europe now. We are supposed to have maybe 10% genes or DNA from Neanderthals, the rest is from the Homo sapiens. And it seems they all started in Africa first. With today's technology, they have managed to find out that all humans alive today are descended from a pool of about twenty thousand people that managed to survive some kind of catastrophe. So we are actually the same people all over, just brought up in different environments and different cultures. That's why I said that killing each other in the name of religion or tradition is crazy. We are born all the same. Religions and traditions are our inventions."

"Be careful who you say that to, old man, or someone might kill you before you help me get out of here."

"You're probably right. I just read at the entrance about that town over there, Moulay Idriss Zerhoun. It seems that it was in that town that Moulay Idriss arrived in 789, bringing Islam with him. Until then, the language here was Latin and they were probably Christians, but who knows? In Sicily, many became Muslims while the Arabs were in charge, but quickly reverted to Christianity once they were sent packing. You see, the Arabs at the time of the Sicilian conquest were more advanced than most Europeans. They also tolerated other religions, especially because they taxed non-believers. So, to avoid paying taxes, many Sicilians simply converted. It's always a question of money."

"Where did you learn all this stuff? Are you a university professor?"

"No, I'm not. I am just older, boring and very interested in history. Every strong tree needs strong roots. Our history is our roots. I read a lot of history to understand the present."

"Maybe you should do more sport and less reading."

"I probably would have if I had stayed in a warm country with blue skies, but after I left Sicily I lived a long time under grey skies. Not a good place to go out and do sport. Inside sports never interested me. Gyms aren't for me. Maybe I'm just not a sport person. Are you?"

"If running away from the police counts, then I'm a full-time sportsman. I did play some football while at school, but most of my friends back home played rugby. You know, in South Africa and Zimbabwe, football was more for black people, while rugby was mostly played by white people. Things have changed now, but my father didn't want me to play rugby because of this legacy."

"You mean real football right? What we in America call 'soccer'?"

"American football is far too expensive to play. Too much gear and too much waiting around. I watched some American football games in a pub in Johannesburg, but I never really understood the rules. The long waiting and the planning they do during the game was good for the long advertisements that took my mind off the game altogether. With real football, you see the players running all the time. When are those girls coming?"

"They are probably taking a picture with every old stone. If you look down there from up here, you can see that they hired a guide, so he'll take them all around and explain the history of every small thing. I do the same when I go somewhere. You know, it's history that brings every old stone back to life. Otherwise, you're just looking at stones. An old beautiful fountain, like the Trevi fountain in Rome, is great to look at on its own, but old building walls or ruins need a bit of history with them."

"Bring me to America and one day we'll come back to this continent as tourists, and I'll take you to the medieval city of Great Zimbabwe in the south of the country. I went once on a school trip. I was probably too young to appreciate the value of the old stones then. Maybe when I am as old as you are now, things will be different."

"Maybe, but I was always interested in history, even before going to school. I remember staying with my grandmother when I was four years old, and loving the story she told me of WWII and the landing on the Americans near her town. I loved the fact I could talk to someone that had been there back then. When I got older and we did history at school, I went back to ask my grandmother more. As a devout Catholic, when my grandmother went to church, she would confess her sins. She told me that after the war ended, during the confession, the priest would tell her not to vote for the devil that came in the shape of the red flag of the Italian communist party. Voting for the devil would have meant my grandmother would have not received absolution for her sins. You see, that's the stuff they don't write in the history books. What I want to say is that I like reading history books, but I know that those were mostly written by the winners, and that key information like my grandmother told me about were omitted. Enjoy history, but logically question it. I'm a medical researcher, and we need to proof the validity of a cure, otherwise it's just a placebo."

Rose and Helen finally came back to rescue Joshua from Enzo's never-ending stream of history.
Helen looked very pleased, but was now tired. "I wasn't even aware that the Romans had made it all the way to Morocco. Luckily, I read about Volubilis

in the travel guide on the plane. It was definitely good to come here. What have you boys been up to?"

Enzo, with a smile, said, "Waiting for you, of course. We enjoyed the scenery and each other's company. Are we ready to drive on to Rabat?"

"Yes, we are."

They departed, and after joining the motorway back in Meknes, Helen enjoyed the mostly empty road. She enjoyed it so much that the Gendarmerie pulled her over for driving too fast. After she agreed to pay the fine, they were allowed to drive on. Enzo and Joshua could not believe how lucky they had been, yet again. Maybe their new, stolen T-shirts made them look even more like tourists. Helen got into the car, not very happy about the fine she had to pay on the spot. She was crossed.

"Stupid Gendarmerie. I'm sure they only stop tourists. What is the Gendarmerie anyway? Does it mean 'police' in French?"

Enzo jumped at the opportunity to impress the ladies. "Do you really want to know? By the way, I'm sorry about the fine, but this is something you'll be able to tell your friends back home."

"Thank you, but I prefer to pick up my own souvenirs and not in paper format. So, what is the Gendarmerie, then? Is it a kind of tourist police like the one they have in Egypt?"

"No, it's not. You see, in some countries, there are two kinds of police. One, the Gendarmerie, like the Carabinieri in Italy, is part of the army or Defence ministry, while the police force responds to the Interior ministry."

"Do you work for the government somewhere? How do you know that?"

Joshua, looking bored, said, "He knows a lot and likes to tell everybody about it. Be ready to learn more stuff."

"Why not? I like to know stuff. So, why do some countries have two types of police force, then?"

"Some countries decided to have two polices forces run by two different ministries, to make the organizing of a coup d'état more difficult."

Rose turned around, "Sorry, I don't speak French. What is a coup d'état?"

"A coup d'état is when the army, or part of it, takes over the power or the governing of a country. If part of the army should decide to get rid of their government with a coup d'état, then the police force could stop them. Also, there would have to be two different ministries in agreement with the coup d'état. It's the same for the police. If they organised a coup d'état, then the Gendarmerie would be there to stop them. So the two police forces are there to keep a balance and to check on each other."

Rose was getting more interested. "Are you saying that those two police forces sometimes compete?"

"I guess you're right, sometimes they do compete."

"What a mess. I am glad we only have one police in the UK." Rose proudly replied.

"Has the army ever tried to take power in the UK?"

Helen stepped in. "Yes, but a long time ago with Oliver Cromwell."

"So, maybe that's why you don't need a Gendarmerie there."

Helen tried to change the subject. "As you're an American, do you know anybody that has gone to Cut&Run to lose a couple of pounds?"

"Don't they have a branch of Cut&Run in the UK?"

"Yes, we do have a branch, but just down in London. I only heard that the procedure is supposed to be good. I'm a bit scared and I don't know anybody I can ask. In the USA, people seem to be keener about plastic surgery than we are in the UK."

"If you ask me, you look good as you are," Joshua told Helen.

"That's very sweet, darling, but I wouldn't mind losing a stone. Rose always calls me 'fatty'."

Rose said quickly, "Come on now, you know I'm joking and that I like you the way you are, darling."

"I know, but when I look at myself in the mirror I wonder how long a young man like Tom will carry on fancying me. So, Joe, do you know anybody my age that has undergone the treatment?"

Enzo said promptly, "No, I do not know anybody in their thirties that has done it."

Helen smiled back. "Sure, but I am just twenty-five, darling."

"I thought so, Helen. I know some people, and they all seem happy to have lost the extra weight. Some have put it back on and gone through the Cut&Run drip procedure three times already."

"They must be rich. What do you mean by 'drip procedure'? Do they put you on a drip?"

"No, they do a small operation so that the fat melted in your body doesn't end up in the stomach and digested again. They kind of bypass the stomach, and your own fat constantly drips out of you."

"Drips out of where?"

"Well, from the same place where the rest of the digested food comes out of you."

Rose, looking disgusted, said, "That must be a disgusting feeling."

"Maybe, but many do it and come back for more treatment. So it cannot be that bad."

"Typical man talking. Do you want to also tell me that giving birth doesn't hurt?"

"No, I know that men don't give birth, but many do undergo the same drip procedure. Is giving birth that bad?"

Rose, now looking crossed, retorted, "I am sure you know all about that. How many babies have come out of you?"

"None, but I have seen many women with more than one child. If it was so bad, no woman that had given birth would do it more than once. I was once kicked in the balls and it hurt like hell. Believe me I would never let someone kick me in the balls again."

They all laughed, and even Rose showed a good sense of humour.
Helen looked at Enzo and said, "Be careful! Once we get out of the car you might have to protect your private parts."

Rose said promptly, "If you're thinking about kicking him there, please do that after we've dropped them in Casablanca and not before. I want to still enjoy my holiday, and this is my kind of diet."

Helen said to Rose, "Oh, yes I do know how you like your belly to be flattened."

Rabat was close, and the traffic intensified. The drive had been fun and they did not realise how fast the time had gone. After travelling for one more hour through the city traffic, they reached the centre and quickly found their hotel. They walked around the Moroccan capital and visited the mausoleum of the early kings. They spent one more great night together, and the day after, they went to the nearby Kasbah with its blue-painted walls. Enzo looked at the sea and thought of his home and family on the other side of the Atlantic Ocean. Joshua had never seen the Atlantic before, and wondered if he would really manage to cross it with his new-found friend. After breakfast, it was time to travel to Casablanca.

Rose looked at Enzo and asked, "Joe, do you like the movie Casablanca?"

Joshua turned around, "Is there a movie called 'Casablanca'?"
The other three laughed aloud.

"I see, it must be some very old film. Sorry for being young and innocent."

Helen quickly said again, "You may be young, but certainly not innocent. Well, at least not since you've been with me. Casablanca is a great movie set during WWII, in a Morocco that was under French and Nazi occupation. Many people that ran away from Europe came to Casablanca, and from there, tried to fly to safety to the USA. You probably haven't heard of Humphrey Bogart and Ingrid Bergman either?"

"Not really. Some old Hollywood actors, I guess."

Helen trying to include him, "Yes, they were, and I don't think they came here to shoot the movie, but I want to see the real place anyway. Marrakesh is a great place, but old. Casablanca looked more modern when we drove past to go to Fes. Guys, we have had a great time, and who knows, maybe one day we'll meet again. And you, Joe, don't forget to send me the information you promised about Cut&Run."

"Well said, Helen. I've had a great time, and I am sure Tom thinks so too. You've also been very generous. Thank you."

Rose, looking a bit sad, said, "No need to say thank you. We also had a great time. Who knows? Maybe one day our paths will cross again. Life is full of surprises."

After a good drive, they arrived in Casablanca, where they spent a bit of time walking around together. Then, they all hugged and parted ways.

Enzo looked at a saddened Joshua. "The holiday has finished, young man. It's time to try to find a way off this continent and over the ocean. I like swimming, do you? Let's see if we can find a boat willing to take us over there for little or no money."

"I had a great time, and I am still amazed by how quickly we fell apart. I liked Helen."

"I hope you haven't fallen in love? Do I need to nurse you? What happened? I thought you said she was too old?"

"I only said that I liked her, OK? I might need a bit of time to get over her."

"You know, I think a long journey on a boat is what you probably need. So let's walk towards the harbour. Any shipping companies should have their office around the port area."

They walked a long time from one of the biggest mosques outside Saudi Arabia where they had parted with the girls to the port of Casablanca. The city was much bigger than they had thought at first. On the way Enzo spotted an internet coffee place where he managed to download a copy of his documents that he had sent to his own email address. He had never needed to download these before and this is why he had not thought of doing that before. Now he thought of a story to tell the shipping company for which it would be handy to have at least a copy of his US passport.

Joshua felt better after seeing that he really had a US passport and was not just a Sicilian. It took hours to find a shipping company. Thinking that maybe their zebra team combination might not be the best, Enzo asked Joshua to wait for him downstairs while he would try to speak to someone. Enzo was soon downstairs and that could not be good news.

"They do not ship to America, but only to Europe. Still they gave me a couple of addresses from companies that do ship to America."

More walking, but the two men were now very keen on finding a way to sail across the sea. After wandering from shipping company to shipping company, they finally found one that could help them. Enzo explained that he had been robbed of his US passport and that he was there in a not completely legal business and therefore could not apply for a passport replacement at the embassy. Practically, he should not have left US soil because of some investigations into his business. After hours of talking, he had struck a deal but the container boat would drop them in Santo Domingo where it was due to stop anyway on the way to the USA. They did not want any problems with the US authorities where they shipped most of their cargo. Enzo agreed for both of them to work on board for no money and to pay two and a half thousand US$ once they arrived in Santo Domingo. He had justified that Joshua was a colleague with local knowledge and connections who had also got robbed and stranded there with him. Enzo thought that once in Santo Domingo, he could ask Julio, his brother-in-law for help. Now he just needed to tell Joshua that he had got a passage for him, but not for the USA.

"Where the hell have you been? You were ages in there!"

"Listen, it was not easy and I had to do some convincing especially to justify our lack of documents and reasons for wanting to go to the USA."

"Are we now?"

"Well, almost..."

"Almost! What do you mean?"

"They cannot risk taking us to the USA on their ship, but they are willing to drop us in Santo Domingo."

"Where is Santo Domingo?"

"Santo Domingo is in the Caribbean just off the American coast, near Cuba if that makes sense."

"Good, but how will we carry on from Santo Domingo to the USA?"

"Easy young man, let's cross that bridge once we get there, shall we? I hoped you would be happy I managed to get us out of Africa. Think about it, as if you don't want to come, I can save some cash. They asked for two and a half thousand US$ to take us to Santo Domingo and on top of this we will have to work while on board, getting there."

"Sorry, I don't want to seem ungrateful. I was just a bit disappointed after you told me that you had found someone who would take us over the ocean. I thought we would go straight to the USA. When will we be leaving?"

"In two days' time. They want us to get on board tomorrow and start working on cleaning the ship. They also want us to be on board the day before the departure as then the rest of the crew will arrive and they will be checked by the port authorities. They will take us to the ship with a delivery van and after unloading stuff, we will remain on board. So let's enjoy one more day in Casablanca."

"I wish Helen were here."

"I ask you again. Did you fall in love with Helen? I think a huge ocean between you two is what you need to forget her. Remember her for what it was, just an adventure and great fun."

"What do you know? Maybe one day I will go and find her in the UK."

"Maybe, but think first about the fact that she might not want you to find her again. Did she give you her home address, phone number or email address? I don't think so."

"What do you know, she might have forgotten!"

"Oh god, you are really in love with her. Okay, fine. She forgot and you will go and find her one day. Anyway, let's walk back toward the harbour. I want to find the dock he described to me to make sure we won't miss it tomorrow."

They went on a long walk and after hours they found the dock where they would embark for the new world. Being tired, they decided to walk back towards the old city centre of Casablanca, but on their way they met a band of young men who started to follow them on their way to the centre. The group of men got very close and overtook them. They felt better until the moment those young men turned around and showed their knives.

Enzo, quickly, "We don't have any money, what do you want?"

One of them that looked like their chief punched Enzo in the face, then the stomach.

Joshua started to shout in French, Arabic and other languages Enzo did not understand until they stopped. Then, one of them carried on speaking to Joshua, while they kept an eye on Enzo who was now folded in two.

"It's okay and they will let us go, but they want at least your jacket and t-shirt first."

"What should I wear?"

"Come on, it is not that cold and I don't care, just take those off and give it to them."

Enzo got undressed slowly at which point they also pointed to his shoes.

"For god's sake those are old worn out shoes!"

"Are you stupid? Stop arguing."

At that point they also pointed to his trousers. Only now, Enzo understood that they did not need his clothes, they just wanted to humiliate him. So he finally got undressed without any more complaints. They all laughed at the middle aged white man in underwear. After they had had enough fun, they decided to leave them in peace.

"How long does it take for you to shut up? You were lucky one of them was from Zimbabwe."

"I cannot go into the city centre in underwear."

"Are you shy? Or feeling cold? Stay there under that arch and hope nobody comes. I will try to find some clothes for you."

Almost an hour later, after what seemed two or three to Enzo, Joshua returned with some Moroccan traditional clothes.

"That is all you could find after all this time?"

"Sorry, next time I will bring you a catalogue and you can choose what you would like me to steal for you. Instead of complaining, think of the guy who is wondering where the clothes he hung up to dry disappeared to. And think of those who will have to walk home in bare feet after visiting the mosque."

"Listen, I did see people in Fez wearing those traditional clothes, but most people here wear western clothes, so it seems odd that all you could find were these clothes. That's all, but thank you all the same."

"Did you flash anyone while I was away?"

"As you are asking, yes. An old woman walked down that small alley there holding a young child. She shouted something in Arabic then pulled the child and walked back. I did wonder if she would ask for help. So when I heard you coming, I was not sure if I should run away or wait to see who was coming. Why did those bastards take my clothes? What was the point of that?"

"They probably did not like you and what you represent to them. "

"What, the rich west they would like to go to, but can't?"

"For example. They didn't like your white face and the fact you did not have much they could take from you. Those kids have nothing to lose. If someone throws them in jail, they have no families or career that is waiting for them. If someone does not have a future to worry about, who cares how long a day is, a week, a month or a life? An ant or a bee are part of a kind of family. But would an ant or a bee on their own care about putting food or pollen aside for their future? I guess they would just enjoy each day like it was their last."

"Anyway, thank you for getting them off me."

"No worries, I had to protect my ticket to America."

"Of course. Well, the ticket says, thank you. Let us go to the city centre now. We need to find a place to sleep."

"No need to sleep. I am sure we can have fun somewhere all night. We will be a long time on a boat with little to do and just sleep."

"Have you not understood? They want us to work all the way to Santo Domingo."

"Fine, old man. Let's see if we can find a place where I can have fun and you can sleep."

The two men walked around Casablanca to try to kill time and carry on playing tourists as they had done with Rose and Helen. They walked around the "Ancienne Medina", then the United Nations Square and the Mohamed V Square from where they spotted the Catholic cathedral of Casablanca. Remembering their time in Algiers, they looked at each other and started to walk towards the cathedral. Not before Enzo went off again about the name Mohamed.

"Look, even the kings here have been called Mohamed for a while. At least they put a number at the end to distinguish one from the other. I guess as a king, it makes you an immortal ruler being always the same name. They just changed the version at the end of the name. Clever. Are you one day going to call your son Joshua?"

"Why not?"

"I told you in Italy is forbidden to give your children your own first name. In the past traditionally they would have named their children with their grandparent's name, skipping one generation. I guess this was done to avoid confusion. In the US we can name our children what we want and then use junior or senior to distinguish between the young and the old. When I lived in Brazil I thought at first that some people were really called junior, then I met some of their parents and it became clear to me that both had the same first name."

They walked into a full church where a wedding was being celebrated. They sat down and pretended to belong to the crowd. Not being properly dressed for the occasion gave them away. An elderly gentleman came closer to them and asked Joshua what they were doing there. Joshua replied that they were journalists investigating Christianity and Catholicism in Africa. Joshua introduced Joe as an American Christian radio presenter. Enzo played the part. The elderly gentleman welcomed them and invited them to join in the celebration of their relatives' wedding. Enzo responded that this would be a great experience, but that they were probably underdressed especially him, wearing local traditional clothes, trying to better fit in with the country's customs. The elderly gentleman introduced himself as Paul and after repeatedly shaking their hands, begged them to join them as they were. They would be very welcome. At this point they were obliged to sit and listen to the whole ceremony in the hope that a celebration with an abundant meal would follow. Their stomachs started to complain, remembering the long past breakfast time. They were lucky. They even got to ride in Paul's car with his wife to the wedding.

"Is Morocco the first country you are visiting on your tour of Africa?"

"Not at all. We also visited Algeria and were very impressed by the cathedral there. A shame that there, we did not find many people in the church."

"Oh yes, I went there years ago. Isn't the altar very beautiful?"

Enzo and Joshua described well the cathedral in Algiers, thus cementing their Christian journalist credentials. Paul explained that he was one of the bride's uncles. They eventually arrived at a beautiful celebration hall that made it clear to them that the freshly wedded couple were not poor. The food started arriving and an almost exaggerating Enzo made the sign of the cross before starting to eat. They got to thank the couple who went around the tables where once more they were introduced as Christian journalists touring Africa. The whole party went well for them until Enzo went to the toilet and came back with an urge to speak alone to Joshua.

"Joshua come, we need to get out of here."

"Why, what happened? I thought we could spend the evening here?"

"When I walked out of the toilet I saw the guy from the shipping company at the restaurant. If he sees me and he knows someone here, he could get us into trouble."

"Why?"

"Listen, as we have no travel documents. I had to invent a story about some business for which we lost our passports. He agreed for his ship to take us to Santo Domingo, I don't want to make him suspicious and change his mind about shipping us there. So let's get out of here as soon as we can."

"Fine. I was just having fun. Be calm and let me ask around if someone is driving back to town near the harbour. It was a long drive and I don't want to walk back."

After asking around, Joshua did find someone who would drive them back near to the centre of Casablanca. They thanked Paul and his wife, then they walked to the car park making sure not to be seen by the people sitting at the bar. Driving them back were two young ladies with their elderly mother. One of the women had an early shift as a nurse at the hospital, so needed to get home early. Her name was Marie.

"Sorry Joe, as you are an American, can I ask you why it is a problem for people in the west to accept women wearing a headscarf? You see many of my Muslims girlfriends here do not understand why this is such a big issue."

"I think this has nothing to do with wearing a headscarf. In the sixties, women's headscarves were also fashionable in Europe and the west in general. The problem is when you want to make a religious statement wearing something specific or even growing a beard. Why do you want to make a point? Do you want to show that you are different or better? In such cases, you are bound to attract other people's attention and not always in a good way. What do your friends think of western women coming to the Moroccan beaches and wearing a bikini? Or even being topless on a beach here. What would your friends here say?"

"If women were to go topless, some would probably think these women are easy to get. Others would even say that they behave like prostitutes."

"What if for these women being topless is normal or even part of their own belief in expressing freedom?"

"I understand you men like to see topless women, but there is no need to go topless."

"There is no need to wear a headscarf either. It's just a statement. In the west many think that some Muslim women are forced by their parents or husbands to hide their hair."

"This is just their tradition."

"Marie, in the north-east of Germany, there is a tradition called FKK, Frei Korper Kultur, or free body culture. In Scandinavia, the mixed sauna is part of their culture. We all have our traditions, but western women going topless on the beaches in Arab countries should not wonder if they are badly judged, right? In the same way, Muslim women wearing a headscarf or more over their heads should not be surprised to be judged in other ways."

"What ways?"

"As I said, many in the west believe that headscarves and other hair covering gear is often imposed on women by parents or husbands. Therefore a woman hiding her hair is automatically seen to be traditional and in her traditional role, thinking a male to be superior to her. This is why she might not get full respect in public. If you present yourself as being submissive, do not expect others to then give you the same rights men have."

"Arab or Muslim women are not inferior to Arab or Muslim men. You are confusing things."

"Tell me, Marie, can Muslim women also take more husbands? Or is it just men who can marry more wives?"

"You know that a Muslim man here in Morocco must have his wife's approval before he can marry another woman?"

"That was not my question. Can a married woman with the permission of her first husband marry a second one?"

"No, this is not possible."

"Would you mind if your husband married a second wife?"

"I am a Christian and I want to marry a Christian. So only one husband for me. Some people in the west have a wife and a lover on the side. In the USA where you are from, people divorce very often, so marriage does not seem to have value any longer."

"You are right, things are changing all the time, but there is no way back. We need to look forward and find new ways."

"What is wrong with the old traditional ways?"

Joshua interjected, "Yes, Joe what is wrong with the old traditions?"

"There is nothing wrong and as a Christian journalist at the radio we often get asked those questions. The traditions or old ways of doing things, are called so, because they were fine in the past. Some of the customs we now call traditions are not that old at all. We humans invent and adapt traditions and customs all the time. You see the first Christians who arrived in America were also much stricter, especially on women's rights. Customs do change. Open women's hair in Europe also used to be a mark of a woman who was free and not yet married. Married women tied their hair up to show that they were taken. In the same way, some women over fifty now cut their hair short."

"I like some of your arguments, but not all. I am also glad my mother does not understand English, my younger sister Theresa just a little bit. I need to get up early tomorrow morning, but I would love if you could join us for a cup of tea. I want to invite my neighbour. She is in a kind of inter-faiths association as she herself is Muslim and worries about her two sons living in Christian Europe. She asks me loads of questions trying to understand, but maybe you could give her better answers. Can you still spare half an hour? Please tell me now as I need to start convincing my mother. She is already cross with me for leaving the party early."

Joshua pushed his leg strongly against Enzo's, begging him not to accept the invitation. Then he said, "Well, we also need to be in bed early as we have an early meeting tomorrow morning."

Enzo, after pushing his leg back into place, "Sure, Marie, it would be an honour, but only half an hour if it will help your friend. Joshua turned the other way so as not to show his disapproving and annoyed face. Finally they arrived at their apartment where on the way up Marie stopped to invite her neighbour and introduced to her the two strangers. What Marie had not mentioned was that the neighbour did not speak English and she would have to translate. They sat at a table where soon a warm cup of tea appeared with plenty of sugar in it already. Marie's unhappy mother was there serving it.

Marie's neighbour, "Please help me to understand why many people in the west do not like Muslims?"

"The truth is that nowadays people in most of the west do not care much about religion, but they worry about terrorist attacks. I am afraid many in the west associate Muslims with danger."

"We are not all terrorists and we cannot be blamed for a minority of people doing stupid things?"

"I fully agree, but imagine if in Muslim countries around the world Christian terrorists were to blow up building or planes shouting Jesus is great before doing so. What would people in Morocco start to think about the Christians living in their countries? Dangerous, right? If those few stupid people, did not do what they do in the name of their God, then maybe people in the west would blame just their terrorist group and not the whole Muslim world. Also we have not seen many Muslim leaders condemning these terrorist actions in the west."

"I am worried about my two sons living in Europe. What do you think they should do to stay out of trouble?"

"They should be fine, especially if they speak the local language, so people around them don't worry about what they might be up to."

"Are you referring to what some Muslim refugees did in Cologne in Germany? My sons would never grope women!"

"We do not know what young men are up to when they're alone, and what they would try to get away with."

"Of course, if those women are asking for it?"

"What do you mean?"

"Well, if these women wore just miniskirts and high heeled shoes."

"Yes, this is the exact problem. In different parts of the world people dress differently and some clothing can send completely different messages in different places. A headscarf, for example, is not well seen in Europe, but is fine here in Morocco. A miniskirt is well seen in Europe, but not in Islamic countries. Please let me say that I do not believe that this has to do with religious values at all. If we would have hibernated a European man in the Middle Ages and defrosted him today, he would react in a similar way to how a conservative Muslim man would at the sight of a young girl in a miniskirt or a bikini. In Egypt I met some Coptic Christians whose customs regarding their daughters were not much dissimilar to those of their Muslim neighbours. So this for me is no religious issue, but one of customs. Women in the west have gained many more rights after WWII and things have changed a lot."

"So women's equal rights means that women can now dress like prostitutes and sleep with who they want. What kind of progress is that?"

"I know you have two sons, but what if you had two daughters, would you not like them to have the same rights men have?"
"Yes, but this does not mean dressing like a prostitute."

"The world is not perfect, but things have changed. In my opinion the biggest problem between the west and the Muslim world is the difference in women's rights. If Muslim men want to be welcomed in the west, they have to respect women's rights there. They are free to behave differently from when they go back home. I do not expect Moroccan women to wear a bikini or miniskirt here just because this is my tradition or custom back home. In the same way, people with other cultural backgrounds need to adapt in the west or go back to the countries whose customs they love and cannot do without."

"So my sons' culture and beliefs will not be accepted in Europe?"

"Nobody will force your sons to become Christians, eat pork or drink alcohol and they can pray to whatever god they like. Everybody in Europe will respect their rights as long as they respect the traditions and culture of their host country. In the west we try to live in harmony, but we expect mutual respect."

"The way my sons were dreaming about moving to the west, I thought they could be living there as freely as they were here, openly professing their religion and respecting the festivities of our Islamic calendar."

"Imagine if we have people from different parts of the world and everybody wanted to celebrate their religion, nobody would ever work and we would just be celebrating each other's festivities. A great party country, but a poor one if nobody worked. Even if fewer people are religious in the west, we still like our festivities as this is when we spend time with our families and friends. Those are our traditions."

Joshua could no longer listen to the two arguing. "I think it is now time to go. I believe Marie's mother has already gone to bed and Marie needs to get up early as we do."

"I am sorry for keeping you up so long, but I was more than happy to answers your neighbour's questions."

"Merci, merci et bonne nuit!"

"Thanks a lot. I could have answered some of the questions myself, but if I had done so, she would have thought I was lacking respect. She's known me since I was a young girl and she has never thought of me as being different because of being Christian. I prefer to keep it this way. Thank you again and tomorrow after work I will need to explain this to my cross mother. Bye now."

The door finally closed and the two men started to walk towards the harbour.

"You are an old mad man. It is almost midnight. I drank that tea as slowly as I could and time stopped all the same."

"Why are you so cross? We had nowhere to go or to be."

"I wanted to try to find a place to sleep, but no chance at this hour now. Thanks to you."

"Sorry, I understood you wanted to stay awake all night."

"Maybe, but not talking about religion."

"I am sorry. When they stole my clothes and you were talking to them, I managed to get out the money I had hidden in the belt. So we could try to find a place to sleep. The problem is that I don't have a valid document, not even a fake one, but if I remember correctly you do have a British passport in the name of Mr. Steven Bennett. What if you get a room on the ground floor and I sneak in?"

"So you had money and I had to steal your clothes and we spent all evening celebrating a wedding and eating for free. Why did you not use your money before?"

"Don't be cross, I did not know when we might need it. As tomorrow we are leaving anyway, I can now spend it."

"Fine, give me some money and let me see if I can find a room for us."

Armed with his British passport, Joshua managed to find a room not far from the harbour where they wanted to remain close. At the reception there was only one person whom Joshua could easily distract by asking for an extra blanket. This allowed Enzo to sneak past the reception and run in. Once Joshua was shown the room and given the key, Enzo walked down and straight in.

"Given the fact that this is my room, you will sleep on the chair."

"Given the fact that you now got an extra blanket, you can sleep on the floor. Thank you."

They slept well and in the morning, Enzo just had to wait for a bit of confusion at the reception before running out of the place. They walked to the place Enzo was told to go and wait for the delivery van to pick them up. The van was more than half an hour late and this had made them edgy. They were really betting on this opportunity to cross the Atlantic. The driver only spoke French, but Joshua understood when after parking he shouted for the American's friends. They were told to jump into the back of the van which drove towards the harbour. Once near the ship, they were let out and straight into a container where they had to wait for one hour. After that immensely long hour, they felt being lifted.

"Let's hope they will put us on the right ship. Imagine if we were sent to South Africa or even Sicily. That would be a laugh."

"Nothing to laugh about at all. Sicily would not be too bad for me."

The container was dropped in place and only half an hour later someone came to let them out and asked to be followed. They were handed some buckets and cleaning material. The man then pointed at a dirty room that looked like the place where the crew would eat. At this point Joshua and Enzo regretted coming out of the container too soon.

"I see, you paid only for two third class tickets."

"I am so sorry you are used to travelling only in first class. Now start cleaning before they change their minds and kick us out. You should be very happy we are on the way out of here."

"Believe me, I am, but I didn't expect to get out of here as a slave."

"I don't see any chains on you and by the way I also have to work. Just think of it as a way of walking across the ocean."

The day passed, interrupted only by the same small man who now and then kept coming back to check their work and point them to the next room to clean. After more than four hours of solid cleaning, the same small man called them, asking to be followed. To their surprise there was no new room to clean, but a table with food on it. They were tired and pleased to have a break.

"With all the work, time has flown and I had not realized it was getting dark. So are you now happy or scared to leave for the first time the continent you were born in?"

"As you know, I don't have much of a reason to stay. I cannot see a future here, so let me try somewhere else. I have been travelling all over this continent for more than a year. The only place I saw many people with pale skin like yours was in South Africa. I wonder how it will be in a place where people with my skin colour are a minority and white people are the majority in charge. I guess we are not going to a majority white country yet. The Dominican Republic as you said has many mixed race people. Right?"

"You will be alright, but coming from Africa it would probably help you if you wore a necklace with a small cross on it. As I said to Marie's neighbour last night, a few bad apples have ruined the reputations for all of them. A bit like those few Sicilian mafiosi ruining my life. We all have preconceptions about other people. Of course, there are idiots everywhere you go and you said yourself most people are good. Just remember that a few idiots ruin the world for the rest of us. So remain watchful."

The small man looked at them and realizing they had finished eating, asked them to clean their dishes, then follow him. They braced themselves for more cleaning, but once more they were surprised. The small man had taken them to a small hidden room where there were some old beds. The man made a sign to greet them and left the room.

"Not too bad for a slave cabin?"

"No, old man, you are right. It could be worse."

From their cabin they could hear the constant landing of new containers that were being loaded on board. Despite this, they soon fell asleep. The day after, they awoke on their own and could not hear any loud noise. They were finally out at sea, navigating the Atlantic Ocean. Joshua could not wait to look at the open sea. They got dressed in a hurry and walked over the bridge where they could see the deep blue sea. Their pleased smiles soon mirrored the sunrise they were watching in front of them. They felt happy. The openness, the nature, the feeling of freedom and not having to hide, brought joy to them. Joshua's face changed to the point that Enzo thought he was a different person. Their happy silent moment was broken by their same little friend, whistling, trying to attract their attention and gesticulating at them, asking to come and see him. They followed the man who this time provided them with some white paint and some brushes to apply this to part of the ship.

"We certainly got our slave master."

"Learn it my friend, nothing comes for free! At least they have taken us on board and some manual labour is not going to kill us. Or maybe you had never done manual labour before leaving Zimbabwe. Even if this is the case, get ready to work hard if you want to reach anything in America, north or south."

"You are right, my first manual work was in South Africa."

"I see. I am sure you are young enough to still adapt to a new life style."

"I don't like manual labour."

"Most people don't, but the alternative is stealing and spending your life in and out of jail. With some help, you might be able to finish your university study and get a job where you don't have to do manual labour. Keep on painting and time will pass faster than just sitting all day looking at the sea."

"Zimbabwe is land locked, Johannesburg is far from the sea, so it might be normal to you coming from an island. This is my first time out at sea. I was really enjoying just looking at it. Now stuck inside here painting, makes me think of those black men and women captured hundreds of years ago, traversing the ocean as slaves."

"No need to be so dramatic, stop crying and go paint the outside. Our small friend did also point to the outside wall. I will carry on painting the inside and you do the outside while enjoying the sea view. But do your part or you are on your own. We are in the same boat. You got me?"

"What do you mean? I am on board the same boat and I will land where you will."

"Don't be so sure, my friend. I am sure they won't let us off the boat before I have paid them the two and a half thousand US$ they asked for."

"Don't worry, old man, I will do my share."

They painted for five long hours before their small friend reappeared and asked them to follow him to a large cabin where they finally met the rest of the men on board. Half of them looked Asian, the rest African. Enzo was the only white person on board and Joshua the only really black one. When they walked in, the rest raised their eyes, lifted their hands greeting and welcoming them in. They quite literally were on the same boat where skin colour and different cultural background did not seem to matter. Some spoke few words of English. The Asian-looking ones turned out to be from the Philippines, the others were mostly Moroccan. Seventeen men and with the two of them, nineteen. After they had finished eating some rice and fish curry, they all cleared their own dishes and as a surprise to them, their small friend did not impart a new task to them. Instead he looked away as if to say they were free for the rest of the day. Enzo had started to think of what to do once they reached Santo Domingo and how to best help Joshua. Not knowing what was expecting him back home in the USA, the last thing he wanted, was to smuggle people. So he started to think of a way to keep Joshua in the Dominican Republic, at least for a time. Now he just needed to convince him that this would be the best thing to do. After the time they had spent together, Enzo felt that he wanted to really help him. Joshua seemed to be a good young man who just needed some support and directions. Somehow he would have to break this news to Joshua, but he had no intention of ruining his cruise over the ocean. It was better to be on land. For a while they sat together admiring the peaceful blue sea and sunset. The good weather and scenery made them forget why they were on that boat. Eventually they looked at each other and wondered how long it was going to take them to cross the ocean. Their small friend appeared again. This time he called them to invite them for supper.

"I think they probably make us work for our food. That's fair enough. I am sure they are all working on this ship during the day. Well, let's walk in before they stop serving food."

"Yes, I am starving. The sea air probably makes me very hungry."

They ate with their fellow travellers and even had a small interaction, exchanging names and places of origin. "Good, yes, well, thank you, OK, good, beautiful sea, sunshine and thank you again for the food." The conversation was difficult, so eventually Joshua and Enzo went to sit outside on the bridge.

"Do you know where the word "posh" comes from?"

"No, but I have the feeling you are eager to tell me."

"As you know, the left side of a ship is called the port side, while the right side is called starboard. The rich British people who boarded the ship in the UK in the nineteen hundreds used to buy a commonly known POSH ticket which meant Port Out, Starboard Home. This meant that they travelled out towards America in an outer cabin on the port side of the boat or looking south where the sunshine would bless them all the way out. They would later travel back home using the SH part of their POSH ticket, which stands for Starboard Home, travelling on the starboard or right side of the boat. In this way, they were again looking south in an outer cabin and enjoying the sunshine."

"This is crazy. In many parts of Africa we need to hide from the sun. So for some of us, shade would be a luxury. I would have bought a SOPH ticket."

"I see, now I understand why we got this cabin. No windows looking north or south. That must be the luxury you were looking for?"

"Yes, right, old man. I have the feeling you are missing your children and cannot stop your urge to pass your knowledge to someone else."

"You are probably right, but I like to learn and to share what I know with others. Sorry for boring you. I guess the problem is that I am getting old and like many older people, I have accumulated some knowledge on a variety of subjects. The sad fact is that nobody wants to know about it, especially now that everybody just asks Google or Alexa. I will probably end up walking around the streets talking to myself. I must be half way there already."

"Then I guess I'd better listen to you. At least until we get to our destination or you will go mad."

"What a clever and kind young man. So I was saying... don't worry, I am joking. I am done teaching for today. Let's walk to our cabin. We are navigating towards those dark clouds and I don't want to get wet."

They walked down to their cabin when they saw their little friend at the end of the corridor knocking on a door. Shortly after, someone opened the door and handed over some blankets. Then the door was locked again. Their small friend carried on down the corridor and had not noticed his two new friends watching him from the other end."

"Do you need an extra blanket? I need one, sometimes I feel cold during the night."

"Not a blanket, but I would not mind a second or bigger pillow."

"Let's knock at that door and ask."

They walked down the corridor and knocked on the metal door. Nobody answered. Enzo also tried. Still no answer.

"This is the only door, but are we sure he knocked or did he use a key?"

"No, I am sure he just knocked on the door and he certainly did not close it. Someone pulled it closed from the inside while he had already walked away."

Joshua started this time to knock on the door with violence, but nobody answered.

"Come on, you probably did not see well from down there."

"I did."

"Listen, you can stay here if you want, but I will go back to our cabin now."

"Sure, let's go back."

They both went to bed, but it was clear that Joshua was unhappy and keen to prove that he was right and that someone had opened the door down their corridor from the inside. Enzo could see his young companion feeling unhappy, so he felt he had to say something.

"Joshua I do not care if you are right or wrong. Whatever is in that room should not interest us. If you want an extra blanket, let's try to ask for one tomorrow morning and stop thinking of what might be in that room down the corridor. Maybe it is something they don't want us to see or know about. Who cares as long as they help us crossing the ocean, right?"

"Sure, no worries, let's forget about that and try to catch some sleep."

The day after, still more painting, then a quick breakfast together with the rest of the men on board. The weather was not as good as it had been the day before, so even Joshua preferred to paint on the inside and begged for Enzo to paint the outside in the cold wind. Joshua argued that he was not used to the cold weather like he expected Enzo to be.

"Of course, yesterday you wanted the sea and the sun shining on you, today it is too cold. Let's kill the old one first, shall we! A bit spoiled, aren't you? Change your attitude, young man, or you won't find someone willing to employ you."

"Okay, fine. But let us paint now or we will never finish and probably won't get any food."

Outside there was much more to paint, and Joshua, after finishing the inside, had started to help Enzo on the outside. After a while, "Listen, I am going in to fetch my jacket. I am freezing out here. And this is no excuse. I will come back."

"You better do so as I will sit down now and wait for you."

Enzo did carry on painting, but he did not want Joshua to stop. Meanwhile, Joshua, after stepping into the corridor down the ship, heard someone at the end of it. He stepped back and then heard the knocking on the door.

Tattara-tatta tatta, then again, tattara-tatta tatta and a third time Tattara-tatta tatta. He could hear the door opening and closing shortly after. Now nobody was in the corridor so he went to his cabin to fetch his jacket and run upstairs to make sure they would finish their painting session and be allowed to eat with the rest of the men on board. Enzo welcomed him back with a smile and reinvigorated, they quickly finished painting. Their small friend came to check their work, nodded okay and with a hand gesture asked them to follow him. They had got used to the routine and standard rice and fish.

"This is not a cruise, but I see how people can get used to this type of life."

"Would you not miss having your feet on land?"

I love the sea and yes, of course, I would miss family, friends and a normal life on land, but I love seeing the sea even in grey weather like this. I don't like the cold wet weather, but I love to look at it from the inside. Maybe I am just old enough. I guess that at your age I would have missed women too much."

"Exactly. I was hoping to meet some mermaid, but those must be just part of fairy tales."

"There used to be mermaids at least during the ancient Greek times when Greeks, Phoenicians and other Mediterranean men were navigating the seas. They certainly missed women. On some islands some women were luring those men with their melodic voices. They often offered their services in exchange for wine, cheese or whatever the men were transporting. Sometimes those melodic voices were luring those men into a trap as once disembarked, some local men would jump out of the bushes, kill those foreign men and steal all they had. That is how the Greek legend about the mermaid was born."

"Where do you find all those stories?"

"I don't just walk around like you. I observe and learn. In Sicily near my town, there is an old place called Erice and there you can still visit one of the temples where those kinds of mermaids were living and luring passing seamen near the shores. A legend says that those few men from faraway lands who slept with the temple main nun or mermaid were always killed. Maybe it's just a legend, but at the time, foreigners had no protection and mermaids could be very dangerous. Some young men must have ended like moths lured to the strong light of a candle. Zzzzzzz, gone."

"Unbelievable. Now you spoiled one of my fantasies and I am scared of mermaids."

"Just forget the mermaids and look at the beautiful sea. Okay, it is still cold, but look, isn't it beautiful?"

They spoke and argued for a while until it got cold and they decided to walk back to their cabin. Enzo stopped at their cabin, while Joshua looked at Enzo and put a straight finger in front of his mouth signalling for him to be quiet. Enzo looked disapprovingly, but said nothing. Joshua carried on until the end of the corridor, then knocked on that mysterious door, tattara-tatta tatta, then again, tattara-tatta tatta and for the third time, tattara-tatta tatta. Someone unlocked the door from the inside, Joshua pushed in and the door was locked quickly from the inside. Enzo was still looking in disbelief from the end of the corridor, but decided to step quickly into his cabin to avoid getting involved. He had no idea what had just happened. So he decided to wait for a while. Enzo felt sorry for what might have happened to Joshua, but he had warned the young man many times not to pursue his curiosity to see what was in that locked cabin. Enzo waited for a long time and was starting to get worried when finally he heard that door down the corridor being unlocked. Shortly after, Joshua appeared with a big smile on his face.

"Now you are dying to know what is behind that door. Aren't you?"

"Not really, I am just happy to see you idiot. I told you to leave it. I also hope you have not upset someone who now wants to throw us overboard. Do you remember what I just said? Foreigners do not have any rights, nor do people travelling without documents on this ship. Do you know how easy it would be for them to get rid of us, with no trace whatsoever?"

"Calm down, old man. I am still alive and nothing happened."

"Why was it so important for you to know what was behind that door? So what's in there?"

"I will tell you only if you will do three quarters of tomorrow's painting job. Is it a deal? You see, secret information has a value."

"No I don't. Anyway, you won't be able to keep it a secret. At least not for long. So good night."

"Okay, you win. I knocked on the door and I found a couple of mermaids."

"So they do exist after all. Why are they locked up in there?"

"I guess they want to sell them to a zoo in the US."

"Come on now. How old are those girls and where are they from?"

"In there, are two adult women from Nigeria. It seems that our small friend is smuggling them into the USA in exchange for sex. But they sent me away before he turned up for his usual evening visit. They promised me that they will tell me more tomorrow afternoon when they are alone. They also begged me not to tell anybody or they will be in trouble."

"Who would have thought that our small middle aged friend was capable of trafficking ladies?"

"This is only possible because rich countries do not allow legal migration. So people smugglers are taking advantage of poor people or real refugees running away from conflicts all around the world."

"Do you propose to just abolish all borders?"

"More or less. The European countries that colonized half of the world should be the first to let people in to pay back in part what they have stolen."

"Joshua, please imagine what would happen if rich countries were to open their borders. What do you think?"

"I guess millions of poor people would arrive there and the poorer countries would have some respite and be able to develop. This, thanks to the help of the rich countries taking in those poor immigrants."

"You don't think that this is a bit of a Utopian way of seeing the world?"

"In the West, you are just worried about sharing the riches your countries have stolen from around the world?"

"What riches or wealth have we stolen?"

"All sorts of natural resources, like minerals, productive land, enslaved people."

"It is true like you said we Europeans have stolen from around the world and it is right that we should do something to help, but the issue is more complicated than just that."

"Do you propose to just carry on as we do and ignore the plight of those in need?"

"I know you are passionate about the subject, but let us think logically about the issue. If natural resources alone make a country rich or wealthy, then DRC (Democratic Republic of Congo) should be one of the wealthiest countries in the world. South Africa, with its gold and diamonds, should be at the top of the list as should Brazil or Indonesia. The oil-rich Arab countries should have the wealthiest populations on Earth. The reason this is not the true, is because it depends on what you do with the natural resources. Gold or minerals are of no use to anybody if you don't have the technologies to make use of them. The oil rich countries are not developed countries and their wealth is dictated by those countries that developed the technologies that need petrol. So even if Europeans and their descendants in North America were to disappear from the Earth's surface, the poor countries' natural resources alone would do nothing to alleviate people's poverty. The right social organization and infrastructure invented and organized by more advanced humans are required to create a prosper society."

"So why not help the poor countries then? Start helping by taking in some poor economic migrants."

"We do already, but a few at a time. Letting millions of poor people in at once would just destabilize the host country's economy. If a large scale immigration were allowed to damage the host country's economy, no one would profit from it. The native population would also get poorer and try to move on, while the newcomers will be in the exact same position they so desperately wanted to leave behind."

"Those poor people just want a peaceful place to live."

"That is not true. The newcomers would certainly want to have access to all those perks the native population already have or they would feel discriminated against. Note that hospitals, doctors and schools are paid for by the host countries' residents who pay taxes there. Newcomers need access without having paid anything into the system. This is charity and heavy economic help paid for by the local taxpayers."

"Just let the newcomers build their own towns and communities."

"Nobody is so stupid as to do that. We have all learned from history. If the newcomers are not assimilated in their host countries' cultures and customs, they will start to undermine them. Eventually they could even ask for a part of their new host country to be separated. Look at Kosovo, Northern Ireland and many more places around the world. Apart from the South Pole there is no empty land to be colonized. Some people have invented fairy tales and religious beliefs in some god somewhere entitling them to a promised land. There has never been an empty promised land. This fairy tale was invented to justify killing those living in that land before the newcomers arrived."

"Are you referring to Israel and Moses?"

"Not only. The Europeans used the same superiority ideology to justify destroying any other culture they met. Their superiority complex meant they felt no guilt when killing those they conquered. If you convince your people that the others are brutal and inferior beings like rats spreading diseases, then they listen to your call of sanitizing or clearing the area from their scourge. The Nazis used the same rhetoric to kill millions of Jews. The Arabs did the same when they conquered and converted to Islam, North Africa, the Middle East, the south of Spain and Anatolia. Preaching Islam and converting the unfaithful was the excuse. Conquering new land and subduing the local population into paying tributes were the real reasons. Before the end of WWII the Japanese nurtured a culture of superiority to any other. The great Chinese Empire did the same, undervaluing the capacity of the few Europeans who had landed on their shores. This is what destroyed their empire. All humans have done this all around the world."

"You are changing the subject and making loads of excuses for the rich countries not allowing legal immigration."

"Fine, then let me put it this way. What would you think about opening Zimbabwe's border to Mozambique and allowing millions of Mozambicans to move to Zimbabwe? The newcomers would want access to water, food, schools and hospitals as the Zimbabweans do. Do you think your fellow Zimbabweans would object to a couple of million Mozambicans moving in?"

"Zimbabwe is no rich country, so we have less to share. And yes, Zimbabweans would probably complain."

"I think they would do more than complain. Even if you ask the refugees themselves if they would mind millions of poor people with other customs or religions moving in to their country, I am sure they would admit that they would not like that."

"So do you suggest everybody carries on as usual and millions of people die while trying to cross the Mediterranean Sea?"

"Now let me ask you a question. What about reciprocal understanding?"

"What do you mean?"

"Let's suppose for example that Germany, where two and a half million Turks live, expected two and a half million Germans to be able to settle in Turkey and expect the same freedoms as Turkey demands for its citizens in Germany. In the same way, if half a million Zimbabweans live in South Africa, South Africa has the right to have half a million of its citizens settling in Zimbabwe."

"Why would wealthier people move to a poorer country?"

"Plenty of people would like a new start somewhere else, but do not trust the poorer and less well organized poor country's institutions. Believe me, if the Germans were to administer a small part of Turkey with two and a half million German people living there, this would flourish as they would bring there their advanced administration and institutions."

"I don't think Turkey or any other country would allow this. Especially not if they were to self-administer the place they settle in."

"So tell me why on Earth the host countries should help if those not able to feed their own population cannot do so?"

"Here we go again. You are just trying to find excuses not to help."

"Not true, I am just trying to think of a way of helping that makes sense. I am afraid opening the borders is not an option as this would only result in chaos and later violence. I know that some well-meaning people in the rich countries advocate open borders. What they don't realize is that the newcomers would completely change the countries they are living in."

"What's wrong if we all get a bit poorer but equal in our world?"

"Nothing at all, but this can only happen gradually. The newcomers need to assimilate in their new host countries and those places need to slowly adjust their economies and infrastructures."

"So you suggest we should wait for you to be ready and meanwhile starve. After the last population growth in Europe at the beginning of the twentieth century, millions of Europeans emigrated to the new world or America. Now the population growth is occurring in Africa, where should we go? Sit around and starve?"

"Joshua you know better than I do that Africa is much larger than Europe and can accommodate its population growth. The problem is in the backward administration of most African countries that does not provide for their population growth."

"This is why I am asking. Why are wealthy countries not helping?"

"Some countries have tried, but we learned that money alone is not the answer. Sometimes it is even a curse."

"Because of the corrupt African politicians?"

"Not just. Money corrupts everybody. People and businesses from the donor countries often force the receiving countries to buy some specific goods that only they produce. This often does not much help the receiving country. Sometimes the giving and receiving ends agree on splitting some of the funds donated. This is difficult to control. You might have heard of the Marshall plan meant to help Europe after WWII. Do you know that 70% was spent on tobacco and cotton? Do you think this was the priority for the starving Europeans? Certainly not, but some corrupt American officials did make loads of money out of the Marshall plan."

"What is your solution then, doing nothing?"

"It is difficult, but the only way I could see this working is with a partnership between a rich and a poor country with the danger that this could be seen as a neo-colonization project. Some people in the rich countries would definitely try to take advantage of such a structure, so this should be constantly policed."

"Why don't we let the receiving country be in charge?"

"You are young, but I am sure you are not so naïve as to think that we should just give money with no questions asked."

"No, but I wouldn't like the white man coming to tell us what to do in our own country. Foreigners don't have the local knowledge needed to help where it is really needed."

"This is exactly why it is difficult. There is no international independent body that can be trusted to be neutral. Well, not yet. Believe me, I come from the country that invented the word nepotism. Nipote in Italian means nephew and nepotism is the system Italians used when distributing state or civil servants' jobs. Giving a key job to a relative or a friend who is not the best person for that task will jeopardize the whole project. Still nowadays in Italy, like in Africa, the elected local politicians are expected to help their relatives by distributing jobs or favours to them. This in the end creates a mediocre system and country."

"It is normal to help relatives and friends, isn't it? It is family right?"

"Sure, but the rest of society will pay the price for it and in the end, all its inhabitants will, even those who distribute civil servants' jobs to their relatives. A country that applies a meritocratic system will always prevail over one based on nepotism. As I said, a country based on nepotism will always be a mediocre country."

"Most likely the word nepotism was born in Italy during the Italian renaissance. So maybe nepotism was not that bad after all. The history I studied taught me that at that time Italy was well ahead of other European countries."

"Yes, sure, in the fifteen hundreds, when all countries were still run by kings and queens surrounded by their relatives and even married them. You are right, that probably was the age of nepotism. That is long gone. I think countries run on meritocracy will stay ahead of those that are not."

"Are you saying that Italy is a mediocre country now? Is this the reason why you moved to the USA?"

"Yes, I am afraid so. Italy is now a mediocre country left behind thanks to its nepotism. First of all if people who are not properly qualified for the job are in charge, they will try to pick up the required skills on the job. This causes long reaction times, harming the whole country. Some of those people taking on those jobs would have been better suited to other jobs for which they had better skills and a more natural inclination. If you like what you are doing, naturally you become good at what you do. If you are doing a job just for the money, then you will be mediocre. That is fine for a few, but if a whole country works this way, then we end up with many people in the wrong job. The result is a mediocre country where many just do the job for the money and have little motivation to do it well. Of course, there are some exceptions, but those few won't help a country. This is why I moved. I met too many mediocre people feeling important because of the expensive suit they were wearing or because of their job title which they never deserved."

"What about racial discrimination in the USA?"

"In some places it can be an issue, but in almost every country you move to, you will need to be better than the next guy, in order to be respected for your skills and work. This is independent of your skin colour. Of course, I have the advantage they only found out that I was a foreigner after I opened my mouth."

"Listen I have enjoyed this discussion, but it's two o'clock and I think we should sleep or I will have to paint double tomorrow."

"Sorry Joshua. I got carried away. Good night now."

In the morning they overslept and their little friend knocked at their door. Joshua opened the door and their little friend pointed at his watch, showing the small hand pointing at number 10. They both nodded their heads, put some clothes on and followed him. To their surprise, there was no painting job on offer. Just a pile of ropes and other tools that needed to be sorted in different places. They started to work and when they turned around to ask if they had to do something else, their little friend had disappeared.

"Listen, I have not even had time to go to the toilet. I will be back soon."

"Sure, but please stay away from the mermaids."

"I know. It's too early to visit them."

Enzo ventured outside and enjoyed the rising sun between the deep blue sea and the pale blue sky. After having taken in as much of it as he could, he walked back wondering how many more days it would take until they arrive in the Dominican Republic. Would someone be waiting there for him? In his mind, he had already decided to risk finding Julio, his brother-in-law, and take it from there. He thought that if the Dominican police were to arrest him, they would just extradite him to the USA. Julio's being a policeman, he thought this might help him, just in case he had to spend some time in the island prison. Eventually Joshua came back, but Enzo had already done half of the work they were instructed to do. Having woken up late, lunch time came early and their small friend appeared again, calling them for their lunch. Sharing a table with other crew members, they managed to understand that the ship would need twelve to fourteen days to reach Santo Domingo, depending on the weather and sea currents. If the weather stayed the same they said that twelve days would probably be enough.

"Twelve days is a lot. How long does a plane take?"

"Between eight and nine hours' flight from Rome to New York.

"Incredible. One day I will manage to get on a plane."

"Of course, I forgot that you have never flown. I took my first flight when I went to the USA. To travel to the rest of Europe, I used to take the train. Flights are now cheaper in Europe, but when I was young, flying was for rich people only, even economy class. Ships and now planes have shrunk the world we are living in. This is why we have rampant globalization with people moving quickly around the globe. Now smartphones have shrunk it even further by showing anybody around the world what is happening on the other side of the globe."

"This is true for those who can afford a smartphone."

"True, but the share of those who can is increasing exponentially. Listen Joshua, we need to talk about what we will do once we get to the other side of the ocean."

"What do you mean?"

"Listen, once there, I will contact my relatives on the island and asked them to lend me some money, so we can both get off the boat. At this point, I am not sure if the Dominican police will try to arrest me. I have still no idea why I was arrested in Italy and if there is an international arrest warrant against me or not.

"So what's going to happen with me?"

"Should they arrest me, I will ask my relatives to help you for a while. But this means that for the time being you would need to stay in the Dominican Republic and learn some Spanish."

"Hey Enzo, I knew you were on the run and I was not sure if I was going to be arrested with you for whatever crap you have done. Of course, I wanted to go to the US, but the time will come and I am in no hurry. Let me also say that I appreciate your help. Who knows, maybe they are not even looking for you in the Dominican Republic."

"As I said, I have no idea and we will see once we get there. I just wanted to make sure you know that I will try to help you. You just need to know that my help will be different depending of my own circumstances. What do you think about finishing your studies in the Dominican Republic?"

"How the hell am I supposed to study in Santo Domingo and in Spanish? Who is going to pay for me to study?

"I am sure some courses are in English, but you should learn Spanish. It can be useful for you anyway. As you speak several languages already, you shouldn't have any problems picking up another one. I can help you with the money. Depending on what you study, I could also help you later in finding a new job. Now forget your past and stay inside the law. If you cause me or my family here any trouble, I will cut you off and you will be on your own. Understood?"

"I knew you were rich from the time I wanted to rob you in Tunisia. I am glad I didn't."

"You should better say you are glad the Tunisian police stopped you."

"Fine, you choose the way you want to remember the time we met. I'll stick to my version of the facts. Whatever way, I am now glad to have picked you up. Now carry on looking at the blue, blue sea while I visit a mermaid."

"Try not to upset our small friends or we could be in trouble or even swimming on the high seas."

"Don't worry. You know I cannot swim."

Joshua walked down towards the cabin, but did not stop there. Instead he carried on until the end of the corridor and then tattara-tatta tatta, then again, tattara-tatta tatta and a third time Tattara-tatta tatta. The door opened and he jumped straight in. The two mermaids smiled at him. They were both young and good looking.

"Thank you for letting me in girls. I apologise for scaring you both last time. What are your names?"

"I am Abebi and my cousin is called Zauna."

"Is he keeping you here as prisoners? Do you want me to help you escape? Do you need any help?"

"No we are no prisoners, we are stowaways."

"Is he treating you well?"

Her cousin Zauna took over, "Yes he is. Sometimes he just wants us to be nice to him. That's all."

"Does this not bother you?"

Abebi, quickly. "What, for having sex in exchange for a big favour?"

Joshua, trying to understand, "Well, yes."

Zauna, looking seriously at him, "Listen, lately we have not had much luck and pleasing a man in exchange for a free ticket has been the least of our worries."

"I am sorry to hear that. What happened to you?"

Abebi with big sad eyes, "We were not poor back in Nigeria. We lost our families and ended up all alone and with nothing. We ended up sleeping out on the street. Eventually someone who seemed kind, took us in. Soon he asked us to sell our bodies in exchange for his help and some small change. We managed to run away, but we had no money and being young women, what men always wanted from us is sex. So we learned to earn our money that way and used it to travel north. In Casablanca we again got into trouble as a gang of men forced us to sell ourselves near the harbour. One day a small man came to take advantage of our services. He was one customer like many others. The day after, we were walking near some anchored ships dreaming that one day we might be able to go to Europe on one of those. Zauna started to cry, reminiscing about our faith. That same small man saw us. He walked in our direction and hugged Zauna. He did not say a word, but made a sign to follow him. We had nothing to lose. He hid us here in this cabin. When the ship was almost ready to leave, he asked us to leave the boat. We pleaded for him to keep us. We were sure those nasty men were still looking for us. We kissed him continuously until he melted away and could not stop smiling. We convinced him all night long. He agreed and here we are. Where are we going?"

"So you don't know? We are going to Lagos in Nigeria."

Zauna started to cry.

"Sorry, that was a bad joke. We are going to America."

Both girls jumped on him, started to kick him down.

Abebi shouted, "You bastard! Go away now. They opened the door and sent him out."

Enzo was still looking into the deep blue sea, when he saw a disappointed Joshua walking towards him.

"Nice mermaids?"

"Yes, but they kicked me out."

"Why?"

"They did not like my humour. Ah, maybe I pushed it a bit too far. As a joke I told them that we were going to Lagos in Nigeria. One started to cry and the other started to beat me."

"You see, maybe you found your vocation, stand-up comedian; like that South African guy Trevor Noah."

"You are funny, you are."

"They will be fine tomorrow. They are probably worried now, thinking you ratted them out. Just try to be a bit more sensitive next time you speak with people you have just met and know very little about."

"Sure, old man. Maybe you should be there to keep me in check."

"I am in enough trouble already and I am not going to look for more. I get the feeling you like them?"

"Yes, I like them, but I don't like how easily they sell their bodies."

"Just think, you would probably do the same if you were born a woman and in a desperate situation. What do you think they do? They close their eyes and let someone else use their body. Surely better than starving. Why do you think there are far fewer homeless women than men? Selling their bodies is a way to keep a roof over their heads. This is more difficult for a man."

"While travelling, some older men offered to pay me. I refused."

"Well, homosexual intercourse requires more than just closing your eyes and thinking of something else. And even then, there are plenty of men who go for it as well. I cannot judge people doing strange things when in distress. I can only judge if I had ever been put in their situation. Luckily, I have not. I am aware of my luck."

"Don't worry, old man. At your age, I think you are out of danger. Anyway, I am not sure what to think of them. Tomorrow I am going to apologise. By the way what kind of job could you help me with?"

"It depends on what you decide to study. Also, I am not sure the university in the Dominican Republic offers all possible courses. What do you want to study?"

"When I started to study I wanted to go into medicine because in Africa we don't have many industries, but plenty of sick people to deal with. Now in the new world, I might have to rethink that."

"I am sure you can study medicine in the Dominican Republic and from there even go to Cuba where they train some of the best doctors in the world."

"Cuba?"

"Yes, Cuban doctors were and still are some of their best exports. Most people just think of cigars and Fidel Castro. Remember that if you are a doctor and have no loan to pay back, you are free to travel the world. If you choose medicine, I would certainly support you. It's a wide field and you can later decide on your specialization. Are you squeamish or dislike blood?"

"I was a bit before, but after running away from home, I have seen a lot that I have not liked, but I learned to deal with it. I guess I am okay now."

"You see, not all that seems bad, is bad in the end."

"I would have preferred to still have a family and be studying in my home country instead of being on the run."

"I understand that it must be difficult to accept this. I just wanted to say that if Sicily would have been a better place and I could have stayed there, I would not have seen much of the world. The fact is that I was more or less forced to move several times to develop my career. It forced me to get to know and see stuff that I would otherwise have never done. Believe me, one day you will be proud of your hard work."

"Easy to say at your age, after you have done the hard work."

"Sure, I understand that one must try to also enjoy the ride to get there. The most important things are your expectations. Aim high, but within your reach, or you will be disappointed forever and be prone to depression. This is a huge problem in rich countries now, where kids have a lot and find it very difficult to top what they leave behind at their parents' homes. They expect to have the same standard of living they had while living in their parents' home as soon as they leave it. That of course is only possible for a few rich people. Like many do, complaining that the world is not a fair place won't help you. As I said before, don't look up, but forward."

"Here we go again with your rant about religions."

"No rant, I am just saying that your faith can be good for your soul, but you also need to do something. In Italy, we have a saying, 'Aiutati che dio ti aiuta' or help yourself that God will help you. I am just saying to you, study or work hard once in Santo Domingo as this is the only way you will make any progress. Of course, feel free to pray to whatever god you want if that helps you. As I said earlier, I have nothing against religions."

"Going back to my future career, if you say that being a doctor would allow me to move freely around the world, I should definitely want to try medicine. Having sneaked through many borders made this clear to me. Thank you in advance and I hope I can trust your words. I learned to trust a Sicilian man's words in South Africa, I hope I can trust yours too."

"Right, some part of me is still Sicilian despite having become a US citizen. I still look deep into someone's eyes when I shake their hand."

Joshua stretched his hand towards Enzo who reciprocated looking him deep into his eyes.

"Listen, old man, it is getting cold out here. So while you are enjoying your blue sea, I will try to find a shower."

"But don't be stupid and leave your mermaids alone."

"Yes, Sir!"

Joshua was tempted but he resisted to knock on the girls' door and carried on towards the shower. Enzo enjoyed looking into the sea, that same sea he had missed for too long while living most of his life in the concrete jungle. Sometimes looking into the sunset, he wondered if he had after all followed the best path in his life. He wondered how it was possible that after all he had achieved he felt envious of the life of Gaetano the poor fisherman who had taken him over to Africa. He knew this was stupid and that had he not left the island and tried to develop his career, he would have always wondered what could have been if he had. Now that he knew, he thought that maybe living with less, but near the sea or even at sea is what he was now longing for. A new idea started to creep into his mind. What if he could convince his wife Carmen to move to Santo Domingo? Suddenly his daydream was interrupted by a thought taking him back to the fact that he was on the run. It was time to get back to the cabin.

"So young man, have you cleaned your body and soul under a hot shower? Are you ready for a clean new start?"

"Have you ever thought about teaching philosophy or selling soap?"

"No, not really. I don't think you can have a captive audience like you, if you are a teacher. Maybe selling soap would be something for me."

"Of course you could teach philosophy. You could even have a full classroom of students who are forced to listen to you and for a whole course. The advantage is that those who decide to study a subject do so voluntarily."

"Maybe you are right and I missed my calling. Have a good night now."

One more day on the boat, but strangely nobody came to wake them up. Their small friend had not appeared. Was he told something by the mermaids? They did not say a word, but both were worried by that same thought.

"Good morning Joshua. Listen, yesterday evening, did you by any chance go back to bother the girls?"

"No, I did not, as I was told. I would not."

"Sorry, I am just surprised about our small friend not turning up this morning. Anyway, let's go upstairs for breakfast to see if he is there and let's hope the girls have not told him anything."

The small man was there having breakfast and greeted them fine when they entered the galley. He either was acting well or still did not know about Joshua's visiting the mermaids. It just seemed that they had run out of work for their two passengers and there had been no need to wake them up.

"Old man, it seems that today you will have the whole day to look at the sea. Put some sun cream on your pale skin."

"How would you like to spend your day?"

"I would like to deepen my mermaids' knowledge, but this can be a risky activity here out at sea. I will study an old sea lion I recently got to know. He might even tell me more about what I should study to be able to gain his sponsorship."

"Good attitude and as a young inexperienced penguin, the old sea lion will teach you one or two tricks. For example, do you know why some babies are born black and some white?"

"I hope this is funny or we will see a sea lion swimming soon."

"Because some are born during the day and some during the dark night. Do I need to take my clothes off?"

"For today, a shower would do. Not bad and I bet this is how you explained the different skin colour to your kids."

"Carmen my wife is not white, but nicely suntanned like many people in the Caribbean. My children are not pale white. They sometimes call me mozzarella. When they are crossed with me, even buffalo mozzarella."

"Do you have buffalo in Italy?"

"Yes, we do near Naples, where they make the buffalo mozzarella they use in their pizzas."

"Did you import or steal them from Africa?"

"Probably, but a long time ago, as the buffaloes seem to have been there from Roman times or even earlier. I don't think they are native from the Italian peninsula, but I cannot be sure. It is possible that the Sahara desert saved your people from the Romans going all the way down there."

"Believe me, it's a bloody long way on foot. I don't think they would have made it. We had to wait for the British to invent better ships and weapons."

"I thought they just bought your land in exchange for some glass beads?"

"I think those were Native Americans. You are getting confused, pale old man."

"I wasn't serious and I wondered how far you could take a joke."

They spent the day engaging with some members of the crew, but with gestures and smiles the conversation was limited and tiring for both sides. After a small lunch of fish and rice, the time had come for Joshua to visit the mermaids. Enzo understood that there was little he could do to stop his travel companion's curiosity and just asked him to be careful. Joshua went up and down the corridor, then stopped in front of the door and started knocking, tattara-tatta tatta, then again, tattara-tatta tatta and a third time, tattara-tatta tatta. The door was unlocked and he quickly jumped in. The two girls smiled and seemed to have forgotten about the end of their last conversation.

Abebi started, "You weren't nice last time you were here. You know you made my cousin almost cry?"

"I am sorry, obviously I had no idea of what you have gone through. I hope Zauna will forgive me."

Zauna stood up and went to hug Joshua who melted like a piece of ice in the hot sun.

"Listen is there anything I can do to help you? Are you in danger?"

Abebi again, "No, as we told you earlier the little man saved us from a horrible situation and I am sure he must be taking some risks hiding us down here."

"We also call him the little man. Do you know his name?"

Zauna looking at the door, "No we don't, as he cannot speak. At first we thought he could not speak English. He did not bother speaking to us in Arabic as we learned the worst words and very little. We asked him some questions, but he smiled and made the sign of the cross with his fingers in front of his mouth. At this point we were sure he was dumb and we felt sorry for him. He is a good man."

"Yes, but he still wants to be paid with your sexual favours, right?"

"You are coming to see us and risking being caught. Are you also in search of sexual favours?"

Joshua was embarrassed and did not like what he heard. Maybe he just hated the fact that they were right. "Let me say that I like you, but I don't expect you to have sex with me."

Zauna, looking at him with a sensual smile, "What a pity. I was looking forward to getting to know you better."

"Zauna, stop teasing him. He seems a nice guy. Don't get some strange idea into his head."

"It's okay. Last time I made her cry, so this is payback time."

Abebi, a bit curious, "By the way, earlier you said we also call him the little man. Who is we? Who are you travelling with and have you told the others about us?"

"Don't worry about my travel companion, we won't tell anybody. Enzo had already noticed you in your room. He prefers to stay out of trouble and was not curious like me to find out who was in this room at the end of the corridor."

"Zauna and I heard people speaking in English and we thought they were other crew members. Are you not part of the crew?"

"Not really. It's a long story. Let's say that we are paying passengers who preferred to board this cargo ship instead of flying."

"Sure, Zauna and I are also paying passengers on this cruise ship. We just use a different currency. We are you from?"

"I am originally from Zimbabwe and Enzo is from the USA."

Suddenly, a noise from the door, tattara-tatta tatta, then again, tattara-tatta tatta and a third time, Tattara-tatta tatta. They all froze, Zauna quickly put her right hand with her stretched index finger in front of her mouth as if to say "be quiet." Then, they heard it again, tattara-tatta tatta, then again, tattara-tatta tatta and a third time, tattara-tatta tatta. By the end of the coded message, Zauna had managed to free part of their luggage stored under her bed and made a sign to Joshua to hide underneath. Joshua obeyed, and Abebi pretended the door would not open quickly so as to gain some extra time. Their small friend came in smiling and bringing some food for them. He sat on the bed and watched the two girls eat peacefully. The girls were trying a one-way conversation to relax their nerves. After they finished eating, the small man pat the bed in a familiar sign to the girls, but it was an action that scared the hell out of Joshua who was wondering if the man was tapping trying to find someone. The small man was looking straight at Zauna who went to sit near him. The small man started caressing Zauna who, knowing what was expected, hugged the gentle man she regarded as her gentle saviour. Abebi, realizing the small man's attention was all for her cousin, slowly caressed the man's arm to warn him that she would go out of the room. This time, Abebi, instead of going to hide in the nearby shower like she had done previous times, decided to visit Joshua's companion. So she walked up the corridor to the cabin Joshua had mentioned to her and, tattara-tatta tatta, then again, tattara-tatta tatta and a third time, Tattara-tatta tatta. Enzo smiled, then

"Stop it Joshua, if our small friend hears you, he might think you're going to see his girls."

Enzo pulled the door and was stunned by Abebi quickly jumping in and closing the door behind her.

"Sorry for surprising you. Don't worry, Joshua told me about you and said you already know about me. I am Abebi. You are Enzo right?"

"Yes, I am Enzo, but where is Joshua? What happened to him?"

"Don't worry, he is fine and he will come back soon. He is back in our cabin with Zauna."

"I see and you wanted to get out of the way."

"More or less. Listen, Joshua told me that you have done some medicine studies. Can I show you a rash I have on my chest?"
"Well, I am not a doctor, but I can see if I can help you. Who am I to refuse to see a beautiful young woman's chest?"

"I thought so."

Abebi took her top off and started to touch her breasts. Enzo started to first look at her breast like a doctor would, but once Abebi's touching slowly turned into massaging, Enzo started to look like a man liking what he was looking at. Abebi stretched her hand, took Enzo's hand and encouraged him to touch her. The message was clear and at that point Enzo was aroused enough to invite her to share his bed. They enjoyed each other's company for a long while.

"Have you ever had a black woman before?"

"Sorry to disappoint you, but I have. You are a beautiful girl and I feel very lucky for what has just happened. As Joshua had probably told you already, I live in the USA where there are people of any skin colour. Why did you ask me?"

"Joshua told me that you are originally from Italy and then moved to the USA. I know many young Nigerian girls end up in Italy in the prostitution racket. I wondered if you had been one of their customers. I know many poor girls travel from Africa to Europe passing Sicily and sometimes stay there for a while."

"I see. Please remember that not all Nigerians are the same and in the same way, not all Italians or Sicilians are the same."

"No, don't misunderstand me. I know that. I also know that if Nigerian girls don't do this job, others will. Life is unfair and I want to enjoy my life."

"In that case, I hope I just helped you a bit."

"You did."

Abebi hugged Enzo and they both forgot where they were and felt like being on a faraway island. Enzo thought that maybe Joshua had been right all along and he had met two mermaids. Their peaceful embrace was broken by someone quickly entering the cabin door. Abebi jumped to the other end of the bed, while Enzo looked up, surprised. Then he smiled at Joshua who had just walked in. Joshua did not reciprocate his smile.

"I thought you would be happy?"

"Why the hell should I be happy?"

"I think I better go back to my cabin to see Zauna. See you later guys."

"What is wrong with you? I thought you were having a good time with her cousin Zauna the younger mermaid?"

"Did Abebi tell you that?"

"No, I kind of assumed."

"You won't believe what just happened to me. What a disgusting experience. I am going to have nightmares for a while."

"What happened? Did our small friend find you in their cabin?"

"Yes."

"Are we now in trouble? I told you to stay away from the girls."

"No, not what you are thinking."

"What then? Tell me!"

"I was in there talking to both girls in their cabin, when suddenly the door went, tattara-tatta tatta, then again, tattara-tatta tatta and a third time, tattara-tatta tatta."

"So he did walk in on you."

"No, it's worse. Zauna freed some space under her bed, to let me hide underneath. Then our small friend laid with Zauna on the bed. Abebi left the cabin and they had sex literally on top of me, twice! That idiot was having sex with the girl I liked above me."

"Almost a ménage à trois!"

"Yes, that is exactly how I would describe it. Not at all. Bastard."

Enzo tried to contain his laughter, but he hardly could. At this point he knew that he was not going to tell Joshua how Abebi had surprised him. Then, he wondered why Abebi did that.

"Stop laughing now."

"Would you not have laughed if that had happened to me?"

"Probably."

"Then stop thinking about it and take it as a man. The gods just punished you for your curiosity."

"Are you suddenly all religious?

"Not at all. It is just a way of saying. Listen, maybe we can plan a bit more of your future so as to get your mind off this little misadventure."

"Fine."

"I know that your dream was to move to the USA, but have you thought further about staying and studying in Santo Domingo?"

"Look Enzo, I was hoping to reach the USA because of English being the official language. I thought that moving to a country where English is not the official language would certainly make my life more difficult. Also, I did not want to move to a country where there are no black people. If you are the only black person in town you will always be the different one, the foreigner."

"Do you mean like if I were to move to Zimbabwe?"

"Yes, exactly. You would pretty much stand out like a white fly."

"I understand you, but black flies are all over the world."

"Very funny. Anyway, I like a mostly white country that voted a black president."

"You know his mother was white right?"

"Yes, but his father was from Kenya and very black. I still cannot understand why in a country founded by European immigrants, they now have something against new immigrants."

"We humans have been on the move for thousands of years. All nations are full of people whose descendants at one point arrived from somewhere. It is just a game of who was there first. Sometimes it is hard for the local population to see that the newcomers have done better than they have. It is also a question of numbers."

"What numbers? Do you mean the number of immigrants?"

"Yes, exactly. During the IT industry boom in California, I saw the number of Indian and Chinese engineers and programmers increase steadily."

"You are not talking about Mexican or South Americans, you are talking about legal immigrants. They certainly have a job and a company that wants them. Why should a US guy worry about them?"

"Joshua, please don't start this again. Sorry to repeat this, but I cannot help you to move straight to the USA. As I said, if you graduate in Santo Domingo you will be able to move to a country that actually needs and wants you. Anyway, now that you learned how to hide under a love couple's bed, you might start a career as a secret agent."

"Very funny, hit me while I am down. Hiding under their bed and listening to them was the last thing I wanted to do. They even banged my head a couple of times. That bastard!"

"Come on, come on. Maybe private detective could also be a career for you."

"Go to sleep old man, you are just annoying me now."

The day after in the early hours, Enzo heard the ship's engine stop. It was too early, so trying not to wake up Joshua, Enzo walked out to the bridge to see what was happening. He could hear a smaller boat engine nearby. Looking at the horizon, he could see a small island. Some boxes were being lowered to the smaller boat. Wherever they were, the island meant that there was land nearby and that they would be soon arriving. Enzo started wondering if Julio his brother-in-law would be happy to see him? He was relying on Julio's help to get off the ship as he had promised to pay on arrival in Santo Domingo. Suddenly, the ship started to move again, leaving behind the small island and a couple of fishing boats that had come closer to the ship to load or unload some goods. The sun was slowly coming up and once more, Enzo could not get enough of looking at the deep blue sea. The fresh air had woken him up and there was now no point going back to sleep. He now felt ready to face reality and was impatient to arrive. A few hours later Enzo felt like many men had felt centuries earlier when approaching land in the Caribbean islands. He felt like screaming "Tierra!" Then he realised it was not 1492 and he was not Christopher Columbus. Suddenly, a loud bang behind him made him jump. He turned around to see Joshua laughing aloud.

"Did I scare you old man?"

"Are you ten? Of course you scared me. I almost jumped over the railing and into the sea."

"Not a problem right? I am sure you can swim and this is your beloved deep blue the sea. It must even be warm. So jump, or do you need me to bang something again?"

"Yes, very warm, and full of sharks."

"Come on, don't be boring and live a bit."

"You said you can't swim. Is that so?"

"Just enough to cross the river at night to escape from my country."

"Just a short river?"

"Yes, but had enough life in it to motivate me to learn quickly. Anyway, why did you get up so early? Bad dreams?"

"Look in front of you. Can you see anything?"

"Finally. It looks like land. Can you feel that?"

"No. Some small boats came closer to the ship, near a smallish island back there. Their engines were too loud and woke me up."

"How long do you think we have?"

"I have no idea where we are, but I am sure we will arrive before dark."

"Good! I think I have had enough of the boat, fish and rice. I am not cut out to be a seaman."

"It could have been something for me, but I worked hard and I was lucky to be in the right place at the right time and listen carefully, with the right qualifications. I cannot complain, but you know, the grass is always greener on the other side. I need to repeat it one more time. I do not care about your past and I will help you to get a new life, BUT no stealing or other tricks once in Santo Domingo or you will be on your own and in prison. Don't waste this opportunity. Do you get it?"

"Sure old man, I get it."

"Good, then let's have some breakfast and come back out later."

Before they could go to eat, their little friend came looking for them asking them to follow him.
Many other of the men they had gotten to know were also there, working hard filling crates with some Moroccan products. It seemed that they were getting ready to unload some of their cargo.

"Damn, they make us work for free until the end."

"Come on, it is better than waiting around, doing nothing. Let's help them and go to eat later."

Three hours later they could finally go to eat something. They had some more broken conversations with the other men on board. They both thought about the two mermaids, but knew that the best time to see them was the afternoon. Maybe they would have arrived at Santo Domingo by then.

"We must be close now. Let's go outside to see how close we are."

They both went out to look and they could see the harbour in the distance and some of the city buildings were now visible.

"Are you happy we are almost there?

"Sure, I am looking forward to see my relatives, and speaking with my wife and kids."

"Are they here?"

"No, but I will call them soon after we meet with Julio, my brother-in-law. By the way, once we are there, I am sure they won't let me get off the ship without first having paid the US$2500 we still owe them. I am sure they will ask you to wait on board until we have paid them."

"I know, you told me already. Don't get nervous now. I will wait for you to come back to fetch me."

They stayed outside for hours seeing the Santo Domingo skyline continuously increasing in size. Someone shouted in their direction, telling them to move to the back of the ship. They did not argue and moved. Joshua then jumped on a pallet. Enzo, worried that he could fall, asked him to come down and told him that the ship could make a sudden movement while manoeuvring inside the harbour.

"Stop being a boring old man and jump up here now."

Enzo looked up, smirked, but started to climb up the full loaded pallet. They both looked at the harbour, which was getting ever closer, when suddenly Joshua pushed him violently over the railing, following him in a big jump and shouting as strongly as he could: "FALL ON YOUR FEET OR YOU DIE"

Enzo had quickly lost his balance and felt himself falling down towards the blue sea. It seemed a dream - one of the many he had had as a young boy when he kept on dreaming about flying. Now he felt like flying, but he was sure this time it was not a dream. He braced himself for the impact. The water was pleasant and he felt lucky that he could still feel his limbs. He thought that if that had been his last hour, at least it would have been a good way to go, in his beloved sea. The need to breathe took him out of the dream or the shock he was in. The salty water rushing up his nostrils did the trick. Still underwater, he could see a white cloud not far from him. Out of the cloud he could slowly see the image of a young black man frantically swimming up. He finally managed to emerge out of the water and take in a deep breath of new air. Shortly after, Joshua's head was also out of the water.

"You BASTARD! Did you want to kill us? Why the hell did you do that?"

"You said that they might keep me until you pay them. Sorry, I did not want to risk that and be sold as a slave somewhere. We worked hard enough to pay for our passage. Stop talking and swim to the harbour down there."

"You are mad! You could have killed us both. Did it not occur to you that maybe you could have told me about your plan?"

Joshua: "Come on, admit it that you would have never agreed to this."

"Probably. Now swim."

Enzo had just finished his sentence when a Dominican police boat appeared and started heading in their direction.

"Great, well done! Now they will arrest us."

The police boat came closer. Then: "Hablas español? Do you speak English?"

"Yes we do."

The policemen helped them onto their boat.

"Why did you jump from the ship? Do you have any ID with you?"

"No, sorry," answered Joshua.

"Did you jump from that ship?"

"Yes. Do you know a policeman from Santo Domingo called Julio?"

"Why?"

"Julio is his brother-in-law."

"Is this true?"

"Yes, his name is Julio Sanchez Martin."

"Sure, John Smith."

"No, it is true, his name is Julio Fidel Sanchez Martin.

"Sit down and dry yourself. We will check this later."

One of the policeman started speaking on his phone and was asking to be given Julio Fidel Sanchez's phone number. After a while the policeman reached him. Then, he passed the phone to Enzo who apologised to Julio and asked him to rescue him. Julio asked to speak back to the policeman who said that they would now head to the police station and Julio would join them there. Enzo noted that at least those two policemen on the boat did not seem to know his face. So maybe they were not looking for him internationally, after all. He was now looking forward to seeing Julio and was sure the feeling was not going to be reciprocated. The police boat started to head towards the harbour, leaving their ship behind them. Some people on the ship had probably seen what had happened, but were happy the police were not questioning them.

"Old man, you owe me $1250."

Enzo looked at Joshua as though he wanted to kill him.

"As you well know, I have no money."

Joshua understood Enzo was not pleased with him, while the policemen laughed and looked towards the harbour. Once they got there, they disembarked and were asked to follow the agents through their local police station. Someone opened a door and asked Enzo to come in and asked Joshua to wait outside. Enzo entered the office to find Julio and a colleague of his in there. Julio shook his hand and then with a stern voice asked him to sit down. The man who looked like the one in charge asked Enzo if he spoke Spanish. Then he turned to Julio to confirm that this man who had just jumped out of a ship in Santo Domingo harbour was really his brother-in-law.

"I am afraid so," confirmed Julio.

"Mr. Dangelo, could you tell us why we have the pleasure of having you visit here in the Dominican Republic? Also, do you often catch a cargo ship and jump off it when at destination?"

"I certainly understand the need to explain my circumstances."

"The last time you came to this country, you landed at the airport. Was that not comfortable enough for you? What on Earth could have forced you to jump off that cargo ship and so put you brother-in-law in such an awkward situation?"

"Please, let me apologize to you and to my dear Julio. As you probably know, the cargo ship arrived from Morocco. After a conference I attended in Rome, I was invited by a Moroccan colleague. I went to Morocco, but there I was robbed of my money and my documents. Those that stole my belongings, threw me in a container that was loaded onto this ship."

"May I ask you what type of conference you were attending and what kind of business you are involved in?"

"Captain, please let me first say that I am also interested in hearing his story, but I want to add the fact that my brother-in-law is a wealthy individual with a high position in the pharmaceutical sector. He is an influential, well known pharmaceutical researcher. He is one of the creators and part owners of Cut&Run."

"Any chances you could help my daughter with her career in cosmetic surgery?"

"Sure, I can."

"My daughter has tried to get in touch with Cut&Run as she would like to open a branch in the Dominican Republic. Can you help her?"

"Please pass your daughter's contact details to Julio. Someone will get in touch with her very soon."

"Mr. Dangelo, it was a pleasure to meet you and I am sorry about your circumstances that forced you to catch a cargo ship to cross the Atlantic. I trust Julio will make sure you stay out of trouble while in our country. By the way, who is the black companion you brought with you?"

"A good man who saved my life and for who I now feel responsible. I will take care of his needs."

"Well, in that case, take him with you. Julio, please provide me with a report by the end of the week. Thank you in advance for your support, I am now counting on you."

"Certainly, you won't be disappointed."

The captain walked out of the room, leaving Julio alone with Enzo. Julio hugged Enzo and shook his hand again.

"What happened? Carmen told me that you were away on some secret business and this is why she was not allowed to know where you were or contact you."

"When did you speak to her? Are they all okay?"

"I spoke to her last week. They are fine and she said that sometimes you worked on US army secret projects, so she thought this was one of those, but she was not told how long you were going to be away. This is the only thing that worried her. Why did you not call them?"

"Let us go somewhere else where we can talk."

"Did the guy outside really save your life?"

"Kind of, please let's go somewhere else."

They both walked out of the room and Enzo asked Joshua to follow them. Once they reached Julio's car, Enzo turned around to introduce Joshua to Julio. Both men shook hands. Then Julio started to drive.

"Joshua where are you originally from?"

"Zimbabwe."

"Have you ever left Africa before?"

"No, Sir. Have you ever been to Africa?"

"I am afraid not. I am not a traveller like my brother-in-law. I have only been to South and North America. Mostly visiting friends. No time for holidays."

Joshua was looking outside of the car window and was pleased to spot some blacks among people of mixed race.

"Joshua what do you think of Santo Domingo?"

"Good looking girls, few white or black people, but many mixed ones."

"That's right. Do you know why people prefer cocktails to drink? Because each original, pure ingredient might be good, but the cocktail magic comes alive when you mix those pure ingredients. We are a good cocktail. You and Enzo are just the pure ingredients, boring on their own!"

Julio carried on laughing looking at Enzo, nodding.

"And that is exactly why I married your sister. Now she makes me continuously drunk. One day Joshua might get drunk on a similar cocktail."

"Yes, that is easily done now that you are in Santo Domingo, my friend."

They finally arrived at Julio's home where his two children run out to hug their uncle Enzo who they have not seen for a long time. Sofia and Isabella jump on Enzo. He quickly apologizes for arriving empty handed and promises to buy them a present the next day. Mariana, Julio's wife comes out also to great him. They all greet Joshua and invite him to follow them inside. Julio and his family live outside of Santo Domingo in a more rural area, in an old family house. Enzo's parents-in-law live at the other end of the house. They are frail, but lively. They soon came to hug Enzo and greet their African guest. Then, they complain to him about having not seen their daughter, Carmen, and their grandchildren for a while. Enzo promise they will be there soon. Julio and Mariana use the central part of the house. The right hand side of the house belongs to Carmen and is kept free for her visits. They had never given up thinking that one day she would come back to permanently live there. Carmen had often blamed Enzo's job for keeping her in the USA. Enzo was well aware of being made the scapegoat, helping Carmen to justify her choice of living in the USA. Julio gave Enzo the keys of Carmen's wing of the house. Eventually Joshua and Enzo were left alone in there. They took great delight in taking off their dirty clothes and having a shower. Without being asked, Julio brought out some of his clothes.

"Is this your part of the house?"

"Yes, this my wife's part of the house. Her parents have never given up thinking that one day we might come back here. Maybe we should. I am keener than she is. Of course, should we move here, she would be expected to conform to the local customs. Me, being a foreigner, I would be excused. I don't think it would ever be an option. But who knows."

"Do you like it here?"

"Yes, I do. Please go and have a shower. I need to wait until you are done. There should be some shampoo in there."

"Yes there is some, but it's no good."

"Why?"

"It says that it's for dry hair and my hair is already wet!"

"Very funny. Get a move now. They are anxiously waiting for us. By the way, note that my parents-in-law do not speak English. So before you smile back, try to figure out what they are saying, or ask me."

"Have I already said something wrong?"

"They jokingly asked you in Spanish if you were another Sicilian mafiosi drug dealer like me. You smiled and answered to them 'Si, claro!'. From now on, please make sure they know you were really joking. They never liked Carmen marrying a Sicilian."

"Seriously, a black mafioso?"

"Listen they love this island. We had to force them to visit us in the USA. They have no idea, nor do they care about people in Sicily. For her parents, you might as well be a mafioso. Capisci?"

"Fine. I got it."

They polished themselves and came out in Julio's clean shirts. They walked into the garden at the back of the house where Julio was sitting in the shade of a tree. After the children joined them, Enzo turned to them and asked them to be nice to Joshua and teach him some Spanish.

"Joshua, Sofia and Isabella will now play Spanish teachers. You will sit and listen to your first Spanish lesson, while I am going to talk to Julio."

Enzo grabbed a chair and sat near Julio who looked keen on talking to him.

"So, tell me Enzo, how the hell did you land here and on a cargo ship from Morocco?"

"Please Julio, don't share this with anyone as I am still not sure about the mess I have landed in."

"It sounds worse than I thought."

"Not for you, but for me. I am still not sure. The first thing I need to ask you is to lie."

"To the captain?"

"No, to your sister. I want you to call her and invent a story about grandma not being well and that it would be better if she came here to see her."

"Why can you not ask her to come here yourself?"

"You see, at the moment, I am not sure about my legal situation and if I call her, I might put her and the kids in danger. Apart from that, they would then know where I am."

"Who are they?"

"I don't know yet, this is my exact problem. You said that Carmen told you over the phone that I was on a secret mission for a while."

"Yes, this is what she said when I last spoke to her. I thought your secret mission was called Barbara or Mary."

"I wish."

Enzo spent a long time explaining to Julio what had happened to him since he had arrived in Rome. Julio listen carefully, trying to understand who could be behind the plot. He fancied himself as an investigator.

"What are your plans now?"

"First of all, I want to see Carmen and the kids, if she can bring them. Also, I need to tell her what happened and ask her if she has noticed any strange things happening while I have been away."

They suddenly heard a voice from behind, "Mi nombre es Joshua y soy nuevo aquí, les gustaría unirse a nosotros en la mesa."

"Wow, they must be great teachers to manage to get so much into your head and in such a small time. Is your head hurting?"

"Claro, si claro señor."

"Just in case you don't know what you said, you asked us to come to the table."

"I know what I said and it does not take Einstein to understand that they are waiting for us at the table."

"Enzo, our cousin Manuel will join us later. I hope this is okay?"

"I am very happy he is coming and I am sure he will like Joshua very much."

"Of course, what there is not to like."

The full table looked like a celebration for the newly arrived. There were many fish dishes as, over the years, they had learned that Enzo loved to eat fish. As soon as Enzo sat down, Carmen's parents asked: "Y cuando llega Carmen?"

Looking at Julio: "I promise that I am going to call her soon and ask her to join me. You see, I am not coming from the US, but I am just back from Europe and Africa."

"Africa? Are you now opening some new Cut&Run branches in Africa?"

"Not really. Some other related business."

"We want to see Carmen and the kids. Please ask them to come soon."

"Sure, I will. Tell them Julio is organizing for her to come soon."

Julio nodded and finally Enzo was off the hock. They all started to dig into their great feast of delicious, local food. Joshua's eyes took up a large part of his head. The poor young man had not seen so much good food since he had run away from his country and lived as a refugee for a while. Suddenly a loud voice interrupted the meal.

"What kind of relatives are you? How can you start without me?"

Julio, looking at Manuel: "What kind of relative always arrives late and let's us wait, eh? Come here and take a seat near this young man."

"Oh, who we have here? Let me see. But first, let me hug my lovely Italian cousin. Enzo did you bring me this present from Italy?"

"No, I brought him from Africa. Treat him well, he is a good friend of mine."

"Sure, I will treat him very well. He seems a bit tired maybe a relaxing massage is what he needs."

Joshua, not knowing what to say: "Sure, maybe later, thank you."

Joshua was a bit embarrassed, especially when Manuel kept on touching his hair and his broad shoulders.

"Don't worry and don't be embarrassed. What is your name, my dear?"

"Joshua"

"Joshua, what a beautiful name. Maybe later you will tell me if it means anything. Now let's enjoy this great food. Thank you all for inviting me."

Sometime later, they had finished eating.

"So tell me, Enzo, is it true what I read about the company you are working for - Cut&Run being involved with the US army and some forced gender change operations around the world?"

Joshua quickly turned his head and stared at Enzo, while listening in carefully.

"Not really my fault."

Joshua leaped across the table and punched Enzo in the face and shouted: "This is for my brother, you bastard!"

Julio jumped over the table to hold Joshua back. Then shouted, "What the hell are you doing? What's wrong with you? What happened to your brother?"

"What the f... I said it's not my fault."

"How could you hear me telling you about my brother's suffering and pretend this had nothing to do with you? What do you mean it's not your fault? Are you or are you not the one who suggested using gender change operations to fight political opponents?"

Manuel, very embarrassed: "I am sorry, I had no idea, I am very sorry. Please Joshua, give him a chance to explain. Why are you so upset with him? Was your brother forced to have a gender change operation?"

"Yes, some bastards came during the night and arrested him. They took him away for questioning. When they released him two weeks later they had turned him into a woman. This destroyed him, his girlfriend and the rest of our family. And this guy here is the one that started this? How can you be part of it? For the money or power? Are you sick in your head? What is wrong with you? Be honest for once in your life!"

"Listen Joshua, I understand you being angry for what happened to your brother, but give me a chance to answer."

Manuel still holding his head between his hands: "Oh my god, what have I done? I am really, really sorry. Please, Enzo, say something. Please."

"I only found out after I was arrested in Italy that what I had once suggested in an internal company meeting had gone out to the wide world. Please believe me that the gender change operation service provided by Cut&Run was only meant for rapists who voluntarily choose to have the operation instead of going to prison. I had no idea this would be used for other purposes."

"How could you be so naïve? It is your fault, after all! You know that ideas have a life of their own. Look what Karl Marx did. Stupid old man."

"Joshua, please calm down and let me speak. Otherwise that is the door and good luck to you."

Joshua calmed himself down and looked at the floor trying to control his temper.

"Our company sometimes collaborates with the US army. Someone in our company suggested a new tactic in the Middle East. Many of the suicide bombers are very young men with little education. Some scrupulous fanatics tell those desperate young men that if they die fighting against the non-believers, their reward will be a place in paradise where 72 virgins will be there, waiting for them. Someone suggested turning all those fanatic leaders who were captured into women. Then they would have to meet their virgins in a woman's body. This was also thought to be a good deterrent for young men wanting to join their ranks."

Manuel, with big eyes: "What about gay, Muslim men? What are they supposed to do with those 72 virgins? Who would ever believe such a story?"

"Well, I doubt Islamic sacred scripture ever contemplated homosexuality as we see it and accept today, in the western world. Many Christians still believe in the flying archangel Gabriel and the Madonna giving birth while she was still a virgin. Anyway, someone was just thinking of a way to reduce casualties. Please believe me when I say that I have never worked for the US army itself and I had no part in the decision to turning enemies of any type into women."

"Still, somehow it was your idea. Do you not know that ideas have a life of their own?"

"Are you suggesting that Karl Marx is responsible for all the people Stalin killed in Russia, or Mao Zedong starved in China? This is absurd. I am really sorry about what happened to your brother, but this is to do with nasty people in your birth country deciding to use gender change operations as a mean of oppression."

"If this is so, why was Cut&Run involved in these kinds of operations for the US army?"

"Again, this is not my doing. Many people work for Cut&Run and I was not involved in this deal. Don't forget those who would have been in jail because of rape and voluntarily changed their sex to become normal, accepted citizens in their country. They must have felt liberated that people were no longer scared of them living next door."

"Yes, I bet them being liberated of their balls made them happy. Good for you to say. How easy was it for you to write this in the safety of your office?"

"What is the alternative you suggest? Do nothing so they are free to re-offend, or keep them in prison until they die?"

"In Africa, we don't have such a problem."

"Neither did we in the west, before women felt free and protected when speaking out. My young and naïve friend. There will always be sex.

Forbidding it won't change anything. Sex is a primordial necessity for men and women alike. It is there to make sure we multiply in whatever circumstances. Many countries simply deny this basic fact of us humans. If forbidding it would have worked, then after thousands of years of prohibition, there should be no prostitution on this planet. Independent of culture, religion or race all around the world we still have prostitution and prostitutes to satisfy our primordial need for sex. Until we have grasped this basic concept, we won't be able to deal with it in a mature manner. Beautiful, ugly, wealthy, poor, healthy or sick people all need to have sex or make love. Call it what you want, but this is the real truth that you need to accept. Once you accept this concept, then you need to think about how to deal with those who are so desperate to have sex that they force themselves on other women, men or children. If we don't accept sex as our primordial need such as eating, drinking, breathing, we won't be able to move forward. Denying this will get us nowhere. Until women in your countries feel free and protected to come out, many issues will lurk in the darkness. Today in the west we can talk freely about those issues, and this is why you see many wrongdoings being reported."

"Most people don't care and carry on with their lives."

"Sure, and if we would have all done that, we would still be living in a cave. Have you ever asked yourself when you turn on some electrical appliance how that electricity is produced kilometres or miles away before it comes out of a socket in your home to power a stove, a television, a radio, or a washing machine? Nothing would exist if we would have all just stared in the landscape thinking of just eating, drinking and sex. I am not big on literature, but one thing I loved reading at school was about the 'ignavi' in the 'Divine comedy'. Dante Alghieri described the 'ignavi' as cowards who, during their lives, had never believed in anything, never been for or against anything. Those who had spent their lives following always a new flag whatever colour it was as long as it meant going the easy way. Dante thought those 'ignavi' would be condemned to run for eternity behind a white flag of no description. Believe me, doing nothing about children starving, about sick people suffering is not just fine. Just staying in your corner and doing nothing for the rest of humanity is a waste of oxygen and resources."

"So would you imprison lazy people?"

"I would not, but the Incas in South America used to do exactly that. You are lucky we are not as far south here and that the Incas are no longer around."

They all laughed and the mood changed for the better.

"Are we okay, now? I am talking to you Joshua. And did I answer your question Manuel?"

"Yes, we are fine."

Manuel, not missing a chance: "Let me hug this young and strong man. Look, he is still shaking."

"This is great. He punches me and he get a hug."

"Come on now. I would also give you a big hug, but I am sure my dear cousin Carmen will get very jealous. Especially if her loose tongue brother tells her."

"I am sure my sister will cope and be careful about calling a policeman, a loose tongue. I think you have caused enough troubles already with your own loose tongue."

"mhmm, mhhmm, mhhmm"

They all laughed again, while Manuel made a gesture sealing his lips with his hands.

Julio looked to Manuel for help: "Manuel, maybe it is better if you take Joshua for a ride on your motorbike. Some fresh air would be good for him. Show him the sights of Santo Domingo."

"What a great idea. Come on darling. You can even drive if you know how to and I will hold very tight."

"Thank you, Manuel. Some fresh air would do me good. Can I really drive? I can, but I don't have a driving license for it."

"I did not hear that, just get out of here you two," said Julio.

Once the two had left, things calmed down. Julio and Enzo were holding on to their drinks and from the end of the table Enzo's mother-in-law with her quiet voice: "Que le hiciste a su hermano?" or what did you do to his brother?

"Nada, solo esta confundido!" Nothing he is just confused.

"Bueno, en ese caso nos iremos a la cama y te dejaremos con Julio, ¡pero asegúrate de que Carmen venga!" Good, in that case we will go to bed and leave you with Julio, but make sure Carmen comes!

"Now that everybody is gone, can you tell me if you are involved with your company turning men into new ladies?"

"For God's sake, Julio. Why don't you believe me and why did Manuel start asking? He never cared before about my job."

"Well, you see there was a high profile case here in our country and on that occasion, your company was mentioned in the local newspaper. We had a family meal and it was me that inadvertently, after reading the article, said aloud: This is the company Enzo works for. Manuel was also present and everybody suddenly got interested."

"What kind of article about what?"

"You see, we are a poor island, but we have still poorer neighbours from the country we share this island with."

"Do you mean Haiti?"

"Yes. Like in many countries, most Haitians are good people, but as you know, very often poor immigrants are the ones most likely to be tempted to commit a crime. Once one immigrant does something bad, the hosting population blames the whole nation, ethnicity or population of the immigrant country. We had a man that had been living in the Dominican Republic for a while. He was a good man, had learned Spanish and many regarded him as a local. He then moved in with his girlfriend, a woman from Santo Domingo. She had a daughter from her earlier relationship with another man. Last year his step daughter was found dead after having been raped. He and his girlfriend, the mother of the 12 year old girl who was killed, appeared on the local TV and newspapers. We in the police searched the whole island for clues and, in the end, the stepfather was accused. He was the last person the young girl had been seen with. He never admitted to the crime and there were never enough proofs of the crime. His girlfriend and the mother of the deceased child, always stayed on his side, believing his innocence. The political situation in the country was heated and near election time. Many people were fed up with Haitian immigrants and most likely they turned him into a scapegoat. People were upset and wanted to see blood. He was condemned. People were hungry for justice and got what they wanted. People were calling for the death penalty, but we abolished it in 1966. At this point, someone found an article about how other countries were dealing with their sex offenders. It was decided that Emmanuel was to become Emmanuelle. The man or woman is still in prison here in Santo Domingo. Now that things have calmed down, people are starting to think that maybe he was innocent after all, and some are starting to blame the company that provided the service for the gender change operation. If they had put him in prison without changing his sex, he could be released to go back to his woman, but he is a destroyed person now."

"It is a very sad story, but why are they blaming a company that provided the exact service it had been requested. Of course, it is always easier to blame the foreigners, but surely they should have not condemned a person without enough evidence".

"I cannot say this too loudly, but I agree with you. I wanted to only tell you why Manuel had taken an interest in your work or company."

"Did you manage to call Carmen?"

"When? I will do so now. Have another sip of wine and enjoy this fresh pineapple. I know you like it a lot. I am going inside to make sure nobody hears me. See you in a moment."

Sometime later.

"Carmen will be here in a couple of days. She just needs to inform work and see who is going to watch the kids or see if she can take them out of school."

"Did you tell her I was here?"

"Of course not. I just told her that mama is not well and she should better come and see her. I worked a bit on her dirty conscience about never coming to see her old parents. Who knows how long they are going to be around? She will be cross with me, but it worked."

"Thank you a lot for doing that. By the way, it is getting late and Manuel has not brought Joshua back. I don't think I will wait up for them. I am quite tired. Thank you for everything you did for me, Julio."

"Please wait, before you go to bed, I need to know what your intention are with Joshua. At the moment he is an illegal foreigner here with no means. What is your plan?"

"He is a good guy and despite punching me, he kind of helped me to get out of Africa. Joshua is a good young man who has made some mistakes, but he deserves a new start. He used to study back in his home country of Zimbabwe. I will find him a room in town and finance his university study. He does not plan to stay in the Dominican Republic forever. Once he qualifies, I will help him find a job. That is, if he behaves. I warned him. Should he go off track, he will be on his own. Please keep an eye on him, but he should be all right. Of course, let me know what we need to do to register him as a foreign student in this country. I will be his sponsor."

"It seems Joshua got lucky when he met you."

"The world is an unfair place and I cannot change this, but what I can do, is to help some of those who cross my path and I think deserves a shot. Maybe one day he will be the one helping someone else. We need to get the ball rolling."

"Have a good night and I might come around tomorrow or the day after, depending on work."

Enzo dived in to bed, but could not sleep. He was missing the background vibrations of the ship's engine he had grown accustomed to. Eventually his brain gave in and his snoring could be heard miles away.

The next day, only the strong sun woke him up just before lunch time. He looked at the bed that had been assigned to Joshua the day before. It was empty and unused. Maybe Joshua met someone or even went back to sleep at Manuel's place. He got up and walked down to the garden where his mother in law asked him again about Carmen. This time he could tell her that her daughter would be joining them in a couple of days. That news took a couple of years off the old woman's face. Then she ran inside to tell her husband. As he had been up for too long he decided to test if the hammock down in the garden would still take his weight. Life can be great. His mind finally woke up. Should he dare to fly back to the USA or stay put? Then he thought that if the authorities were able to get him in Italy, they would have certainly got him in the Dominican Republic. He was no Lucky Luciano hiding in Cuba with the help of Batista. Still, staying away would have made them more suspicious or even made them believe he was guilty. His kids were in the US and Carmen would certainly not want to move back to Santo Domingo. He was confused, and decided to postpone making any further decisions until Carmen arrived. Maybe she knew something he didn't yet, or so he hoped.

Enzo was shaken awake by two children, violently pulling both ends of the hammocks.

Sofia and Isabella were smiling showing all their teeth, very happy to have surprised their uncle that was getting seriously sun burned.

Mariana, after telling her children to stop pulling their uncle out of the hammock: "I am glad we came to find you. A bit more time straight under the sun and you would have been in serious pain. Take care of your pale skin."

"Thank you. Believe it or not, I did not have any sun in my face when I fall asleep."

"You know that this is stronger than your Sicilian sun. You grow vines, we grow coconuts here. Anyway, I heard Carmen is coming. This is great. I have not seen her for a couple of years. She does not seem to be missing the sun as much as you do."

"Yes, that is probably it, or maybe she does not want to hear from her parents for the thousandth time that she should have married that rich guy who fancied her at school and stayed here all her life, near her family."

"Maybe she should not tell them that your well paid job forces you to stay in the USA."

"Maybe. Anyway, it's great to see you and the kids. I see you are all well."

"Sure, we are doing fine. Julio's job is secure and that small plot of land we have grows most of the stuff we eat. We cannot complain. Sofia and Isabella are still young. The problem will start once they finish school and need to look for a job or a rich husband."

"That was our generation, Mariana, I don't think they want to rely on husbands."

"Talking of jobs, this reminded me about that article on the local newspaper where they mentioned your company name. Are you involved?"

Julio arrived and intervened: "I think I better answer this question after what happened last night. In short, Enzo is not involved in any of the gender change operations. He is not a surgeon, just a medical researcher. Is this right?"

"This is correct, Julio. By the way, Joshua did not come back last night, so maybe we need to pay Manuel a visit."

"Let's go. Mariana we will come back here later. So, enjoy my parents' company for a while. I am sure they will love to see Sofia and Isabella."

Julio and Enzo got into the car and drove off towards the opposite part of Santo Domingo where Manuel lived."

"Is Mariana not getting on with your parents?"

"She is, but you know how it is with you wife and her parents-in-law. It is fine, just like text book. Of course, it does not help that ours are the only grandchildren here. They would like to see them all the time and they often tell how they would better deal with the children. Times have changed and they are hanging on to old ways of doing things. Mariana teaches part-time and my parents think she should stay at home to take better care of me and the children."

"I see, but still better than Carmen's relationship with my parents. A stupid relative in Sicily made some comment about Caribbean women. Since then, she won't set foot in Sicily anymore."

"Yes, she told me about that at the time. I cannot blame her. I understand that this must be difficult for you."

"Yes it is. The traffic seems to have increased a lot since I was here the last time."

"Like everywhere and this is why Manuel prefers to drive a motorbike."

"This reminds me of a funny thing I saw when I was in Germany for work. A colleague of mine rode a motorbike after we left the office and remained behind our car the whole time. The day after. I asked him why he stayed in the queue and did not just go to the front at the various traffic lights we passed. He told me that in Germany if you drive your motorbike in front of the traffic light, all cars will beep at you. I laughed and told him about the time as a student I was driving my Vespa in Palermo's horrible traffic jams, back in Sicily. He said that he was aware of other countries as he had seen the same while on holiday. A couple of days after he was once again behind us and after he beeped at us, he demonstrated to us what he had said and rode his motorbike to the front of the red traffic light. Several cars beeped and I had to laugh. I could not believe them beeping. I don't understand this, as the motorbikes drive away quickly in front and do not hinder anybody. Well, every country has some strange things they do. This is a German one."

"It does sound German to me. If people had to queue here, many would never buy a motorbike and the queues would be longer. I have never been to Germany, but I am sure that as a policeman I would prefer the law abiding German drivers to the people on this island."

"Probably, but don't be too sure."

Enzo rang the bell and a smiling Manuel came out onto the balcony.

"I am coming out into the open. Please wait for me."

"Listen Enzo, Joshua spent the night with me and he might be a bit embarrassed to come down and face the music. Please go easy on him."

"Manuel, I am happy you both had a good time and as long as you didn't do anything illegal, it's none of my business. He is an adult and I am no judge. Have I ever judged you? Have I ever questioned your life style?"

"No, you are right, but maybe this is just because we are related."

"Not all. It's none of my business. I live in the US and I am a US citizen now, but I am no prude. For all that I care, the president of my country could sleep with a donkey, and this is not why I vote for a person. Whatever you do in bed or in a barn is your own business. I care how you deal with me or politics if you are a politician. Please, never doubts this about me. Now, where is hat young African Homo? Just joking, I won't tell him that".

"You just did as I heard you, asshole."

"I hope you also heard what I said before."

"I did!"

"Then all is sorted. Your relation with Manuel is none of my business. We just wanted to make sure you both were all right. We called Manuel's phone, but he did not pick up. This is why we came. I slept a lot and it's a bit late. Maybe tomorrow we need to look where to register for the university or better first of all for a Spanish course. Also, we need to find a place for you to live."

"If he wants, I don't mind him staying here for a while."

"That's a great offer, Manuel, but I need to hear from Joshua if that is fine with him."

"I guess at the beginning, it would be easier until we know where the school will be."

"Fine that's settled then. Should we eat together around here somewhere?"

"That would be a great idea if Mariana and the kids were not waiting for us with my parents."

"You are right. Are you then staying here or coming to see us later?"

"Joshua and I will eat here and join you later for a glass of wine or some coffee. Is that okay?"

Enzo and Julio left Manuel's house with a smile and jumped into Julio's car.

"I had never thought Manuel would turn that wild boy around. Did you see how mellow he was? It seemed a different guy from the one who punched you last night."

"I think he was just embarrassed and he has still not come to terms with the fact that he has just spent the night with a man. I wonder how drunk he was."

"Better to say that he spent his first night with a shemale. Anyway, that makes it a bit better for you as Manuel has taken an interest in Joshua and will be keen to help him."

"I hope it lasts."

Mariana was very happy to see them back and stop answering her mother-in-law questions. Enzo ran around the children that inevitably reminded him of his own. He missed them now more than ever and was hoping Carmen would be able to bring them with her. Their cousins, Sofia and Isabella, had not seen them for a couple of years. The last time despite, his children speaking little Spanish, they were able to somehow communicate.

"Listen Enzo I don't want to start any arguments, but seeing that your friend Joshua has not come back with you and there is no danger of someone punching you, I would be interested to know how you got involved in a company that turns men into women?"

"Mariana, as I said, I was not involved, nor am I involved in those kind of services provided by a department of the company I work for."

"Why did your friend punch you?"

"Because, like you, he misunderstood my role in the company. Anyway, why are you so interested in my job and that article which I understand appeared months ago in the local newspaper?"

"I am not sure if you know, but I teach in a school on a part-time contract. You know, in the morning when the kids are at school. On some days, I teach in a school supported by a NGO. This NGO supports single young mothers in learning a profession, so for them to become economically independent. You see, things have changed since that guy was turned into a woman. Now those single mums find it very difficult to find a new partner. Many men are now scared of starting a relationship with a woman who already has children. This was not an issue before. Now it is, so bad, that some just hide their children with their grandparents and in a couple of cases some young mothers have abandoned their children in the hope of being able to start a new life. This is terrible. Some have tried to give their children up to adoption. Even this is horrible."

"I agree it is a sad affair, but you don't think that if the man, as you said, had not been turned into a woman, that if he had just been put into prison, that those men would still be worried to start a new relationship with a woman who already has children?"

"Maybe, but I think that things have got worse now. It seems men are far more terrified of becoming women than to be put in jail. The jail sentence existed and some men still raped women. This new law and procedure your company provides is affecting those poor single mums."

"I think with time, things will get normal again and people will forget. Men cannot stop falling in love with women who already have kids."

"To me it seems they have stopped trying."

"Remember, Mariana that turning men into women is not my job and it has never been."

"I am glad to hear you are not involved and I am glad you are here. Even better, I am looking forward to seeing Carmen. Listen, I have already helped in the kitchen and if I carry on talking to you, she won't be asking for my help anymore."

"Is she really that bad?"

"No, but I cannot be told one more time how to better cut the salad or fry the vegetables. We have a good mother-in-law, but she is set in her own old ways and I cannot always pretend not to hear the annoying things she says just to avoid discussions."

"In that case, go ahead, is there anything apart from my work that you wanted to speak with me about? And where is Julio?"

"Julio was sent to fix some furniture. She asked him to do that some months ago and thanks to you he finally came here. Now he cannot escape. Don't worry he will soon come out again.
Ah, yes, I wanted to ask you about migration? As you know, many Dominicans live in the US and many young ones dream of one day moving there. Is Mr. Trump going mad?"

"Mariana, I am sure you will understand that Dominicans would not be happy if all poor Haitians who wanted to do so, would move to the Dominican Republic. There has to be some kind of control. Plenty of people in the world would love to move to the USA. If they were to allow everybody to move there, the USA would no longer be what it is today. A country can only digest a certain number of new arrivals in a given time. In Italy as a child, I had to study the Roman Empire for a long time. The rise and the fall of the Roman Empire. Once the poor and ignorant barbarians invaded the Empire, everything was lost. It took hundreds of years for part of Europe to recover. I have been living in different countries myself and met many Italians living outside Italy. Many of those migrants remember the good old days back home and long to go back. Often they don't like the mentality and customs of the place they moved to. They would like the job and money they now have in a country where people behaved like in their home country. That makes no sense."

"Why? I can understand those people as many Dominicans in the USA or Canada do miss the warmth of the Dominican people."

"Sure, that part I agree with, but what we need to understand is the reason why the economy in Italy or the Dominican Republic does not work as well as in the USA, Canada, Germany, or other rich countries. Those rich countries' different ways of doing things is why their economies are doing better. If you look around the world, you will notice that the richer countries are those that are better organised. Are Italy or the Dominican Republic famous for their organisation?"

"I don't think so."

"In short, this is why our economies do not work as well."

"Are you saying that the mentality of the people of the poor countries is the cause of their bad economies?"

"Exactly. If nobody follows the rule, or better, if those who don't follow the rules are not punished, why should anybody else follow the rules? Of course, if the rules are fair for everybody, people are more willing to follow the rules. I don't know about here, but when I used to live in Italy those who managed to avoid paying taxes were regarded as heroes such as Robin Hood. This would not be the case in Germany or other countries where people believe in living in a country with a fair tax system. We Italians are relaxed about applying the rules, but then complain about things not working. The rules must also be fair and easy to understand. This is not the case either. It's just a mess and this is why the economy does not work as well. Money alone cannot solve the issue. You can fill up the tank of a car, but if the engine does not work, you will still have to push it."

"You are not answering my question about migration?"

"Sorry, you touched a sore point. I think that people want to migrate to richer, better organised countries. We can agree that the problem would not exist if their own countries worked better. We cannot expect to mismanage our own countries and then just move to another one. It's like stopping cleaning our houses and once it is so bad that we can no longer live in them, just moving in with a neighbour who has kept his house clean."

"No offence, but you moved to another country."

"Yes, you are right. I did move at a time when fewer people could afford to travel or even knew how life was in another country. Since the invention of the smartphone in 2007 people have a window to the world in their own hands. Nowadays everybody can check and see things in other countries. That is fine, but people are not able to move to other countries as they please. There are now almost eight billion people on this planet. In the west we have little understanding of this, but in China they are far better at crowd management."

"Do you mean that we all need a dictatorship?"

"No, but we need rules. Imagine for a moment if the Chinese government were to allow everybody in their country to move freely and then one hundred million people would like to move to Shanghai just because there are more jobs and better hospitals there. How can a city cope with those numbers? Imagine if an average of twenty million tourists wanted to visit Santo Domingo every day, or Rome or Venice, or London, or New York. This is our future, it has already arrived. China is becoming ever richer. Imagine if just twenty million decided to buy the best houses here in the Dominican Republic. Those would not be poor people, but wealthy individuals who would like to buy a house in the sun. Do you think you could live here as you do now?"

"Are you trying to scare me with those nightmare scenarios?"

"No, I just want you to understand how scared people are in those countries where millions would like to move to. They are aware that their lives would change. It is not just a case of letting one million individuals in. This would be a never ending stream that would destroy the receiving countries. I think migration needs to continue, but this can only happen in a controlled manner."

"Now I am worried about the future of my children."

"When they are older, there will be ten or more billion people on earth and they will survive, but life will be different. Changes will be slow and people will get used to this new way of life. All around the world the population has already started to concentrate in mega cities. This will leave more space for nature and food production. Those changes are already happening and more are creeping up on us. Trump is just saying what many feel and others will soon do the same all around the world."

"What should people do? How do we create a better future for our children?"

"We need to fight for quicker changes in our own countries. I also feel we need to tackle this internationally. It is not possible for some countries, because of traditions or religion, to support the constant growth of their population without having the means to feed them. This is irresponsible. In advanced societies when a couple has too many children and cannot feed them, the state intervenes not just with food. Imagine if your neighbours kept on having children and expected you to work harder to feed them. Would you think this to be fair? No family would. No country either. What if the host country were to internationally be granted the voting rights and the right to speak on behalf of its guests?"

"What do you mean?"

"Imagine now that there are one million Italian citizens living in the USA. In this case the USA would have the right to speak on behalf of one million Italians on the world stage; and in the Italian government. Not only that, but the USA should have voting rights in Italian internal matters for the number of Italian citizens it hosts and feeds. Also, if one million Italian citizens live in the USA, then one million US citizens should automatically have the right to settle in Italy. In this way, those countries that feed the population also have the rights to talk on their behalf. Many countries that could not feed their population would think twice about constantly exporting people or encouraging new births. Believe me, that with this system in place, those who have moved to other countries would be encouraged to assimilate and take a new nationality. At the moment those who cannot feed their population behave like irresponsible parents."

"Those ideas could make you many enemies. I would not say this too loud."

"This is just my opinion. You asked me about migration and maybe you got a much longer answer than you wanted. I am sorry, but there is no simple solution to the migration problem in a world of eight billion people that can now easily travel everywhere."

"In our school we read an article about rich countries always needing new immigrants to keep their economies growing. So if they need immigrants, then that should make it easier for people to get there."

"This is true, rich countries always need new immigrants that take up the jobs that the locals are no longer prepared to do. As I said earlier, it is a question of letting in the people the economy needs and not too many to destroy it. Opening the border to everybody will benefit nobody. It's just a question of numbers."

"I still think the current situation is inhumane and something should be done."

"I agree with you, but opening all the borders won't help anybody. We need to tackle the issue at the root and stop the need for people to move in the first place. We need to find a way to develop the economies of some countries that are far behind in their development."

"What if those countries want to keep their traditions and ways of living?"

"Their traditions and ways of living should also include a way to feed their offspring. If this is not the case then obviously their traditions or ways of living are the root of the problem."

"You sound extreme."

"The truth is always hard. There is no way to sugar coat this. I am just a realist and no dreamer. Do you think that if around nine thousands years ago humans had not started to cultivate plants and farm animals, that today we would have been able to feed a population of eight billion people?"

"Probably not."

"What do you think happened to those people who hung onto their nomadic traditions?"

"They were exterminated by those who were no longer nomads."

"It sounds harsh, but it is the same at work. If I don't constantly update my skills, I will no longer be needed by my company. Traditions and ways of living must continually adapt to the new circumstances or will die out with those who hang on to them. The same goes for religions. Please never say to anyone what I am about to tell you. Believe me, even before Christianity, Islam or Judaism were born, humans already had their religions. What happened to those? Once people worked out that fire is not lit by a god, but that even humans could light it up, few carried on believing in the god of fire. What do you think will happen when people stop believing in the flying archangel Gabriel, the Immaculate Conception of Mary, or in a paradise that cannot be to everyone's taste? Do you really want an angel playing the harp for you all day? I prefer jazz."

"I thought you Italians were great Catholics? Make sure you don't speak to Carmen's parents in the same way."

"I am a gringo now, but I am not stupid. Why should I destroy or attack her beliefs? The reason I speak freely to you is because they cannot understand English."

"I finally fixed the leg of that table, two chairs and a wardrobe. Is Mariana telling you what we did in the last two years since we saw you?"

"Not really. I think I was boring her trying to answer one of her questions. And I think we solved most of the world's problems."

"I wish. Now I need to join you both with a good drink to forget the sad reality you spoke about."

"Not sad, just realistic!"

"Too realistic for my taste. I prefer to still be a dreamer. After our talk I understand better the phrase, ignorance is bliss."

"I am sorry, Mariana, I did not want to depress you. My secret is to enjoy life to the full, especially the time spent with family and friends. Maybe next time let's speak about lighter things."

"Since Mariana started to teach those young mums, she is more aware of social issues. She knew that all before, but of course it's different when you are every day confronted with it. By the way, my mother said to be ready for dinner at eight."

Mariana, looking to the kitchen door into the terrace, "Does she need help preparing?"

"Sofia and Isabella are helping already, but I am sure she won't mind an adult in there."

"Of course, I will help the girls out. Being a policeman, Julio probably agrees with your views on migration."

"What views on migration?"

"Nothing, I just said that opening all borders is a utopia and won't help anybody."

"Yes, I agree. We know something about migration here in the Dominican Republic. We share Hispaniola with Haiti and they are having a tough time, so many try to come here. At the same time many people from our country have emigrated to other countries. We understand the issue from both sides. Then you are a migrant yourself and have just brought one here from Africa."

"I just said to Mariana that only a slow process can work or there will be chaos and killing."

"Mariana is right, being a policeman I kind of agree with you."

They carried on talking into the night. During the evening Julio received a call from Carmen confirming the flight details and asking him to pick her up. Enzo asked to borrow Julio's car, to pick up his wife and surprise her. Julio was not keen on lending him his car knowing that Enzo did not have any valid documents nor driving licence with him. As a policeman, it could be embarrassing for him. Julio managed to dissuade him and have him wait at home for them. Thinking about it, it was probably better not to show his face at the airport, where the police might have a picture of him. He really did not want to risk it and not see his wife and children.

The day after, all the rum and wine they had drunk was still in his cloudy head. He did not regret a good night, talking to Mariana, then Julio and playing with their children. In the late evening even Joshua and Manuel had joined them. Joshua looked less embarrassed probably helped by a good portion of rum. He felt he needed a good breakfast and loads of water followed by a good strong coffee. The not-too-hot start to the day was what he needed. Maybe the clouds were just in his head. Father-in-law walked past him, mumbled a good morning in Spanish and smiled at the sight of his face. Mother-in-law also smiled, but nudged him kindly to the kitchen and gave him a mug of water and started to prepare a spicy vegetable omelette. Enzo walked up to her and kissed her forehead. She laughed and without saying anything waved her index finger at him. After throwing down drinks and breakfast, he headed straight for the hammock in the garden and wondered if moving to the Dominican Republic was not a bad idea after all. Looking at the slightly grey sky through the vegetation looked to him like a dream. Or was it? What had been the point of all his hard work? Was it not good enough to find two palm trees and stretch a hammock between them? Yes, this was his new project, just enjoy life on a hammock. Probably still the rum talking, but he did not care and soon feel asleep. The sun did wake him up after it had started to roast his forehead. Enzo jumped up and ran to the bathroom to pour some water over his hot head. It was early afternoon and in a couple of hours, Carmen and his children would land. He was looking forward to embracing them, but also to know a bit more about his situation with the authorities in the US. Mother-in-law looked busy in the kitchen, working hard despite her old age and the different malaise a woman of that age has. Enzo walked in and asked if he could help, but Carmen's mother threw him out. She was a woman of her generation who did not think men belonged in the kitchen. Enzo always liked to watch her cooking. He wanted to learn from her, but she often looked at him as an intruder. He needed to kill some time not to be too tense about the waiting, so he decided to go for walk. While walking around, some of the elderly greeted him. He waved back, seldom recognizing those who greeted him. He was the Italian who had married Carmen. This is how many remembered him. Over the years, he had met many in Carmen's house. He could only remember a few of them, but in order not to offend anybody, he made sure to greet back anybody who greeted him. He walked around the streets waving and smiling back now and then until he reached the sea he loved so much. He looked into the wide sea and realised it was not that long ago that he had arrived from the other side of the ocean. That made him aware of his adventurous and lucky trip. At fifty, he had not expected to be exposed to such an adventure, but maybe this had been exactly what he needed to pull him out of the ordinary cycle of life. The smell of rotten fish reached his nose, ending his romantic thoughts, prompting him to resume his walk. After leaving behind a row of fishing boats, he had in front of him a stretch of free open beach. What a pity. It was time to start walking back and avoid missing Julio return from the airport.

Julio arrived. He was hiding upstairs. After Carmen had greeted her parents, Julio asked her to help him carry her luggage upstairs to her room. Julio let Carmen walk into the room first. She was stunned to find Enzo in there. They hugged, but she soon pushed him away, "Why are you here? How long have you been here? Why did you not tell me you were here? What happened?"

"Sorry for the surprise. Believe me, I did not plan this. I need some time to tell you what happened. Are you not happy to see me?"

"Of course I am, but I don't understand why you came here to see my family on your own."

"Listen, I will explain, but first it is very important that you tell me what you were told about my absence and lack of communication."

"Jim from your office called me to say that you were on a kind of secret mission working for the US government and I should not tell anybody. Is it true?"

"Who told you that?

"Jim. Was it true?"

"No, it is not true at all. I cannot understand why they would tell you that."

"Jim told me that I should not be worried because you had been called to help the military forces in a delicate matter and I should not mention this to anybody. They also told me that I would receive an official letter apologising for your absence."

"Did you receive the letter?"

"Yes, it looked like an official government document. If you were not on an official military mission, where the hell have you been all this time and why did you not call us?"

"Listen, I swear I will tell you the truth, but please let me first hug my children. Go and help your mother bringing the food out and later after dinner I will tell you everything. I promise."

"Be aware that I told the kids that you were away for work in a place where there was no phone reception and no internet. They thought you must be on Mars, so it's up to you what you want to tell them."

"Thank you, Carmen."

Enzo went to find his children in the garden who were overjoyed to see him. Then when asked where he had been hiding, he replied that he was on a secret mission in another country. His son Johnny asked him if he was working for the mafia or for the CIA. He laughed and answered, sorry to disappoint you, but it was neither of them. Julio, Mariana and their children joined them as well. Later Manuel and Joshua turned up. Joshua was introduced to Carmen as Enzo's new African friend. Carmen had been worrying about some new woman being in Enzo's life, maybe a midlife crisis. Maybe she was wrong and her husband's midlife crisis had turned him gay. She was even more convinced after she saw how affectionate Manuel behaved towards Joshua. The more she waited, the more her curiosity grew. She could not wait any longer. Could she trust him or would it be a cover up. Then she heard of Joshua punching her husband at that same table a couple of days earlier. She tried not to show it, but she was sitting uncomfortably all evening. The fact that Enzo kept on enjoying the never ending supper with the family grew in her the suspicion that this was his delaying tactic. She was tired but determined to stay awake until all had gone. Enzo seemed unaware of his wife sitting on tenterhooks. Eventually the guests went home, the parents apologised for retiring to their bed, the kids had dropped, exhausted, and were carried to their beds.

"Joshua seems a good guy. Where did you meet him?"

"In Africa."

"Did the US army or your company send you to Africa?"

"No, I escaped to Africa from Italy. All the refugees coming to Europe via the Mediterranean Sea gave me the idea to go the other way. And you know, I don't work for the US army."

"Why on earth did you have to run away from Italy and why through Africa?"

Enzo started to describe his adventure, making sure to omit Rose and Abebi.

"And who is Joshua?"

"I met Joshua in Tunisia shortly after I had landed there from Sicily. Despite the way we met, he later helped me get here from Africa. It would have been harder without him."

"Why did you not just go to a US embassy?"

"Because I still have no idea why I was detained by the Italian police. Do you think they would have believed or listened to my side of the story? I want to be in the US with my lawyer near me."

"You could have called us? We could have sent money or a ticket?"

"I am still not sure if someone was spying on you. I did not want to endanger you and the kids. If I had called you, whoever asked for my arrest could have tracked me. This is why I had no mobile phone on me. I also made sure Joshua did not have one with him either."

"What is your plan now?"

"Tomorrow I want you to call George, my lawyer. Do that from a public phone and ask him when he can fly to Santo Domingo for me. If necessary, remind him that he still owes me for his sister's and his son's operations. Tomorrow I will also go with your brother Julio to the police station and report my US passport as stolen. Once George is here, I will go with him to the US embassy in Santo Domingo to request whatever temporary document I need to board a plane to the US. I want George to be there for the eventuality they make some trouble at the embassy. By the way, when is your return flight date?"

"We are due to return in a week. Should we go to bed now?"

"You could have said this earlier if you wanted me so much?"

"Calm down, boy. After seeing Joshua's tender relationship with Manuel I did wonder if at your ripe age you came to discover different pleasures in life."

"Don't worry, my dear. I still prefer women and in particular the one in front of me."

"Well you never know. Taste can change with age."

"Has your taste changed over the years?"

"Sure it has. When I was young, I liked the skinny Mediterranean elegant look. Now with age I am coming to appreciate the more experienced middle aged American look with a small, but growing beer belly."

"That was a great answer that deserves to be rewarded with a night of pleasure with such a middle aged American stallion. Welcome to paradise!"

Then he slammed the bedroom door closed. Their relationship had gone through some rough times, but the bedroom was the place where they often settled their disputes or calmed things down.
The day after, Enzo entered the kitchen, surprising Carmen by talking with her mother in a reassuring way. He pretended not to detect the mood, smiled and asked for his usual coffee. Took his mug outside and patiently waited for his wife to join him. As it was too quiet, he enquired of his children's whereabouts, it was a good excuse to re-enter the kitchen. Carmen answered that Mariana had come by to pick up the children and take them to their cousin's schools.

"Enjoy your coffee in peace while the children are away and I catch up with my mother."

Enzo got the cue and walked out again.

One hour later, "What was that all about?"

"She saw you arriving alone and then she heard us talking loud into the night. She asked me if our marriage is in danger. She thinks last night we were having a fight and that you had come here earlier to get some space and expected me to run after you. She clearly doesn't know me well."

"What do you mean?"

"Do you seriously think I would run after you after what happened last time?"

"I guess not. Does she know about that time?"

"No, she does not. Anyway, I explained that you were around here for work and that we had planned to meet up here afterwards. I am not sure she believed me, but at least she pretended to. Listen, is Joshua going to stay with Manuel? What is your plan for him? My mother asked me. Some of the relatives have seen Manuel with him and asked her about him."

"I intend to help Joshua in finishing his studies and I am trying to convince him to take up medicine. He wants to migrate to the USA. I told him that being a doctor would certainly help him."

"Is he going to be one of your social projects?"

"You know me. I cannot change the world, but if I can, I would try to improve the life of someone who crossed my path. He is a good boy who just needs a sponsor like me."

"Did you know he was gay before he arrived here?"

"No, I didn't know he also liked men. I saw him in Africa being interested in girls at least that was what he said. Anyway, I don't care with whom he sleeps. This makes no difference to me. I will help him if he wants."

"Manuel seems happy at the moment, but be prepared for when the romance ends. I don't want my parents or Julio having to face the consequences of your new social experiment. Please don't misunderstand me, I like what you are doing, but I don't want my family here having to deal with it."

"Don't worry, we will find him a school and a room somewhere. I don't expect he would have to stay a long time with Manuel."

"You should ask Mariana. She knows a lot about schools in Santo Domingo."

"I certainly will. Please don't forget to call George later."

"I have not forgotten. I will try at ten from the house opposite. You know my parents' friends, Luis and Maria. I will call from their home."

Later in the afternoon.

"Where were you all this time?"

"They had not seen me for a long time and asked me to stay for lunch, so I did. Anyway, I called George who was busy, but he kind of understood this is an urgent matter and will arrive in two days."

"In two days?"

"Come on Enzo, he is a busy lawyer and you cannot complain about having to wait two days. Have a rest and try to sort Joshua's stuff out before we leave. By the way, do you have any idea at all, why they arrested you back in Italy?"

"Not at all, and I am racking my brains trying to understand why? Believe me, I have not done anything wrong, but my current guess is that someone whom I know might have implicated me in something."

"Mafia, drugs, work?"

"I don't know and this makes me crazy. Did you notice anybody following you or anything strange coming out here?"

"Nothing at all. Ah, wait! Someone swapped seats on the plane, mid-air and came to sit behind us, but at the time I did not think much of it. Maybe he wanted to sit close to us, but I have no idea."

"Did you see him again at the airport?"

"Just when collecting the luggage."

"Who knows? I have decided to find out. I cannot hide forever. Maybe it's better if you call Manuel, asking him to pick me up or to bring Joshua here to discuss what to do."

"Sure, I will do."

Later Joshua arrived alone.

"Hi Joshua, good to see you again. Do you like the island?"

"Good to see you as well and thank you for bringing me to this sunny island."

"Are you having a good time and do you think you could spend some time here?"

"It is not that I have much choice apart from being deported as an illegal immigrant?"

"Listen Joshua, I will try to help you, but only if you want. You should not do anything for me. I am happy to help you, but I don't have to. If you prefer to go back, tell me now and I will get a plane ticket for you to return to Africa."

"Why don't you get me a plane ticket to the US?"

"Very funny. There is no way they would let you in. Remember that I am a US citizen and I have no intention to hide an illegal immigrant. Of course, you could try your luck crossing the Mexican border as an illegal, but I won't be helping you with that. One day, with the right qualifications, the doors to the USA will open automatically for you. I suggest you embrace this opportunity and make something of yourself. I need to know for sure before I leave this island in a couple of days."

"Days? Are you leaving already?"

"Yes, I will be leaving in a couple of days if all goes well."

"What do you have against illegal immigrants crossing over the border to the US?"

"Listen Joshua, I understand why people in desperate conditions try to reach a wealthier country and realize their dream, but you need to also understand that there is a reason why those illegal immigrants are kept illegal for years once they cross the US border."

"Why is that?"

"You probably don't know, but in European countries such as Italy, Germany, France and others, you cannot be an illegal immigrant and have a legal driving licence with your name on it. As an illegal, you have no access to medical care or schools for your children. Any citizen or foreign person living there must register with the local authority and only then can you have a driving licence, medical insurance or enrol your kids in school. In the USA, newcomers can remain illegal for years."

"So what?"

"This is a way to have a two-level society. The illegal ones won't of course be able to protest for better pay or better working rights. You are kept as a slave and nowadays this has nothing to do with the colour of your skin. The only difference is a person's legal status in the eyes of the local authorities. In the Roman Empire there were plenty of white slaves from conquered lands. They lived amongst Roman citizens who had free citizens' rights. Note that not all Romans had white skin. Some Roman citizens came from the North African provinces and even those had full Roman citizens' rights if they were not slaves. In India they still have the Indus caste of the untouchables. This is a way to keep people in an inferior status and to take advantage of their work without having to fear any legal request for better pay or work conditions. Some people in my country might be appalled at the idea of the Indian caste system, but are blind to their own underclass as long as they get cheap food and cheap cleaners. In the UK one important point made before the Brexit referendum was the in-work benefit claimed by new immigrants coming from poorer EU countries. The in-work benefits are an invention to keep salaries low while allowing the financial market to prosper and raise the cost of living in a country. Many British people were opposed to the newcomers getting the same in-work benefits and so discriminated against fellow EU citizens. British people living across other EU countries would have hated to be discriminated against, but many back in their home country thought it perfectly fine to treat newcomers differently. We can find similar situations all around the world. The point is that I want to help you in a legal way that believe me, will profit you in the long run. Still if you prefer to leave and walk to the US border, I won't stop you, but I won't support you either. Believe me, you will have a much better life here as a student than in the USA as an illegal immigrant. So what do you want to do?"

"I want to stand on my own feet and I am not yet sure what you will want in return from me. Nothing is free. Am I right?"

"Joshua, I don't want anything apart from loyalty. I was luckier than you and was born from parents who could afford to pay for my education and were also willing to do so. I am prepared to help those who are less fortunate than I am. I also wanted to tell you that just being in the US does not make you richer. There are plenty of poor people in the US, especially black people."

"Are you saying black people are still discriminated against in the USA?"

"I am saying that because of their poor economic conditions, many black Americans have little chance to improve their social status through education which in the US is mostly open to rich people. You can of course take a student loan and come out of university with a huge debt that turns you into a paid slave who is forced to accept any job offer that comes your way so as to be able to pay it back. Mostly, it's not the skin colour, but wealth that counts. I am not sure if you remember. I told you before we left Africa that today in the US, the people with dark skin who have the best jobs out of all the blacks are not US citizens, but well educated Nigerians."

"That's a joke."

"No, it is not. In the USA, what counts is money, citizenship does not count that much. Wealthy foreigners have better chances than middle class US citizens have. This is why I tell you to study here and then if you want, move there. Maybe poor Americans should move to Cuba and study there. I guess they are not allowed to."

"Okay, I got it. Do you want to make of me a new Anthony William Amo?"

"Wow, I am certainly surprised you are aware of Amo's story."

"We read about him when I was back at school in Zimbabwe."

"No, don't worry, you are not my social experiment. Believe me, you are not the first black person I have met. I have black colleagues in my job, so I won't need to test your intelligence. Luckily, times have moved on since the eighteen hundreds, but if you want, you can consider me your Duke of Brunswick-Wolfenbüttel, your protector or better still, your sponsor until you are ready to fly on your own."

Joshua stretched out his hand and looking Enzo straight in his eyes, nodded. Shortly after, Johnny and Mary ran to the end of the garden to hug their father, then suddenly turned around and looked at the other man standing there.

"Is this your friend, daddy? Is he the one who came from Africa with you?"

"Yes, I am Joshua, and you are...?"

"I am Mary and this is my brother, Johnny. Did you have a monkey as a pet back in Africa?"

Johnny, quickly, "A lion would be much cooler!"

"Yes, and eat you for breakfast. Anyway, it was nice meeting you and now I better go to pick up Manuel. Yes, grandpa don't look at me like that, I will avoid the coastal road, grandpa."

"Daddy, why is he calling you grandpa? Do you have other children in Africa?"

"No, don't worry, you and your brother don't have any brother or sister in Africa. Compared to him, I am an old man. This is why he calls me grandpa."

"Can I also call you grandpa?"

Johnny started to run around the garden shouting, grandpa, grandpa, grandpa!

"No Mary, imagine how upset your real grandparents would be."

The evening arrived and all sat at the table including Manuel and Joshua who sat near each other. Then Enzo moved to sit closer to Mariana.

"How did the kids behave at school?"

"All fine, they had fun with their cousins and I am sure they learned some new Spanish words."

"Great. That is exactly what I wanted to talk to you about."

"Julio mentioned something, but go ahead."

"Julio is a clever person as I have not spoken to Julio about this yet. My plan is for Joshua to be a university medical student here on the island. As you can imagine, he will need to learn Spanish first. I think our cousin Manuel has already started teaching him, but he will need proper schooling."

234

"Where is he going to live?"

"Well, this is my second problem as I need to find a room or small affordable flat for him not far from the centre. I will pay for the rent, deposit and school."

"I will ask around and I am sure we will find some accommodation and a proper course for him. If he is gay, then it might be even easier as I work and help in a centre for single mothers. Joshua could even help teaching English while he is still learning Spanish."

"That all would be great apart from the fact that he is not gay, maybe bisexual. So I am not sure what would happen if we put a cock alone in a hen's stall?"

"I see, don't worry, we will work something out, but I won't be the one breaking up Manuel's romance nor will I be blamed for all eternity."

Enzo looked around to make sure Joshua and Manuel were not listening.

"Sure, but we know Manuel, he will soon get bored of his new toy or maybe Joshua will. This is why we need to soon find accommodation for the young man before the honeymoon is over."

"Don't worry, tomorrow I will ask around. Actually, let me send a couple of messages with my phone. I know a friend of mine whose mother recently passed away and the children want to rent out the old place as it is, before they decide what to do with it. For the time being, this could be a great place to live near the Santo Domingo town centre, not far from one of the schools I go to teach. How long are you and Carmen going to stay?"

"A couple of days. I need to wait for a friend to fly in from the US and then we will leave together."

"Someone from work?"

"Yes, kind of."

The family kept on chatting away with the occasional neighbours popping in to say hi to Carmen and her family. Then, a little sound and Mariana looked down at her phone, typed something and turned to Enzo.

"Enzo, my friend confirmed Joshua can move in next week on Monday."

Manuel, quickly turning around, "Joshua is moving where?"

"Sorry, Manuel, but I will go back home soon and I need to organise some accommodation for Joshua before I do so. I don't expect you to put him up for the rest of his life?"

"Why did you not ask me before, and have you asked him what he wants to do?"

"Listen Manuel, for me you can live together from now to eternity, but should you change your mind while I am back home, then he will have a place to go. By the way, as I understood, the place is not far from your flat and conveniently close to the school he will need to attend to learn Spanish."

"I understand, but it would have been good to ask me first. I might have also known someone who could have helped."

"Don't be offended Manuel, I just asked Mariana and she happened to know about a free small flat in the centre of the town."

"Joshua, are you now going to move out?"

"Only if you want me to."

"It's up to you where you live, but if you need, there is a place for you."

The evening went by pleasantly into the night with good food and drinks. The day after Enzo managed to rent the small apartment for Joshua and with Julio's help they applied for some official and legal documentation for Joshua to enrol him as a foreign student sponsored by Enzo. Having to sort out Joshua's immediate future took Enzo's mind off his thoughts about organizing his own documents at the US embassy. He had to wait for his lawyer, Bob, and then go with him straight to the US embassy and ask for a new passport. He had a copy of his passport, but he knew that was not going to be enough to board a plane. Being this the second time he had lost his passport outside of the country, he knew that he needed to report his loss of documents to the local authorities first and then present the police report to the embassy. Julio took him to the main police station helping him to file his passport as lost or stolen. He was not sure if he had left it behind at some restaurant or if it had been stolen in his hotel. This is what they wrote on the police report. He was sure this was not going to be questioned. Julio did then call Mariana and both visited her in one of her schools, where she helped enrol Joshua in a Spanish language course. They did not have enough students to start the course, but Enzo agreed to pay more to speed up the process. In the late afternoon, Enzo went back to meet Joshua.

"Hey grandpa, I want you to know that I am really grateful and that I will try my best not to disappoint you. I really appreciate your finding and funding my accommodation and the school. One day I will try to pay you back if I can."

"Have you ever heard of Karma? What goes around comes around! I have met many idiots in my life, but also many people who have helped me. I am paying back to you what they have given to me. I hope one day you will do the same and pass on the bucket with a couple of bucks."

"I will try."

"Please stay out of trouble. I know this place is full of beautiful girls blessed by the sun, but make sure you don't get anybody pregnant as you will have to own up and become a daddy. Don't do this too early. So have fun as you deserve at your age, but be careful not to ruin your life and some girl's life. I need to also ask you for a big favour. Whenever the story with Manuel ends, please let him down easily. Manuel is a romantic who believes in love. Please don't break his heart."

"What if he leaves me?"

"Even then be kind to him and not bitter. I understand you are having fun, but I don't want this story to spoil the good relationship I have with Manuel. He won't leave you, he keeps on falling in love with young strong wild men like you. So be kind."

"I'll try."

"I'm going to see my wife and kids now or they will start to wonder where I am now. Tomorrow I will be busy all day, but if all goes well, I will be flying back home by the end of the week and we will keep in touch over the phone. Once your official documentation has been sent to you, you will be able to apply for your own smart phone and we will keep better in touch.

Once you start to feel confident, write to me in Spanish. This should help you practise."

Enzo had to wait for Julio to drive him back as he did not want to risk driving without a driving licence and embarrass his brother-in-law after all he was doing to help him. On the way back to his parents-in-law, "Listen Julio, I know that your parents miss Carmen and have promised her their house, and you their other house in town. We also know how much you love that house with the large garden. As it is most unlikely that we will ever move here it seems fair to me that in the far away future once your parents are no more, you should get their house instead. I will speak to Carmen about this. I know your parents won't write this down despite our asking them, but be sure that we will pass the house over to you. You have always been helpful to us and a great brother to Carmen. So we think you deserve this."

"I appreciate what you are saying, but I am not sure I want a house my parents don't want me to have."

"Luckily, we don't have to decide about this yet, I just want you to bear this in mind and decide then when we will have to."

"Thank you. I will keep this in the back of my mind."

One more family evening passed, mostly being entertained by their children and neighbours coming and going. The morning after came and Enzo could not wait for Bob to land. Carmen drove him to the airport and Bob's plane landed on time. Bob was surprised to also see Carmen there, but Enzo explained that he had no driving permit.

While driving into Santo Domingo, "How did you lose your driving licence? Drinking? Is this why I am here? It's very nice of you to drag me to this pleasant island and pay for two days of my work, but Carmen did not want to tell me the reason you want me here."

"The truth is that Carmen could not tell you. I will explain everything while we are driving to the US embassy in Santo Domingo to request a new temporary passport for me. Otherwise I cannot fly back home."

Enzo explained his unexpected arrest in Italy and his adventurous journey back to the American continent.

"As you don't yet know your legal situation in the US, what would you like me to do at the embassy?"

"Nothing at all, if nothing of you is needed. I want you there in case they decide to arrest me. I need you to be there just in case."

"Have you considered hiding out here?"

"Briefly, but it makes no sense. As I told you, I really have no idea why they are after me."

"You must know."

"Yes."

Carmen struggled to find a parking spot, but once they did, they entered the US Embassy, who directed them to the consulate section dealing with the loss of travel documents. Bob sat outside, waiting to be called in, but he never was. Enzo was surprised that he was not stopped or questioned. The consulate employee checked the copy of his passport for authenticity, called the US mainland, received confirmation, and told him to wait outside to be called back in later to retrieve his temporary travel document, which he could use in the next five days to fly back home. He felt relieved and stupid at the same time.

Enzo, having left the Embassy relieved, shouted, "Why didn't I go straight to the US Embassy in Tunis and fly back home from there?"

Bob smiled, simultaneously amused and pleased for his client.

"I never had an easier job. Thank you!"

"I am both surprised and pleased, but this is only the first part of your task."

"What's the second part?"

"Once they give me my travel document, I will book a ticket on your same flight back so we land together. Just in case they should arrest me when I set foot on US soil."

"Sure, that makes sense. Now I also understand why Carmen was adamant that I stay for two days and fly back on the third."

"Today I will take you to lunch, and then you have the day all to yourself. We have a family invitation to attend to. The hotel I booked for you is in area not far from the lively centre, and there are plenty of bars around there."

"Thank you! And don't worry, I'll find a way to amuse myself."

During the meal, Bob kept asking Enzo about any possible clues or activities prior to his journey to Italy. Something that could have possibly caused his arrest. After a long chat, neither of them were any the wiser. The day had finally come when he would fly back home with Bob, just one day earlier than his wife and children. He did not want to expose his wife and children to him being publicly arrested at the US border.

"What seat number have you got? Are we sitting close to each other?"

"Sorry, Bob, we won't be sitting together at all. I'm in business class, near the front of the plane."

"I see you prefer to travel in style."

"Not really. This time I just wanted to travel with you, and there were no seats left in economy."

"Well, in that case I can confess that I am also in business class, but I didn't want you to think that you were paying me too much."

"Don't worry, Bob, you aren't known for being cheap, but for being good. Which seat number do you have?"

"8A."

"I'm in 7A, so watch my back."

"So you did think of everything."

"Have a good trip, Bob, and speak to you after we land."

They landed in LA and went through passport control. The border agent even made a joke about naïve US tourists having their passports stolen when on holiday in the Caribbean. It seemed like nobody was after him. Bob carried on watching him from behind.

"Well, my friend, I must say that this has been the easiest and most pleasant job ever. I have never earned easier money. Thank you. Gracias!"

"I'm happy it went this way. Please keep your phone on you at all times, as I'm not sure what will happen in the next few days."

"Don't worry, I will."

Enzo went back home, and called Carmen to inform her of his uncomplicated entry into the USA.

"Are you sure you aren't trying to hide something from me? Some new woman?"

"Is this is funny to you? I'm going crazy and I have no idea what happened to me. Anyway, on Monday I'm going to turn up at the office, and see how they react and what they say."

"Do that. That's a good idea. Maybe tell them you were abducted by female aliens that raped you every day."

"Have you thought about becoming a comedian?"

"Did they have three breasts? Or two in the front and two on their back?"

"That's such good idea. I might suggest this to our company. Not just breast enhancement, but doubling too. Should I schedule an appointment for you?"

"Try suggesting that and they'll call the guys with the straitjacket. Then you'll be gone for even longer. Good luck."

"You started this, I just carried on with it. It's just a good idea."

"No, it's a stupid idea and you know it. We're both tired and talking nonsense. So, see you tomorrow."

The next day, Enzo went to the airport to pick up Carmen and the children, who were happy to be reunited. In the evening, they retired to their bedroom.

"What are you looking at?" Carmen asked.

"First of all, let me say that you are a great-looking woman. And second, I was wondering how you would look with two more breasts on your back. Come here, give me a hug."

"Stop caressing my back, looking for something that isn't there. Bloody men, it's never enough."

"You started this, and now I can't get it out of my head."

"That's your stupid, childish imagination."

"And you, stop touching my bum."

"Why, I was only wondering if you could do with a second penis at the back to be used once the one in front gets tired."

"You never stop, do you? I really think it's time to sleep and dream of a world with people who have multiple sexual organs."

"No, thank you, those are called nightmares. Good night."

Monday came, and Enzo went to work, pretending he had not missed a single day. He wondered about the reaction he would get from his colleagues and manager. The receptionist welcomed him back, saying that she had not seen him for a while, and asked him if he had been on a company trip outside the country. He nodded. Most of his colleagues did the same, welcoming him back as they had done on other occasions when he had been working on a longer project that had needed his presence elsewhere. Not being satisfied with his colleagues' reactions, he decided to walk into his manager's office, where again, she welcomed him back and was pleased that he had finished working on that special, secret military assignment she had been informed about. It seemed that wherever he turned, he could not find out anything more about his abduction in Italy. At this point, he even started to doubt his own mind. Had he really been arrested in Italy, been taken to a Sicilian prison, and eventually escaped? Travelled through North Africa and over the Atlantic to the Dominican

Republic? Joshua was real proof of what had happened to him. Had someone given him some drug to make him believe that everything was just a dream? He went through his emails, and retrieved the documentation he had emailed himself from Rome after he had attended the conference. He was relieved to find confirmation that the conference in Rome had really happened. He needed some rest. He knew that back home, Carmen would have bombarded him with questions he was not ready to answer. Then, he remembered his old bar, near work. He had not been there for a while. A chat with the barman and a couple of drinks were exactly what he needed. Then, a phone call.

"Why aren't you answering my messages?"

"Sorry, Carmen, I've been busy at work."

"Have you found out anything?"

"About my new project, not yet, darling. I'm not sure when I'll be off for that consultancy job. Listen, I just need another hour here and then I'll be back home."

Carmen understood, as "consultancy job" had been their code for years. It meant that it was not a good time to talk. Enzo knew that this would worry Carmen even more, but he had no intention of passing any details over his mobile phone. Enzo went home after many more drinks, and relaxed enough to be able to easily answer Carmen's questions. Several days went by with nothing out of the ordinary, so much so that Enzo was becoming paranoid, trying to interpret any movement or gesture that was slightly suspicious, but nothing. So, once more after work, he headed to the same bar he had been to the week before. Same barman, same drink. After knocking back a couple of shots, the barman turned to him.

"Enzo, I'm sorry, but I forgot to say that after you left last week, a man came in asking for your name."

"What did you tell him?"

"The truth. I said that I only know your first name, Enzo."

"Did he ask you anything else?"

"No, he left the bar shortly after you did. I thought he might have caught up with you. Didn't he find you?"

"No, he didn't."

Enzo looked at the screen showing some football game, and carried on enjoying his drink. He was even more puzzled now. Who was that man asking for his name? Then his mind drifted, thinking about how much he had changed since moving to the US. In Italy, he used to always go out with friends, but now he was comfortable being alone with himself. It had not been easy getting used to solitude. He remembered it being a painful process. In his new life, there was no "comitiva", or group of friends one always called before going out. One or another would always come out with you. In his new country, everybody was always too busy, and eventually he had stopped asking for company. In a way, he was too busy himself to join some sports club and plan a weekly meeting with some players who were not necessarily his friends. He had tried to play squash with some colleagues, but they all had a long way to travel back home. There was never any time for idle chat. He had learned to become an American, like those lonely men he had seen on US TV series like "Cheers".

Now he was one of them. Now he also understood that type of life, such a far cry from the sunny island where he was born, where people spend most of their time outside under the blue sky, and are forced to speak to each other, unprotected by walls and dim lights. He was still deep in thought when the barman came closer, served him the drink he had ordered, and with a nod, pointed to a man sitting near the door. Enzo understood. That man was the one who had asked for his name. He returned the nod, making it clear that he had understood. Then, pretending to turn around to look for the restroom, he took a look at the man in question, and could not remember having ever seen him before. If he had asked about his name, certainly he would make the first move. He swung around his stool, back to his previous position. The man got the message, and started to act nervously. Enzo looked for a possible escape route, should the man be armed. The man stood up and left the bar. Enzo thought about whether it would make sense to follow him, but he had to settle his bill first. In the time the barman needed to fetch his change, the man had walked back into the bar, now looking even more nervous, and walked towards Enzo, who now was imagining one of those gangster films when someone is shot at close range. So he stood up, ready to run if needed. Even the barman stepped away from him. The man came closer, then pulled his right hand from his jacket and stretched it out towards Enzo, who was ready to jump up. Enzo glanced down at the empty, outstretched hand that was waiting for a handshake.

"Mr. Dangelo, my name is Alexander Collins."

"Mr. Collins, how do I know you? I apologise, but I don't think we ever met. How do you know my name?"

"Mr. Dangelo, you are a well-known man."

"I hope it's for a good reason."

"Mostly, but not only."

"Have you come to find me to complain about something?"

"Not really, but we need to speak in private."

"As I don't know you or your intentions, this place is private enough for me. Joe has served me plenty of drinks in the last few years, and he has listened too many of my secrets."

"Maybe, but I would prefer to meet you somewhere else tomorrow afternoon, after you leave work. Please come to this swimming pool, and we will meet in the hot tub, outside the one you often go to on Wednesdays after work."

"You certainly know my habits. Sure, see you there tomorrow."

Once Mr. Collins had left the premises, the barman came closer. He looked relieved, and smiled apologetically for having quickly stepped away to the other side of the bar.

"Listen, Joe, you moved back so quickly and quietly that it seems you aren't new to that sort of experience. Have you ever experienced anyone getting wacked in this bar?"
"I'm terribly sorry, but my instinct for self-preservation might have kicked in. No, luckily I've never witnessed anyone being killed in front of me."

Enzo went home and told Carmen about the encounter and his arranged meeting for the next day.

"Be careful!"

"I will be, but at this moment I'm more curious than worried."

The next day, everything ran smoothly at work, and as he had agreed, he left the office and headed to his usual swimming pool, where for years he had satisfied his longing for the Sicilian Sea he missed so much. Enzo walked out to the hot tub, and planned to get in while he waited for Mr. Collins, but found in it a young couple enjoying each other's closeness. That was his meeting point, and he had no intention of staying outside in the cold wind. He decided to play the role of the strange, awkward man, and started to intensely stare at the couple from afar. It did not take long for the young couple to feel uncomfortable and look back at him, annoyed and disturbed. Eventually, he won the staring competition, and the young couple climbed out, loudly mumbling about old weird man who should not be allowed into the establishment. Like a proper winner, he could now occupy the conquered new land, the hot tub. He was not waiting long when Mr. Collins climbed out of the pool, and he looked pleased to find Enzo in the tub. Mr. Collins had to pass in front of the young couple that had mumbled aloud something Enzo could not quite catch, but could well imagine.

"Good afternoon."

"Hello, good to see you."

"Those young people warned me about you."

Enzo stood up and embraced Mr. Collins.

Mr. Collins, puzzled, said, "Sorry, I don't understand."

"Don't worry, now that they think we are good friends, they'll finally leave. I had to get them out of this tub just before you arrived."

"I see. Anyway, I wanted to meet you here because there are microphones, smart phones or people close enough to hear us."

"Understood. I hope you will explain to me how you know my name?"

"I want to warn you, and I hope to convince you. I know you have worked and are working on an interesting science project partly financed by the US government."

"Plenty of governments around the world fund science projects."

"We both know that, but some inventions can be dangerous for the whole of humanity, and I'm sure a man like yourself will understand that."

"You're right, sometimes ideas have a life of their own. Sorry for sounding cynical, but why are you so worried about humanity? Who are you working for? And besides, I'm no Einstein, nor am I working on some new kind of atomic bomb."

"Mr. Dangelo, I wish more people were worried about humanity."

"I agree with you, but we both know, that people have an insatiable appetite for resources that makes us all selfish."

"Even if this is true, I'm still prepared to do something to fight our worst instincts."

"This is certainly admirable, and you've won me over. Who are you representing? Who are you working for?"

"Mr. Dangelo, you understand that who you work for is not who you are. Before telling you who might be supporting me, I want to explain why I came to find you. I promise that I will disclose who is behind me once you have given me the time to explain."

"I'm enjoying the hot tub. Please, go ahead."

"We are aware of your collaboration with the US army, even if it was indirectly. You are aware of the fact that some of your inventions have been turned into destructive tools or weapons. We are now particularly worried about one of your latest projects involving insects."

"Are you talking about taking control of some insect motor actions?"

"Yes, exactly."

"This project isn't a secret at all, and there have been plenty of public presentations about it. I'm not sure I can tell you more than you already know about this."

"Aren't you also involved in a variation of the project that deals with implementing genetic changes to some of those insects?"

"In a supporting capacity, as I'm not an expert in genetics. I'm just helping some colleagues who are geneticists."

"Are you aware of what they are trying to do?"

"Not really, I only help on the insect motor research."

"Mr. Dangelo, your colleagues are working on a new, devastating weapon. The war of the future will not use conventional weapons. Tanks, ships and planes will only be used for transport. Some countries have been heavily investing in all types of drones. Some are as small as insects, and can already travel unobserved behind enemy lines. Some are used to map the area, others can already carry explosives. Some carry a tiny droplet of curare and other deadly poisons that will sting any human in their way. Your company is going even further. Instead of building tiny drones, it will reprogram insects that will be able to easily reproduce in their millions. With your help, they will be able to direct the insects wherever they want. They call those Cyborg bugs. Your colleagues will have those insects secrete a poison, deadly to humans, from their genetically modified glands. Do you have any idea what could happen if those insects escaped from the lab and reproduced freely outside?"

"I'm sorry to hear that. Please believe me when I say that I was not aware of their final objective. But I still don't understand how I'm supposed to help your cause."

"Mr. Dangelo, we are aware of your opposition to the US army using your invention to melt people's fat and kill them. Certainly, this was not your original intention. In addition, we know that you have been against the forced gender and sex operations that have been partly supported by your company. I know you were against the use of human fat for the production of food."

"How do you know that?"

"Partly from your public interviews and partly thanks to some spies' investigations."

"Who are you working for? The Russians, Chinese, a competitor? By the way, let's get out of here. We've been here too long and some people have started to circle around us. Let's go upstairs to the steam bath. It's always empty there."

They walked inside, passing the young couple, who smiled at them.

"They think we're gay. Smile back to reassure them."

Mr. Collins smiled back as he was asked, and then followed Enzo upstairs into the empty steam bath.

"Do you remember Julie Wilson?"

"So you work for the Russians too. Can I call you Sasha now?"

"If you prefer!"

"Why do you think the Russians would do a better job with this technology?"

"They wouldn't. As you said, we are all selfish humans. The Russians just offer me protection. My mother is Russian, my father is American."

"What happened to Julie?"

"Julie is fine. She was the first to provide us with some information about you. Anyway, I don't need any information. I just want you to stop working on this project by simply refusing. We are also targeting other people working on this project. I'm not spying, and I don't want to sell any vital information or data to anybody. We just want you to stop working on this."

"You will understand that this is not easy for me. They will ask me why. It's not as simple as 'stop working on this'. As you can imagine, if I drop out of the project they will simply employ someone else. Maybe I'm not as important as you think I am. By the way, do you happen to know what happened to me recently?"

"We know you were arrested in Italy, but I'm not sure why. I'm also not sure how and when you were released. Probably some other parties were involved. I told you. You are working on something very dangerous. Just stop!"

"I get your point, but I need some time. I don't know what I'm going to do just yet."

"Mr. Dangelo, I'm the nice guy, but I don't know who they might send after me."

"Am I in danger?"
"After what happened to you in Italy and what they asked me to do, yes, you might be a target now. Maybe it's time to retire."

"I'm too young for that."

"Maybe too young to retire, but not old enough to die. Your kids will miss you, and you're rich enough to enjoy life in Florida, the Dominican Republic, or even Russia."

"Don't be offended, but Russia is too cold for me. Also, a bit too poor."

"Not so poor."

"Once cleaning ladies in Western Europe and USA stop being Russians, then I might believe you."

"Not only cleaning ladies, but also scientists, professors and doctors."

"Tell me, Mr. Collins, how many American or West European cleaning ladies do you see working in Russia? None. Never believe the statistics, look at the people, and especially at the poor. Anyway, I've received your message and as I said, I will think about it. Let's get out of here. Now I'm too hot."

They shook hands and separated. Enzo went swimming for a while, thinking about what to do next, and feeling sure that eventually someone else would get in touch with him. Once he got home, Carmen asked for any news. After Enzo told her, she realized that Enzo was working on a dangerous project that had upset someone, and had probably caused his arrest in Italy. Enzo knew that what Mr. Collins had told him about Julie could not have been true, as the project in question had not even started back then. That was the first warning. Now he knew that someone else would come forward in the next few days. That evening, he went to bed and spent a long time staring at the ceiling, lying in bed, not able to close his eyes. Then he started wondering about why people don't paint anything on their bedroom ceiling.

This took him back to his childhood, when sleeping at his grandparents' old house. The rounded ceiling was covered in old frescos from some unknown artist. It was great to look up at those angels flying in a light blue sky. The small amount of light peeping through the wooden shutters was strong enough to create a somehow magical atmosphere. He remembered not really appreciating the masterpiece, but he remembered it being somewhat pleasing. Strange how the things and people around you mould you into what you become. Growing up in a country full of art everywhere makes you long for aesthetic beauty, but only when you move away from it do you start to miss it. You can only miss what you no longer have. Thinking back to his youth had been a pleasant break, but soon enough, he was again haunted by the curiosity of knowing what was going to happen to him in the days to come. Who would come forward? Should he really retire, as Mr. Collins had suggested, and start contemplating a life away from risky research projects? Would he be allowed to do so, or would this move attract the attention of others? Then his mind went back to his meeting in Rome, and he remembered being asked by an Italian colleague about the insects' project, "Dave2". After what Mr. Collins had told him, he understood that "Dave2" must stand for David and Goliath. The small, remotely-guided insect swarm was David, and Goliath must be the enemy to take on. He had been envious of his colleague, Dave Manston, thinking they had used his name. He had not been the only one to believe that. Dave had played a minor role in the project, but played plenty of golf with one of the project managers. They had never said so in public, but many were not pleased with the project's code name. It now seemed obvious that, like him, many of his colleagues had no idea of the final aim of their project. Everybody just worked on a small module or part of the project. It is as if they were working on the mechanic timer used in a bomb that would kill thousands. The one that built the timer would have no idea of how people would use that item. Still, this was no excuse, and that new, terrifying weapon was not something he would like to help create. Would his removal from the project resolve anything, apart from making him feel better about himself? Or should he do something and go public, jeopardizing his family future? What if another country got there first and used that weapon against his own compatriots and family? How had he gotten into this mess? Now it seemed that his business was even fishier than Gaetano's. Gaetano, the Sicilian fisherman who had taken him to Tunisia. In a way, he had almost come full circle, he thought. He had left Sicily, partly to avoid any involvement with the mafia, whom he despised, and now he had ended up working on a project that could be regarded as criminal. What was he supposed to do? Daytime came too quickly.

"Why were you so restless last night? I think you should consider quitting your job. I know you're too young to retire and I know you'd be restless without something to do. Maybe you could write a book, like you've been wanting to do for a long time. Think about it. You're putting your family in danger."

"You're probably right. I can't just jump out of the boat. I need to be careful and get out without rocking the boat. For the safety of those inside, and so as not to create too high waves."

"Be careful. I support you in your decision, but think about the children."

"I do, and that's why I couldn't sleep. Now you probably wish you had married that doctor from Santo Domingo as your parents had wanted."

"Did you marry the woman your parents wanted? I don't think so. I guess we deserve each other. Go to work, but have a cold shower first to wake yourself up. Your face looks like an un-ironed shirt, and it's too early to iron."

"I love you too, darling."

Back at the office, Enzo tried to find the Dave2 project paperwork. He was trying to find any details that could point to its final purpose. Nothing, as he had expected. The module he was working on was just related to the insects' remote control. Then he remembered that he had collaborated with an entomologist to determine how many of a given type of insect they needed to remotely control, in order to guide an entire swarm. Maybe controlling few, key members of a swarm would have been enough to indirectly control the whole swarm. The entomologist team worked closer with the geneticist team. He decided to casually arrange to meet his colleagues from the different teams for a coffee, and find out how far along they were with working on their Dave2 module. In the afternoon, he managed to meet Sue and John from the geneticist's team. They told him that they had long stopped working on the Dave2 project, and were now working on a new project for some beauty clinics. They were trying to have insect secrete the poison used by the cosmetic industry for Botox injections. What the colleagues were surprised by was the fact that their aim was to have single insect secrete enough poison to kill a person. The idea was to require fewer insects, and to dilute the poison used for the Botox. They had been told that now, different type of poisons were used in the beauty industry. Sue and John had shown some concerns about some of those insects escaping from the lab and secreting enough poison to kill the first person in their way. They had voiced their concerns to management, who reassured them that nobody wanted to create a minuscule monster that would kill people. They had also been reminded of the fact that their international competitors were not sleeping, and that some were already working on similar projects. They were also told not to forget that their end of year bonus was linked to the project's good results. Enzo was now sure that the new project Sue and John were working on was also related to Dave2, but decided not to alarm them. He was now sure that Mr. Collins had told him the truth. After work, he went back the bar. As usual, he walked into the bar and greeted Joe, the barman, who smiled and started to prepare his favourite drink without asking. "Double or normal?"

"Double please, I'll take a taxi if I need to."

Enzo stared at the screen showing an old football game. He had learned to like American football. Many times in the past he had been told that soccer was for suckers, while football was for real men. He never cared enough to argue about sport, so he got used to just smiling in response. Being accustomed to European football games, at first, American football seemed slow to him. They always stopped and discussed in the middle of the game. He was used seeing twenty men running back and forth for ninety minutes or longer. From a bar stool, he preferred American football. There were more breaks, and time to talk to friends or nearby people. The cheerleaders weren't bad, either. Each time someone walked in, he would look up, hoping someone would approach to talk to him, but many just walked past without stopping. Finally, someone entered who he did not expect. Julie walked in. He had not seen Julie for years. She walked straight up to him. A kiss on the cheek, and sat on the stool next to him.

"Long time no see, but still the beautiful lady you always were."

"Thank you. You haven't changed much either."

"Thank you for lying. Did Alexander send you?"

"Yes, he thought I might be better at convincing you."

"Do you remember what happened the last time we were together?"

"Sure, but a little bird told me that I wasn't the last woman you had on the side. Didn't you enjoy the time you had with me?"

"I had a good time, but back then I didn't know you were spying on me. Are you telling me that you could be the reason for me leaving my company?"

"It seems that some people are willing to pay for you, and others are willing to stop you from what you're doing. I have no idea. I was just told to ask you."

Julie leaned closer to Enzo, and in that exact moment, Carmen walked in. If her eyes were laser beams Enzo would have died on the spot. She walked energetically towards Enzo, then turned to Julie and shouted, "What the hell are you doing here?"

Then she turned back to Enzo. "What the hell are you doing here with her? Haven't you learned your lesson?"

"Listen, Carmen, I know you're upset, but give me a chance to explain. Do you really think I would've sent you a message saying that I'd be here if I wanted to meet her in secret?"

"That's the only thing that's saving you right now. I'm not done with you. Why is this bitch here now? Did you forget what you promised me, and all the pain she caused us? Why would you do this to your children?"

The barman, once again, slowly retired to the other end of the bar. Enzo looked at him and shouted, "Don't worry, she's not armed!"

"My dear Carmen, you have nothing to be upset about. He hasn't done anything. And remember that last time, he left me to come back to you."

"Leave us alone, and stay out of our fucking life!"

"OK, now you're exaggerating and you're annoying me. Does he know about Jason?"

Carmen face changed colour. There was a sudden silence.

"So ladies, who is this Jason?"

"I have nothing to say to this bitch." Then Carmen walked out of the bar.

"Do you want to know, who's Jason?"

"Well, I guess it seems that this 'Jason' is some person in my wife's life. Yes, please tell me more."

"Jason is his acting name. His real name is Matthew Houston."

"Has my wife been taking acting lessons?"

"More like Romeo and Juliet lessons."

"I see. And you know this because you've been spying on us. Am I right?"

"Her Jason doesn't work for us, and he never has. I guess many organizations and countries are interested in what you're doing. Does this make you feel important?"

"Not really, I would prefer to have a much simpler life."

"Yes, but remember that you would have missed out on meeting me, and I think that despite everything, we had a good time. It was my job, but I can honestly say that it was a pleasant one."

"I guess you aren't cut out for normal life, without spying or playing the part of the honey in the honey trap."

"Honey, I'm home! I guess you're right. Normal life always seemed dull to me. I fell in love at a young age. I even got pregnant. Then I found him in bed with my younger sister. That opened my eyes. I decided right there and then, that a nine-to-five job with a family in suburbia wasn't what I wanted. We're just passing through, and we only get one ride. I want to have fun."

"Do you really not care about Russia?"

"Not at all. The fact that I speak Russian does help me get some jobs for them, but right now, it's not them who are paying me to try and convince you."

"Now tell me, what does this 'Jason' or 'Matthew' have to do with my wife?"

"Are you jealous?"

"I will be if she's fallen in love with him."

"I don't know about that. She certainly has, or has had a relationship with this ex-actor. He is gorgeous, so I'm not surprised she fell for him. Doesn't this bother you?"

"A bit, but I'm also honest with myself, and I know I had my fun elsewhere as well. I can't really blame her. We've been together for a long time. I can't expect that spark we had to stay alive forever. I still thought we had a great relationship going. I'm sure in her heart she suspected me having some affairs, so I can't blame her for having a bit of fun while I was away."

"Aren't you originally from Sicily? I thought people from there were very old fashioned and had little time for women's rights or needs?"

"Time have changed there, too. Anyway, I might originally be from Sicily, but I'm not stupid. Who's paying you now?"

"I can tell you that it's not the Russians, and you're free to believe me or not. As Alexandre told you the other day, stay out of it. Drop the project, retire, do whatever you can. Just get off this boat or it will sink with you in it. Capisci?"

"You're talking about my life and career. Who makes you think that I can simply stop and leave the company without getting into trouble with my employer and their customers? As you just reminded me about Sicily, I'll tell you what used to happen there periodically. Different mafia families would court, and eventually invest in companies that were doing well. They poured dirty money into those companies, which thrived for a while. This always worked until those clans had a power struggle. Guess who paid the consequences? As usual, the normal people and the companies' owners who had wanted to carry on working in peace, and had been forced to accept their investments so the mafia could launder their money. The poor guys running those companies got caught in the middle of their criminal associates' war and got gunned down. To add to their families' injury, after their deaths, the Italian police accused them of being part of the mafia organization themselves. In short, who makes you think that 'jumping off the boat', as you say, would be as simple as just that?"

"I never said it was going to be simple, but we can provide some help with your transition. We know you have enough money, but you might need protection."

"I see. Now, tell me again who this 'Jason' is."

"After I failed to check on you, and your wife convinced you to save your marriage, they thought that your wife would still be angry with you. They thought that she would be keen on revenge. They decided to lure her into a honey trap. Without knowing, your wife has been informing us of your whereabouts and projects for years now. I don't think she knows, but her phone is bugged, and so is that beautiful leather bag you gave her for her birthday two years ago. GPS tracker, microphone transmitter, etc."

"Now I know why they told me in the shop that it was the last one of that model and they would give me a 50% discount. They even took it to the back to give it a special cleaning because it had been in their shop window. God they were good. Honestly, I never thought of it because I never imagined anybody would be interested in listening to what I say."

"It's not us, but your employer, or better, their largest customer, the US government, who is keeping you under surveillance. You are foreign-born, you travel a lot and you speak foreign languages. They just needed to be sure they could trust you. Nothing special."

"Are you also working for them at this moment?"

"Maybe?"

"Enrico Fermi, Albert Einstein and another researcher working here were kept under surveillance, as I am sure they kept their own important US citizens. This is no surprise, but I still have no idea about what happened to me in Italy."

"What happened to you in Italy?"

"I see you won't be much help to me in solving that puzzle."

"I understand now why you were so happy to see me when I walked in."

"Not true. I was just happy to see this beautiful woman coming to kiss me. You understand that to me, right now, you represent more trouble than pleasure. When I met you for the first time, I was under the illusion that you actually liked me as a man. Now I am older, wiser and not ruled by my testicles."

"Or you just know who I am and what my job is. Listen, we weren't in love, but we had a good time and I grew fond of you. That's why I don't want anything bad happening to you. You're still young enough to enjoy the rest of your life, so retire now."

"Thank you, Julie. I appreciate your effort, even if this is just part of your assignment. I need to think about what I'm going to do. Please tell whoever sent you that I'm not happy collaborating in a project that could cause a human catastrophe. Many have talked and written about human self-destruction, but I don't want to be one of the executioners. In theory, I want out, but I need to find a way to disentangle myself from this dirty mess. Also, I now need to find Carmen and talk to her about this good-looking 'Jason' fellow."

He arrived home and walked into a quiet house.

"Where are the children?"

"I organized for them to spend the night with their friends. I think it's better if they don't hear our conversation tonight."

"You're probably right. Who wants to see or hear their parents arguing, right? What happened, Carmen? Who is this 'Jason'?"

"What did Julie tell you about him?"

"Maybe it's better if you start telling me about Jason first. I'm sure Julie only told me part of the story."

"Did she tell you anything about your arrest in Italy?"

"No, she didn't have any idea, and on this count, I think I can trust her. She seemed surprised when I asked her."

"Are you going to see her again?"

"I had no intention of seeing her again, but I can't promise that she won't surprise me at another time. Anyway, stop trying to change the subject. Remember that now I know that she's just a spy and she was never in love with me."

"Yes, and the first time you met her, you didn't remember that you were a married man."

"Tell me, was Jason your act of revenge? How long was it for? Are you still seeing each other? Are you in love with him? What did you two speak about?"

"So she told you about him."

"Carmen, remember that after what happened between me and Julie, you made me go through hell. I have the right to know why you started this relationship with Jason, and what I especially want to know is if this is still on going. Is it? Again, did you fall in love with him?"

"I was mad at you. I also missed your attention. You were travelling a lot for work, and I knew in my heart that you must be having some close contact with other women, being away for all that time. So I decided to have some fun, too."

"Was it just fun? Anything else?"

"Why are you asking me if I fell in love with him? Don't you care that I slept with someone else?"

"Carmen, I still love you, and for me, love is greater than sex. I hate the idea of you having sex with someone else, but far from my eyes means far from my heart and mind. If it was just fun or revenge sex, I don't care. I need to know if I can trust you. Can I trust you? Do you love him?"

"Is this how you see our relationship now? Have you slept with other women just for sex?"

"Don't try to turn this around. Do you love Jason? Can I trust you? What did you tell Jason?"

"I'm sorry. I don't even know anymore. I know that I complained to him about your long absences for work. You were always away on some trip. For a while, I spent more time with him than with you. I also had no idea that he was a spy, nor did I think that your job was important enough that someone would go to such lengths to know what you were doing. How could I have known?"

"Neither did I, until I was arrested in Rome. Did you ever leave Jason alone in this house?"

"Maybe a couple of times."

"Great, so the whole house is probably bugged. When was the last time you saw Jason? How long ago?"

"Maybe a month. The last time I saw him was before you left for Rome."

"Listen, Carmen, I think you need to clear your head. Is Jason really, what you want? You need some time. I have a lot on my plate right now, and I need time to think on my own. I don't yet know if I can trust you, as I see you aren't even sure yourself, yet. Think about your future, and if you want to spend more of your life with me, or not. I'll go to a hotel and I'll get in touch at some point. I need some time and I need some space. Tell the kids I'm away on another business trip. I think they cope with it better than you do."

"Where are you going? Don't be stupid, you need help right now."

"Thank you, but I'd prefer to be alone right now. Thanks to you, this house is bugged now. I'll call you later, and when I get arrested or killed, your decision might be easier."

"They didn't bug the house to listen to me. It's your job's fault."

Enzo slummed the door and walked out of the house. He walked a couple of blocks down the street, when he heard a car slowing down behind him. Then it suddenly stopped. The window of the car slowly rolled down.

"Hello sir, do you need a ride somewhere? Maybe to a hotel?"

Enzo looked at the car to figure out if it was a taxi. It was not.

"I'm fine, thank you. I'll call a taxi soon."

A man got out of the back of the car, stopped in front of him, then stretched out his arm, pointing to the empty front passenger seat. It looked like an offer he would not be able to refuse. He looked back at the man, who opened his jacket slightly to show part of a gun concealed under his belt.

"I usually call the taxi myself, but I guess you're a new type of service."

Enzo got in, understanding that the second, harder convincing phase had started. Julie had warned him. Then, from the back he heard a known voice, "How are you doing, Enzo? Are you still working on crazy ideas?"

"James, or better, Mr. John Austin. What the hell are you doing here? Why did you need to kidnap me? You know I would have willingly come to see you!"

"Sorry Enzo, I'm afraid I'm only a small cog here, and it wasn't me who decided how to pick you up. Anyway, I'm glad to see you again."

"Who are you working for Mr. Austin? By the way, do you mind if I carry on calling you 'James'?"

"No problem at all. I had gotten used to being called James. Believe me, I've been called worse things."

"I can imagine. Do you mean 'Jack', for example? How on earth did you end up in Denmark working with Francesco? And who's sending you now?"

"I'm just a private security contractor."

"The new foreign legion, right?"

"Come on man, we haven't seen each other for a while and you want to offend me already? Do you think I'm picking you up to answer your questions? Or maybe we want something from you. What do you think?"

"It seems you caused me loads of troubles already by inappropriately using some of my ideas. So if you're looking for new ideas, try Francesco."

"So I guess you haven't heard."

"What?"

"Francesco was found dead in a Sicilian holiday home not far from the beach. I'm sorry, I know your friendship went a long way back."

They stayed silent for a little while.

"Listen, about your ideas, as you always said and Francesco used to repeat, ideas have a life of their own. Once out of your mind and mouth, they're free to be snapped up. Call me snapper if you want. Add that to my list."

"James it's great to see you, as I had no idea you would make it back alive. Tell me, what's the reason behind this encounter?"

"As you just said to your wife, you need time to be alone and think for a bit. We're taking you to a hotel, and tomorrow I'll meet you there at nine for breakfast. Your colleagues and managers have been informed of your early meeting with some government officials. Don't worry, everything is covered. Please don't do anything stupid, as there's little that I'll be able to do to save your ass. This time, you are in big trouble. I'll tell you more tomorrow. This is the hotel. Please don't drink too much, as we have a long day ahead of us tomorrow. Bye, Enzo."

Enzo entered the lobby and mentioned his name at the reception, where they did not even ask for his check-out date. He did not even have to show a document. He knew he was now definitely in big brother's hands. He went to sleep, now knowing that the US government had kept him under their control, and had probably stopped him in Italy for whatever reason. After he had finished his dinner, he looked outside, and thought to himself that this cell looked much better than the one in Sicily. Outside his room on the fifth floor, he could see many trees in the parking lot, not just one. His mind was far away when someone knocked on the door. He guessed someone had come to pick up the dirty dishes, so he slowly went to open the door, where he was stunned. Abebi was there, smiling at him.

"Come in. How did you find me?"

"James called me and told me you would be here."

"How the hell did you meet James?"

"I am really sorry and I hope I didn't cause you any troubles?"

"I don't know yet. I am already in all sorts of troubles. Just tell me, how did you meet James?"

"Shortly after we arrived in the US our small friend kept his promise and let us go free once we were in the harbour. We didn't know where we were at first. Then we found out we had arrived in Savannah a port town in Georgia.

From there we caught a ride to Charleston with a truck driver. We were exhausted, so I fall asleep. The driver was kind enough to let Zauna have a nap on his cabin bed. I was awakened by Zauna screaming. The driver was trying to get friendly with her. She kicked him and he shot her leg. I got scared and hit him on his head with the fire extinguisher. We ran out of the truck and started running through fields. We reached a small town where it was clear we were not from there. Zauna was still bleeding. We went into a church and someone there started to take care of us. Then a police car arrived. I explained what had happened. They drove us back to the truck, where the police found out that the driver had been taken to the hospital as I had hurt him badly. They searched the truck and found the stupid driver's smart phone still recording a video of the empty cabin bed. They could rewind it and saw that we had told the truth. They took us back to the police station where they registered us as illegal immigrants from Africa. They questioned us non-stop. One of the questions were if we knew anybody living in the USA as this might help us staying here. Under pressure, we gave them your name as we knew nobody else in this country."

"I see."

"Can I sleep here tonight?"

Enzo took her arm and nudged her out of the door while he followed her out. He closed the door behind him. Then lowering his voice as much as he could, "Listen Abebi I am in some kind of troubles. There are microphones and cameras hidden in the room. This is the reason James brought you here. We will need to behave and keep for yourself anything you don't want to share with the police. Understood?"

"Sure, but I don't have anywhere to go."

"I said you can stay, but behave."

They walked back in and turned on the television loud enough not to feel observed. Then Enzo took paper and pen from the desk and started to write something on it. Abebi tried to read, but she couldn't as Enzo was curved over it, making sure no hidden camera could see what he wrote.

"So tell me Abebi back in your country, had you learned any skills that you could use here to find a job? Can you cook?"

"I worked as a part time florist. Yes, I can cook. I can also use a computer."

"Depending on what James tells me tomorrow, maybe we could find a job for you."

"What about my illegal status?"

"Yes, we would need to see what your best options are. I will try to help you if I can. Some time ago, someone also helped me. This is my turn."

"Are you not a self-made man?"

"That to me sounds more like masturbation. There are no self-made men. Everybody needed another to climb the ladder. In some countries there is no ladder to be climbed, just a wall dividing and protecting the haves from the have nots. In better organized countries, there is a ladder that can be climbed. That social ladder is the infrastructure kept alive by thousands of people guarding the border, policing society, making sure water, electricity and data cable reach our homes and places of work. Some people are just arrogant and mostly ignorant of the fact that their success was only possible because of all those people working hard to keep the infrastructure in place. I guess you got a much longer answer than you had expected. Don't get me started or I'll bore you to death."

"You are not boring me. I find this interesting and I am very sorry I cannot thank you for your lesson."

Abebi smiled in a provoking way, while Enzo looked at the ceiling trying to remind her of the situation.

"So tell me Abebi, why did you leave Nigeria? Looking for a better future or what is the reason?"

"Our families Zauna and mine were invited to a big wedding north of Lagos. We wanted to travel together and were in the car with Zauna's half-brother, Godfrey. Our parents and other relatives shared a bus ride. The party was great, but when we travelled back, we got back much quicker with Godfrey's car and waited a long time for the bus with our relatives to arrive. It never did. It was dark and maybe the driver had been a bit drunk. We don't know. The bus hit a lorry carrying petrol and caught fire. There was an explosion and nobody survived. Zauna and I lost our families and anybody that could economically support us. We suddenly were alone and needed to earn our own living."

"Sorry, I didn't want to upset you by reminding you of the past."

"It's my destiny. Maybe because I had to meet you."

"Abebi you are a young, good-looking woman. I am middle-aged man who is married with two children and currently in big troubles."

"Is your wife American?"

"No she is originally from Santo Domingo the Dominican Republic in the Caribbean."

"I am hungry. Can we go to the hotel restaurant or do we need to stay in this room all the time?"

"No you are right. We can go to the restaurant downstairs."

They took the lift. They were alone, Abebi went close to Enzo took his hand lifted it to her breast to remind him of their first encounter. "There are no cameras here," she whispered in his ear. They kissed until the lift told them that they had arrived downstairs. She exited first and walked slightly ahead as she knew where she was going or so she looked. Enzo saw her entering a side room from where she quickly exited to pull him in. It was the ladies restroom outside the hotel restaurant. She pulled him all the way into one of the partitions and they kissed with passion. Enzo could not resist her and let himself go. They were making love when they had to freeze as a woman entered the cubicle next to them. Once they were alone again, they carried on passionately. Eventually satisfied they walked into the restaurant having gained an appetite.

"You certainly know what you want and how to get it."

"I am young, but the last year I've learned a lot. First of all, life is too short and I should make the most of it. I won't measure my life in the amount of years I live, but how. Quality for me is better than quantity."

"Yes, live life like every day is your last, but then you get old and boring like me. Especially if you have children and are responsible for them."

"Maybe that time will come for me, but I am not there yet. You see many men have used me in the last months. Now I learned how to use them."

"It certainly worked with me."

"I know, just practising."

They had a good evening together and went back to the room each to their own bed. Enzo could not wait to see James and hear what was expected of him. For the time being Abebi's treatment had relaxed his nerves. The morning arrived and they went down to have breakfast. Not long past, James arrived.

"Good morning. Did you both have a good night sleep? I guess not. I know Enzo always had a weakness for the dark ladies. And this one is very pretty as well. Abebi, in the lobby you will find a young blond man from immigration that will need to ask you some questions. Don't worry he won't take you anywhere. Enzo and I will need some privacy."

"I understand. See you later."

"Now I think it is better if you tell me why you think I am here?"

"I don't want to offend you, but until now you have not shown me any budge or official document, so you could be a spy. Why should I tell you anything? Who are you working for, at this moment?"

"You have a point. I am working for an agency that cooperates with the US army."

"I see you are a kind of Guantanamo bay. You do the dirty work that the US government does not want to be seen doing. Right?"

"If you want to see it that way. It's alright. Someone needs to do this and it's not a bad job."

"Well, it's still your choice. I am still puzzled about the interest people have in me, a middle of the way scientist. You make me feel far more important than I am. I am honoured and annoyed at the same time."

"You know that you have been working on and off on some project with military interests. The latest project you were involved in, had something to do with mini drones. I believe this has awakened the interest of the US military, but also from many other governments. It has become a race and you are one of their stallions. And by the way that is not what Abebi told me."

"Would you like to have someone poking around in your private life?"

"Enzo, you know that you are a key scientist and with foreign roots. We need to be sure you stay on the straight and narrow."

"Why was I arrested in Italy? Actually why were we arrested in Italy?"

"Believe me it wasn't us. In Europe, some countries no longer trust us and they prefer to work alone. They are worried about what we are doing, so we now worry about what they are up to."

"Are you saying that the Italian government in a complot with other European countries decided to kidnap me to squeeze important information out of me?"

"They mostly wanted confirmation about what they feared. Also they wanted to show that they can strike out without our or NATO help."

"They were playing with fire and by doing so sacrificed the life of poor inspector Cammarata. He only had a couple of years left before retiring. His daughter Rosanna will get married next month and her father will no longer walk her down the aisle."

"I liked inspector Cammarata. I am sorry to hear he died. Any more macabre news you want to share with me?"

"No, no more thanks god. Just a good one. We tracked down the guy that drove you to Mazara del Vallo, I think he was called Carlo right?"

"What did you do to him?"

"Nothing, he is working with us. His escort agency is now going global. Anyway, listen you will need to keep on working on the various projects you are working on right now. Not share any of the information with anybody. Some foreign agencies will try to stop you or even poach you. Be aware that should you jump the line or stop working, you will be in trouble. Most likely, you will be accused of treason. I am the nice guy they decided to send to tell you that. Toe the line and you will be fine."

"So you have just been sent to tell me to carry on working as usual?"

"Practically yes. As I said I am the nice face of the US government. Believe me, this is one of the most pleasant jobs I had to do."

"Recently I have been thinking about retiring. What would be wrong with that?"

"I am afraid this will not be seen as a valid option. Again this would be treason as you would abandon your country when it most needs you. Would you not call this betrayal?"

"Are you not slightly exaggerating?"

"Listen to me. Some politicians are worried and think that the entire nuclear arsenal that has worked as a deterrent will soon be obsolete. What's the point of having thousands of nuclear missiles when an army of tiny creatures that are able to move across borders undetected will soon be our nightmare?"

"Did they tell you what they are trying to achieve? You seem to know more than some of my colleagues actually working on the various projects."

"I have been doing this job for a while and I learned to connect the dots. You know those highly specialised folks they just know their area of expertise and some never bother to look over the edge. You are a clever man; you must have known what their final aim was."

"Maybe I did, but pretended to look away. Nobody likes to work on building the next guillotine, but someone always will. Listen I feel the pressure and would rather get out, before I get hurt."

"I am sorry you feel that way. What should we do with Abebi?"

"Why are you bringing Abebi into this?"

"They say that you already shared some secrets with some foreign countries. In Italy while in captivity and with Julie during your love affair. Now they say that you could be charged for smuggling illegal immigrants into this country. That's heavy stuff that would allow them to lock you up for a long time. Think of your family as well. You have two children and certainly, you don't want to spoil their future. They are not asking you for much just carry on as usual and keep your mouth shut outside of your company. Especially with your wife that likes to share your secrets with other men."

"Men or just a single man?"

"Maybe just that Jason. I admit that even as a man I can see why women fall for him. I guess this is why he is always assigned to ladies jobs. I have to deal with the men. We know that Abebi and Julie, were not the only ladies you got to know closer after you got married. Believe me that your whole past would be part of the investigation and Carmen will not like that a bit. Again, it's very easy to just carry on as usual. We are not asking you to do anything else that you would not have done before. We know you have been contacted by some people and will be contacted even more in the future. We are keeping an eye on you, but also protecting you. Just stay clean. Avoid leaving the country. Maybe you can still go to visit your wife's family, but no further than that. We need to know you are safe."

"And under surveillance right?"

"Yes! This is for your own protection."

"Can you help Abebi and Zauna settle down?"

"Depends how nice they are to us."

"Well, I cannot influence that."

"No worries I was joking and I wanted to see if Abebi had broken your heart."

"She is a great girl and I think she genuinely likes me. She is half my age and has a great young body. But that's all."

"Do you care about her and her future?"

"You know I care about people, most likely more than you."

"People like Joshua?"

"I see, you have done a good job. Yes, Abebi, Zauna and others I met in my life."

"You are a good man and US citizen remember that. I hope you will keep it that way. I know you had a situation with Carmen and told her that you need some time away. This room is yours until next Sunday if you want. After that, do me a favour and move back home, so that I can tell my superior that all is fine and you have returned to your normal life."

"I am not really free to do as I please it seems."

"Nobody is my friend. Nobody is. I am sure better times will come, but until the next thing comes on their agenda this is what they are all concentrating their attention on right now. Listen I have to go to speak to the immigration guys about Abebi. What do you know about her?"

"Not much apart from what she herself told me. She was unlucky, but I am sure if given the chance she will make a good new US citizen one day."

"As you know there are plenty of poor people in this country and they never got a chance."

"They never crossed my path."

"I see what I can do for her. Let's see maybe she is a good runner. When are the next Olympic Games? It was nice seeing you again. Keep developing new technologies for this great country big head. Together we will keep on top of things."

"Is there any way I could contact you if I need?"

"Here my email and phone number, but avoid calling me. Keep clear of troubles. Abebi will soon be back. See you around big head."

Enzo felt relieved to know that he had not been yet charged of any wrong doing and could carry on his life as usual. First some of his ideas had been misused now he knew to be working on an evil project. Would his country misuse the new technologies he was helping to create? Would he feel responsible? He knew that he was not the kind of person to be able to look the other way and pretend it was not his responsibility. He was just a small cog in a huge machine. Maybe a vital cog without which things might not have developed. Would other countries not be even more irresponsible with this new technology? He felt the weight of the world on his shoulders and needed a heavy drink to draw those thoughts. He remembered his youth days dreaming of inventions carrying his name. Now he was known for a weight lost solution, the ED bomb and forced gender change operations. Not a great record and now he was about to add participating in the creation of killer insects. "One more drink please." A few drinks relaxed Enzo, until a hand touched his back gently.

"Are we ok with James?"

"As I told you I am in trouble and it's probably better if you don't know much about my problems. Believe me it would not help you nor me. I am trying to be polite, but stay out of it."

"Sorry I won't ask again."

"What did they want from you?"

"They asked me about you. I only told them about our romantic encounters."

"Why did you do that? Why should they care?"

"Not true, they asked me about many details."

"Perverts. Anyway did they say anything about you being able to stay here?"

"They said it depends on how you will behave in the next months."

"I see. Listen Abebi; they told me that I should go back home with my wife soon. I will stay here for a couple more days and you can stay with me. I need to make a call to see if you can stay with George a nice colleague of mine that got recently divorced and hates living alone. Maybe he could put you up for a while."

"Thank you. I hope he is a good guy."

"George is a good guy. I will talk to him later. Now let's see if they have a swimming pool or hot tub in this place."

"What's a hot tub?"

"In this case I really hope they do have one."

"I have no swimsuit with me."

"Take this money and cross the road. There is a shop that should have something for you."

"You don't want to come and help me choose one?"

"Abebi this is my golden cage. If I get out of here they expect me to go back home or to work."

"OK. Will you be in your room?"

"Yes, don't worry."

Enzo walked back to his room scratching his head. Should he now go back home and tell Carmen everything preventing James from using what he knew to blackmail him? Or would that cause Carmen to walk out on him and take the kids away? Coming clean with Carmen seemed the better option, but how could he help Abebi after having told Carmen he slept with her? He picked up the phone.

"Hi George, how are you doing? Listen I wonder if you're still living alone. Are you? Ok, good that's great. No sorry, I am really sorry your wife has not come back. Sorry, I didn't mean it that way. Please let me explain. I know a girl that needs a place to stay for a while and you told me that you hated being alone in your big house. No she is not American. I am sure she is clean. What about on Thursday after work? Great, I will be there. Sorry again. See you then."

Abebi came back and went straight to the bathroom from where she came out wearing her new swimwear. Enzo turned around and could not hide feeling very attracted by what he was seeing. Abebi smiled pleased. Enzo forgot his precautions and walked to her like a moth to a flame.

"I thought you wanted to show me the hot tub?"

"It can wait!"

Later they made it to the hot tub and later still they went to the restaurant to have dinner together. Abebi excused herself and walked to the restroom. On the way there she noticed a young man walking in and looking nervously around, but she was on a mission and so carried on walking anyway. Enzo was contemplating the bottle of Chilean red wine that reminded him of the time he had visited that country. He took the bottle to read the label when suddenly heard a loud noise and a gun being fired. Only when he turned around he realized that he had been the prime cause of that commotion. On the way back from the restroom, Abebi spotted again that nervous young man, but this time he seemed to be extracting a firearm from his jacket while walking towards Enzo. She had managed to hit that man with a chair, but this caused the man to turn towards her and shoot her in right arm. Now she was on the floor losing blood, while that young man was being kept on the ground by some hotel security personnel. Enzo turned to Abebi trying to stop her bleeding and holding her in his arms. Most of the other guests and personnel had run out, but few were taking pictures or filming. One of them asked, "Why did he try to shoot you? Do you know him?"

"No, no, I don't know him, call an ambulance. "

The ambulance arrived, while some agents were taking that young man away. Enzo kept looking at him, but could not remember ever seeing him before. He now knew there were to be in bigger troubles. Some wanted to kill him and they knew where he was. The police asked him to stay at the bar. Shortly after James arrived.

"Well, honestly I didn't think I would see you so soon again. Did you recognize that guy that tried to kill you?"

"I have never seen him before. I seriously hope you will find this out."

"We will try, but let me know if you remember something. That girl turned out to be your black angel?"

"Definitely a black angel. She certainly stopped me from becoming a white one."

"That worked out well for all of us."

"How?"

"She saved your life so you will forever be indebted to her and even more willing to help her now. We can easily throw her out of the country if you won't play ball. In short we got you by the balls."

"I see."

James left and Abebi was taken to the hospital surrounded by local journalists praising her for saving Enzo's life. Not long past and his mobile phone rang. Carmen had seen the news that her husband had nearly been killed in a hotel bar.

"Now I know where you are hiding. Are you ok? The news said you were nearly shot. I know you needed time, but after this, I needed to see you."

"I understand and it would be great to see you. I would have come home tomorrow anyway. Come here. I am waiting for you."

Carmen arrived and she hugged him still at the bar.

"I am glad you're alive. At first I wondered, who is that lady who saved your life? Then I realized that to me it was more important to know that you were alive no matter what will happen between us."

"Thank you a lot for that. Carmen, what we have is something special and I don't care if you were massaged by someone else. I haven't always been faithful myself, so I am not the one who can judge you. I was hurt for you betraying my trust and easily falling prey of a spy. I need a life partner that can trust. Can I?"

"Who is she?"

Enzo had been waiting for that question and had considered how to answer it. If he told Carmen the truth he would destroy their relationship or lie, and hope she wouldn't find out for a while.

"She is a colleague I am working with at the moment."

Carmen had wondered how she was going to react to his answer. Should she call his lie and start a fight that would end up with separation and divorce or let it slip through until the kids were older or even out of the house?

"A very loyal colleague if she is prepared to take a bullet for you."

"Yes you can say that aloud. We are all very dedicated to our job in our company."

They looked in each other's eyes silently agreeing to accept each other's lies for a bit of quiet family life. Enzo raised his glass moved it towards Carmen. Carmen did the same and they toasted to a calmer future.

"Listen Carmen, I will sort things out with the police here and I will be back home later."

"Why did the guy try to kill you?"

"I have no idea and I hope the police will find this out. They caught the guy and I am sure they are interrogating him right now."

"Do you have any idea about his motive?"

"At this point, I can only imagine that he was trying to avenge someone who was killed with one of the new weapons developed with my help. But I am not sure yet."

"Are you now proud of having taken part in developing some weapon?"

"What do I always say, ideas have a life of their own. All the projects I have been working on, were never originally meant to create new weapons. At least not to my knowledge."

"Are you telling me that you don't know what you are actually doing?"

"More or less. Nowadays it's very complicated and difficult to explain. Imagine a tank being built by sourcing each component from a different factory. The people in each of these factories have no idea that they are actually producing a tank. In the same way, I am working on modules or part of a large project whose final aim we often don't know."

"So why was he trying to kill you if a whole team was building something?"

"That's a good point. Well, maybe this is due to the fact that I have been the team leader on several projects and I have been speaking publicly about some of those. Like the one I was invited to at the conference in Italy before they arrested me."

"Isn't it time you stopped working for this company? You don't even know what you are doing anymore."

"I have tried and I was told that in doing so, I would put myself and my family in danger."

"Are they blackmailing you?"

"Yes. They need my help and want me to prove my loyalty to my country in a moment of need. Well, that's what I was told. They told me to carry on as usual."

"Do you want me to stay here?"

"No, go home now and make sure the kids are alright. I will come home tomorrow."

They hugged as good friends do, then she left. Shortly afterwards, a man walked straight to him and introduced himself.

"Hi I am inspector Kobalsky and I am working on your case. You had a lucky escape today. You have a black angel."

"How is she doing?"

"She is fine and will soon be out of the hospital. Maybe in a couple of days. She said you will pay her medical bill. Nothing comes for free not even angels."

"That's fine, but tell me about the man."

"I was actually going to ask you first. Had you ever seen that man before?"

"No, I have no idea who he is."

"Mr. Dangelo, have you invested in a company called Blowout? Or better are you a partner in that company?"

"Yes, I am. I liked their new idea and joined those guys to make it happen."

"Can you please explain to me what services or products does Blowout provide?"

"Different products, but the first one they pitched to me was a way to extinguish fire."

"Interesting. How does it work?"

"They are two young clever guys who got upset by seeing forests burning. They wanted to find a way to quickly extinguish large wood fires. They created some special chemical bomb which explosions quickly sucks the oxygen out of the air towards the explosion removing it from the surrounding area, so depriving the fire of the oxygen it needs to burn. It is even cleverer because H_2O or water is the result of the implosion. This also falls on the burning forest. You see that I could not resist, but had to help those guys turn their brilliant idea into reality."

"Any more ventures you helped them with?"

"They had another brilliant idea to fight flooding. They invented a powder that when thrown on water, turns quickly into a kind of hard gelatine or silicon. So if applied to the hedge of the flooding, the water contour turns into a strong gelatinous wall made of the water itself and blocks more water coming down."

"They seem clever guys, but those are not the details I was looking for. Going back to their fire extinguisher implosion -- What is the impact on any living creatures that are near that implosion?"

"Yes this was the down side. The quick lack of oxygen does kill those living creatures nearby, but note that the fire would have killed any creatures nearby anyway. At least we can now stop a fire quickly, safe the forest and any creatures where the fire has not yet arrived thanks to this invention."

"Sure this is good. But are you aware that your young brilliant partners also sold the product to a company called Future arms?"

"No I did not know that. Anyway what has this got to do with that guy trying to kill me?"

"Future Arms commercialised a new weapon using the same concept, but focusing on its destructive potential. The explosion and consequent implosion leaves any leaving creature around, including humans without oxygen; so these die suffocating. By the way I had to laugh when I find out how he linked you to that bomb."

"How?"

"Guess what they named the bomb?"

"You must be joking?"

"Those brilliant young guys probably were. The oxygen sucking bomb is called the Dangelo 1."

"Bastards!"

"The man we arrested is from the Caucasus region and we still need to confirm his real name. It seems that some member belonging to his same organization were killed in the mountains in the Caucasus. One of those killed was his younger brother. It seems that you didn't know that new weapon had your name on it. Are you going to sue them? Or is there a reason why they did that?"

"Mr. Kobalsky, do I really need to answer this question?"

"Well, I was told to expect full collaboration from a new US citizen keen to show and prove his loyalty. Not to talk about his attempt to smuggle a Nigerian girl or two into this country. Were they right to say so?"

"I see. I helped those guys by funding some of their great ideas aimed at helping the environment. One day they came up with an idea about miniature drones flying at high altitude. I was aware of several projects using mini drones developed by the company I mostly work for. To avoid a possible conflict of interest, I had to turn down investing in their miniature drones. I guess this is why they might have decided to compromise my name. At first I had said I would help them, then I found out about my main employer investing in that area and I decided to withdraw my financial support. I think for a while they were in financial trouble and almost went bust. They called me several times for help, but I told them to find some other backers."

"A private Russian investor provided the missing funds. To understand the issue I called your young partners who confessed that after being dropped by you. To save their company and livelihood, they accepted the collaboration of a new investor without checking first their environmental or pacifism credentials. They sounded disappointed and a bit resigned like you."

"So we are all victims?"

"That is what I am trying to find out here. Peter and John, your brilliant young pacifist friends with their new miniature drones idea, have now disabled or better said dented this country's main military muscle."

"How?"

"Please tell me what you know about their mini drone's project."

"As I said I didn't participate in that venture!"

"Don't take it the wrong way, but we will decide if this is the case."

"I only know that they wanted to fly those miniature drones very high in the sky to measure the atmosphere methane and other gasses content. They mostly needed funding to test different options to recharge those tiny machines batteries in flight using solar cells, methane captured up there or just by using gravity by letting themselves fall down from time to time. I knew this part would take a long time and I told them that I was not sure they would ever make money from this."

"They are brilliant young entrepreneurs and they managed to create self-recharging miniature drones."

"I am happy to hear they succeeded, but tell me how they now pose a threat to this country's military might?"

"Please wait a second. I need a drink."

"Good idea. Two beers then?"

"I am working, so a coke would do for me."

"Sorry, could you bring two cokes please? Thank you."

"Again, how have they put this country in danger?"

"Those autonomous mini drones can remain in the air for a very long time. It seems that some of our military planes have been downed by those drones. We were not sure at first, but now we know that some Russian, Chinese and British planes have suffered the same fate."

"How?"

"It seems those miniature drones are very cheap to produce on a larger scale. They are made of a kind of hard material similar to ceramic that can perforate metal and glass."

"How, by landing on it?"

"As I said, these are made of hard material and carry a small amount of explosives on them. They fly in swarms and build an almost invisible wall or net in the sky. Any aeroplane hitting at high speed, that invisible wall is perforated by several of those mini drones damaging the electronics of the plane or even killing the pilot. It seems that several countries are very interested in buying or manufacturing those miniature drones. In time, this could render military aviation almost useless."

"Interesting story, but I swear to you that I am not nor I was ever involved with their drones project even if they called it Enzo 2."

Mr. Kobalsky laughed aloud and stretched to grab his coke.

"I don't know what they called their mini drones. I think we are done for the moment and now I have loads to write down. Please keep our conversation to yourself and as promised, please move back home soon."

"I will move back home tomorrow. Do I need to worry about protecting me and my family or is my dear country looking over me?"

"Don't worry, you will be under observation for a while, but make sure you stay in public places where everybody can see you."

"Thank you and have a good evening."

It was now time for Enzo to find out how his black angel was doing. Once he was back in his room, he called the hospital where she had been taken. The nurse put him through.

"How are you? How are you feeling?"

"I am fine and I am glad you finally called."

"Where were you shot?"

"Don't worry my breasts are fine. They pulled the bullet out of my left upper arm. They said I was lucky, but I might suffer some pains in my old age."

"You were lucky and so was I. I am very sorry and I feel very guilty. I am also glad your breasts are still fine."

"It's not your fault and if I had to die for someone, let it be for a person that was good to me."

"Abebi, my wife saw what happened on the news and came to see me. I told her you are a work colleague. Bare that in mind should you ever meet her. I was told by the police to return home. Tomorrow, I will be back home. Do you know how long they will keep you there?"

"They say another couple of days."

"I will organize a place for you to stay, while you get better. Take my number and call me once you know they are releasing you from there."

"Are they going to deport me?"

"I think for the moment you are safe and my responsibility."

"Who is going to pay for the hospital bill? They already asked me here."

"Of course I will. This is the least I can do."

"Who is trying to kill you?"

"Someone that does not like me."

"No really, don't joke. I am not in the mood."

"He was trying to avenge his brother and some friends that have been killed by a bomb named after me."

"I knew you looked clever and dangerous. That's what many women like in a man."

"Maybe, but I am not proud of it. All my life I have been trying to improve our planet, but it seems that whatever I do turns into a nasty tool of destruction."

"It's not your fault if people use your ideas for other means or twist your words to their advantage. You see, when a mother gives birth, what comes out of her is a new independent life."

"They gave the bomb my last name."

"I must admit, that doesn't look great. Are you called Kalashnikov?"

"Very funny. Get well soon! I will be in touch, but let me know if they let you out."

"I think they won't let me out until I pay their bill. Thank you for calling. I would give you a big hug."

It was time to throw himself on the bed, stare at the ceiling and think what to do next. The morning arrived quickly and it was still dark when he got back home. He made it look like the usual business trip away from home. He put the suitcase back upstairs and had small presents for the kids that were ready to go to school. Carmen looked pleased to see him back home, but unsure of what would happen next. When asked by Carmen, he told her the reason of his attempted killing as the police had told him.

"Are we all in danger now Mr. Dangelo 1? Will someone else not try to finish the job now? Ah, by the way my cousin Manuel has now thrown Joshua out of his flat. Maybe you should call Joshua."

"The one that tried to kill me seems to have been a lone wolf. He was trying to avenge his brother. I was surprised how fast the police was there at the hotel. They must have been there already. What happened in Santo Domingo?"

"Well, it seems that Joshua brought a girl home and Manuel made a surprise visit."

"Where is Joshua now?"

"He has moved to the accommodations you found for him. I thought Joshua was gay?"

"I think he was just confused and loving Manuel's affections."

"Have you ever been confused? Did Joshua confuse you as well?"

"Come on Carmen. I have never been confused, but I know that plenty of people have been. Were you ever confused in your younger years?"

"Are you saying that I am old now?"

"I certainly did not. Are you cross with me?"

"I am not cross just annoyed that while you seem to find time for other people, I am left alone dealing with our children. Our children I said not just mine."

"I am sorry. Can I now do something to help?"

"It's probably better you stay away from them or they will also be in danger."

"That is not my fault."

"It never is."

She walked away and slammed the door behind her. Enzo was annoyed, but knew that she was partly right. He had spent long hours at work and many weeks away. He had worked hard and was economically in a good position to slow down and spend more time with his family. He could stop, but he was now forced to carry on. He needed to find a way out.

A couple of days passed and all seemed to be going back to the good old times. Then Abebi called and Carmen pretended not to be bothered by it. Enzo pretended not to notice her reaction either. She always liked to bite her lips while chopping vegetables. It was clear that tension at home was building up. The black angel had saved his life, but upset Carmen. Nevertheless, he felt obliged to help her even more and was prepared to strain his relationship with Carmen. He drove to the hospital to pick up Abebi settle the bill and took her to George. George looked pleasantly surprised by her good look.

"Thank you George for doing this. I need to tell you that Abebi arrived to this country illegally, but the authorities now know about her presence and are checking if she will be able to stay or not. This should take some weeks. Of course, I will keep you informed. She has enough money to pay for herself."

George seemed reassured enough and at first sight happy to have some company. They hugged with Abebi before he left her there. She was pleased to be out of the hospital and into what looked a welcoming home. Now it was time for Enzo to go back home and reassure his wife. He felt a small weight off his shoulders and managed to look around long enough to notice that a car was following him. To be sure, it was not just his paranoia, he stopped to fill up and the stalker stopped to fill up as well. Was he paranoid or was he being followed. He thought that the way to find out would be to stop at the next petrol station on the way.

"Hi Carmen, it's me. Are you ok? Listen I might be paranoid, but I think someone is following my car. No, no need for that. I am sure both our mobile phones and landline are tapped. So I think that I am not just talking to you right now. Anyway I might be wrong, but you never know. I am on my way back and should be home in twenty minutes. No problem... I will see you later when you are back from school. Say "Hi" to the kids. No, I won't forget to order their new phone headsets. Bye now."

The next petrol station was only a few blocks down the road. Enzo parked and pretended to buy something in the shop inside. The stalker car was gone. He had just been paranoid. He started the car and got the car back on the road, then turned the radio on. The music was good and his mind started to think of an escape plan on how to get out of the mess he was in. Then suddenly something cold touched his neck.

"Do as I tell you and you will be fine. Turn on the second right."

Enzo turned right, then right again and then left. He wasn't surprised of what was happening, but very curious to know who his kidnappers were.

"Where are we going and what do you want from me?"

"Someone wants to speak to you. We are driving to him and he will explain."

After some driving, they arrived at a three storey underground car park probably to guarantee bad reception. In there they asked Enzo to enter the back of the van after having forced him to totally undress. The van had two young men in it who gave him a bathrobe and without saying a word pointed to a chair. He sat down and realized they wouldn't be able to answer any questions. Some more driving, then he could feel the van driving down again. Eventually they got him into a lift and directly into a spa and a steamy room where two other men were sitting.

"Hello gentlemen, I hope you will explain to me why I was invited to this strange party?"

"Mr. Dangelo, like many these days we are interested in your advanced research. We are aware you have been put under pressure and believe me at the moment you're one of many scientists feeling that same pressure. You see, it seems that we have entered now a post nuclear age. Large weaponry are on the out and a mini or micro army of semi intelligent devices will decide who will be in charge of our future."

"Sorry for being direct, but who do you represent?"

"We represent concerned Europeans that are worried about some of your company projects you are working on".

"I thought the US and the EU were working together."

"We are partners in crime and defence, but I am sure you are well aware like anybody else that the US is spying on us. We just return the favour, or trust."

"The changes that are currently occurring are a game changer. We want to be sure we won't miss out. As the US is suggesting we need to reduce our defence dependence."

"It seems you are both up to speed on our development. You probably already know more than I do. Why am I here? I am just an employee and a very small cog in a very large machine."

"Because of your social engagement. We are aware that you won't be prepared to just follow orders without thinking of the consequences."

Mr. Dangelo, I am from Germany were many people are law abiding and have learned to trust their government. In good times this is great, but if you know our history, when a bad government was voted in, German citizens carried on abiding racial discrimination laws just because their government asked them to do so. We know Italians only respect laws that make sense to them and from experience they are used to distrusting their government."

"You are forgetting that I am a US citizen now."

"We are well aware of that, but we are also aware of the fact that as an older Sicilian you have strong principals. Stronger than any citizenship you may be holding. We are not here to corrupt you or to turn you into a spy. We are here asking you to carry on your work as usual. We are only asking you to inform us if things fall into the wrong hands."

"You're asking me to spy on my country?"

"You see, it's a question of choice of words. What you are now labelling as spying, we would call acting responsibly and consciously."

"Okay, then spying for a good cause like Geoff Snowden. Right?"

The man in red, "Again, this is your choice of words. Anyway, we are well aware that you and your colleagues are under intense observation, so we will no longer get in touch with you. If you have something you need to share with us, go to the Italian consulate pretending to need some documentation from your relatives in Sicily and ask for Signor Salvatore Mondiale."

"Wow, that's a good choice of anonymous name."

"Too obvious to be true," replayed the man in blue.

"What if I refuse to collaborate? After all, why should I trust you Europeans who I am sure got me arrested in Rome? In the US, I am a free man."

"We can make sure you are arrested in the US if required. Mr. Dangelo, you know better than I do how easy it is to incriminate someone from Sicily who has plenty of dodgy friends. Not to talk of the fact that you are already accused of smuggling illegal immigrants."

"Are you blackmailing me?"

"Another unfortunate use of words. We would call it a collaboration for the building of a safer world. We need you as much as you need us. We are in it together. Remember that we are all on this beautiful blue planet. The unique place in which our children will have to share their future. This is if this space will remain inhabitable. Mr. Dangelo, we want to just appeal to your conscience."

"I agree with most of what you said, but to fully trust you, I need to know why I was arrested in Italy and what I am going to tell those people who currently observe every movement of mine. They will certainly want to know where I am now."

"We needed to find out to what extent you were involved and how much you really knew. Too many sensitive research projects carried your name. Interrogating you cost inspector Cammarata his life."

"I am very sorry about that. I thought he was a good man who was looking forward to his retirement."

"He served his country well. For many of us, personal gain alone is not what drives us. I hope you still think this way. Some people only care about themselves. Some care about their family alone. Some care about their town or region. Some care about their country. Some care about every human. Some care about our planet. Where are you drawing your circle, Mr. Dangelo? Are we in it? I hope so. You are now a citizen of this country. We respect this and are only asking you to care about the whole picture, not just a small part of it."

"I understood. What am I going to tell them about the time I have been off their radar?"

"Mr. Dangelo, it might come as a surprise to you, but there are plenty of concerned US citizens who have formed an underground movement to keep their government in check. Those concerned are mistrusting of a government controlled by powerful business lobbies. Anyway, they arranged this meeting and you have just been here to this spa for a back pain treatment. On your way out, you will find a bag with the clothes you left behind in a prison near Palermo. In your jacket pocket, you will find a doctor's receipt advising you to come to this place. Your wife has been asked to collect you in about twenty minutes' time. We wish you great success in your work and a conscientious career."

Enzo nodded, showing his agreement and got out of the steam bath. Just outside the door, he found the bag he had left behind in Sicily. Luckily, the bag contained some fresh clothes too. Near the bag, was his jacket with the promised documentation proving that his doctor advised him to go there for a scheduled treatment. He showered and got dressed quickly to run out to his wife who greeted him with, "I didn't know you had such bad backaches. Are you feeling better now?"

"Who told you I was here?"

"Betty from your office called to say you had some problems with your back and they had brought you here. Are you feeling better now?"

"I am okay now, thank you. Probably just old age creeping up on me."

Enzo had decided to keep the truth to himself to protect Carmen and to avoid unnecessary questions he wouldn't be able to answer. At work, all seemed normal and a couple of colleagues asked if his back was now fine. He laughed at some old age jokes aimed at him, while pondering how well organized the people who had kidnapped him were. That meant that he had to calculate well his movement, avoiding trusting anybody in his own company with what he did or said. Suddenly, someone came into his office.

"Enzo, you are also invited to a meeting at eleven. Should we drive together as it is in the new office across town? Check your email, but I am sure your name is on the list."

"Sure, why not! I still need to go through my emails today. How long do you think we need to get there?"

"Probably twenty minutes."

"Okay, then let's meet downstairs at around 10:30."

At the meeting, Enzo realised that all those present had, at a time, worked together on the remotely controlled insect's project. Eventually the speaker started.

"Dear colleagues, you might be wondering why you have been invited to this meeting at such short notice. Well, our government has asked for our help. It is needless to say that several different government agencies have been and still are some of our major customers. Nevertheless, today our government is appealing to us not just as a supplier, but also in our national interests. You might have realized already that those present here today are those individuals working on our special bug or Cyborg project. As you can imagine, we are not the only company or country working on such a project trying to harness the living resources of our country. It's needless to say that what is discussed here today should not be shared with anybody outside this team. Please keep everything to yourself; this is also to avoid turning your loved ones into possible targets. Remember that the less your friends and families know, the better it is for them. We now need to step up our game to be able to defend our country, our livelihood and our families. Some of you might be surprised by my tone and language. I am aware that we are no army nor a government agency, but we have been asked by our government to do our part to defend our land. We are aware of foreign powers and criminal organisations alike trying to acquire key technologies. They are also attempting to lure our scientists and experts away, so as to gain access to key knowledge and possibly to slow us down in our endeavours."

Someone raised his hand.

"Yes Mike, what's on your mind?"

"Jack, I am sorry, but you are using a military tone and I am not keen to be working in an army. I love my country and members of my family have served this country's military around the world. Some never came back. Are we at war?"

"Mike, I appreciate your interjection as I am sure you said what many others are also thinking right now. Again, keep this to yourself. A couple of weeks ago in a small hamlet in upstate New York several people were found dead. They were slowly poisoned by bad drinking water. The place is occupied mostly by wealthy retired people who have a habit of enjoying several cups of tea or coffee each day. It seems that the local lake and source of their drinking water was purposely poisoned. In the lake they found a large number of decomposing insects. It seems that those insects were previously unknown in this area. Entomologists are currently trying to identify the insects and are trying to understand why their decomposing had poisoned the local water source. Last week the police had to force open a room that had been rented at the top floor of a New York house. People downstairs had been complaining about constantly increasing noises upstairs. They could not find the owner and nobody answered at the door. The firemen were called and once they forced their way in, they found the apartment full of large insects that kept on flying out of the open windows. Later some children in their neighbourhoods confirmed that they had been observing large numbers of insects flying north for months. A neighbour reported her cat dying after having eaten one of the insects that had fallen down from the sky. It seems that someone had rented the room months earlier and bred insects in there. People don't remember anybody going into the room. The place is owned by a company that rents accommodation online. The given credentials have been checked and are false. At this point we are partly speculating, but after weeks the entomologists involved still cannot find a known insect type matching the one found in the apartment and decomposing in the lake. Some entomologists have asked for an investigation as they have started to believe this to be a genetically engineered insect. No animal has previously been known to release such strong poisonous substances when decomposing. It is clear now that this is a man-made insect and problem. It could be a coincidence, but in the affected hamlet I mentioned earlier, live some of our politician relatives. One of our president's relatives who lived there is now dead."

"What other places are also affected?"

"Thank you, Alice. Similar incidents are being investigated in Florida and Arizona. It might not be war or 911, but to me it seems like a targeted attack. This is why we need your help."

"Why have I not seen anything in the news yet?"

"The stories that have been in the local news were about an increase in the level of cancer due to environmental causes. At this time, nobody has correlated the three instances, as the government agencies have made sure to clear the decomposing unknown insects from the water sources. Anyway, I know that due to the importance of this project, some of you are under the influence of some government agency. I agree that this is a violation of your privacy, but we need to also understand the importance and gravity of the situation. We need to be able to trust all of you to be doing the right thing. We are all people and we have our own different views. I am not asking you to blindly support our government, but I want you to think for a moment and realise if you would prefer an autocratic country or a criminal organisation to gain access to this technology first and endanger us all. I know our democracy is not perfect and needs reforming, but would you really prefer a foreign power or criminal organisation to force those changes on us? Ah, by the way, we also know that some of you have extramarital affairs. I don't care, but I would walk a straight line right now and avoid wrecking your families with the evidence gathered by the state currently watching you."

"What if we leave or change our job and stop working on the Cyborg bug project?"

"Thank you, Shanice. I am not sure, but I guess it depends on the reason. If you stop working because you decide to stay at home and bring up your kids, then it is okay. If you start a new job with a competitor or even worse, you move abroad, then I am not so sure. By the way, early retirement will not be accepted as a way out. This would be understood as betraying your country, not just your company. Are there any more questions before we start talking about how best to proceed with the project? As there are no further questions, let me say that from now on we will have a team meeting every Tuesday at the same time. Now like our adversary, we have managed to breed insects that are born with a partly programmable surface. This allows us to remotely control their movements. Entomologists are a rare breed and we are trying to add more to our team. At the moment, we are trying to identify insects that are naturally used to follow a leader. Once we have found the best type of insects that fit our purpose, we could implant in them a micro GPS detector to allow us to control the location of an insect swarm via satellite and direct them to the location we want. Until now, we have purposely created sterile insects. This is to avoid affecting the natural environment. Our ethics committees are currently discussing with some politicians if this is still the way to go. At this point, we believe a small number of insect larvae were shipped to this country and multiplied here over a very short time. Those insects were suicidal but not sterile. To us, those are still an unknown type of insect. We don't believe there was any cross-pollination, but we are not sure. In the areas near the poisoned lakes, more dead birds than usual were found. We believe these must have eaten some of the poisonous insects. I reiterate that we still sterilise the insects we are working with. As I said, we might stop sterilising them in the future. We are currently working on different branches of this project. Some of you are working on insect swarms that might one day replace pesticide. Others are working on swarms of insects that will be attractive to eat, but will cause the death of those doing so. This is for other kinds of pest control. Now we come to those parts of the project the military is interested in. Some swarms of insects could one day be used to attack humans hiding in caves, jungles, etc. Some insect swarms will be used to devastate crops and starve the enemy. Some insect swarms will attack other insects. Finally, some insects will be made tasty and palatable to most humans. The military are also very interested in those. Imagine food flying itself to the soldiers at the front. If when fried they tasted like burgers or chicken, few would complain especially if they were first put through a mixer. Some important points we are concentrating on are, what is currently the engineered insect with the best flying range? What is currently the engineered insect that uses the fewest calories when flying?"

Many like Enzo were surprised to be catapulted to the front line of a war based on small modified creatures. It was fascinating and scary at the same time. When looked close up, some insects' behaviour was terrifying. Worse still, they were asked to help with the production of new weapons. The majority were not keen on the idea, but felt compelled to oblige. From a third to half of the scientists asked to help were, like him, foreign-born naturalised US citizens wary of having to demonstrate support to the country that had taken them in, helped their careers and offered a better standard of living. They all knew that someone somewhere was already working on this technology. It was a question to strike first or at least have a powerful deterrent. Enzo's dreamed of being able to walk away and have no part in it, but he knew this was not the time. Then, while he was still deep in his thoughts, someone put a hand on his back.

"Enzo, how do you feel about that? We are all in the same boat. Let's try not to destroy it, shall we?"

"Well said, Carl. I think we have no option."

They all felt united in their endeavours and in part loved to work for a common cause. They had been critical of the speech, but soon realised that it worked. Now they were no longer just working for their salaries and bonuses, but to protect their families and country. Was there a touch of nationalism or just patriotism? The urgency of the matter seemed slowly silencing of any doubts they had previously voiced. Even the usual more critical individuals were enjoying the new sense of comradeship. Enzo was enjoying the new atmosphere at work and even Carmen had remarked noticing in him a reborn interest in his work and positive motivation to go to work. So much so, that she had made an obvious point of wanting to join him and his colleagues for lunch. Enzo knew she wanted to make sure his new positive attitude for his job was not because of a new female colleague joining his team. The week after, at the next Tuesday meeting, Jack was once more welcoming them, but he was not showing his usual smile.

"Dear colleagues, here we are again a week later. Once more, I need to ask you for discretion and not to share anything we will discuss here today. As many of you are aware, we are now investing much more in hybrid micro technology involving genetically enhanced insects. I am afraid some competitors around the world have once more used a new weapon based on small-modified creatures to sabotage our military might. At the beginning of this week, at three different US Air Force airbases, some military jets exploded on the ground before being able to take off. When it first happened, they thought of a technical defect, but after looking closely into the matter, it seemed that the engines or reactors had exploded after reaching a given temperature. The curious thing was that all four planes that were trying to take off had all been affected by the same exact problem. We now know that has happened at three different US Air Force bases. At the three bases, newly qualified pilots were taking off to celebrate their first flight as fully-fledged US Air Force pilots. It became clear that this had been a well-timed coordinated attack. How could someone have sabotaged several aeroplane engines at three different military bases? Only when they checked the engines of the other planes that had not taken off, did they find them full of insects. Those looked at first like common flies. Only when an entomologist looked more closely, it found those were not ordinary flies. We now have some of those flies here in our labs. Catherine will now come to the front to explain what she has found out."

"Thank you, Jack. I will try to explain, but those of you working on related issues, please feel free to come to see me for an in-depth discussion. By looking more closely at the insects in question, we have found this to be a genetically modified species based on one originally from sub-Saharan Africa. This species can withstand high temperatures and reproduce easily. These flies live together in large numbers. In their original or natural form, these flies would simply burn when exposed to an unnaturally high temperature. This is where the genetic modification comes into play. The main structure of the captured insects seems to differ from that of their natural cousins. The ones that were captured at the three different airbases have a base structure genetically modified, which contains an explosive substance that only explodes when an unnatural source of heat like that from an aeroplane engine is applied. A single one might cause a tiny hole, but hundreds or thousands of them exploding at the same time were able to damage the aeroplane engines."

"Hi Catherine, I am Bob. Does this mean that all planes are affected? My wife is supposed to fly back home from L.A. in five hours' time."

"I am supposed to fly to Houston this evening. Are we all grounded?"

"No Claire, I don't think so. I would not put my hand in a fire, but until now, it seems that no civilian aeroplanes have been affected. It seems those flies only nest in two different types of aeroplane engine. These seemed to have been somehow coded to favour a certain type of nesting environment provided by those engines. We are still studying their very unnatural behaviour. I said that I cannot guarantee the new type of genetically modified flies will not appear in the next days, months or years. The only comfort I can give you is that none of the damaged planes managed to take off at all. Their engines exploded before they could lift off from the ground. Nevertheless, a couple of pilots have died because after the engines exploded, the plane hit some buildings in front of them at high speed. Of course, in normal circumstances the planes would have had enough runway length to take off and not hit anything. As always, in such circumstances we are trying not to alarm the whole country and not to disrupt the normal functioning of our economy. At the moment, we have made sure all plane engines are inspected before starting the plane. Until now, we have managed to find and remove those flies from military machines only. We have not yet found the source and nobody has claimed responsibility for these actions."

"At this point do we know if this attack was executed by the same people or organization that poisoned the water with the decomposing insects?"

"Sorry Bob, but like you, we are all still guessing. As the weapon used is similar, we currently assume so. Like you, we are all wondering about their next move. We have been asked to help identify possible future targets. Any ideas?"

"Every nuclear power station and nuclear rocket launch facility. They won't need any nuclear bomb if they manage to detonate our own. It would be a tragedy and a nightmare."

"Thank you, Enzo. Why specifically those objects?"

"Catherine, over the year I have written extensively about the danger of those kinds of locations as they are easy targets for any enemy. This is the way some non-nuclear powers can perpetrate a nuclear attack on us and using our own weapons. Years ago during an interview I gave, I made it pretty clear that while I understand people's buying guns to defend themselves, they need to be aware that many criminals better adept at using guns could use the same to kill the gun's owner. This is the same thing."

"What about the Pentagon and the White House?"

"Yes Bob, they have already increased the security around those possible targets. Well, if you get any new ideas, please let me know. Now let's talk a bit about our work progress. Our team in Albuquerque have identified the changes in the DNA that caused the decomposing insects to become poisonous. We can now create the same type of insects, but this of course was not the aim of our research. We are working on a way to quickly identify the substance released by those decomposing insects to be able to quickly stop the pollution of drinking water sources. We are now focusing on detection, so we are building a database of insects and their predators. This could help us in our detection and elimination of a new threat. If there are no further questions, I thank you all for your participation. May I ask Dave and Enzo to remain here as I need to discuss a further point with both of you?"

Once they had all left.

"So Catherine, what have we done wrong? I hope this is not about my asking you out more than ten years ago?"

"No Dave, this is not about your asking me out while you were still married. I don't think Enzo would be interested in that story anyway."

"Not really, but it sounds like fun!"

"No, it wasn't as his wife ran shouting into the restaurant, and totally surprised me. I won't deny that it was great to see Dave showering in a rose Zinfandel. His white shirt turned pink on the spot."

"You see! I knew you had great memories about our date. And despite that, you never gave me a second chance. A hard heartless woman you are."

"Maybe, but I love you dearly as a colleague and friend. Can we talk business now?"

"As long as you can make use of a man with a broken heart?"

"Yes I can. So back to business."

"It has come to our attention that both of you have dealt before with some of our business branches in Africa. The genetically modified insects we are currently studying are originally from that continent. We would appreciate it if you could recruit some local help or even fly there and organise some expeditions if you need."

"What kind of information or help are you looking for?" asked Dave.

"We are lacking the local knowledge of those insects' behaviour, stuff you won't find in a book. And if we are lucky, someone there might have heard of some foreign companies collecting or breeding insects."

"I have only been to our office in Cape Town in South Africa".

"I don't know what or where, but any help would be appreciated. We are currently in the dark. By the way, we are all patriotic here, but I forgot to say that if you help us solve this puzzle, the government would be willing to invest a quarter of a million dollars in one of your pet projects. What do you say?"

"I will try my best for my country, a quarter of a million dollars and for a second chance with you, Catherine."

"What about your wife?"

"I am divorced now."

"Why am I not surprised?"

"I guess I will leave you to it and start calling my contacts in Africa. Bye, Catherine."

"Bye Dave."

Enzo started to wonder if Abebi or Joshua would be able to help him identify those insects and their predators. He had not heard from Abebi or Joshua for a while, so it was time to get in touch with them. He had also wondered why George had not even texted him as he had promised. That afternoon, straight after leaving the office, he decided to drive past George's place and speak to Abebi. George came to the door in a dressing gown. He seemed embarrassed. Enzo tried to cut through the ice, "How are you, George? Is everything okay with you? Where is Abebi?"

"Who is at the door, darling? Come on, come back to bed!"

"No need to be embarrassed, George. I am glad you are getting on fine with her."

"Do you want to come in?"

Abebi came at the door to see for herself.

"Hey, it's you! Where have you been? Is your wife not letting you out of the house anymore?"

"I am glad you are having a good time. You see some of us need to work sometimes. I just wanted to know how you were doing and please give me a call at my office number as I need to ask you some questions about Africa. Don't worry, it's about work."

"Africa? I am intrigued. Sure I will call you tomorrow after lunch time."

"Great. Speak to you tomorrow. Bye, George."

While just outside the door, his mobile phone rang.

"Hi Carmen, what's going on?"

"Julio rang. He wanted to speak to you about Joshua."

"What has he done?"

"I am not sure, but he said you should call him back as soon as possible."

"Sure, I will do so once I get home in half an hour. See you soon, darling."

As soon as he got home, Carmen had to relay to him what Julio had just told her.

"Julio said that Joshua is seeing a girl who belongs to an important family on the island. This could cause us problems. Julio is worried about it. Please give him a call."

After calling Julio, it was clear that Joshua's possible romance could jeopardize his own future on the island and cast Julio and Carmen's family in bad light. It was time to do something, first of all speak to Joshua. Maybe even suggest a trip to Africa. He had also been told not to leave the US. James or John Austin were the only ones who could help him.

"Hello James, how are you? Yes, it's important. Yes I am sure. Can we meet?"

Two hours later, Enzo was sitting at the bar of the hotel where someone had tried to kill him. While sipping his drink and waiting for James to turn up, he thought, of how lucky he had been for Abebi to be there. That could have been his last day, but before he could indulge in deeper thoughts, he felt a hand on his shoulder. "Hi Enzo, have you not yet learned to stay out of trouble?"

"Are you called trouble?"

"There are probably enough people who would say so. Anyway, good to see you. So what's going on?"

"James, I have an idea and I need your help or the help of your friends."

"Did I understand correctly that you are voluntarily pitching your idea to me?"

"Well, it seems you were capable of turning some of my ideas into reality, so you are the man I need."

Then Enzo started to tell James of his idea to take with him Joshua and Abebi on a mission to Africa. He was worried that they would never accept if they knew they couldn't come back. He needed for James to find some political backing to guarantee Joshua and Abebi a safe return to the new continent. They needed some legal documents they could use for travelling.

"I'll see what I can do. I will get in touch."

"When?"

"Enzo, keep your cool. It won't be me taking this decision. I promised I will let you know as soon as I get an answer. Now I have to go. See you, my friend."

James disappeared as quickly as he had appeared. James seemed to love his job. One could feel he was not just in it for the money. Now it was time to go home and call Joshua. Once he got home, Carmen asked him straightaway if he had called Joshua and sorted things out.

"Carmen, I promise that I am working on it. I will call Joshua now."

"Hola, puedo hablar con Joshua por favor? Con quien hablo? Maria? Y Joshua? Hi Joshua, how are you?"

"Hey Enzo, how are you doing? Did you forget me on this island?"

"Sorry Joshua, I have been busy at work. By the way, there is a chance you could help me with my job. Well, I might need to go on a business trip to Africa and it would be good to have someone with local knowledge with me. Well, let's just say that this is what I told the people in my company. What do you think?"

"Enzo, did you forget I have no legal documents yet?"

"No, of course not! Part of the plan is to get my company to sponsor your new documents. That would be great right?"

"Yes, that would be great. When do you need to go?"

"We need to wait for the paperwork. I will call you back once I know more. Bye for now."

Carmen had been listening to the whole conversation and looked at him like an enormous question mark.

"Are you going to Africa with Joshua?"

"Would that not be a great way to get Joshua out of Santo Domingo for a while and away from the precious local beauty?"

"I guess so. I am just not keen on your taking off again."

Enzo took Carmen's hand and then he put his index finger in front of his mouth to signal to her not to say anything. They walked to the nearby park where Enzo told Carmen that he was not supposed to be, but he wanted her to know about what had been disclosed to him at his job. He thought the house might be bugged and he had left both their mobile phones at home just in case those were listening in.

"I understand the issue now and I am glad you told me about it, but why the hell you seem to always get involved in stuff like this? You are not working for the CIA or the US government, are you?"

"Carmen, I am very sorry, and of course you would know already if I were working for the CIA. You are right and I have no idea why I seem to always get stuck in such situations. I can only say sorry again."

"Are you aware of the fact that you have two kids and they have seen very little of you while growing up? You are either working until late or away on a trip. Why did you marry? Why did you have kids?"

"Carmen, I know it's no excuse, but I am just one of many people having to work until late."

"Enzo, please spare me that. Many people have to work until late because they need the money to survive. Thanks to your hard work, we are lucky and you no longer need to work."

"Carmen, please be reasonable. Do you really want me to retire and spend all day at home with you? Believe me; I don't think you would like that."

"Are you saying I am unreasonable because I want my husband to spend more time with his family? I even married a Sicilian and Sicilians are supposed to put their families above anything else."

"Come on, Carmen, no need to start with the stereotypes now. I know you are angry. Please let's stop now."

Suddenly they spotted their daughter walking towards them. Enzo was very surprised.

"How did you know we were here?"

"Mamma put a note on the fridge. Dad, your mobile phone has been ringing all the time. It's ringing again."

"Thank you darling, please walk Mamma home. I will take this and come back home in a bit."

Carmen looked very annoyed at him, took Mary's hand and started walking back.

"Hi, Enzo speaking, who is there? Hi James, I didn't expect your call back so soon. What is going on? Sure, come to the same bar. I will be there in half an hour."

At the bar, James was already there and not alone. The other guy looked far more formal than James and he looked like official government material.

"Hi Enzo, this is Robert and he seems to be very interested in your idea."

"Mr. Dangelo, these here are two US passports for Abebi and Joshua. As you can see, they are valid only for six months. We want you to move quickly, preferably in the next few days. Would you be okay with that?"

"I feel some urgency, but that will be fine. Why so urgent?"

"James will carry on being your direct contact and will give you some more details. He will keep me up to date. Nice meeting you."

"James, what's going on?"

"It's not what you wanted? You know, it is very difficult to keep you happy. Anyway, a double whiskey on the rocks will lose my tongue."

"I thought in Denmark you had stopped drinking whiskey?"

"Yes, I had in Denmark, but then that bitch left me and I found whiskey was the only thing left waiting for me at home. Anyway, what did you want to know?"

"Why this urgency? What happened?"

James looked around and then after putting on a serious face and starting to look at his glass, started to say that something bad had happened. Two nuclear power stations had been forced to stop. Another was being attacked as they spoke. Genetically modified insects seemed to be the weapon. The insects had somehow managed to reach the atomic reactor's cooling water reservoirs; reproduce for a while then they started to absorb most of the water. Eventually the reactors could no longer be cooled down and no fresh water could be pumped in without first removing the blown up strange creatures. The heat eventually caused it to burst; ironically causing a chain reaction and a consequent explosion that damaged several components of the reactor. The situation was desperate and the US government was trying all possible options.

"And by the way, you are one of these options. God, they must be really desperate to bet on this dead horse."

"Are you forgetting that you have bet on this dead horse once or twice already?"

"How could I forget? Your strange ideas have been great for my career. It rhymes so well that I should make it into my motto. Anyway, when will you be ready to leave?"

"Well, my wife will kill me, but I guess I could go in two days."

"Don't worry about your wife. I will make sure she will be more understanding on your way back."

"James, please leave my wife out of it."

"Don't worry, we won't physically touch your wife. We just know some of her girlfriends. Leave it to me."

"Now I am really worried."

"So you will fly to Santo Domingo first to pick up Joshua. Then, as I understand, you are also going to take Abebi with you. Is this right?"

"Yes, this was my intention. By the way, do you know what happened to Zauna? I didn't hear a thing after she had been injured. Abebi told me she was alright, but nothing else."

"Abebi is right. Zauna is okay, don't worry about her. And the last important thing I need to tell you is that we believe you should start your search for bugs in Angola. They have a feeling the first load of insects might have come from a cargo plane arriving from Angola. I think you already speak some Portuguese, so it should not be difficult for you."

"I have never been to Angola and I always wanted to go, but I know nobody there."

"Perfect, how lucky can you get? I am sure you will make new friends there."

"What about the expenses?"

"Count those as the price for the two US passports."

"I see. Don't ask what your country can do for you. Think what you can do for your country."

"Exactly what a real American would say."

They bid farewell and James was gone. Enzo stayed to finish his drink and use his phone to book a flight to Santo Domingo, when suddenly his phone rang and he could no longer click on the BOOK NOW button. Really annoying, but he had to take it, it was a call from work.

"Hi Bob, what's going on? I see, yes, I will be out for a couple of weeks I guess. Somewhere in Africa. Yes, I will send you updates."

Bob had called to say that they had been informed that one more nuclear reactor had to be turned off. They now had problems cooling them down and were worried about an American Chernobyl. Enzo went home and explained the situation to Carmen. To save their marriage, he had to promise that this was going to be his last mission alone and that next time she would fly with him. In his heart, Enzo really hoped James's magic would work on his wife. It was time to pack and wait for the kids to return from school before going to the airport. He had called Abebi on the way home and she had seemed very happy to hear from him. George lived close to the airport, so he had decided to leave his car there as he had done often before. Once he arrived, George was not there and Abebi was very happy to see him. Abebi jumped on his neck and hugged him.

"What happened? The last time I saw you two, you looked like a couple on honeymoon."

"Yvonne happened. She came back and was more than surprised to find me here. I saw that George still loves her. Still confused and with tears in his eyes, he asked me to find a new place to stay. Great timing. Let's get the hell out of here before they come back."

They put her stuff in the car boot and drove to the airport.

"In truth I never liked Yvonne, but she seems to be the love of his life. They met in college, then she fell for her manager at work and broke George's heart. She is good looking and likes everyone to know when making an entrance. I can't stand women like her. But George loves her. Anyway, have you ever wanted to go to Angola?"

"Angola? I am not even sure where it is in Africa. Certainly not near Nigeria. I thought you needed someone with local knowledge?"

"Does it matter, as long as you got a US document you can travel with?"

"I guess not, but are you sure they will allow me back?"

"This passport does not expire for six months. By the way, we are first flying to Santo Domingo to pick up Joshua. Do you remember him?"

"Vaguely. I think he liked my cousin Zauna very much. If you like boobs then you like Zauna."

"What kind of question is that? All heterosexual men like boobs, but not just that."

"Don't worry, I know men and what they like. Don't you think?"

"Okay, Abebi, you win this one."

They finally boarded the plane to Santo Domingo. Abebi embraced the warm air as soon as she got out of the plane. It reminded her of Nigeria. Julio was there to pick them up. Making sure Abebi could not understand he spoke to Enzo in Spanish, telling him how glad he was that he was finally dealing with the issue. Julio reiterated several times that he could lose his job. He told Enzo that one of his superiors wanted to speak to him personally. Julio dropped Abebi at his home where Joshua was supposed to appear and drove Enzo to a private villa outside the city.

"Listen Enzo, they told me to let you in and wait outside. So I will be here waiting for you."

Enzo nodded, walked down the path and into the building. A young girl obviously working there asked him to follow her. Finally, a well-dressed mature man came out.

"Hello Mr. Dangelo, nice to finally meet Julio's famous brother-in-law."

"Great to be invited here and I hope I am not famous for the wrong reasons?"

"Thank you for coming straight to the point Mr. Dangelo. Maria, please bring us a couple of cold drinks."

"Please let me start by saying that we have known Carmen's parents for a long time and our families have mutual respect. This is why we are sometimes prepared to turn a blind eye to minor issues. Let me say that smuggling an African into our country is no minor issue, but given the trust between our families and the fact that you took over the financial support of the new African student, we decided to once more turn a blind eye. Now you will understand that having already turned a blind eye means that doing it again would really make me blind. As much as I love Carmen's family, I don't fancy going blind and losing my job due to disability. Do you understand, Mr. Dangelo?"

"First of all let me say that I appreciate your giving me the chance to make amends and repair anything that I might have broken, starting with the trust between our families. I am not sure if you have been informed about my plan to take Joshua on a business trip with me. This will give the young man a chance to refocus. Of course, please let me know what else I can do to help?"

"Mr. Dangelo, Julio had told me that you were a reasonable man and I am more than happy to agree. I am also more than happy to hear about your upcoming trip with your assistant, Joshua. By the way, I heard that in six months' time, some better professors will be starting to teach at the school where Joshua is enrolled."

"Well, in that case we shouldn't miss such a great opportunity. I will make sure the school is informed."

"Mr. Dangelo, it was a pleasure to meet you. Please give my regards to Carmen's family."

As soon as he was out.

"How did it go?"

"Hey Julio, calm down, my friend. All is sorted and we will leave tomorrow. Now it's time for me to see Joshua."

They drove home where Mariana, Sofia and Isabella were very happy to see him. Uncle Enzo had brought some sweets boxes from the airport and some perfume for Mariana. Joshua stood up to hug Enzo, but Abebi who was sitting close to him seemed to have started her magic spell on him. That girl was right and somehow had learned to turn any man's head the way she wanted. Enzo hoped his feelings were right. That would make his job much easier.

"So tell me why you need a Zimbabwean and a Nigerian girl to help you with a business you have in South Africa?"

Enzo threw Joshua's temporary US passport on the table then said, "This is why!"

Joshua grabbed the passport, "Man, this is crazy. I got a real US passport with my name on it and I have never set foot on US soil. Who are you? James Bond?"

"James Bond is British. Maybe Tommaso Crociera or Tom Cruise in Mission Impossible."

"Wow, that's amazing, but it is only valid for six months?"

"Baby steps, my friend. One day you might get one that lasts longer. First prove to them you are worth it before they give you one."

"Fine, when do you want us to leave?"

"Tomorrow, flights are booked for Miami, then Houston and Luanda from there."

"How long will we be gone for?"

"Not sure yet. Don't worry, I have already spoken to your school."

Abebi cleverly put her arm around Joshua's neck. He seemed to like her attention. After a duty call at Carmen's parents' house, Enzo was happy to retire to the room Mariana had prepared for him. Trying to smooth things over for the troubles Joshua had caused, Enzo called Mariana aside and gave her a bundle of US dollars asking her to use those towards the girl's education or whatever they needed. Mariana tried to refuse, but Enzo insisted until she put the bundle away. Joshua had gone to his place to get his stuff together and promised to be back on time the day after. Abebi had tried to tag along, but Joshua said that it was better he went alone. Julio and Enzo both really hoped he would not get them into more trouble before departing. The morning arrived and as promised, Joshua was there on time. Julio and Enzo exchanged glances with sighs of relief while sipping their morning coffees. It was time to greet everybody and drive to the airport.

On the plane, Joshua looked very happy. He was flying to the USA. Abebi was sitting between them.

"What if I get out of the airport?"

"Sure, you can do that and hide while the police hunt you down or you could just stop asking stupid questions and start behaving like an adult. So what will it be?"

"God, you have no sense of humour old man."

They eventually made it to Houston and from there, boarded a plane to Luanda. The cabin attendant made announcements in Portuguese which rendered the atmosphere more exotic already. Joshua and Abebi did not feel like going back home at all as they had never considered going to Angola. Being both English speakers, they were looking to Enzo for help in translating anything Portuguese they read or heard. After the long flight, they took a taxi to the centre of Luanda, a city of more than eight million people. Enzo had booked three single rooms. Abebi and Joshua looked pleased with his choice of accommodation.

"Listen guys, go to your rooms and let's meet down here in one hour. I know you're a bit tired, but it is now time for you to know what we are here for."

They disappeared to their rooms to reconvene in a quiet corner of the bar. There, Enzo started sharing part of the stories that concerned the US security department. He showed them some pictures of the genetically modified insects they were after. Abebi did not remember seeing anything like that before. Joshua was not sure. He might have seen some of them near a river, but was not fully sure. With no real plan, they went to bed.

During the night Enzo's mobile beeped, signalling an incoming message. It was from James.

"Hi Enzo, I was told you have arrived. I am not sure if it helps. The insects that arrived on a cargo plane from Angola, were transported in crates with Spanish writing on them, not Portuguese."

Enzo thanked James and started to think if this information could be useful at all. He stared at the ceiling, hoping for some inspiration. Then it struck him. Years earlier he had visited Cuba and several museums there. In one of the museums, he remembered seeing a world map showing where Cuban military personnel or doctors had been sent to help around the world. He had been impressed to see that a small country with little resource had had such a wide reach and imprint on the world fight for socialism. The Angolan MPLA who fought for independence from the Portuguese then fought in the country's civil war. The MPLA had support from the Soviet Union and Cuba. In Cuba, of course, they spoke Spanish. Cubans send military, but especially doctors to help their cause. As a qualified doctor, he knew Cuba as a great centre for medical education. He knew that even now poor Cubans had better access to medical help than poor Americans. Maybe he could try to speak to someone from the old MPLA members. That was a plan he could go to bed with.

The day after at breakfast, he explained that he would sell themselves as some journalists interested in the recent history of Angola. Joshua and Abebi would pretend to have one grandparent each coming originally from Angola, but not sure where exactly from. With that plan, they managed to find a tour guide who would find for them some old MPLA members willing to speak to them. They spent days interviewing old members of the MPLA and some mentioned warmly the support of the Cuban doctors who had helped them. On the fourth day, there was finally light at the end of the tunnel. An old man finally mentioned a place, Cazombo, where some Cuban doctors had decided to stay. They all exchanged glances, pretending it was time for a lunch break. They had heard enough to write a book on MPLA fighters. They thanked the tour guide, then asked him how best to get to Cazombo as they would like to interview some Cuban doctors there. João, the guide, quickly saw an opportunity and offered himself as a guide. They accepted and agreed on meeting the day after when João had promised to turn up with a large Range Rover and a driver who would drive them all to Cazombo. They went back to their hotel rooms. As soon as Enzo had entered his room, he realized that someone had gone through his stuff probably trying to find some valuables. Some money, a phone charger and an old camera were missing. All the documents were there. He reported what had happened at the reception where they apologised and swore this had never happened before at their hotel. It was time to sleep and forget about the things that had been stolen. The day after, while they were still having breakfast, João came in to inform them that he and the driver were waiting outside for them. It was time to see the interior of the country. It was time for adventure. Five hours away, the town of Lombe was their first destination. As soon as they had left Luanda behind them, the countryside started to open up as did Enzo's mouth who started to tell them about the Portuguese being the first Europeans to circumnavigate the south tip of Africa and establish some posts on the African coast. Joshua listened for a while then exploded.

"This is your history white man. We have our own. The history of the people who were living here and saw those strangers building some settlements near their villages. The history of those who later the Portuguese enslaved."

Enzo felt the need to apologise as he realized he was the only non-African person in the car trying to tell them about African history.

"Sorry Joshua, you are right. This is our European history. The history of the pale-skinned people who were intrigued by what seemed at the time an inscrutable continent. The truth is that I have not come across a book of African history written by an African in a language I can read."

João seemed amused about their arguing and tried to stay out of the discussion, preferring to speak to the driver beside whom he was sitting.

"I like you, pale old man, but please don't try to teach me about Africa."

Enzo, trying to make good weather, "Fine, I will stop telling you about Africa if you tell me you knew about MPLA and the Cuban doctors before embarking on this mission?"

"No, I did not, old man. My grandfather never told me about it," answered Joshua cleverly remembering to play the role of an Angolan descendant tracing his roots. Both turned around to see Abebi crying.

"What's wrong?" asked Joshua while stroking her hair.

"Are you emotional about being back in the country of your grandparents?" asked João proudly.

Abebi nodded and turned her face to the outside scenery passing by, while wiping her tears. Enzo realized that the countryside and the journey were probably reminding her of the relatives she had lost while they were driving back from a wedding. The single event that had changed her life trajectory. They stopped to eat on the way. João described the landscape, making it clear to Enzo who the tour guide was in the group. In the late afternoon they arrived in Lombe. João warmly greeted the owner of casa Maria. Maria was a strong and smiling lady renting the rooms for the night. She asked at what time they wanted to have supper, then welcomed them into the house. It looked like João had definitely brought other people there before. João asked all to try to have an early night, reminding everyone of the eight-hour trip he was expecting of them the next day. He made it clear that it was best to leave before 7 AM.

Maria prepared Muamba de Galinha, an Angolan chicken dish, for them. Enzo liked it, but not as much as the Calulu de peixe he had had in Luanda the day before. Enzo asked Maria if they had kissangua, a non-alcoholic drink he had learned about on an Angola guidebook he had read on the plane there. Maria apologised and explained that kissangua is drunk mostly in the south of the country, but she offered kapuka instead. Enzo was always curious about drinks and dishes unknown to him, so he asked to try kapuka. He quickly realised kapuka was definitely an alcoholic drink and a strong one as well. Now all wanted to try it. Apart from the conscientious driver, all kept on drinking kapuka until late. The morning after, a rooster just outside Enzo's window provided the needed alarm clock at half past five. Straightaway he knew he had drunk too much and could not remember how he had managed to go to bed. Also he did not remember taking his clothes off. He was desperate for a glass or bucket of water to quench his thirst and dampen his headache. He stumbled around to get dressed in what he could find. Opposite his room there was an open door, so trying to find water, he slowly pushed the door open to see a bed with Joshua and Abebi half naked and still half embracing. It seems they had also enjoyed kapuka too much and got very friendly. He thought that they must have brought him into his room and undressed him. He finally made it to the front of the big house where Maria hugged him good morning and, smiling, handed him a large glass of juice. He downed the first one quickly and asked for a second. Adão walked in, looked at him and smiled. Behind him, João, who repeated the same, then went close to his ear and whispered, "Please be generous with the lady of the house. You all made a bit of a mess last night."

Enzo could only nod to comply. Then he asked João if he had taken him to bed. João, laughing, said no, then looking at Maria, nodded to say she did.

That was embarrassing. Enzo could not remember a time he had behaved worse with someone he did not know. Kapuka was definitely off his list. He now started to look apologetic to Maria every time she walked passed him. She kept on smiling back at him. João finally decided that it was time to wake up Joshua and Abebi. Enzo pointed towards their room to say feel free to do that. João went and walked back laughing. Shortly after, Abebi and Joshua walked out looking embarrassed. It looked like they had not planned to sleep in the same room, but the kapuka had helped them decide to do so. They packed their belongings, downed a couple of coffees and silently loaded the car. Enzo, looking as apologetic as he could, asked Maria for the bill and gave her more kwanza than he had been asked for. She looked happy, hugged him and made him promise to stop at her place on their way back. He obliged and they finally departed.

They soon fell asleep, leaving Adão and João talking amongst themselves. Three hours later Enzo was woken up, by one more bump in the road that jolted all around in the car. Adão apologised and then smiled. Abebi and Joshua seemed awake, but not talking. Enzo decided to break the ice, "So did you have a good night?"

Nobody answered for a while.

"Come on guys what happened? It was just kapuka."

Abebi then suddenly exploded, "Have you ever slept with a black lady?"

Enzo was more than surprised by that question.

"Why on earth are you asking me that?"

"You asshole!"

Enzo was more than puzzled now. Abebi had always been good and grateful towards him.

"Listen Abebi, last night I got so drunk like never before and I cannot remember anything. So let me apologise for anything offensive that I might have said while out of control. This morning I already apologised to Maria for our behaviour."

Joshua was staying well out of it, but Abebi did eventually come around.

"Sure, of course you apologised to her first. Did you apologise for being too loud during sex with her or for starting to touch her breast while we were all still sitting at the table?"

"That bad? And I slept with Maria?"

"Who do you think undressed you? She asked if you had ever been with a black lady and you answered, no."

"And that is why you're so cross with me? How can you be so cross for something I said while so drunk? I am sorry for getting so drunk and for offending you."

Then Joshua finally decided to open his mouth, "Come on old man, can you not see that she might be a bit jealous."

"Jealous of me and waking up between your arms? You must be joking."

Abebi almost stood up in the car, "You're both idiots. I am not jealous of a middle aged married man. I found it very offensive that even when drunk he could not remember to have been with a black lady. As if it had meant nothing at all to him."

"Abebi, I am very sorry and I still have no idea why I answered in that way. Do you think drunk people are in control of what they are saying or doing?"

João had had enough of the shouting and quickly announced that they would soon stop for lunch at a place he knew. João added that they all needed a break to cool down. All agreed by remaining silent. One more hour passed while the passengers in the back kept admiring the landscape and jumped up at every road bump, trying to soften their landing. They finally deviated from the main road down a smaller track. At the end of it there was something that looked like a farm. Adão and João seemed happy to quickly jump out of the car. They were offered a meal that included cassava, something that pleased Enzo who had never tried it before. Mango juice was all they drank. They soon departed all looking in a better mood. The early start had not helped softening the kapuka blow from the night before. One more hour into the drive to Luando, Abebi decided to rest herself on Joshua. Enzo was pleased to see the mood on board had improved. He then started a conversation with João asking him how he and his family had survived during the civil war. João recounted his experiences as a young boy, making sure to say that both sides suffered and that it had been a war between Angolan brothers. He added that his parents and those of Adão's might have still thought along old tribal lines and fought against each other as part of MPLA and the UNITA. João repeated to make it clear that his family was on the MPLA's side, while Adão's family supported UNITA. Enzo was keen on learning about Angolan history but the young passengers were very bored. It was almost dark when they finally drove into Luando. A lady walked out of the house, welcoming them in. João looked at Enzo and whispered, "Be careful Enzo, Maria is a widow. Señora Magdalena's husband is inside and he is a very strong man."

Then he laughed and walked in.

Enzo realised that kapuka had ruined his reputation at least on this trip. This time he felt guilty about sleeping with the landlady after the passionate discussion he had had with his wife. Could he ever be a faithful husband? Now he was not sure anymore. He knew that Carmen would not accept kapuka as an excuse. He felt like calling home, but the telephone reception in Luando was very bad. When the new landlady asked for how many rooms they needed, Abebi shouted the first, asking for a double while she put her arm on Joshua's shoulder. Enzo was pleased as he hoped this would help Joshua forget his girl in Santo Domingo. It had been a long day with an early start. They all seemed keen to have a quick bite and throw themselves onto their beds.

The morning after, Enzo woke up in a much better mood and could remember the day and evening before. João had told them that their next trip to Luena would only take about five hours. So there was plenty of time for a late breakfast. Enzo realised the others were still asleep. Bernardo the landlord welcomed him to the front room where the open front door was letting the sun in. Without being asked, he was given a coffee. Bernardo asked him why they were travelling to Cazombo. Enzo explained about the documentary and his two companions' Angolan ancestors. Trying to change the subject, Enzo asked, "Is the economy doing fine now?"

"Certainly better than during the war, but like in many other countries, a small number of families control a large part of the economy. The rest of us need to ask their favours."

Enzo, trying to cheer him up, "Oligarchy are running most countries around the world. You see once someone manages to take hold of the country's resources, they will stop any new development."

Bernardo looked him into the eyes, "This is why during our independence struggle and civil war we had hoped for a better and fairer government."

Enzo lifted his mouth from his cup, "I guess after the collapse of the communist dream, the country reverted to the colonial ways of doing things. Every society needs a template. We are all a bit lost right now as our western democratic governments are failing to adapt as well. People see a minority taking all the spoils and betraying the rest by not paying their part in taxes."

Bernardo, looking disappointed at Enzo, "So we are left with no new ideas or ideology? Don't you think we need hope and a new revolution?"

Enzo saw Bernardo's eyes lightning up, bringing some of his memories of youth back.

"Don't worry, things are quickly changing and a new revolution will eventually come. Will you be ready?"

Bernardo started to laugh out loud.

"Well, if I don't have to wait for long, I will be here if they need me."

João, and the others soon appeared. Joshua looked broken. Enzo could not resist, "Did you sleep well?"

"Definitely not. Abebi kept tossing and turning all night. She hit me every time."

Abebi smiled, "Maybe I wasn't tired enough."

"Maybe you need your own bed," replied Joshua.

Señora Magdalena walked in with a large breakfast tray that concentrated everyone minds on the most important task at hand.
After breakfast they were soon on the road to Luena. João keep on answering questions about the landscape and recent Angolan history. When he got tired of listening to João speaking English, Adão would just turn on the car radio blasting some Brazilian music out of it. They had a good ride and in good time they arrived at Luena, their last stop before moving on to Cazombo the day after. In Luena João had no favourite place he knew so they decided to find a guesthouse close to the road to Cazombo. Despite picking on each other, Abebi and Joshua decided to share a double room again. Enzo could not resist, "Are you sure you don't need two singles?"

They left him behind without answering. João made it clear to them that the next day they had a long ride in front of them, therefore it would be better if they had an early night. Being deep in the country, Enzo had hoped to start seeing some insects similar to the ones they were looking for, but Luena turned out to be a much larger town than he had expected it to be. The day after, they managed to leave before eight and nobody uttered a word whatsoever before ten. As they were coming closer to their final destination, Enzo started to question João about the Cuban likelihood of wanting to speak to him. João reassured him that his friends in Cazombo had already arranged a meeting with the Cubans. Six hours already into the journey, João told Adão to go off road down a track where some sitting lorry drivers outside made it clear there was good food to be had there. They celebrated being almost at their final destination by drinking some beer. After a good lunch of chicken and rice they got back on the road until they had to stop to fill up the car. Enzo stayed in the car with Adão, while João went with Abebi and Joshua into a nearby shop looking for some water and toiletries. Adão started the engine. Enzo was sitting in the back reading a map he had downloaded on his smartphone when suddenly Adão departed leaving the others behind. Enzo at first thought he might be turning the car around, but when he carried on driving down a different track he realised something was going on. He looked into the rear view mirror to find Adão's eyes, but Adão was just looking where he was driving. Before Enzo could say anything, Adão had stopped the car and pointed with his hand to the right. Enzo could see a pick up car with two men dressed in paramilitary clothes. One came close to the car, then speaking Spanish, "Señor Dangelo? Tienes que venir con nosotros en el coche."

The man asked him to go with them in their car. Enzo saw no other option and jumped in the pick-up car. They started to drive further into the jungle. At this point he started to wonder if Adão or even João had arranged this meeting. It looked like he needed to be patient and wait. When he asked the men where they were taking him, he got no answer. After what seemed to him a long silent drive they finally stopped at a well build wooden hut. They asked him to follow them in. They let him wait alone for a while, then an older man walked in.

"Mr. Dangelo, do you prefer to speak English or is Spanish okay for you? You are used to speaking Spanish to your wife Carmen, right? Do your son John and your daughter Mary also speak Spanish or just English?"

It was clear they knew who he was and there was little point hiding much.

"As you rightly said, I can also carry on in Spanish if you prefer."

"Mr. Dangelo why are you here? I don't believe you are here to open a new branch of the various businesses you are involved with. Please don't waste our time and your own. Are you here on a spying mission?"

"I am sure you have heard of our documentary about the recent Angolan history?"

The man turned around and shouted to the men outside to bring him a bag. Out of the bag he took an iPad on which he showed some photos to Enzo.

"Are those insects part of your Angolan history documentary? I will give you one more chance, don't waste it."

"Fine, you win. We are looking for those insects. Are they from this area?"

"Mr. Dangelo, who are you working for or better, who sent you here?"

"Maybe the US government."

"Mr. Dangelo, you are playing a dangerous game and getting involved in stuff that you should not. But we might be able to help each other."

"How can I help you?"

"Mr. Dangelo, you can pass a message to your American friends. Like an insect, Cuba might be small, but even a small poisonous insect can sting and kill an elephant. A small tiny mosquito can do loads of damage until you find a cure for it."

"Are you not worried the elephant might put its heavy foot on the mosquitoes' nest?"

The man laughed, then carried on "An elephant moves very slowly and there are plenty of mosquitoes' nests. Lift the embargo and leave our country alone. With no money or resources, we have built a better health care system and a fairer society than you have. Leave us in peace and we could be a prosperous neighbour you could even trade fairly with. But on equal terms, not as slaves. Tell this to your friends. The men will take you to your friends in Cazombo. Tomorrow evening, we will come and get your answer. Have a good evening and enjoy your stay in Angola. It is a beautiful country."

The same men drove him to Cazombo. João soon came out of the building, apologising for what had happened to him and swore he knew nothing about Adão's plan to kidnap him. Then Joshua and Abebi ran out after hearing João apologising so profusely. Abebi hugged Enzo, who after looking at Joshua's face, exploded, "Don't be jealous, she is just happy to see me alive. Aren't you?"

"Sure, old man. I am very happy to see my return ticket still in one piece. Do you have something to tell us?"

"Are you sure you want to know and be taken away into the jungle instead of me?"

João looked up with a stern face, "I think it's better if Adão and I go out for a walk round the town now. See you later."

They quickly walked out and disappeared from their sight.

"You can talk now?"

"We no longer need to pretend with our documentary story, well at least not with the Cubans. They knew my name, that of wife and kids. We have no cover and it seems in Luanda it was a pretend robbery. They showed me a copy of the photos I had showed you before."

Abebi looking worried, "Are we in danger?"
"Seriously, I don't know. It's a dangerous dance where we can get stung. Anyway, now that we no longer need a cover story, you can stay out of the way. After all, they kidnapped just me. Enjoy the place and take it easy."

"We will, but are you going to see those Cubans again?"

"They are supposed to get in touch with me tomorrow evening after I have got in touch with the people who sent us here. I think that it is better for you if tomorrow evening you stay out of the way."

Enzo tried to find a quiet place with a landline and called James.
"Hey man, where have you been? I hope you have something important to tell me."

"James, I think I am onto something, but they have a clear message for our politicians."

"Who are they?"

"Some Cubans."

"Could we not just bomb the hell out of Cuba?"

"Sure, but they are not just in Cuba and by the time you find them all around the world, we will be in big trouble."

"What do they want? Money?"

"Come on James, they are people who don't care about money. They are doctors who would be able to work anywhere in the world and have a good life. What makes you think that you could just buy them? If it had been that simple, don't you think the CIA would have just paid Fidel Castro? Cuba is not like our country where the richest one is merely elected. All around the world, 90% of people are sheep who can be bought with grass or money. Those are lions defending their territory."

"Hey comrade Enzo, have they turned you into a communist?"

"No, sorry, I forgot you had no principles and cannot understand people who cannot be bought. Anyway, is there any chance you can involve some politicians and tell them that they want the Cuban embargo to be lifted?"

Enzo could hear James laughing very loudly. "That's funny, but I will pass this on."

"James, they want me to give them an answer tomorrow evening. What should I tell them?"

"Try to buy time. Tell them we need time."

"Enzo, I will call you later."

"Sure, speak to you later. Bye now."

Enzo didn't feel James had taken him seriously. He felt he had no other choice but to just tell the Cubans that they needed more time. He called Carmen to reassure her. It was a sleepless night and even during the day, Enzo looked tense. He could not wait for the meeting. Abebi and Joshua had made their own plans and disappeared after breakfast. João and Adão had gone to stay at a different place. João asked Enzo to call him should he decide to drive somewhere. Enzo started to feel lonely. In the evening after ten, he felt he had waited for too long. Nobody had turned up at the bar where the meeting point was. Eventually he thought that two hours longer than agreed would be enough, so he decided to walk back to his room. He had just walked out of the bar when he felt a hand on his right shoulder. He jumped, surprised, and quickly turned around.

"You asshole, what are you doing here?"

James could not stop laughing, then asked, "Where are your communist friends? Where are those assholes?"

"How long have you been here?"

"Calm down, Enzo. We have been tracking you all the time and when you left Luanda I decided to fly in. I guessed you were on a good trail. It's late now, but let's have a beer here then we'll drive you to your place. Tomorrow you should try to get in touch with your communist friends again."

They had more than a couple of beers, while Enzo tried to convince James that those were serious people standing up for their country as some patriotic Americans would be prepared to die for their country. Enzo was not sure he was getting through to James, but he could only try. James and the other two men with him drove him back to the hotel. Abebi ran out to hug Enzo and was surprised to see James. She quickly asked James about her cousin Zauna. James smiled, replying that Zauna was fine and had already got a permanent visa for the US. Then James asked Enzo to bring him the bag with the insect photos as they were worried those could end up in the wrong hands. Enzo asked Abebi to fetch the brown bag in his room. Abebi obliged and brought the bag to James. They wished each other good night, then the car drove away. Enzo was still walking into the building when he heard an enormous blast and felt a hot wind coming from behind. He turned around to see James' car ripped apart and in flames. Everyone came out to watch. Enzo could not believe James had just been blown to pieces. He was now in Cazombo and the Cubans might be thinking he wanted to ambush them. They could have killed him as well. He was now wondering what their next move would be. The Angolan police arrived and asked the people at the hotel if they knew the victims. Enzo said he knew one of them and his name was James. He didn't know his last name. Enzo had managed to convince the police that James was just a fellow American whom he had just met at the bar and who had kindly offered to give him a lift. They asked for their reason for being in Cazombo, then left after getting his phone number and passport details. They would get in touch with him if they needed. Once the police realised there were no Angolans killed they seemed only interested in collecting information to file a report as soon as possible. The hotel owner, Eduardo, apologised for the police interrogation and said that from time to time there are some foreigners involved in precious wood or minerals. He explained that they sometimes get involved with corrupt politicians and end up being killed. Enzo thanked Eduardo and when he was gone, turned to Abebi, "Why did you ask James about Zauna?"

"James helped Zauna by turning her into his lover. She lived in a flat he paid for. This is why I could not move in with her. Once he found me there and told me to never to sleep at her place again. I got the message."

"I thought James already lived with a woman."

"Has this ever stopped a man having another woman?"

"I guess not. I am just surprised because he seemed to love his partner."

"He did, this is why he shared Zauna with Samantha."

"I see, now I understand. I think it is time to go to bed."

Joshua finally looked up, "What are you going to do now?"

"Tomorrow I will call João and my colleagues in the US. Try to sleep now."

Despite not being his best friend, Enzo could not believe James had just been killed and this while trailing him. The Cubans were sending a strong message. He was wondering how the US would react now and he was caught in the middle. He never thought he was going to be involved in international politics when he had decided to study medicine. It was going to be another sleepless night.
In the morning he waited to hear for people to move around, then he walked out of his room in search of a strong coffee. Eduardo the landlord gave him a coffee when Enzo's phone rang.

"Good morning, yes it's me, who is calling? Rick Molden, how can I help you Rick? Yes, I am sorry, I was aware, James has passed away. Sorry to interrupt you, but had James informed you about our operation and the reason he had suggested I fly to Angola? Okay, then let me say that those people have a simple message for the US government: Lift the Cuba embargo."

This time nobody laughed. Rick carried on telling him that things were worse still. More nuclear power plants had been turned off and now instead of producing electricity they were consuming a lot of it to keep their reactors cool and prevent them from exploding. They agreed to speak later in four hours' time. He had been too loud and now Joshua and Abebi had joined him for breakfast. They both looked at him for news.

"Things have got worse, but I am worried they still don't take the Cubans seriously."

Joshua looked up, "I think they are. Have you looked outside the window?"

Enzo stood up and went to the door. The road was full of army trucks. He asked Eduardo who said that they had arrived during the night and were searching the surroundings. Eduardo carried on saying that the people in Cazombo would not betray the Cuban doctors who had taken care of them for years while the government in Luanda had not cared much about the population in the interior. Trying not to attract the attention of the military, Enzo went back into the building to sip his second cup of coffee. Suddenly, an overdressed man walked in, looked straight at him, walked to his table and stretched out his hand looking for a handshake.

"Good morning, Mr. Dangelo. I apologise for interrupting your breakfast, but we need to talk. I am from the US embassy in Luanda and have just flown in to see you."

Then, the man looked at the other two sitting at the table. Without uttering another word, Abebi and Joshua got up, looking at Enzo, "We will be in our room if you need us."

"Sorry, I didn't catch your name."

"Call me John Smith, if you like."

"I see. John, can I say that this army operation I see outside of the door is like trying to use a missile to kill a bird. What are they doing?"

"More to the point, what are you doing in this country and especially in this town? We had no issues here until you turned up. What kind of documentary are you supposed to be shooting here and for whom?"

"Mr. Smith, I am sorry. I thought you had been informed."

"Informed about what and from who?"

"Please call this number and speak to Rick who is a colleague of James Austin's, one of the guys who was blown up yesterday."

"In that case, you need to stay here and don't move until I have spoken to this Rick."

Mr. Smith spent little time on the phone, then looked very irritated at him.

"Was this a kind of joke? Rick said he doesn't know any Enzo or James. You have caused enough problems here. We will send you back to the US and let the police there take care of you. Be ready in one hour and don't leave the building before then."

Enzo realized that his had been a secret mission and he was on his own. His mission had failed. He decided to call João to apologise for his departure and pay him for his return trip without passengers. Adão looked at him and whispered, "Em Luanda, encontre o bar do Rio de Janeiro."

They greeted and quickly walked out of there. Enzo informed Abebi and Joshua of their sudden departure. A couple of military vehicles drove them outside to a clearing where a small aircraft was waiting for them. They landed in Luanda in the late afternoon.

"Stay in this hotel and enjoy dinner inside. You are being guarded and tomorrow around lunch time you will fly to Houston where the police are waiting for you. If you're clean, they will let you go."

"Mr. Smith, could you tell me why we are being sent home?"

"Mr. Dangelo, I don't know and I don't care why you are here. My job is to make sure our relationship with our Angolan friends is kept on good terms, something you had started to change. I am serving the United States of America and you are making my job difficult. As you have no official business here, go home. I hope I was clear enough. If you leave the hotel or try to escape, I will have you arrested and deported in handcuffs. Am I clear?"

Enzo realised he was talking to a wall, "No worries, we will stay here and tomorrow we will be out of your hair."

Mr. Smith left, leaving two of his men sitting in the hotel lobby. Joshua looked around, "I have been in worse places and they even have a bar on their terrace. I'll drop my bag in the room and see you on the terrace bar in thirty minutes old man."

Enzo nodded and took the lift up to his second floor single room. Later on the terrace they had a great view. Joshua looked down at the streets of the historical centre, then turned to Enzo and asked, "Why do they have so many businesses named after Brazilian drinks or cities?"

"I thought you found me boring when I explain things?"

"I guess that I have strangely missed your boring explanations in the last couple of days. Anyway, do you know?"

"Brazil, like Angola, was a Portuguese colony, but one of the richest ones. For the cultivation of coffee and other products the Portuguese enslaved many people in Angola and transported them to Brazil. For hundreds of years there were ships constantly crossing the Atlantic between these two countries. It was a triangle. The Portuguese would sail from Portugal to Angola to get the slaves, then to Brazil to take their human cargo there, and finally from there back to Portugal with coffee, gold, etc. After Brazilian independence, some in Brazil tried to unite the country with Angola and create a Brazilian empire. Of course the European powers of the time did not approve and this never happened. The Portuguese language they have in common also makes the cultural interchange easier. Have I bored you enough?"

"Good enough, thank you."

"What Brazilian name did you see?"

"Look opposite the hotel there is a great looking place called, Bar Rio de Janeiro. I wish we could go there."

Enzo stood up and looked at the bar. "I wish that too, but let's enjoy this bar and the great view."

Not long after, Enzo remembered what Adão had told him. He lent on Joshua, "Joshua, listen, I am supposed to meet someone in the Rio de Janeiro bar. I have a plan."

"Why do you want to get all of us arrested?"

"Since when have you got so scared?"

"I am not scared old man, but now I have something to lose. If you remember back when we met, I had nothing to lose. Therefore I had no need to respect the rules. If we screw up here and especially if you're killed, we get stranded in Angola. Do you get me? So don't play with my future, old man."

"You got a point, but this old man who is currently investing in your future is asking you for help. Believe me, if we don't sort this mess out the world we know will change and so will your future."

"Okay, what do you need from me?"

"I looked at the back of the hotel where I saw some large rubbish bins on wheels. I will hide in one of those and you will roll me to the other side of the road, on that corner. I will then try to get out of the bin and into the bar. Abebi should wait until a large truck or bus covers the sight of the bin from this side of the road then call me to let me know. So Abebi, you stay here and enjoy a long drink and keep an eye on the road and on a brown bin crossing it. Okay?"

The men ran down to the kitchen of the hotel where a man tidying up was surprised to see them walk in. They called out to him. Once out of the kitchen, Enzo showed him three hundred US$ and asked him to help them. Enzo also asked the young man to give Joshua his hat and uniform. Luckily, the bin was half empty. They took something out and put a plastic bag in covering the rest. Then Enzo jumped in. Joshua, enjoying his new look, started pushing the bin over the road. One of the men guarding the entrance turned around, attracted by the noise they had made. He soon turned back. A large truck drove down the road and after hearing his phone ring, Enzo quickly jumped out of the bin and ran into the bar. Enzo felt he was definitely getting too old for these sorts of actions. While walking in, he realised he had made no plan to get back to the hotel. Joshua and the hotel kitchen helper hid behind the corner. Enzo ordered a beer and started to look around him, trying to identify any possible contact or messenger. Nobody there, so he started to wonder if there were many bars called Rio de Janeiro in Luanda. After having waited for half an hour in the bar and nothing had happened, he decided that he had risked enough and was time to roll back. When a large group of people left the bar, he joined them and for once he was lucky and they walked past the bin into which he jumped back. The two men waiting around the corner quickly rolled him back. Enzo was more than happy to jump out.

"Shit! What is sticking to my back?"

Joshua started to laugh while taking off his uniform.

"It looks like someone must have thrown an ice-cream in the bin, while you were in the bar and you have collected it with your bottom."

After Enzo cleaned his sticky trousers, they walked back to the terrace to find a couple of well-dressed and good looking guys talking to Abebi. Joshua could not hide his jealousy and quickly walked back. Before he could make a scene, Abebi stood up, "You see, I told you I was not alone. This is Joshua my boyfriend and this is Enzo my manager. These are Manuel and Antonio. These guys have been keeping me company while I was waiting. Don't worry, I was in secure hands as they are with the local police force."

"I am a captain," replied one of the guys quickly, while still shaking hands with Enzo and Joshua.
"Anyway, have a good evening and enjoy your stay in Luanda."

As soon as they were gone Joshua had to let it out, "We are risking our lives and you cannot wait to speak to other men."

"Come on, Joshua, she has not done anything wrong. Anyway, are you together, you two?"

Abebi, looking at Joshua, "Not that I know of. Are we?"

"Joshua, I thought so."

"I am glad to hear you say that. By the way, someone brought me this envelope shortly after you left."

Enzo started to laugh aloud. "All for nothing. This is the message I was waiting for. They want us to go to Chipera in Mozambique."

Joshua, annoyed at hearing that announcement, "Can we not fly back to the US now? How on earth will you manage to get there?"

"I actually like your company, so you are coming with me. And I don't know yet how we will get there."

The morning came and so did the car that was picking them up to drive them to the airport. Before passing security, an embassy employee told them that he would now leave them there. He also reminded them that missing the flight back would have meant being arrested and being kept in an Angolan prison for a while. They told him not to worry and went through the security checks. Once on the other side, Enzo noticed that a flight for Lusaka in Zambia was leaving twenty minutes before their flight just a couple of gates down from their gate. "Abebi and Joshua, please don't argue and stay close to me. I said don't argue, so stop looking at me like that."

Joshua bit his tongue. The plane to Lusaka had started to board. Enzo waited until the last passengers boarded. Then, just before the man checking the tickets was closing the door behind him, Enzo went to him as he wanted to ask a question. Then he turned around, gesturing to Abebi and Joshua to follow him, and they did. All three boarded the plane to Lusaka. Joshua had to sit on his own, while Abebi and Enzo got the last two seats at the back.

"How did you manage to do that?"

"The power of two thousand dollars."

"Why are we flying to Zambia? I thought you wanted to go to Mozambique?"

"Abebi, you are beautiful, but you should learn some geography."

"No need to be rude, old man. By the way, you realise our luggage will go to Houston, right?"

"We will buy what we need at the airport."

"Who buys stuff in an expensive airport?"

"People like us who have lost their luggage."

They landed in Lusaka where, after some necessary shopping, they found a hotel.

"Do you still need a double for you two?"

They both nodded.

"See you down here in an hour. We need a plan."

Once in his room, he decided to call Rick.

"Hello, is Enzo speaking. Do you remember me? Yes, you do. And why did you not remember me when the guy from the US embassy in Luanda called you? I see, a secret mission. Is there any point in my carrying on here and being taken seriously or should I abort my mission and return home? Yes, I told you that I have a contact. Yes, those are the people who killed James. They are not joking. You know. What did they do? I see. Listen the best thing would be for me to give them a contact number or email address so they can communicate directly with you and take me out of the loop. I see. Okay, send me the contact details. I will do. Speak to you tomorrow then. Bye."

Enzo enjoyed a warm shower and put some new clothes on. At the reception he asked where to rent a car or maybe one with a driver. The receptionist told him to wait at the bar, promising to him he would find a driver and send it to him in the next hour. He ordered himself a gin and tonic as he hoped it would also be good against malaria. Joshua, looking at his glass, "Perfect drink for an old man."

Enzo subsequently turned around to the barman shouting, "Two cokes for these kids, please!"

"I actually fancied a beer."
"Sorry, but in my eyes you are too young for that."

Enzo smiled like a happy little child. Abebi, looking at both, "Isn't it time to grow up, you two? So what is your plan, wise man?"

"That's just a fancy way to call me old. Anyway, we are waiting for a driver and we will ask him to drive us to Mozambique."

"Would it not be easier to fly there? We drove for days to Cazombo to be flown back in a couple of hours."

"Joshua, the place where we need to go has no airport and is just six hours' drive away from here."

Abebi, looking serious, "Any news from the US?"

"I am afraid more bad news. I should not share this with you, but I will do just in case I don't survive this mission. I think you ought to know: A new species of insects has been identified as conducting electricity better than copper does. These insects were used to create conductive flying chains that have been used to interconnect high power lines so as to short circuit them. Thanks to those insects, several US cities have now lost power. Many people have died as a consequence of the lack of electric power. This time, it is possible that swarms of insects might have flown directly from Cuba to many southern US states. Some US politicians and armed forces generals are discussing the bombing of Cuba."

The driver finally arrived to interrupt their grim discussion. He introduced himself as Wilson. He said that he could drive them to the border town of Luangwa and from there he was sure that once they passed into Mozambique, they could find a driver willing to take them to Chipera. He apologised, but explained that he was not allowed to take his car outside of Zambia's border. They had no choice and accepted. Wilson would pick them up in the morning after nine.

"I am happy people speak English here. I feel more at home." said Abebi.

"Do you only speak English?"

"I also speak Ibo and Edo."

"How do you count or swear when you are cross?"

"I guess mostly in English."

"Then your mother tongue is English."

"And you, how do you count or swear?"

"In Italian of course. Italy is where I grew up. And you, Joshua?"

"I swear in English, but I also speak Shona. The only thing for which I am grateful to the British colonial bastards is the English language."

They had an early night but during their supper they tested munkoyo, a non-alcoholic drink made from maize and the roots of the munkoyo tree. They also tried a couple of bottles of mosi, the local beer. Northern Rhodesia or Zambia now, had been independent since 1964, but the breakfast on offer was still very British. They all enjoyed it and were happy to jump into the car when Wilson appeared. Wilson believed he recognised Joshua's Southern Rhodesian or Zimbabwean accent and Joshua confirmed this to him. Wilson spoke some Shona to Joshua which made him very emotional. It seemed that Joshua suddenly realised he was not far from what was left of his family. Abebi hugged him. They had filled up on breakfast and soon all three passengers fell asleep. Hours later, still snoozing, they enjoyed the scenery with some commentary from the driver. Luangwa used to be called Feira which means market in Portuguese. On the opposite riverbank is the town of Zumbo in Mozambique. In 1856 David Livingston had passed this way. Finally, arriving in Luangwa, Enzo went to find a place to sleep. At this point he wanted to speak one more time to the US before needlessly passing the border. He was not yet sure of what he could offer. At least he needed a serious contact name to pass on. What could he ask the Cubans to do to prove they were really orchestrating the whole thing on their own? More than anything, he needed to know if there was a point in risking his or better, their lives. Enzo handed over to Wilson the amount of Zambian Kwacha they had agreed plus a tip and said goodbye to Wilson. They found only a small guesthouse that could offer to them a room with three beds.

"Are you sure you will be able to cope, you two? No double room for the love birds tonight."

They laughed and asked if there was any food around as they had had no lunch and it was now late afternoon. The owner of the place said that he could offer some fresh fish from the nearby Zambezi with beans and rice. They were also offered a couple of glasses of chibuku, an opaque homemade beer. It was time to call Rick.

"Hi Rick, do you have any news for me?"

Rick explained that many politicians he had spoken to would prefer a military solution. Those he thought he might be able to sway were worried about mass migration out of Cuba once the embargo was lifted. Most were still not convinced the Cubans alone were behind this. They thought the Russians or Chinese were helping them, so he felt they needed tangible proof that the Cubans would be able to stop what they had started. Rick also told him that no official representing the US government can be a contact and that he would have to deal with them on his own. Enzo could not believe he had been left alone again. Once more in his life he promised to himself not to get involved in such adventures. Now that he had come so far, he decided to try speaking one last time with the Cubans and then go back home. The day after, they crossed the river on a local fishing boat. Before they disembarked, the fisherman looked Enzo straight in the eyes and said, "It is better you all leave your mobile phones here. You will find them back at the guesthouse when you go back."

Enzo understood that they were being tracked by the Cubans. In Zumbo, a man with a pick up car offered to give them a lift. As there seemed to be no other option, they hopped in.

"Enzo, I am a bit scared. I admit it has been fun, but why did you bring Joshua and me here?"

"Sorry if you are bored. I thought together that you would help me blend in."

"Bloody old man. Did you seriously bring us here just for the colour of our skin? Did you think our company would make you less white?"

"I guess so. Not less white, but maybe better accepted by other black people."

"Is that the way it works where mostly white or pink skinned people like you live?"

"Please don't be offended now, this is not a racist thing. Everybody is more accepting of newcomers if they are introduced by those of one same tribe. It works the same way between people with the same skin colour. As a Sicilian, I was more quickly accepted if someone local introduced me. I guess this is just human nature. As a young man in Sicily, my father always used to tell me, don't tell me where you are going, but who with. He meant that if he saw and trusted the friends I was going out with at the time, he would feel reassured."

Then a sudden jump forced them to concentrate on their landing back down on the bare metal of the car. After two hours, they left the main road and drove down an even narrower track. At the end of it they saw a disused wooden hut. This time a middle aged woman looking like a tired doctor came out to greet him.

"Mr. Dangelo, welcome, and I am happy to finally meet you. As a medical researcher and doctor, I admire your cure for obesity and even your suggested gender change operation for rapists. Some find this a harsh measure, but having been raped myself as a young woman, I think this is the appropriate punishment. Of course, I disagree with your government using such measures against captured enemies. I guess for me it would be worse if they could also turn women into men, but that's for the future. Anyway, please tell me, how did you end up getting involved in this political issue?"

"Please call me Enzo. I guess you didn't study medicine to end up getting involved in this mess either?"

She laughed, "Yes, you can say that again. But as a mixed race woman of poor parents who were living in almost enslaved conditions before Fidel came along, I owe my education and chances in life to those colour-blind revolutionaries. You see, for me, Ché Guevara or Fidel are not just names printed on a t-shirt. They are my life. So tell me now, what are we going to do about our countries? Needless to say, that if they involve the army as you did in Cazombo or if you attack Cuba, we will badly retaliate. As you can imagine, we are well prepared for such an eventuality."

"I seriously hope we will be able to solve this peacefully, but I will not deny that there are some hot heads who would prefer a military response."

"We know about that. You see your country's weakness is that everybody can be bought and in the US money is paramount. So we have plenty of spies willing to share facts and information with us. We are poor, so we don't have this problem. Whoever works for us is obviously not just in it for the money. Those Cubans who are only after the latest unnecessary gadget have already left Cuba for Florida. Honestly, I am glad they have. Once they are there for me, they are no Cubans anymore. They can keep them."

"Don't you think some left because they had nothing to eat?"

"I have never seen a person starve in Cuba. How could we educate everybody for free and have a free-of-charge national health service if we were starving? Tell me, then, why are so many students from poor countries studying medicine in Cuba? Don't believe your country's propaganda, Mr. Dangelo. What is causing our suffering is the economic embargo forced on us by your inhumane country defending the interests of those criminal slave traders who moved to the US after our great Cuban revolution. As you were born in Sicily, you might have heard of Lucky Luciano and his friend, Meyer Lansky. I'd prefer to die than to see any Cuban land returned to those criminals. What have your friends in the US told you? What do they want to stop the embargo?"

"First of all, the proof that you will be able to stop what you have started."

"And then?"

"The reassurance that should the embargo be lifted, no mass migration out of Cuba will occur."

"Anything else?"

"No, this is it."

"Good. For the migration issue, we have no intention of allowing our people to leave our country en masse, especially not for the US where those racist old Cubans have set up camp. On this piece of paper I have written some GPS coordinates. Ask your people to start a big fire at this exact location in two days' time. On the third day we will expect strong signs that the embargo will be lifted otherwise we will carry on our mission to the bitter end of bringing the US to its knees. Let me say that I hope this won't be necessary. I have nothing against American people and I hope one day we will be able to live near each other as good neighbours. It was good to meet you, Enzo. Have a good ride back to Zumbo and a good flight home the day after. Please leave Africa soon. I won't be able to guarantee your safety if you don't do so. Some in my organisation either don't trust you or worse, have relatives who have suffered because of inventions linked to your name."

"Thank you, and I am sorry about the suffering I might have indirectly caused to any of those you know."

They bid farewell and were quickly driven back to Zumbo. Then they went across the river back to Luangwa. They went back to the guesthouse where they were given their mobile phones back. Enzo called Rick and passed on the information and the coordinates. It was too late to drive back to Lusaka, but not to arrange for a driver to take them there the morning after. After buying the three plane tickets online, he announced to his anxious travel companions, "Tomorrow we will fly to Atlanta. Are you happy now?"

Joshua looked unsure.

"What's wrong, young man, I thought travelling to the US was your dream?"

"Yes, it is or it was. I am so close to my family and country here."

"Joshua, I won't force you to get on the plane. It's your choice."

"Sorry Enzo, I don't want to seem ungrateful, but Sarah, that Cuban lady, was dedicating her entire life to her country and the Cubans. Now that the Zimbabwean government has changed, maybe I should do the same."

"Joshua, you have a whole night to think about it. Let me say that if you decide to stay here and if you need my help, I will still be prepared to finance your education."

Abebi hugged Joshua.
The morning after, they were woken up early by a strong knocking on the front door of the little guesthouse. A black car was parked in front followed by two police cars. A white man in a suit walked in shouting, "Where is Mr. Dangelo?"

"I am here. Sorry, do I know you?"
"Very funny. You were supposed to board a plane from Luanda to Houston, but never did. We finally managed to track you down. Get your stuff now. We will escort you to the airport now and make sure you board a flight back to the US."

"We can go now. Please let me show you that I have already purchased a flight back to the US. This is my booking reference number and time of departure. By the way, did you come just for me or for all three of us?"

While he was still checking his flight booking details, "All of you will have to fly back. We don't want any of you in this country. Am I clear?"

333

"Sure, no problem. As you have seen, I have purchased three tickets."

Enzo was looking at Joshua, trying to guess what his final decision about staying or going would be.

"Kind of ironic, isn't it? They are now forcing us to go to a place you were not allowed to go to before. Anyway, you can still fly back if you want. Please don't do anything stupid now. Think of it as having just been given more time to decide what you really want to do with your life."

They were driven back to Lusaka airport with a police escort. The police escort helped them drive quickly through the traffic of Zambia's capital city. This time they were escorted all the way to the gate and two policemen waited until they had boarded their flight to Atlanta. It was a long flight and Enzo wondered if the police was really expecting them at the other end as the embassy guy had told him. There was nothing he could do, but wait. He also hoped Rick had managed to follow the instructions that the Cubans had given him. Enzo was longing for a peaceful time at home with his family. After the plane landed they saw a police car following the plane. The cabin attendant requested Enzo, Abebi and Joshua to disembark first. All other passengers had to wait, seated, while they were let off the plane first.

"Wow, are we that special?" Asked Joshua, looking at Enzo.

"Yes, and for once this has nothing to do with the colour of your skin."

Abebi looked at him, "Please don't start him on this."

Two police officers asked them to follow them. They were taken to the airport police station.

"Mr. Dangelo, as far as I see, you have been sent back home as an unwanted guest from Zambia and Angola. How did you manage that? Why, and what problem did you three cause over there?"

"This is my employer's phone number. I was on a mission for my company that is currently collaborating with the US government on a security issue. I am not sure if I am allowed to share those details with you."

"You will understand that if you cannot share the details, we have a problem and I cannot let you go."

Joshua, losing his temper, "This is ridiculous, this man just risked his life for this country, paid all with his own money and you want to arrest him? What kind of country is this?"

"Maybe you will be able to tell me more about the reason you got kicked out of Africa?"

"Sorry Enzo, but I have no patience for this. I don't know how you can cope with this stupid dance."

The policeman looked seriously at Joshua. "So tell me, why on earth were you kicked out of Africa?"

Joshua, pointing to Abebi started to talk, "We both were trying to trace our birth parents. You see, we were adopted as babies, but in reality we were sold to wealthy Americans who could not have children. Enzo and his investigative company were trying to help us find our birth parents. The Angolan authorities did not want us to dig into this old stuff and bring to the surface a trade in babies that they had during their civil war period. This is why they wanted us out of there."

"I see, but why did you end up going to Zambia?"

At this point Abebi felt she had to contribute, "Because we had found out that my birth parents were Angolan, but during the war, were refugees in Zambia. We were on the right track until we got found out and forcibly taken to Lusaka airport."

The police had had enough and after checking they had no penal record in the US, just let them go free. Once outside the police station, Enzo put his arms on their shoulders and started to laugh.

"How did you get that idea?"

"I have been around you long enough old man. I thought that if they were not prepared to believe the truth, then I needed to invent a story they liked. Sometimes people don't really want to know the truth. They prefer to hear a story they can believe in. This is especially true if the story is based on their prejudices. When he kept on saying Africa instead of Angola or Zambia, I knew I needed to provide him, a typical American, with an African story."

"You are learning fast. It's really time I retired."

They all laughed and walked to catch their next plane home. Finally landed, Enzo turned his mobile phone back on and it started to ring straightaway.

"Hi Rick, how you doing? That's good, right? I see. Well, I am not sure now. No, I have no contact number for them. Listen, they won't do anything until the embargo has been lifted. You know now what they want and what we need to do to stop this. I think we have done all we could here. Bye now."

Joshua and Abebi were hanging on to every word of his. "Arrogant idiots! This country will have to learn not to be top dog anymore."

"What happened?"

"It seems that they actually followed the instructions and started a big fire at the GPS location the Cubans had given us. Shortly after, they saw a large number of insects arriving and going straight into the fire. One of the nuclear reactors is now free from bugs and will soon be back online."

"That's good, right?"

"It is, but then they tried to remove the bugs from another nuclear reactor using some kind of robots. The bugs started to explode in a chain reaction and the fire is now out of control. The whole area will be contaminated. The population in the towns nearby are being evacuated. The news talks about a technical accident. Now small fires are starting all over the shale gas fields. It seems new insects are flying near them and igniting themselves. I hope they finally understood that they will need to act. Listen guys, I need to get back home. For now, I will put you up in a small apartment near my office. I will call you tomorrow."

Enzo dropped his travel companions and drove straight home. Carmen seemed genuinely happy to see him back. It was late and the television was on in the background when finally the news he had wished for was being communicated. The US government was thinking about lifting the Cuban embargo. Enzo jumped up.

"This is great! If this works out, I have an idea of what I want to do now."

Carmen looked straight into his eyes, "I think you have shared enough ideas. I think it's time you retire, step back and listen to my idea. What if we moved to Santo Domingo? My parents are getting old and need me there. You like the sea, eating fish and walking on the beach there. You could finally get the dog you always wanted and never had time for. Isn't that a great idea?"

Carmen had managed to plant a seed in Enzo's mind.
Enzo's eyes showed that Carmen's idea was taking on a life of its own.
This had already started to change Enzo's future life and he had no idea.

Printed in Great Britain
by Amazon